KERRY McGINNIS

Out of Alice

PENGUIN BOOKS

PENGUIN BOOKS

UK | USA | Canada | Ireland | Australia
India | New Zealand | South Africa | China

Penguin Books is part of the Penguin Random House group of companies
whose addresses can be found at global.penguinrandomhouse.com.

First published by Penguin Random House Australia Pty Ltd, 2016
This edition published by Penguin Randon House Australia Pty Ltd, 2017

13 5 7 9 10 8 6 4 2

Text copyright © Kerry McGinnis 2016

Cover design by Alex Ross © Penguin Random House Australia Pty Ltd
Text design by Samantha Jayaweera © Penguin Random House Australia Pty Ltd
Cover photographs: Background © Chris Hakanson; Girl © Oleh Slobodeniuk/Getty Images
Typeset in Sabon by Samantha Jayaweera, Penguin Random House Australia Pty Ltd
Colour separation by Splitting Image Colour Studio, Clayton, Victoria
Printed and bound in Australia by Griffin Press, an accredited ISO AS/NZS 14001
Environmental Management Systems printer.

National Library of Australia
Cataloguing-in-Publication data:

McGinnis, Kerry, 1945- author.
Out of Alice / Kerry McGinnis.
9780143786108 (paperback)
Subjects: Country life--Australia--Fiction.
Man-woman relationships--Australia--Fiction.
Alice Springs (N.T.)--Fiction.

penguin.com.au

This one is for my brothers
and for Judith

1

1994

Sara Blake settled back in to her bus seat with a thankful sigh as the big vehicle slid smoothly through the streets of Alice Springs. Her muscles, which seemed to have been tensed ever since she had fled Mildura, relaxed, along with the nagging impulse to look behind her.

Safe at last.

But she wouldn't think of that now. It would be better to concentrate instead on her new job. To work out how she was going to justify her lack of teaching experience to the mother of her young charges. *Governessing and some housework*, the ad had read. Surely any reasonably intelligent person could manage that? It was just a matter of working out the right approach to her new employer – show that she was willing and adaptable, and hope it would be enough.

Sara found herself watching the passing scenery, which had the glamour of difference. She had spent her life in the city of Adelaide and this was her first visit to the Alice, as the locals called it, the isolated little town set in the bowl of the Macdonnell Ranges. It was only early September but she still found herself unused to the heat, and the vivid light. The pace was slower too, in everything, as she had learned on Monday. Arriving from the airport, she had taken the taxi driver's advice on a budget hotel on the riverbank, and had then tried to book her onward journey.

'Not till Wednesdee, love,' the snaggle-toothed owner advised her, a practised hand reaching for the stack of sun-faded brochures on the desk. 'On'y three buses a week – on Mondees, Wednesdees and Fridees. Not to worry, but. Plenty to see in the Alice.'

'But I was told there was a bus every day.' Sara suspected he simply wanted an extra night's booking.

'So there is. The dog runs up three days an' back two.'

'Dog?' she repeated, wondering about his sanity.

'Greyhound,' he said patiently. 'Like I said, she runs to Darwin Mondee, Wednesdee, Fridee, an' comes back Tuesdee and Thursdee. So you can book your seat tomorrow and be off at the crack of dawn Wednesdee. Which gives you a full day to see the sights.' He beamed and waggled the leaflets at her.

He had spoken the truth – except about the early start. A mechanical fault had delayed them for several hours, during which Sara's anxiety levels had steadily risen. It did no good to tell herself she was being absurd, and that nobody but her new employer knew where she was. It wasn't until the diesel motor turned over and the door sighed shut that she finally relaxed and could gaze out upon the scenery that so exactly resembled the paintings of Albert Namatjira – copies or prints of which could seemingly be found in every shop in Alice Springs.

Perched high above the bitumen, cocooned within the shaded windows and air-conditioned comfort, Sara watched the scenery pass: low, rugged ranges tinted purple and ochre, red soil, white gums, an untidy scribble of olive-green scrub and the odd taller tree whose dusty grey leaves gave off glints of silver in the vivid light. The sky was cloudless, a pale enervating blue with edgings of pink that may, she decided, have something to do with the window colouring. There was nothing to see – the occasional car roof passing below her, dark clouds of birds that periodically took wing from the road's verge, and endless vistas of scrub and rocky ridge, and red desert. The other passengers were mostly silent, wrapped in their own thoughts, only the infrequent murmur, too indistinct to decipher, breaking through the hum of the diesel motor.

Sara wondered where the stations were. She couldn't even see any cattle and yet she understood that the land north of Alice Springs was all divided up into properties. Sometimes a windmill showed on the skyline to support this theory but her eye wasn't quick enough to discern the dark shapes of cattle standing among the thin scattering of scrub. The visible landscape was dreary beyond belief and as the first couple of hours passed without change to the view from her window she started to wonder if she hadn't made a hideous mistake.

Then the bus began to slow, the passengers all stirring in their seats to crane ahead. Sara saw that they were entering a town – well, scarcely that. A collection of shabby buildings scattered across an open flat, a dusty racecourse with a crooked stand, a black tank and mill set beside a shallow creek, and up ahead a roadhouse with a further scatter of buildings at its back. There were no shops, no paved streets, just dirt tracks between the houses. A sign, pockmarked with bullet holes, announced that this was Charlotte Creek. Sara had reached her destination.

2

The bus driver, a short-tempered man in his forties with a paunch and thinning hair, unhooked the microphone and addressed his passengers.

'Right, folks. This here's Charlotte Creek. The only reason I'm stopping is to let one of yous off. That'll take five minutes. Now, you might reckon that's time enough to have a smoke or grab something from the roadhouse. But you won't be eating it on the bus and if you ain't back on board when I am, yous'll stay here.'

'When do we get to eat, then?' a man from the front seats queried, his tone petulant.

'Ti-Tree Roadhouse, sunshine. Same as it says in the bus schedule.' He pressed the door release and Sara hauled her smaller bag down from the overhead rack and exited the bus into a blast of heat and brilliant light that the coach's tinted windows had diffused. Her other bag was unceremoniously dragged out from the compartment beneath the passengers' seats and dumped on the dusty ground. She thanked the man, who ignored the courtesy as he rearranged the remaining luggage. A few moments later the driver's door clunked shut, the passenger door followed and the big vehicle moved off, blurring the incurious faces gazing down at her from the windows as they pulled away.

Sara stared after it, momentarily wishing she was still aboard. The Stuart Highway, and the bus, ran all the way to Darwin, which was at least a city, with streets and shops and proper houses – not this godforsaken-looking dump. What to do now?

She recalled her new employer's voice on the phone: *The bus stops at Charlotte Creek. That's as close as you can get to us on public transport, but the mail comes through Fridays so you'll be right. When you get to the roadhouse, ask for Harry. Sometimes he runs a bit late, but he'll bring you out.*

First things first, then. Sara donned her sunglasses, then towed her dusty case into the shade of the building. The roadhouse had fuel bowsers out the front, and the building sat back behind a post and rail fence that enclosed a scrap of green lawn. Metal steps that winked in the light led onto a long, shaded verandah and a door veiled by coloured plastic strips. A couple of native trees completed the attempts at a garden, but at that it was the best on view. The rest of the houses – shanties? – sat behind sagging enclosures containing perhaps a tree or a collection of tired-looking pot plants, and vehicles of various ages and decrepitude.

Immediately next to the roadhouse was another huge tank and a great slab of concrete flooring beneath a roof, as if the builder had got that far and given up; or perhaps, Sara thought, wiping her sweaty face, he had thought better of walls. This certainly wasn't the climate for them and it was still early in September. She wondered with some trepidation what December would be like.

There was nobody about. Presumably the inhabitants of Charlotte Creek had learned to ignore the traffic along the bitumen. Sara could see a battered-looking Toyota LandCruiser parked at the shady end of the roadhouse. Harry's, perhaps? Deserting her luggage, she went to find out.

The public room was dim and blessedly cool; banks of louvres front and back allowed for a cross flow of air and showed up the framed photographs on the wall. There were pictures of rodeo action, of huge road trains, one of two kangaroos boxing against a rising sun. Above them was a heavy timber rail with collections of numbers, symbols and letters burned into them like strange arcana from a foreign land. There were tables and chairs, a wide bar, the glass face of a huge, humming refrigerator, shelves and display cabinets – and then suddenly a male figure shooting to his feet exclaiming, 'Shit! Of all the friggin' mismatched junk I've ever seen —' He wrung his right hand, then sucked at the knuckles, catching sight of Sara hovering just within the door as he did so.

'G'day.' His gaze took in the slim figure in jeans and shirt and he jabbed a finger at his hat brim, lifting it slightly. 'Sorry for the language. Didn't know you were there.'

'I came on the bus,' she said. 'Are you Harry?'

'Nope. Jack Ketch. Which Harry did you want?'

'I don't know,' Sara confessed, flushing a little as she saw his brow rise. He was tall, lean looking and long faced; he was about thirty, she judged. He wore a khaki shirt, rumpled and stained, and the rest of him was below the level of the bar. 'I didn't ask,' she said. 'I'm going to a property called Redhill and I was told to get off the bus here and Harry would pick me up. Only he might be late so – well, I'm wondering, how late exactly?'

'Coupla days,' Jack Ketch replied. 'Mail comes Friday. Didn't Beth say?'

Sara closed her eyes in vexation. 'Oh, God! He's the *mailman*. I didn't realise. Yes, she did say, only I – well.' She glanced around. 'I suppose I'll just have to stay here till then. They do have accommodation?'

'Nope.' The man cheerfully contradicted her. 'Hang on.' He went to a door at the back and bellowed, 'Mavis! Customer.'

Somewhere a door slammed and shortly a plump, white-haired woman clad in a skirt and scoop-necked blouse entered the room. Her hair colour belied her age. She had an ample body with firm upper arms, and an unlined face save for the deep squint lines about her hazel eyes, which embraced Sara with a welcoming smile.

'G'day, love. What can I do for you?'

'She's got herself stranded,' Ketch answered before Sara could speak. 'Waiting on the mail to get out to Redhill. She's Beth's new governess.'

Sara closed her mouth and frowned at him, her stomach twisting nervously. 'How do you know that?'

'You told me.' He glanced at Mavis. 'By the way, that fridge of yours is cactus. Made of tin and glue. I cracked the bloody pipe and I'll need an oxy torch to fix it. Then it'll want re-gassing. So I'll run her out and bring the oxy gear back, but you'll have to get the gas out from the Alice. Harry might fit it on if you catch him in time.'

'Right, well, that's no drama.' The woman called Mavis smiled at Sara. 'Not to worry, it's all sorted. What's your name, love?'

'Sara Blake.' She eyed the rough-looking man. 'Did he – is he offering to drive me?'

'Yeah, Jack'll see you right. What about a cuppa before you leave?' Her eyes twinkled. 'You must be peckish. I know that cranky sod of a driver, all rules and schedules. If he had his way, his passengers wouldn't even breathe.'

Sara glanced at her watch, realising that she was hungry. It was after two. 'Thanks very much,' she said gratefully to Mavis. 'If we've time?' She looked at the man. 'How far is it?'

'Plenty of time,' he assured her. He reached to shake hands, his own none too clean, the nails rimmed with grease. 'Only a coupla hours, but a cuppa's a good idea. So, Sara . . .' His gaze swept over her from head to foot. 'What brings you out here?'

Nettled by his inspection, she said primly, 'The job, Mr Ketch.'

He grinned, seemingly amused. 'Jack'll do. We're not big on formality in the mulga.'

'No? So how far is it to Redhill, Jack?'

'I just told you, a coupla hours.'

'Oh.' It seemed an odd way to measure distance, but Mavis was returning with the tea and a substantial plate of sandwiches so she asked for the bathroom, then settled down to satisfy her hunger before they left.

It turned out that the battered Toyota Sara had seen was Jack's. He brought it round to the front of the roadhouse, loaded her luggage, then pulled the passenger door open to sweep away the clutter on the seat.

'You'll have to get your feet round the water bottle,' he said. 'Hop in and we'll be off.'

'Thank you.' Sara had taken the opportunity while being conducted to the bathroom to ask Mavis about Jack. She didn't intend getting into a vehicle with a stranger whom she knew nothing about, but the woman had laughed at her fears. 'Lord, you're not in the city now, love. Everybody knows Jack. He's fine.' It was reassurance of a sort, she supposed, though the state of his vehicle came as a shock. The cab was coated with dust and a large rifle was secured in a rack across the back, above the seats, the covers of which looked as if they had never been washed. Her thoughts must have been plain to read.

'Sorry about the mess,' Jack said. 'She's a working vehicle.' Three flies had entered with them and buzzed noisily about the window. His hand shot out to slap them against the glass, the sound and sudden movement making her jump. 'Curse of Oz,' he commented, wiping the mess off on his jeans. 'Now you've seen this,' the wave of a hand indicated the dusty nothingness beyond the bitumen, 'how long d'you reckon you'll stay?'

'Till the job's over, I expect,' Sara responded tartly. 'Why would you even ask?'

'Hard to get good help in the mulga. It's not everybody's cup of tea. The last girl quit after a fortnight.' They crossed the bitumen and shot off down a narrow track between the grey scrub at which Jack jerked his thumb. 'That's mulga, by the way.'

Sara stared at its unvarying sameness and the barren-looking red soil beneath. 'It all looks very – very parched.'

'Yeah, well, there's a drought on. Has been for a coupla years,' he said dryly. 'That's why.'

She immediately felt guilty for not knowing. Seeking to change the topic, she asked, 'Are you employed by the roadhouse? And if you are – don't get me wrong, I'm not complaining – but why are you driving me to Redhill?'

'Why not? I'm going there anyway. And no, I don't work for Mavis. I'm a fencing contractor and, for my sins, the district's Mr Fix-it. She's got a problem with her fridge.' He shrugged. 'I'm helping her out.'

Sara was aware of his gaze upon her, taking in the straw beach hat, and the undisciplined riot of red curls about her sweaty face. He sniffed discreetly and she hoped it was perfume he could smell and not the perspiration on her body; she folded her hands to hide the pink sheen of her nails that all at once seemed frivolous and rather silly in this barren setting – as if they might reflect poorly upon her capabilities.

She studied him in turn, noting the dark hair under his grease-stained hat, the glimpse of grey eyes when his head turned towards her. He had high cheekbones and a couple of days' dark stubble on his jaw. She said lightly, 'And this includes knowing everyone's business? Even strangers who have just arrived?'

He laughed. 'Got you going, did it? Beth Calshot's my sister, so when you said you were headed for Redhill . . .'

'I see. Not hard to work out, then. This other girl, why did she leave?'

'Because of who she was, I suppose. A European backpacker. Danish, or German, something like that. Said she'd worked on *foms* before. But our "farms" are a bit bigger and further apart than anything she knew. The isolation got to her, I guess.'

'That's understandable.' Sara gazed around at the landscape, at the dull red soil and grey scrub with the narrow ribbon of bumpy road unspooling through it. She could see no living thing; even the stray tufts of grass looked dead, and much of the timber – the mulga, Jack had called it – was broken off in swathes as though a giant windstorm had blasted through, flattening the trees as it went.

'What happened here?'

He twisted the wheel to avoid a hole. 'Bungy's been pushing scrub. We all do it.' Reading her incomprehension, he explained. 'Stock can eat mulga, but you have to push it for them. Cattle aren't giraffes.'

'I see. Would this Bungy be Mr Calshot?'

'Nope. Bungy Morgan. He owns Wintergreen, which we're currently driving through. He's Redhill's western neighbour. North and east is national park and south is Munaroo. So you've got two neighbours, and the rangers at Walkervale, in something like,' he squinted, doing sums in his head, 'say, six and a half thousand square miles of country.' He glanced at her with a humorous lift of his brow. 'You want it in kilometres, you'll have to convert it yourself.'

The areas were staggering. Sara blinked. 'I see then why that poor girl found it hard.'

'Ah, well,' Jack said. 'It's desert, you need big areas.' They rattled across another grid and a half-dozen crows rose cawing from a carcass beside it. Sara glimpsed the desiccated frame of a cow, its horns and jaw and empty eye socket. A brief whiff of corruption overlaid by the smell of dust and they were past. He nodded at the windscreen. 'Right, here we are. Welcome to Redhill.'

Sara gazed about her, saying doubtfully, 'I don't see a homestead?'

'That's miles away yet. I meant, we've crossed the boundary and we're now driving on Redhill land.'

'Oh.' Feeling foolish, she fell silent again.

3

The country had changed without Sara noticing. Grey mulga had given way to a scattering of different trees where the fence ran and beyond was an open plain, grassed over with pale feed. She stared and swallowed, overcome by sudden dread. The feeling was as intense as it was inexplicable. Her hands clenched and a cold sweat broke over her body. She swallowed convulsively but her mouth filled again as her stomach churned. She gasped, 'Stop! Please stop!' Jack slammed on the brakes and she tumbled out and ran a few paces before bending double to a bout of helpless retching.

Jack took his time about exiting the vehicle, for which Sara was grateful. When he finally reached her side it was with a plastic cup of water to rinse her mouth. 'Did you get a fly?' he asked sympathetically.

'No.' Sara's nausea had passed as quickly as it had come and the dread with it; her heartbeat was back to normal and all she felt was embarrassment. 'Sorry, I don't know what came over me. I just felt . . .' It was impossible to say *terrified* so she let the sentence hang.

'Maybe you're a bad traveller,' he suggested. 'It's not the best road.'

Sara gave a shaky laugh. 'Honestly? I wouldn't know. I've never been off the bitumen before. It's probably the heat. How much further?'

''Bout an hour.'

'Okay.' They started again and Sara, seeking distraction from her whirling thoughts, said, 'All this grass, why don't the cattle eat that?'

'They can't reach it.' The succinct reply stumped her, and seeing it he explained. 'No water. Len's hoping to punch a bore down here some day, but the chances aren't good. This is the Forty Mile block; people have drilled here before without success.'

Puzzled, she said, 'I thought it was Redhill?'

'So it is. The Forty Mile's just the old name for a section of a mining lease that was incorporated into Redhill twenty years back. The miners never hit water on it, though.'

'Still, if things are so bad, isn't it worth the gamble?'

'Probably,' Jack agreed. 'But first you've got to get the rig. It costs a lot to get 'em out on site, especially if you can't guarantee more than one hole. And at the end of it you could still come up dry.'

'I see.' A glint of silver caught her eye. 'What's that?'

'Microwave repeater tower for communication.'

'Ah. For a cattle property,' she remarked, 'there doesn't seem to be many cows. I've only seen one so far – and it was dead.'

'Time of day. They're on the waters now. You'll see a few when we pass Canteen bore, about fifteen k from here.'

Sara lapsed into silence again, a little frown between her smooth brows. She ought to say something; Jack would be wondering if she was having second thoughts. Her hands moved on her lap, the right index finger flicking repeatedly against her thumb, a habit she was scarcely aware of. She felt washed out, but not – thank God! – as if a migraine were imminent. That would surely impress her employer, to turn up prostrate after catching the bus on the wrong day. It was certainly desolate-looking country – there seemed to be no end to the sky and the pinkness she had glimpsed in it before was nothing to do with window tinting after all, but dust. Pretty really, layered above the blue with the dull grey sheen of the scrub below it.

Five minutes short of the hour Jack had stipulated, they drove through the horse-paddock gate and Sara caught her first glimpse of Redhill Station, a flash of metal roof and mill sails, and a complex of drab buildings. The largest, an open-fronted shed, had the word *REDHILL* spelled out along its length in letters a metre high. The other smaller buildings she would later come to recognise as feed and saddle sheds, a chook pen, the men's quarters, the meat house and, foremost, the homestead.

It was set in a railed and netted enclosure full of shade trees and lawn. After the dusty hours on the road the green was a sudden feast for her eyes. A red cattle dog came racing to meet them as Jack pulled in by the front gate, where dusty oleander bushes dropped blossoms of pink and red. He switched off and in the sudden silence Sara heard the creak of the mill wheel turning on the flat, the cries of the cockies lining the tank's rim and the sound of hammering from the sheds. Then the dog barked expectantly and Jack pushed his door open.

'G'day, Jess old girl. Well, here we are, Sara. Come on in and meet Beth and the kids.'

Beth Calshot was a lean, wiry-looking woman with long brown hair pulled back into a ponytail that accentuated the thinness of a face marked with sun wrinkles at the corners of her brown eyes. She wore khaki shorts and a blue singlet top that outlined the sparse shape of a body from which all softness seemed to have been stripped. Seeing them, she trod quickly down the five steps leading from the wide front verandah.

'Mavis rang,' she said. 'I'm so glad you've come, and early too.' She shook Sara's hand with a firm grip. Her nails, Sara saw, were short and unpainted. 'How do you do? Did you have a good trip out? Call me Beth. I do hope you're going to like it here.'

Sara was warmed by the welcome. 'I'm afraid I misunderstood your message about the mail, what day it ran. It's lucky Jack was there to rescue me. I hadn't realised the distances involved.'

'Oh, but it's not really far —' Beth broke off anxiously, then grimaced. 'Oh dear, will you listen to me? Of course, you'll make up your own mind about that. Now, would you like a cuppa before you unpack? What about you, Jack?'

'Please, but first I want to check if Len's got any gas. You girls go ahead. I'll bring Sara's gear in.'

'Right. You didn't get it fixed, then?'

'Cracked the damn pipe. Where're the kids?'

'Getting the goats in. Kitchen's this way, Sara.'

Beth led the way through the central section of the house. Dining-cum-lounge, Sara noted, with a heavy polished table and sideboard juxtaposed with cane chairs and a television.

'Satellite TV,' Beth said quickly, catching her glance. 'We've got *some* mod cons.'

Sara smiled. 'I'm sure.' The kitchen space was crammed with a coldroom, freezer, a slow combustion stove obviously not in use, and a smaller gas model beside it that was. Beth lit the gas while Sara continued her survey, seeing sink, cupboards, breakfast bar and a pine table where, she guessed, most meals would be eaten. The dining room, she thought, had a special-occasion look about it.

'Take a seat,' Beth invited. 'Tea won't be a moment. Do you cook, Sara?'

'Yes,' she answered, surprised. 'I enjoy it. Nothing fancy, just ordinary meals.'

Beth nodded. 'Good. Not that I'll expect you to do much of it. But now and then, perhaps.' She made the tea and, with an economy of movement that spoke of long practice, dumped mugs, sugar, milk and a tin of biscuits on the bare tabletop, before seating herself opposite. She turned the pot several times. 'The thing is, the reason you're here is because my son is not well. Sam has acute lymphoblastic leukemia. He's eleven.' Her throat moved as she looked at the younger woman. 'He needs regular chemotherapy and that means monthly trips to the Alice. He will get better,' she said forcefully, picking up the teapot, 'but it means that I need someone in the schoolroom with Becky to oversee her lessons, and to run the kitchen when I'm away with Sam. Len, my husband, used to share the driving with me and we'd take Becky too, but with the drought . . .' Her brown eyes studied Sara and she sighed wearily. 'There's another trip coming up. That's why, right now, I'm desperately hoping you won't be taking the next mail out.'

'I'm so sorry about Sam.' Sara added milk to her cup. 'The poor kid, that's truly awful for him, and you.' She felt a surge of dismay at the news, wondering just how sick he was and how it would affect her job.

'I know. And he's so damn brave about it all.' Beth's voice wavered momentarily. 'It's not a pleasant treatment. It makes him so ill. Anyway, that's the job,' she continued, pushing the biscuit tin at her guest. 'Becky's nine and she can't afford to miss any more schooling. Sam's way behind, of course, but that can't be helped. When he's well again . . .'

'Yes,' Sara agreed meaninglessly. The tea tasted funny; she took another sip, schooling her expression. 'How long has he been ill?'

'This is the second year, and the treatment could last another yet. But if it makes him better —'

'Of course.' Sara hesitated, asked anyway. 'Jack said something about your last governess leaving?'

Beth grimaced, skin tight over prominent cheekbones. She looked as gaunt as the barren landscape outside, nerves stretched tight by worry and fear for her son. 'Gela was Swedish and only nineteen. She couldn't stand it. I suppose it *is* lonely for outsiders. I've had two others come, both young, but neither stayed. That's why when I heard you were older – well, I thought you'd handle it better.' She gave another grimace, this one comical. 'You're the last person I should be saying this to!'

'It's okay,' Sara soothed, feeling sympathy for the woman. Beth seemed stripped to essentials. Fear for a child could do that, she supposed. Or perhaps it was the cost of living out here. She was suddenly ashamed of the nebulous fears that had driven her to this isolated outpost. If their circumstances were reversed, she couldn't imagine this plain-spoken bush woman doing as she had, because some man had frightened her. She'd probably take a shovel to him instead.

'If it would only rain.' Beth sighed, then gave a small grin. 'You'll hear that a lot, Sara. It's all people can think of, when the rain will come. Things will be so different then. This is pretty country, you know, in a good season. Really it is.'

'I'll have to take your word on that because I've never seen anything so – so empty and desolate. We passed a few cattle at a tank, and I saw a dead cow and some crows, and about a billion grey trees. And that was it.'

'Mulga. Yes, but the sand country grows on you, if you let it. Well –' Beth stood and collected the dirty mugs – 'don't be afraid to ask the kids about the place. They know how it all works, the land, the stock. They can teach you heaps. Because you'll find everything easier if it makes sense, if you know why things happen.' A smile flashed. 'I need you to like the place, to stay. Anyway, there're the goat bells now. Come on out and meet your pupils.'

The children were at the goat yard, which lay between the last shed and the distant glitter of old bottles on the station rubbish dump. The animals milled about the yard where their young had been penned for the night, watching the women's approach with calm, yellow eyes. Jess, the cattle bitch, accompanied them, sniffing Sara's shoes before silently migrating to her companion's side.

This was Sam, the taller of the two children. He was plainly unwell, with that thin, fine-drawn look of chronic illness. He moved more slowly than his sister and the felt hat he wore rested almost on his ears, as if his head had somehow shrunk. He had Beth's brown eyes, but the flesh below them looked bruised against his pale skin.

'Hello,' he said politely in response to his mother's introduction. He looked puzzled. 'It's not Friday. How did you get here?'

'With your uncle,' Sara responded.

'Uncle Jack's home?' the little girl squealed. 'Cool. Are you gonna teach us now, instead of Mum?'

'Yes, Becky,' Sara said. 'But I hope you and Sam are going to help me learn about the station too. There's so much I don't know. For instance, why have you locked up the baby goats?'

It was Sam, amazed by her ignorance, who answered. 'So we can milk the nannies in the morning.'

'Oh, so you use goat's milk. Is it nice?'

He shrugged, at a loss. 'It's milk.'

Beth smiled faintly. 'Not helpful, Sam.' To Sara she said, 'You had some in your tea.'

That explained the odd taste. Feeling a fraud, Sara smiled at both children. 'There, you've already taught me something.'

'I'm gonna see Uncle Jack,' Becky declared and took off at a run.

Sam stayed behind to walk soberly back beside his mother, whose hand came to rest on his shoulder. 'Okay?' she asked softly.

'A bit tired.' Quickly he added, 'I'm okay, Mum. It was just a long walk.'

'Early night, then, I think.' She spoke lightly but Sara saw the strain in her face, a look she would come to associate with Sam's down periods when his energy levels were low or his appetite off. Of course the worry must be constant for her, so far from the ambulance service and hospitals. Sam's illness would be a tremendous burden for any family, she thought compassionately, but how much more so for one way out here?

4

At the house Beth glanced at the lengthening shadows. 'Dinner won't be long. But there's time enough to shower or unpack if you want to.'

Sara did both. Her room opened onto a side verandah and contained all she would need. There was, she was glad to see, a ceiling fan, and a bed with a white coverlet and two pillows, patterned drapes at the French doors, a dressing table and a narrow wardrobe. A bulky roll on top of it proved to be an old-fashioned hooked rug – for use in winter, she deduced. Slipping off her shoes, Sara lay down to test the mattress; she yawned, settling her head onto the pillow. It had been a long day. Moments later she had drifted off, to wake to a persistent knocking and Becky's voice calling that dinner was ready.

It was still warm although the sun had set while she slept. Night enfolded the homestead with a blackness Sara had never experienced before, and somewhere out in it a diesel engine thudded monotonously. They would eat in the dining room.

'To celebrate your arrival,' Beth explained, 'and to prove we can be civilised.'

Becky, plainly pleased with the novelty of it, had set out linen placemats and had begged to use the good plates as well. 'I did the table,' she told Sara proudly.

'And you made a lovely job of it,' Sara responded.

The little girl beamed.

The men arrived, heads wet from recent showering. Jack hoisted an eyebrow at his niece, who was fussing with paper napkins. 'What's all this, then, Squirt? Putting on the dog for Sara?'

Becky giggled. 'It's a party, Uncle Jack.'

'You'll be giving her ideas. Next thing she'll want a rise in pay.' But he winked at Sara as he spoke and she smiled back, amused by his relentless cheerfulness. He'd shaved and scrubbed his nails and, now that his hat was off and she could see his face properly, he wasn't bad looking. The white stripe across his forehead where his hat habitually rested was startling at first, but Beth's husband had it too.

Len Calshot looked older than his wife, a rangy six-footer with sun-damaged skin and big freckled hands. His hair, a lighter brown than Beth's, was thinning, and there was a bloodhound droop to his cheeks, which, with his dark eyes, gave him a mournful look that vanished when he smiled. He welcomed Sara in a low voice, then settled himself before the casserole dish to serve out the meal, passing each plate as it was filled to Beth, who added mashed potatoes.

Jack was seated across from Sara. Once they were all eating she asked, 'Have you found whatever it was you wanted for the thing you were repairing?'

He grinned. 'That's one way of putting it. Yeah, I did. So what do you think of the place, Sara?'

'Leave her be, Jack,' Beth admonished. 'Don't put her on the spot like that.'

'Actually I like it. It's so peaceful. You've a comfortable home, Beth. Is it very old?'

'Oh, yes. Eighty-odd years since this house was built. Len's fourth generation, you know. We upgraded the homestead when we got married: put in the coldroom and the gas stove, built the bathroom. The old bathroom was outside under the high tank: ghastly in winter! The house is beginning to need attention now, and the floors are well overdue for resurfacing. The climate's very hard on timber.

But it's not likely to happen this year – or next. Drought takes every-thing, you see.'

'I notice the laundry is outside. Why's that?' It was a separate building next to the wood heap; she had spotted it on her return from the goat yard.

'Because of the copper,' Beth explained. 'Len's mother used to scrub the clothes on a table, then boil them. It was 32-volt power back then on the stations, if they had any at all. We've progressed to a washing machine since, so feel free to use it, but only when the diesel is running, please. It pulls too much power from the batteries otherwise.'

'You're not on the grid?' She caught Sam's look of surprise and something very like a snort from Jack, but Beth's tone was serene.

'Heavens, no. We have a solar rig and battery bank. Sam can explain it to you. He knows all about alternative energy.'

Beth bent a quelling look upon her brother and began collect-ing plates. 'Who's for pudding?'

Len, who so far had said little, asked, 'Where's home for you, Sara?'

'Adelaide. It's where I was born, educated and worked until now. Except for a week or so in Mildura, of course.'

'What did you do?' he persisted.

'Oh, office work at the Commonwealth Employment Agency.' She smiled at Sam. 'It was very dull. Coming here's the most exciting thing I've ever done.'

'When I grow up,' Becky struck in, 'I'm gonna be a pilot for the Flying Doctors.'

'Good for you. I wish I'd thought of that. I *did* work in a cake shop once, though,' Sara admitted, eyes twinkling at the children.

'Did you get to eat any?' Sam asked.

'Sadly, not often. It was mostly sweeping and washing up.'

'I wouldn't have stayed,' he declared, curling his lip. 'Not in a shop.'

'I was in high school. I needed the money for books. What do you plan on doing when you're grown up, Sam?'

'Help Dad, of course.' His bald skull, which looked so vulnerable in the light, turned towards his father. 'And when he's as old as Pops, I'm gonna run Redhill myself.'

'And if he gets sick again,' Becky chimed in, '*I'll* fly the doctor out to make him better.'

'Sounds like a plan,' Sara nodded.

''S'a good one,' Becky agreed complacently. ''Cause when I grow up I'm gonna marry Uncle Jack, and he's gonna keep my plane working so it won't *ever* break down.'

Jack looked at his sister. 'In that case I reckon I need two helpings of pudding to keep my strength up.'

Jack left immediately after the meal, the bright lance of his headlights cutting a way through the dark paddock. Becky went out to see him off, then scampered back to the kitchen where Sara was helping clear up, while Len watched the news.

'Quick, Sara, come and see.'

'Why aren't you cleaning your teeth?' Beth asked sternly.

'I will, Mum. I want to show Sara the sky first.'

'Make it fast, then. Has Sam gone to bed?'

'Yes. Come,' she tugged Sara's hand and they went together to the verandah and down the front steps. 'Shut your eyes,' the child commanded, 'and wait.' A few moments passed. 'Okay, now look.'

Sara lifted her head and her breath caught on a gasp. She had never until then seen the night sky in its natural state. There was no chance of doing so in the city and even Mildura's lights had cast glow enough to diffuse their splendour. But here the myriad stars glittered above her, pulsing with every breath she took. How had Paterson put it? *And at night the wondrous glory of the everlasting stars.* They spread across the arch of the heavens like the glitter of diamonds against black silk. Beside her Becky swivelled, slowly naming the constellations.

'That's the Milky Way and there's the Saucepan, see? And the Seven Sisters – only there aren't really seven. Well, there are, Dad says, only you can't see them all. That's the evening star setting, low down there, see? And that bright one's the pointer for the Cross coming up.'

Sara was amazed. 'How do you know all this?'

'Dad told me,' she said smugly. 'You like it? I'm glad. That's where I'll be flying one day, up there where the stars live.'

'It's beautiful.' Sara looked down at the blur of the child's upturned face. 'Thanks for showing me, Becky. You're a very lucky girl, and I'm not the least surprised you want to fly.'

They didn't keep late hours at Redhill. The children were well asleep by nine and the adults too had retired. Sara switched off the bedside light and lay listening to a silence broken only by the whirr of the fan and the faint creak and splash of the mill turning in a vagrant breeze. She had left the French doors ajar and the breeze whispered softly through the room, cool on her skin. She wondered if Jack had reached the roadhouse yet, and what would now be done to fill the vacant position she had left so hurriedly in Mildura. If it seemed a week since she had got off the bus at Charlotte Creek, the actions that had driven her to boarding it belonged to another age.

It had all begun that afternoon at the beach.

Normally Sara wouldn't have gone there: as a redhead she wasn't a beach person. Her pale skin was unsuited to exposure, and her thick wild crop of curls would claim their own penance when the spray and boisterous wind were done with them. She had stood at the top of the sand, clutching her hat and takeaway coffee (disappointingly lukewarm) and wondered why she had come. It had been the impulse of a moment on a dull Sunday afternoon. A walk on the beach and a coffee. Where was the harm?

It had been an unusually warm day in late August and the place was crowded with sunbakers and surfers, there were kids with spades, boys with boogie boards and a half-dozen youths down at the water's edge tossing a bright plastic ball about. Even as she watched, a gust of wind took the soaring ball and spun it inland. Heads swung like a choreographed dance to follow its flight as two of the youths began to run. The ball might have been aimed towards her. Mouth slightly open, she craned upwards, watching as it sailed closer. Just as its volume blocked the sun, turning the coloured sphere black, a third person, a man she hadn't even noticed till then, gave an exuberant leap to head it and his flying elbow rammed her shoulder, knocking her to the beach.

Was that when the terror hit her – or was it the moment before? She was no longer sure; she knew only that she was sprawled in the sand in an explosion of coffee, confusion and gibbering fear. Light was blinding her, fear sucking away her senses. There was sand in her hair and on her face, coffee soaked her blouse and dripped from her arm and she was panting as if she had run a marathon. Her shoulder hurt and one shoe had come off. She had raised a trembling palm to block the light and saw above it the loom of her assailant's face and reaching hands, and terror had taken over.

'Get away from me!' She thrust herself backwards, scrabbling awkwardly. Her mouth opened to scream and the man had hastily stepped back.

'Jesus, lady! Look, I'm sorry.' Her face, to his surprise, was bone-white against the undisciplined riot of her hair. 'It was an accident. I didn't see you.'

Sara's panic had vanished as suddenly as it had come. She flushed, feeling angry, foolish and embarrassed. Her heart was racing, her mouth dry, and she wished only to be elsewhere. She rose unsteadily, searching for her bag and hat. The former had flown open when she fell, vomiting its contents across the sand. The man had crouched to collect her things and half the beach with it, she thought crossly, watching him shovel up her belongings. He snatched her hat in passing as it bowled away on the wind, the vigorous shake he subjected it to doing nothing for the straw.

'I do apologise.' He eyed the blouse and grimaced. 'And for that, too. God! Nice going, Mike. I'm Mike Markham, by the way, off-duty cop. Please, let me buy you another coffee to make amends.'

'It's all right,' Sara said brusquely, eager to be gone. She registered only his general appearance: well built, dark hair, olive skin. Perhaps a Mediterranean heritage? 'An accident, no apologies needed. I didn't really want the first coffee anyway.'

She had walked away, ending the encounter, and had thought no more of it at the time, save for the mild annoyance occasioned by the stained blouse and the subsequent discovery that her address book had been overlooked in his mad scramble to retrieve her belongings.

Well, it didn't matter. She had the information elsewhere and there was nothing of a personal nature in it: business contacts, the salon where she had her hair done, the SES – where was the harm in being prepared? – her mother's current number. Sara felt her lips twist at the final thought. It said everything about her relationship with Stella that she had to write down her phone number.

Sara sighed and pushed aside her hair to let the fan cool the pillow, which had become unpleasantly warm. Even though the sun was long gone the house still retained its heat. If it had only been the man, she reflected, she could have braced him, demanded to know why he was following her. But it was that blinding instant of terror she had felt as he loomed above her that was the problem. She was cautious in her dealings with men, as any young woman alone in a city in the nineteen nineties was wise to be, but she wasn't afraid of them as such. Only this one. She should have demanded a reason for his persistence the day after that first encounter at the beach, when he'd bobbed up beside her on the pavement as she left the office to buy her lunch. He'd had two takeaway coffees in a cardboard holder and had called her by name, claiming to have learned it from a co-worker in the office. She had snubbed him and stalked off – a mistake, she thought now. Better if she had taken the coffee and found out what he wanted. At the time she had mistakenly put his interest down to her looks. Sara knew that men found her attractive, but when she was still a teenager her mother's promiscuity had aroused a fastidiousness in her daughter that baulked at easy conquests. She would not allow herself to be the subject of a pick-up in the street. Whatever her contemporaries might do she had no inclination to sleep with casual dates.

After that there had been no reason to believe she would ever see the man again. And if, a week later, she hadn't developed that migraine . . . Sara shuddered, thinking of it. She had suffered them intermittently for years, the headaches starting soon after the car crash that had blanked out all memory of her early childhood. Sara had been six or seven when it happened, but had only the haziest recall of being in bed for an unspecified time, and being forbidden to go outside. During puberty the headaches had developed into full-blown migraines, crippling in their severity. She had come to recognise the warning signs though and the moment her vision splintered into flashing light she had informed her boss and left to go home.

And that was how she had seen him, the man from the beach encounter, coming out of the alleyway dividing her flat from the dry-cleaners' business next door. She had watched unseen as he strolled away and then, rendered all but incapable, she had staggered indoors and collapsed into the helplessness only migraine sufferers know. Afterwards, her careful search of the flat had convinced her that he had been inside it. There was no open-and-shut evidence to support her belief – nothing was missing, nothing she could point to to prove it had she called the police, but the subtle signs were there. Remembering it now, Sara shivered, feeling afresh the violation of what had been her home. Then, the next morning at work, an extravagant bunch of flowers had been delivered to her desk with a note from Mike promising to ring her. She had stared at the bouquet as if it had been a nest of snakes, wondering what sort of sinister intent lay behind their arrival. Had she unknowingly attracted the attention of some twisted control freak intent upon forcing his way into her life? You heard about such people and the lengths they went to to achieve their ends. Well, she was not about to play. The dread that had swept over her at their first meeting was warning enough.

It was no wonder then that her boss's fortuitous offer of a temporary transfer interstate, following almost immediately after the flowers, had seen her jump at the chance to be somewhere else. In a fever of motion she had packed up the flat in which she no longer felt secure, stored her furniture, and cancelled mail and phone. Steeling herself to the task, she had also rung her mother, who currently lived three suburbs over, to tell her she was coming to see her. Sara had given a day but not a time to avoid arriving to find her mother out, a not unusual occurrence – Stella excelled at evasion. But this time, rattled and fearful as she was, Sara intended to have some straight answers about the past.

However, when she had arrived, early by design, she had parked her car around the corner, expecting to catch Stella in her housecoat. Instead, to her horror, she had found the same man from the beach knocking at her mother's door and peering into the front window.

Pressed into a hedge, her heart in her mouth, Sara had watched as he banged again, flat handed, against the door, then strode to the next-door neighbour's house. The colloquy that followed was brief. When the door closed he had punched a fist into his palm and then got back into his car and drove off. Sara had waited ten minutes, then went to tap on the same door only to have it wrenched open and a glaring householder confront her with a snarl.

'What the hell is it now?'

'I – sorry to be a nuisance.' She was startled by his aggression. 'I was looking – that is, wondering about the woman next door?'

'Gone,' he barked. 'Yesterday, I dunno where, and I don't care, got it? Now, if you don't mind, I'm tryna watch a match.'

The door had slammed on his final word, leaving Sara seething with fury at her mother's duplicity. Stella had agreed to see her. She should have smelled a rat right then, she told herself. When had anything ever been that simple and straightforward with her mother? From all through her growing years, she could only count on one hand the number of times Stella had ever delivered on a promise or answered a straight question. Sara had not expected much from the visit, but this was madness – unless she had already planned the move and simply hadn't bothered to mention it? Sighing, Sara admitted that was possible. The only time she ever heard from Stella was when she was between jobs and wanted money, which Stella expected as her right. Sara's temper rose with the return of one particular memory.

'It's no more than I'm due. I did plenty for you and don't you forget it, miss.'

'Newsflash, Mum. That's what real mothers do. Not that *you'd* know anything about that.'

She had had her face slapped for her pains. It always surprised Sara how fast her mother's scarlet-tipped hands could move. Her figure had thickened with middle age but she still carried a trace of the bold attractiveness she had owned in her youth, with her strong features and the dark hair an unlikely shade of blonde. Standing thwarted in the empty street, Sara reflected that she had never found a single thing that she shared with her mother – neither looks, colouring, nor taste. The woman was as complete a stranger to her still as somebody plucked randomly from the far side of the earth. But there was no time now to remedy that, supposing she ever could.

The man had driven off, but if he knew where her mother had lived, what would he unearth next? With the hair prickling on her neck, Sara slid into her car and drove away.

By the Sunday she was gone.

Mildura had seemed a haven at first – a warm one, it was true, but she no longer felt hunted. When the eight weeks of her tenure were up, Sara decided, she would apply for another regional posting. She need never return to Adelaide, for the Commonwealth Employment Agency was nationwide. The idea was strangely liberating – and yet it was shattered to a million bits the following Friday afternoon when she had spotted her stalker amid the throng of shoppers in the street where she worked.

Something had changed in the night. Sara lifted her head from the pillow as the steady background *dom dom* of the diesel motor slowed and died. She held her breath waiting for the fan to cease turning then relaxed as it continued. Of course! What had Beth said? They had a solar rig and battery bank – so now, presumably, the power was coming from the batteries that were charged by the array of solar panels she had glimpsed earlier. Sam had said he would show her how it all worked tomorrow. Her thoughts turned to the children, to Becky's ambition and energy, and Sam's quiet reserve. She had envisaged little horrors, spoilt and unruly. They seemed like good kids, she thought, yawning deeply.

Sara's eyelids fluttered and fell, and the intermittent splash of the mill carried her into a dream of two children digging in a shallow creek, like the one they had crossed in the horse paddock. They were building an underground cubby but the dry sand kept caving it in. *Bum! Bum! Bum!* the boy swore angrily. In the dream his face was hidden under a large-brimmed hat. Was he Sam? The sky dazzled when she looked up, and the glitter of gum leaves twisting against the glare made her eyes water. There was so much they could do. *Bum!* she yelled, flinging herself into a somersault, and the boy laughed, temper forgotten, and stood on his head.

Eyelids twitching, the sleeping Sara smiled, her breaths coming soft against the pillow.

5

Sara woke with a feeling of wellbeing and lay for a moment considering the fragments of a dream that faded even as she reached for it. Roger had wanted children, but she had not felt ready for them. They had married when she was nineteen, having known each other for less than six months, and divorced two years later when she had come to see that her feelings for him sprang not from love but from dependence. She had never told him much about her childhood – her excuse being that she remembered so little of it – only that she and her mother, Stella, didn't get on. She had said nothing of the loneliness of knowing herself unwanted, of the deep desire for something that was missing from her life. She had feared her father until he vanished into the hospital, subsequently to die – from what, she never knew. And Roger had known nothing of how, despite her best efforts as a child, she had signally failed to win anything beyond a hard stare from her mother and a dismissive *Go on, go outside and play*.

Throughout her brief marriage she had secretly blamed her lack of desire for a baby on her own unhappy experience. Children had always been for her no more than a faint possibility, far in the future. She had her flat, her work and Roger to rely on, and for a while it had seemed enough. But now, remembering Becky's upturned face, and the tender worry on Beth's as she watched Sam, she found her certainties shifting. As if some part of her suddenly yearned to hold a child in her arms.

In the meantime she had overslept; the realisation jerked her upright. By quite a bit too, judging by the sounds she could hear beyond her room.

By the time Sara reached the table the children had almost finished eating and Len was leaving. He had a disreputable felt hat on his head and a packet of sandwiches in one hand.

'Morning, Sara.' His gaze sought his wife. 'I should be back by five. The wireless'll be on in the cab. Call if you need me.'

'Yes.' Beth glanced at Sam and away again. 'He'll be fine. How did you sleep, Sara?'

'Like a log,' she confessed. 'Sorry I'm late. I plainly need an alarm to wake me.' Beyond the windows the first grey hint of day was growing and lights burned in the kitchen.

'That's okay. School doesn't start till eight. We do keep early hours but you'll see the wisdom of it when summer comes. I'll find you an alarm clock. That's a pretty blue top. Toast? Or would you rather have eggs?'

'Thank you. Toast is fine.' Sara poured tea for herself and talked to the children while she ate. Sam had missed a year's schooling. He looked more rested this morning but his physical strength was obviously limited. Sara decided against the walk around she had planned and asked him about the property instead.

The taste of the tea reminded her. 'Who milks the goats?'

'Me and Mum,' Becky replied. 'Sam used to help but the yard's too germy.'

'Germy?'

'The manure.' Beth had overheard. 'Infection is a risk we try to minimise.'

'Of course.' Sara stacked cup and plate and rinsed them at the sink. 'I'll just clean my teeth, then you can show me your work, Becky. And Sam, you might explain to me how the School of the Air works. It comes on the radio, doesn't it? So we'll all be having lessons today.'

'The school's in the Alice,' Sam explained. 'The teachers call us when it's our turn so we get to talk to her, but not to the other kids. Each class has one session a day.' The brevity of the explanation, she thought, showed his familiarity with an obviously complex operation.

Sara had been nervous about this part of the job but the morning went well. The children knew what was required and made no effort, as Sara had half feared, to play up. Becky was a bright child, articulate during the on-air lesson, gabbling her answers to squeeze in her own breathless snippet of news. 'Guess what, Mrs Murray? Our new governess is called Sara. She's got ever such pretty red curls.'

'That's interesting, Rebecca,' the disembodied voice answered. 'Welcome, Sara. Let us stick to the lesson, though. Now, Billy, what number comes next?'

'Seven, Mrs Murray,' piped a new voice.

'Beat ya!' Becky crowed to Sam, who scowled back.

'I was gonna tell her about Sara. You shoulda let me! I'm older than you.'

'So what? It's *my* news too!'

Sam was behind in his work. Watching him struggle with a paragraph, Sara also suspected he had poor reading skills. She would have to do some remedial work there, teach him to break the words up and sound them. She found a passage in his reading papers and they began on it, but his concentration soon flagged and by lunchtime he had developed a headache. Beth dosed him with Panadol and sent him to lie down.

'Is he okay?' Sara was concerned.

Beth sighed. 'Yes and no. He's been getting a few bad heads lately. It could be that his eyes need checking. Kids with ALL,' she explained, using the medical abbreviation for the disease, 'can suffer all sorts of latent effects from the treatment – learning difficulties, stunted growth, problems with vision. I'll get his eyes tested next time we're at the hospital. He might need glasses.'

'It must be so hard.' Sara caught a slipping comb, scooped up a handful of curls and pinned them back in place. 'Do you have much help on the property?'

Beth was making sandwiches for lunch. 'None. Len does it all now. We employ men for the musters, but we haven't done one this year. Len and Jack between them can handle what needs doing. It's mostly pushing scrub, bore maintenance, lick runs, repairs – there're always repairs when you can't afford to replace equipment.'

'Does he work here, then, Jack?'

'He helps out, and he's the district's general handyman. That's why he's fixing Mavis's fridge. Alec, he's Mavis's other half, is a great bloke but he's useless with tools.'

The kettle shrieked. Sara found the teapot and hunted along the shelf for the tea.

'Blue tin, at the end.' Beth pointed, setting aside Sam's meal. 'He can have it in his room,' she explained. 'Do you have siblings, Sara?'

'I was an only.' Her smile was crooked. 'My mother told me often enough I wasn't wanted, so there was never going to be a second child.'

Beth looked shocked. 'That's too bad. *Not* happy families, then?'

'No. What about you? Were you a happy kid?'

'You bet!' A reminiscent smile touched her lips, deepening the creases about the brown eyes. 'Jack and I both were, but I don't know about my poor mother! I was a terrible tomboy. Always on a horse, or down at the cattle yards or catching snakes. That was our big thing for a couple of years – we were mad about snakes. God, when I think back!' She slapped the last sandwich on the plate and rewrapped the bread. 'The last one we ever caught was a big brown – longer than I was tall. It could've killed us both and a couple of horses, too. We had it pinned down with a forky stick and were arguing about how to bag it when Dad turned up.' She grinned. 'Jack got the walloping of his life. Bit unfair, seeing as I'm two years older. I was yarded up in the house and garden for a month over it, and I had to learn to sew. I was going to run away a dozen times.'

'So you grew up on a property. Near here?'

'Closer to the Alice. Arkeela Downs – Jack's got it now. It's only small, five hundred square miles. He sold off most of the herd to settle our parents in town the year before last. A good thing as it's turned out, because he got the rain we didn't last summer, so there's agisted stock on it at present. Right.' She closed the fridge door and picked up Sam's plate. 'Lunch. I'll go see how he's feeling now.'

At three o'clock when school ended, Sara walked down to the horse yards with the children, carrying one side of the feed bucket with Sam. They had spoken to her of their ponies and she had pictured roly-poly Shetlands, but the reality looked like full-sized horses. Becky's was a bay mare called Star (for the mark on her face, Sara learned) and the odd-coloured gelding with the crooked blaze was Sam's.

'He's called Lancer.' His young owner rubbed the horse's face.

'What do you call that colour? He's a sort of red,' Sara observed.

'Yes, he's a red roan. There's heaps of different roans: red, blue, strawberry. When it rains we could teach you to ride. If you stay,' he added.

'I plan to.' Sara looked doubtfully at the animal. 'I don't know. He's awfully big. I've never been this close to a horse before.' She raised a tentative hand to pat the dark, muscled neck. 'Do you like living out here, Sam? I mean, wouldn't you rather be in town, go to a real school, have friends?'

The hat brim tilted as he looked at her. With his bare skull covered and the sun on his face, he looked almost well. 'Why would I? This is the best place in the whole world. Besides, there's always been Calshots at Redhill.' In a tolerant tone older than his years he said, 'Droughts pass, you know. This country's had heaps of 'em. Dad told me there was one so bad back when my granddad was young that the camels died, which means there can't even have been mulga left.'

'Imagine that,' Sara said feebly. 'So when you grow up you'll stay here, just like your dad?'

'Course.' He switched back to tour-guide mode. 'See the little birds on the ground over there? They're called peaceful doves. They come to eat the grain the horses spill.'

6

By the time ten days had passed, Redhill, though completely different to her quiet city flat, set in its shady street, had come to seem like home. Sara had thought she might miss the privacy the flat had given her, the peaceful evenings and lazy Sundays by herself. She had been solitary as a child and it had become a habit – she had grown to adulthood with acquaintances rather than friends – but she needn't have worried. She settled into the rhythm of family life as if born to it, welcoming the children's noise and spats and Beth's even-handed way of dealing with them. Sam might have been ill but he wasn't a saint. He frequently snapped at and teased his sister, who gave back as good as she got.

'You can now see the advantage of being an only child,' Beth wryly remarked one day after separating the two. 'Or were you lonely? Did you ever wish you had a brother or sister?'

'I think I'd have liked one,' Sara admitted. Hidden in the mist of half-forgotten things was a yearning she sometimes still felt for something dear she had missed. She had always assumed it was a playmate, but since meeting Beth she'd thought it could simply have been a mother's love. You could tell that Beth never forgot for a second that she was foremost a mother. Whereas her own childhood recollections of Stella's face had too often included a momentary blankness of expression, as if Sara's very existence had slipped Stella's mind. Perhaps if her father had survived things might have been different, but Sara doubted it. She retained no clear picture of him, only vague and disturbing memories of a threatening shape like a giant shadow on the wall, and hints of some hidden fear. She remembered his presence more than his person, and the relief that had followed his sudden disappearance.

He's crook and gone to hospital, Stella had said, face hard as she had puffed on a cigarette, *so I don't want no noise outta you. Go outside.* The child Sara had been glad to escape. She was no longer sure if it had been weeks or even months before she'd asked about him again, but they had moved house in the interim. Stella had delivered the news of his death in the same unemotional tone in which she had spoken of his original absence.

Does that mean he's not coming back? Sara could scarcely believe her good fortune.

Course it does, you little ignoramus. Gawd! Stella gave her a look of pure dislike. *I was never cut out for this parenting malarkey, and Vic oughta have known it.*

'And you're truly not finding it too lonely here?' Beth's question broke into her thoughts. 'The drought's to blame that it's quiet. There's usually more social stuff happening – the campdraft and the races. Mavis organises the odd dance, and there're the CWA meetings. Country Women's Association,' she explained. 'A good excuse for us all to get together. They used to be monthly but nobody can afford the fuel for the extra running about now.'

'No, I'm perfectly happy, truly I am,' Sara assured her. It was the truth. She hadn't thought about her stalker once in the past week, and the memory of that paralysing fear that had so unnerved her had faded. Every day was crammed with interest. 'I'm beginning to think I've missed a lot, not having children around. Maybe I should have trained as a teacher. Do you know I'm finding both your kids' speech a bit old-fashioned? Why is that? Becky actually said *Goodness me* this morning, like some maiden aunt in a play.'

'Really?' Beth said. 'I honestly hadn't noticed but I suppose it's because they've only ever had adult company. Oh, they see other station kids a few times a year, but they're in the same boat, aren't they? Don't worry about it though, parents with older children who go to boarding school say they soon pick up the teenage talk.'

They saw little enough of the men, who left early and returned on dark or later, the bang of their vehicle doors the signal for both arrival and departure. Jack came and went, either helping his brother-in-law or called out by the neighbours to fix something mechanical. Anything from a bulldozer to a wireless apparently lay within his remit, and the loss of the latter seemed the biggest problem. The one in the office at Redhill ran daylong, the burr of static and machine Morse occasionally interrupted by phonetic call signs and the gabble of a message.

'It was all radio before the phones came,' Beth said, turning the bread dough out of the bowl. 'Now, dust it with flour and knead – pull it towards you, then turn it and pull it again. That's it. We knew the sound of everyone's voices even if we'd never met them. People from north of Katherine to the other side of the Alice. It was great. We all knew what was happening where. It's different now, though, with the phones.'

'More convenient, surely?' Sara suggested, adding, 'Heaps of places out here have girl's names, don't they? There's Alice, Katherine, Charlotte Creek.'

'Mmm. Alice Springs was named for Sir Charles Todd's wife. He just got the river for himself. Katherine – I don't know. Charlotte, though, was named for a camel.'

'You're kidding me!'

Beth grinned and sprinkled more flour. 'Okay, cut the dough in half now and shape the loaves. She was a cow camel, died in the creek bed that's named for her. Dunno why. Might have been the collywobbles, old age, thirst, even . . . Camels made this country, opened it up for settlement, I mean. The pioneers built roads with them, delved dams. They were the only transport at one time. Very tough animals.'

'Still.' Sara smoothed her loaves and lifted them into the greased bread tins. 'Naming something – why wouldn't a man think of his wife or his mother first? Why pick a camel?'

'She's the one that died.' Beth laughed. The sound was so infectious that Sara joined in, bringing Becky to investigate, more than a little jealous at being left out of the joke.

When she had flounced off, Beth sighed. 'She knows Sam's treatment is nearly due again. She hates me going off and leaving her.'

'So that's it,' Sara said. 'I thought he was quieter than usual, poor kid.'

'Yes, the treatment's not pleasant but the side effects are worse. It's hard on Becky too; still, right now he needs me more.' Beth looked troubled. 'It's only natural she should feel jealous and neglected, poor mite, but at the moment all my energy feeds into keeping Sam going. I can only do so much, and I *will* make it up to her.'

'Perhaps I'll think of a project to occupy her,' Sara suggested. 'Something she can feel is special, just for her.'

Beth's face lit up. 'Could you? That'd be brilliant. We leave Monday and I'll be back late on Wednesday, unless Sam needs to rest. Sometimes he does. Jack'll be here to help out with the chores. You can leave the goats and the diesel and the watering to him. There'll just be the four of you to cook for and Becky's lessons. Don't worry about too much housework or the washing. I can catch up when I get back.'

'I'm sure I'll manage okay,' Sara said. 'You just concentrate on Sam.'

Beth ran water into the bowl, saying, 'You're a godsend. Make sure you always soak the dough off the sides. If you scrape at it, you can nick the surface of the bowl and let in bacteria. That'll ruin other batches of dough. I've ordered extra bread this week so you shouldn't have to bake, but you'll need to do it next month.'

'He needs treatment that often?'

Beth nodded. 'Yes. Once it would've meant going to the city. We're so lucky it's available in the Alice now.'

Sara could only admire the woman's determination to make the best of the tragedy that had overtaken her family. There was a survival rate of ninety per cent among *all* sufferers, so her pupil's chances were better than good. His mother always spoke optimistically of the future, hiding her dread of that other ten per cent, save for odd moments when Sara had seen her eyes resting on her son's face, her own unguarded. A growing hum broke into her thoughts. 'Is that a vehicle I hear?'

'It will be the mail. He's a day late this week, remember?' Beth glanced at the clock. 'Time to put the kettle on.'

Becky came in, letting the door bang behind her. Beth winced.

'Don't slam it, Becky. I've told you before.'

'I bet Sam's allowed to,' she said.

Her mother ignored this. 'The mail's coming. Would you like to show Sara where Harry's special biscuits are kept?'

With a bad grace the child yanked the corner cupboard open. 'Back there.' She pointed.

'Becky!' Beth said warningly. 'Bring them out and show Sara properly. Is the school envelope in the office, Sara? Good, I'll get it.'

She went out and Sara knelt beside the child, peering into the cupboard. 'They must be pretty special biscuits,' she offered.

'Yeah.' Becky mumbled. She hauled the tin out and prised off the lid. 'Mum makes them for him.' Her glance flickered to Sara's face, her look suddenly calculating. 'You wanna try one?'

'Why not? Ginger, are they? Yum. My favourite biscuit.' She took one, bit into it and chewed. A few moments later the heat hit her. 'Aaagh!' Sara sprang to her feet feeling as if she had ingested live embers. Hurriedly she spat the remaining contents of her mouth into the sink and splashed cold water over her burning lips, but it made no difference. She could hardly breathe; her mouth and gullet were on fire and her tongue felt red hot. Involuntary tears poured from her eyes as she pressed a hand to her swelling lips.

'*Becky*!' Beth, re-entering the kitchen, saw and understood what her daughter had done. 'You wicked girl! How could you be so mean to Sara?'

Looking suddenly scared, Becky dropped her gaze. 'I never made her eat it,' she whined.

'And I didn't make Sam sick,' Beth snapped, yanking the fridge open. 'It's not Sara's fault you're unhappy. Tell her you're sorry this minute – and I hope you mean it! Here,' she proffered a glass of milk to the sufferer. 'This will help, and I'll get you some bread. I'm so very sorry, Sara. Sit down and just sip, try not to touch your face. You might've got some on your hands.'

Sara's eyes continued to tear as if her body was trying to douse the inner fire. She could feel her lips swelling, stretching taut and shiny across her face. 'What is it?' she gasped.

'Cayenne pepper, I'm afraid. There's enough in those biscuits to stop an ox. I haven't heard you apologise yet, Becky.'

'I'm sorry,' the child muttered. 'I didn't think it would be that bad.'

'You can see it is,' Sara said, her voice severe. 'It wasn't a nice thing to do and your mum is right. Hurting people won't make you feel better. You have to find other ways of doing that. We'll talk about it tomorrow.' The milk helped a little, though its effects only lasted while she held it in her mouth. 'Why cayenne?' she gasped between gulps. 'What have you got against Harry?'

'He loves ginger biscuits and a pinch of the stuff is part of the recipe. Only he complained they had no bite so I kept upping the amount. He reckons I've finally got it about right.'

'He must have asbestos innards, then!'

'He has. That's why they're kept apart, so never feed them to anyone else.'

'I'm not likely to. Talk about a weapon of mass destruction. You could fell armies with that mixture.' Sara set aside her empty glass and breathed through her open mouth to help dispel the heat. 'I'm going to wash my face and hands, maybe that will help. If not, I'll try ice.'

7

Harry Ellis's left arm was missing far enough above the elbow that the short sleeve of his shirt covered the stump. When she'd met him briefly the previous Friday, Sara wondered how a disabled man could manage the job he had, but Len brushed off her query.

'He does okay. I've seen him use a shovel and he can change a tyre. And he carries a wireless.'

'What happened to his arm?'

'Guess they parted company.' He said it without a trace of a smile, only his eyes crinkling a little at the corners. Len had a dry wit that was totally unexpected in such a self-effacing man. 'I knew a bloke once who had a three-legged dog. He was a bit like old Harry – ran with the rest and could jump just as far as any mutt in the pack.'

Sara, holding a cold washcloth to her lips, was remembering his words as the mailman hooked a finger in the screen door and nudged it open with his foot. A man of middle years, he was wirily built, the skin of his good arm burned to a deep tan by a thousand suns. He had an amazingly large nose, bushy grey brows and a head of grey hair. He let the door close gently against his stump, swung the mailbag onto the table while at the same time dropping the half-dozen magazines he had clamped in his armpit.

'Mavis sent 'em,' he said. 'Thought the kids might use 'em for school.' He winked at Sara. 'So how's the country treating yer?'

'Very well, thanks, Harry.' Her face felt hot and tight, but if he noticed, he didn't remark on it. She tidied the magazines into a pile and poured tea for him as he dropped his hat and sat down.

'She'll make a bushie.' Beth had opened the bag and was going through its contents. 'She's even survived one of your biscuits.' Becky, mute in the corner, hung her head.

'Whoa!' His brows rose. 'That was game of yer.' He bit into one himself and munched contentedly. 'Good as ever, Beth. One of these days I'll bring you me recipe for curry.'

'Thanks all the same, but I doubt we could swallow it.'

'Good for you. A bit of 'eat cleans out your pipes.' He swallowed gustily from his mug and smacked his lips. 'I'm carrying extra rations for the park this week. Seems they've got a bunch of scientists out there, counting the hairs on bush rats, or some damned thing. Typical townies. Turned up without so much as a loaf of bread between 'em, so Clemmy put in an urgent order. Oh, and Mavis is talking about a fundraiser for the doctor sometime in the 'olidays. A Saturdee, anyway. Said I'd pass it on.'

'Thanks.' Beth found a biro and wrote on the calendar hanging on the wall. 'It'll depend how Sam's feeling.'

'How is the young fella?'

'He's fine, thanks. I'm taking him in again Monday. I'll be home by Friday but, just in case, Sara knows where your biscuits are.'

'Good-oh.' He clicked his teeth suddenly. 'Damned if I didn't nearly forget. Man needs his 'ead checked for 'oles! I ran into old Bungy on the road. He said to tell Len that Kingco's sending a driller out to their prospecting camp. Bungy's gonna borrow him to get a hole put down. He thought Len might wanna do the same.'

Beth straightened in her seat. 'But that's wonderful news! Having the rig in the district will cut the cost enormously. Did Bungy say how long it would be round for?'

'Don't reckon 'e'd know.' Harry emptied his mug and stood up. 'Well, I'd better kill a metre or two. Thanks for the cuppa, Beth.

I left yer chook food on the loading dock.'

'Thanks. Len'll shift it when he gets home.' Beth handed him the outgoing mailbag. 'See you next week.'

'Yes, goodbye, Harry,' Sara echoed, collecting cups. A few minutes later the truck door slammed and the engine fired. There was still a residual burn on her tongue as she prodded gingerly at her swollen lips. 'Who's Clemmy?'

'A ranger at the national park. That's Harry's next stop. She and Colin have been there, oh, six or seven years now. Becky was just a toddler when they came. She's very pretty – small, blonde, wears these sexy little shorts; looks about eighteen but she's got to be nearer thirty.' Beth smiled ruefully. 'Makes the rest of us seem like dried-up old sticks, but she's so nice you have to like her. Funny thing is Colin's just the opposite – skinny as a rail, no conversation, hides behind a great black beard. They're both very dedicated to the park.'

'Any kids?'

'Not yet, though Clemmy says they want them. What about you, Sara? Do you ever think about it for yourself?'

'Having children?' Sara pulled the plug and wrung out the dishcloth. 'Sometimes. If I remarry, I think I'd like a child.'

Beth looked surprised. 'I thought you were single?'

'I am now. Divorced. Roger wanted children, but I wasn't ready then. Still, it wasn't the only reason the marriage broke up. Anyway,' she finished lightly, 'there's not much I can do about it now.'

There was a hint of a smile in Beth's brown eyes. 'Oh, I don't know, there's Harry. And old Bungy's still a bachelor. You never know your luck in the mulga.'

On Monday morning Beth and Sam left for Alice Springs in the family station wagon. Sara, bidding the boy a cheery farewell, thought he looked pale and fatigued. The bruising that had suddenly appeared on his arms didn't help either. He was listless at breakfast, eating little, and Sara couldn't help but be aware of both Len's and Beth's silent concern.

Len went off to continue work on the engine he was dismantling; Jack, apparently, wasn't the only mechanic around. Jack himself had returned the previous day after a brief absence, dumping his gear in the men's quarters and turning up for dinner, to Becky's obvious delight.

'Have you finished at the roadhouse, then?' Sara had asked. 'Nothing left to mend?'

'Not till the next time Alec does something stupid,' he'd said. 'I've been with old Bungy at Wintergreen.'

'Fixing things?'

'Divining for water.'

Len had looked up from his plate. 'How'd it go?'

Jack's look had been doubtful. 'I wouldn't say he has the best prospects. He's gonna drill anyway, but what's there is scrappy and I reckon it might be deep too. The best pull I got was north of Fiddler Creek and it's a bit too close to his other bore there to suit him.' He shrugged. 'I suggested he drill there and pipe the water to where he wanted it. Maybe he will, though he's a stubborn old goat.'

Len's loose cheeks wobbled as he shook his head. 'Man, it'd cost. The poly you'd need . . .'

'No more than a dry hole – a *deep* dry hole.'

'Yeah, well, not good news for us either, then.'

'Maybe not. Still, it's a fair step from his northern boundary to the Forty Mile and different sort of country. Could make the difference.'

'Yeah,' Len had agreed but Sara saw that his gaze had returned to Sam, picking at his dinner, the hollows in his thin cheeks accentuated by the overhead light. Outside in the warm darkness Jess was scratching herself a hole; her tail thumped against the steps at the sound of their voices, then the sound of her digging continued. She was a quiet dog, devoted to Sam, and Sara had noticed how closely she had been sticking to him, as if, in the manner of dogs, she was aware of the imminent separation.

Now Sara stood at the gate under the oleanders, watching the dust column rise behind the station wagon as it vanished down the paddock. Becky had gone off without saying goodbye to the travellers. Sara would have to do something to cheer up the child. She listened to a magpie carolling from the branches of a garden tree and eyed the lawn, which looked very dry. Beth had said the men would see to the outside chores but she supposed she could turn on the sprinklers. There wasn't much she recognised in the garden, save the lemon and fig trees, and then only because of their fruit. Perhaps she could get Becky to make lemonade for smoko? The girl loved her brother, but Sara had also seen how she resented him always getting the larger share of her parents' attention.

Between supervising schoolwork Sara swept the house, moved the garden sprays around and baked a batch of patty cakes, popping back into the schoolroom periodically to ask Becky largely unnecessary questions – which bowl was the Mixmaster's, where was the dustpan kept? By smoko time Becky was happily involved in squeezing lemons and icing the cakes.

'Great job!' Sara praised. 'I'll make the tea while you stir the sugar into the lemonade. What a team, eh?'

'This is fun,' Becky said. 'What'll we cook next?'

Her methods seemed to be working. Sara tapped her chin thoughtfully. 'We-ell, what's your favourite pudding?'

'Frog's eyes. Yes, please, Sara!' She clapped her hands.

'*Frog's eyes?*' Sara echoed and heard Jack laugh behind her.

'That's tapioca pudding. Great choice, Squirt! It's the best.'

'Really? Well, then,' Sara said gamely, hoping there would be a recipe somewhere. 'I'll see what I can do.'

'Tomorrow arvo,' Jack said as he drank his tea, 'I'll be going out to Kileys bore. Might be room for a pint-sized person.'

'Yes!' Becky cried. 'And Sara too?'

Since their little talk following the biscuit episode, Becky had been penitently solicitous of her governess.

'If she wants to come. Great cakes.' He helped himself to another. 'Up to her, really.'

'I am sitting here,' Sara said. 'What about some details before I decide? Like, how far is it, and how long will it take? I have dinner to cook, remember.'

'It's a bore about twenty k out. We'd leave after school – say three o'clock, check the bore, boil the billy and return. Allowing for everything short of a wheel collapse, we'd be home by five.'

'That seems doable,' Sara agreed. 'I would like to come, thank you.'

'That's settled, then.' He favoured Becky with a stagey wink. 'You reckon she might pack some of these cakes for smoko?'

'You might need to take more grease for the mill,' Len put in from his end of the table. 'The tin was about empty last time I was there. The cakes are great, Sara. Just shows –' his eyes twinkled – 'here I was thinking city women couldn't cook.'

Jack grimaced. 'Marilyn certainly couldn't. So, is the job living up to expectations, Sara?'

'I told you I didn't have any preconceptions,' Sara replied, wondering who Marilyn was. Of course she had been too desperate to even consider what her new life would be like. 'But I like the life. Especially the mornings. It's so wonderful waking to the birds instead of traffic.' She relished the sound of the magpies, the crowing of the cocks that mingled with the half-caught dreams that sometimes played at the edge of consciousness. Before coming to Redhill her dreams had been less frequent and those that came were darker, and filled with a nebulous anxiety. Jack was watching her and she tossed her head self-consciously. 'I think I must've been a country girl in another life.'

'You're right about the mornings, though.' Len stood and

pushed his chair in as Jack also rose. 'Best part of the whole day.'

'I think so too. What time should Beth reach the Alice?' There, she was even beginning to sound like a Territorian.

'She'll ring when she does.'

'Should I fetch you – if you're round, of course?'

'Just take a message; we'll speak tonight.'

'Of course.' She had forgotten it was all STD out here. Sara rose, crooking her finger at her pupil. 'School, Becky. We have to finish early today because I've got a special project planned.'

'What?' She bounced eagerly to her feet. 'Tell me!'

Sara smiled. 'It's a surprise, but a nice one, I promise you. Go and get started on your sums while I clear up.'

'Will you be long?'

Sara reseated a comb and wrinkled her nose at her. 'Depends. I have to find a recipe for frog's eyes, remember.'

8

When lessons were over Sara produced the ringbinder she had filled with sheets cut from manila folders to serve as an album. 'It's a scrapbook,' she explained. 'I thought you might like to make your own collection of pictures and stories about yourself and your life on the station. Because it is sort of special, you know. People like me, from the city, don't understand it at all. So it'd be like a pioneer's diary. You can cover the pages in pretty paper if you like – your mum gave me some gift wrapping – and you can draw pictures and colour them in, or cut them out of magazines and paste them, or use photographs. Whatever you like.'

Becky fingered the stiff sheets, eyes bright with dawning possibilities. 'Did you make one when you were a kid?'

'No, but then, I had no one to help me, or buy me things. Your mum said you can raid her sewing box for bits of lace and ribbon. And if you keep your birthday cards . . .'

Becky nodded vigorously.

'Well, there's heaps of pictures on them you could cut out and use. What do you think?'

'Oh, yes! Are you gonna help me?'

'To start you off, but it's *your* book remember. And when it's done you might even want to take it into town to show Mrs Murray. You do see her sometimes?'

''Course. At the School of the Air break-up. We always go to that. And the sports days. I can show Nan too, and Pops. Wait'll Mum sees it! You have the best ideas, Sara! I'm so glad you came. I like you heaps better than Gela. Sam does too, only he won't ever tell you. That's 'cause he's a boy, Mum says.'

Sara was touched. She said lightly, 'I'm glad to hear it. As it happens, I like you too, chicken. And Sam. Come on, then. Let's get started.'

The following day school had just ended when the peremptory blast of the Toyota horn announced Jack's arrival at the front gate. Becky whooped and ran, Sara following more slowly. It seemed wrong to walk out leaving the house unlocked. Jess, lying under the oleanders, swivelled lion eyes to watch them pass.

'You're sure it's okay? Even the windows are open.' Sara wedged the cake tin under the seat. She wore a long-sleeved shirt of pale blue over jeans, and had enlivened the straw hat's crown with a matching blue scarf.

'Jess is here. You try getting past a cattle dog,' Jack replied. 'Here, wriggle over, Squirt, and tuck your feet back. You got enough room there, Sara?'

'Yes, thanks. Heaps.' The rifle, clipped in its rack, promptly nudged her hat off. She dumped the hat on her lap, fingering the scarf. 'So, where's this bore?'

'North.' He jerked his chin as he set the vehicle moving. 'And strictly speaking it's a well, not a bore. There's about three hundred head running on it.'

'So it's quite important,' Sara guessed, and caught the affirmative dip of his chin.

'They all are. Water's precious out here, so we check 'em regularly. Don't do much else really these days, apart from pushing scrub – that's the mulga we knock down to feed 'em.'

'It'll be a long drive, if that driller Harry spoke about does make one for you out where all that dry feed is,' she observed.

'It's called the Twelve Mile,' Jack said, 'the plain, that is – part of the Forty Mile. And you're right about the distance. Incidentally, you don't "make" bores, Miss Blake, you put them down.'

'You do? Sounds like getting rid of an old dog,' she said straight-faced and caught the edge of his grin from the corner of her eye.

Once through the horse-paddock gate Jack turned up along the fence, heading north, crossing over the shallow creek that ran through the paddock.

'Skippers,' he said.

'What?' Sara caught up. 'Oh, the creek. Skipper who, then?'

'No one. Skipper was a nag.'

'Of course. I understand that Charlotte was a camel. Funny sense of priorities you people have out here.' His lips twitched and she settled back, enjoying the drive despite the roughness of the track and the fact that there was nothing to see but scrub and sky. The sheer emptiness, coupled with the knowledge that there wasn't another soul (save Len), within two hours' drive in any direction, was somehow invigorating.

The change in the country, when it came, was disconcertingly abrupt. The harsh red soil and grey scrub vanished and there was suddenly a diversity of shapes and colours in the timber. A smudge of ochre ridge grew in the distance, glimpsed through the taller line of timber that she had come to recognise as a watercourse. There was even an emu; Becky pointed it out.

'There – by the conkerberry bushes.'

'I see it,' Sara assured her. To Jack she added, 'The hills are pretty. Is that where Redhill got its name?'

'Yep. We're a practical lot out here. Walkervale's named for Tom Walker, who pioneered it. And it's said Wintergreen came about because there was good winter rain the year it was taken up. It doesn't happen often but when it does . . .' His face softened. 'Well, it's worth seeing.'

'You love it, don't you? Beth said you've got a property too, is it like this?'

'A bit,' he conceded. 'Desert country but more stone. Miles of spinifex ridges, a couple of good springs in the hills and the rest is like this place – mulga, and great herbage when it rains, but it's basically a battler's block. My parents managed on it but things are tighter these days. There's Kileys.'

Sara searched ahead, then spotted the glitter of a mill wheel above the trees. Myriad thin tracks Sam had told her were cattle pads wove in towards it, and the bare ground all about the bore was darkened by years of dung. Cattle stood and lay about under the trees, their ribs and hipbones prominent. Jack drove slowly past them to stop in the shade by the creek bank. He switched off and the silence brought the buzz of flies into the cab, the squawk of a white cocky, and the drag of the working mill rods.

'Well.' He thrust his door open. 'I'll go check things. Reckon you girls can get a fire going and put the billy on? There's matches in the glovebox.'

'Yes.' Sara didn't intend admitting that she had never built a fire. Becky helped, gathering up handfuls of dried gum leaves that proved very combustible. As the blue smoke curled up into the pyramid of twigs and larger branches, Sara had a sudden, brief flash of memory – a family picnic with just such a fire and a billy heating beside it. The image was gone almost before she could grasp it, lost in the aromatic smoke. The smell of the burning leaves must have triggered it, she thought, staring blindly at the crackling flames. But who was the family involved? Certainly not Stella, who had nothing but scorn for 'the sticks'. But for Sara to have the memory, surely she must have been there?

Becky was returning from the bore with the filled billy. Her mind in a whirl, Sara took it from her, casting a doubtful look at the water. 'Is it clean?'

''Course! I got it from the outlet, not the trough.'

'That's okay, then, I think. Oh,' Sara remembered in dismay, 'I didn't bring any cups.'

'Under the Toyota seat.' Becky rummaged to produce three enamel pannikins. 'The green one's Uncle Jack's.'

Sara stared at their blackened interiors. 'Well, they definitely *aren't* clean. Come on, a bit of sand will work wonders.' She sploshed a little water into one of them and headed down the shallow creek bank.

'It's only tea stains,' Becky protested.

'And this will get rid of them.' Sara wet a little sand and scoured the enamel. 'See, you have a go. You have to wet the sand, though.'

Becky's enthusiasm soon took over. Sara let her finish the job, reflecting that she was a good kid, eager to try anything new. The creek sand was coarse and scattered with tiny spiral shells and millions of gum nuts from the white-trunked eucalypts lining its bank. She wondered if the seeds were ever washed to where they could grow. It seemed unlikely in such a desert place, but only water could have made the creeks, so they must occasionally fill. She wished she could see it. A whiff of burning gum teased her nostrils and she found herself remembering the children of her dream. They had been at a place somewhere like this, the sand as loose and as hot against the thin soles of her sandals. She could smell the gums and the moisture trapped beneath the deep sand. *We could dig a soak.* The ghostly words trickled through her mind and she recalled her own eager reply. *Yes, let's!*

Sara jerked herself back to awareness, blinded by light. She had left her sunnies in the vehicle. Where had that voice come from? A shiver went through her as if something cold had traced a line down her spine. Cicadas shrilled and the long fingers of the eucalypt leaves spun in the heated air. She mopped her face on her sleeve. She was sweating but her skin felt cold. What was wrong with her? She turned towards the bank, meaning to find her sunglasses, and saw instead a man's dark outline looming above her. Terror blanched her face. She shrieked, 'No!' then the blackness roared over her and she fell into darkness.

9

Sara woke to the heat of sun-baked earth at her back. It took her a moment to remember where she was, then she saw the man's shape crouched beside her and recoiled before recognition overtook her instincts and she relaxed. 'What happened?' Her head spun as she sat up.

'Take it easy. You fainted.' His gaze left her to find Becky watching big-eyed beside him. 'It's okay, Squirt. Could you get me a cup of water? Good girl.' The child scampered off and Sara reached vaguely for her hat that had fallen off; she felt shaky and light-headed, and wilted before Jack's accusatory gaze and the sudden harshness of his voice. 'You scared the crap out of the kid, shrieking like that.'

'I'm sorry,' she said stiffly, embarrassed. 'I don't know what —'

'Drink this. You're probably dehydrated.' He thrust the cup at her and waited, frowning while she drank.

'You want to tell me what's going on?' His tone had moderated. 'You saw me on the bank, squawked like a frightened chook, then dropped like a poleaxed steer.'

Her face reddened and she bit her lip, not meeting his gaze.

'Maybe it's not my business but Beth's not here, and Becky's my niece so . . . You don't suffer from epilepsy or anything like that, do you?'

'Of course I don't!' she cried, stung. 'I'd have said if I did.

Anyway, I hold a driver's licence. And I can't be both a hen and a steer!' Sara caught herself and reined in her temper. 'Look, I'm sorry. Perhaps it was the heat. I've never fainted in my life. That's the first time ever! So if you're worried about Becky, you needn't be. Where is she, anyway?' She looked frantically around.

'Making the tea. She's okay.'

'With boiling water and an open fire?' Alarmed, Sara struggled up, briefly dizzy again as she bent for her hat.

'She's a bush kid.' He spoke calmly. 'She's been making billy tea for ages.' He took her arm as she climbed. 'Go and sit down. You need tea with plenty of sugar, and I'm serious about your liquid intake. It's easy to get dehydrated out here.'

Becky, her face grave, was sitting on the trunk of a fallen gum; Sara joined her there. 'Sorry, chicken. Did I scare you?'

'A bit.' Sara felt the child's scrutiny, read the uncertainty in her dark eyes. 'You're not getting sick, like Sam, are you? He fell down like that too, right at first. His face went all white and he went to sleep just like you, only he didn't yell.'

'I'm sorry,' Sara repeated gently. 'That must've been awful for you. But people can faint for all sorts of reasons. Your uncle thinks I haven't been drinking enough water. *I* think I just got too hot. Look, let's have some cake. That'll make us all feel better.'

It worked with Becky. She was soon chatting away again. Jack squatted on his heels near their log, drinking from the green pannikin, his previous suspicions of her fitness seemingly forgotten. Not that she blamed him. He was obviously fond of his sister's children and it was bad enough having one of them at risk . . . She fought to keep her mind from replaying the incident and was visited with an idea instead.

'Becky,' she said, tossing away the dregs of her tea. 'I want you to pick a few leaves off all the different sorts of trees and bushes you can reach. Can you do that, do you think?'

'Yes. Only, why?'

Sara smiled. 'You'll see. It'll be something for your book, another surprise.'

Later that evening, with Becky asleep, Sara asked Len if she could use the printer in the office. Jack had gone off to the quarters by the time she had finished, and shortly after he left Len excused himself and she heard his bedroom door shut. Night shrouded the homestead; the diesel was off for once and somewhere nearby a mopoke was calling. Sara trod quietly out into the garden to gaze at the starry expanse of sky, stiffening as she felt a cold touch on the back of her leg. Thoughts of snakes shot through her mind, then sense returned and she stooped to fondle the dog's head.

'Jess. You miss him, don't you? Never mind, he'll be home soon.' The dog's tail swung against her knee, then Jess padded off and Sara returned indoors. When she was in bed she finally let herself think of Kileys bore and what had happened there. Below the frustration and fright bubbled a small measure of excitement, for she was almost certain the tiny instant of recall was a memory. She had first thought it a dream, but it seemed too real for that. Besides, dreams didn't come with olfactory and sensory impressions. She had smelled the gums, and the burn of the hot sand had been real. It was no dream. She and the little boy had been there – well, not to Kileys, obviously, but they had played in a creek very similar to that one. The question was, where? And why had she screamed at the sight of Jack? Though it hadn't been at *him*, she knew, because she'd been dazzled by the sun and had only seen his shape. Just, she suddenly realised, as she had only seen the shape of the man, who had subsequently stalked her, that day at the beach, the first time the sense of terror had overwhelmed her.

Sara knotted her brows, staring into the blackness. The only light came from the illuminated dial of the alarm clock on the dresser. The darkness of the room was like her memory, she thought, the tiny pinpoints on the clock face the pitiful segments of all she could recall. It was as nothing set against the dark, but she had to hold to it and struggle with the blackness until something was forced to yield. Only when the glitter of yellow light had grown to flood the room would she know what was hidden within it.

Something had made her faint and, whatever Jack had said, it wasn't dehydration! Abruptly Sara remembered the incident in Mildura and bit her lip. And she'd told him today's fainting spell was a first. Damn! She had never intended to lie, which reminded her again of her stalker and that sent her thoughts uselessly back to her reason for being here. Weren't deliberate omissions a form of lying, anyway? There was so much she hadn't told him but how could she, when so many things made so little sense? Sara wished there was somebody she could talk to about it all. Beth, perhaps, if she were home and unburdened by Sam's illness, but she couldn't lay her problems on top of the far more urgent ones her employer already had.

Beth had rung earlier that evening but Len, returning from the office where the phone was, had simply shaken his head at his brother-in-law's lifted brow. 'Not so hot,' he'd murmured. 'She thinks they'll wait an extra day in town. Sam's feeling a bit tired.'

'Well, it's a long trip,' Sara said, her gaze on Becky. 'I thought I was never going to reach Charlotte Creek when I came out.'

'Yes.' Len twigged, and injected heartiness into his voice. 'A good sleep-in and an easy day, that's all he needs to be as fresh as a daisy.'

'Is that like a fresh horse?' Becky wrinkled her brow. 'How can a daisy be fresh?'

Sara turned her palms up in bemusement, and it was left to Jack to sort out the difference for his niece between a frisky mount and a newly opened flower.

In the morning it was Jack who came in with the milk bucket while Sara was turning chops in the pan. She raised pale brows at him, her fiery curls neatly confined by two combs.

'I didn't know you could milk. Is Becky with you?'

'Morning, Sara. She's finding something for her hair.' His own head was bare. The muscles swelled in his forearm as he lifted the bucket and strained its contents carefully into the milk pan ready for scalding. 'Milking's easy enough. I learned as a kid; we always had goats. Milk and meat in one parcel.'

'Sara, can you help me, please?' Becky proffered a scrunchie in one hand, the other holding her gathered hair. Sara turned off the stove, combed the girl's ponytail with her fingers and secured it.

'Phew, you smell awfully like goat. Go and have a really good wash.'

Becky giggled and ran off making bleating sounds. Jack, rinsing the bucket at the sink, said abruptly, 'You're good with her. The last girl was hopeless.'

'Thank you.' Sara heard the approach of Len's boots and the light patter of Becky's returning feet. She said quickly, 'Later I'd like a word, about yesterday. If you have the time?'

The grey eyes rested on her face, then he nodded. 'I'll make some.'

Sara cut lunches for both men, fed Jess and the hens, started the garden sprays and bustled Becky into the schoolroom with the reminder that her lessons had to be finished in time for the mail.

'But it's only Wednesday!'

'I know, but there's lots of work still to get through today and tomorrow. Besides, if you work hard this morning, you'll have time to do another page in your scrapbook. And I've made you some special sheets, see?' She showed her the paper printed over with the various leaves collected from Kileys. 'Maybe you could write a little story on them about yesterday – having tea in the bush at the bore, with Uncle Jack, and picking these very leaves.'

She touched their outlines.

Becky's eyes lit up as she gave Sara a swift hug. 'You have the *bestest* ideas!'

'Don't I just? Let's get started, then.'

10

The men were home late that evening. They had been pulling Canteen bore, Len told her, and would be starting back at first light to complete the job. 'Would've camped if we'd had the gear,' he said. 'Could you manage a five o'clock breakfast, Sara?'

'Of course.' It seemed awfully early. 'What's the rush?'

'Water,' Jack grunted. Neither of them had showered yet and their clothes were smeared with rusty-looking mud – or muddy-looking rust, Sara couldn't decide. 'The tank's empty so the cattle don't drink till we've fixed the mill.'

'I see. What shall I do about the goats?'

'Let them out,' Len said. 'Their kids'll take care of the milk.'

'Right.' It was at moments like these that Sara was most deeply aware of her ignorance. Even Becky would've known the answer to that, she thought, and felt foolish for asking. Both men appeared tired so she got the meal on the table quickly, and later shook her head when Jack moved to pick up the tea towel. 'Becky and I will do it. Is that the phone?'

Len answered it, sticking his head into the kitchen some five minutes later to say, 'They'll be home tomorrow, Sara.'

'How's Sam?'

'Better, Beth said. He had a fever, but he's brighter now. She thinks he's right to travel.'

'That's good.'

Len vanished into the bathroom and Jack went out yawning, calling goodnight from the door. Becky, putting away the last pot, looked expectantly at her.

'What shall we do now?'

Sara stifled a sigh; she had planned to watch television, but current affairs wouldn't interest Becky and it wasn't yet her bedtime. 'You could read a book,' she suggested without much hope. Becky had already complained that her books were boring. She reiterated it again now with vigour.

'Okay.' Sara gave in. 'We could think about another page. What if we find some pretties to paste onto it first, then decide on a theme, what it's to be about?'

'I want to make one about us, for Mum,' Becky said. 'I could put all our faces on it. There's heaps of photos of me and Sam, and Mum and Dad and Uncle Jack. And I could put in Jess and the horses. I wish I had one of you too, Sara.'

'That's nice, but maybe you should just keep it as a family thing. Have you got a snap of the homestead? You could put it in the middle with all the faces around it.'

'Yes! And a ribbon in the corner. Only, can you tie a bow, Sara? Mine never turn out right,' she confessed sadly.

'I'm sure I can, chicken. Your mum is going to be amazed.'

Becky beamed.

The clamour of the alarm dragged Sara from sound sleep, its strident urgency impossible to ignore. Groaning, she rolled over, shut it off, and got up reaching for her wrap. In the kitchen she lit the gas for the kettle and a pan of eggs, which would be quicker than chops, and was setting the table when the men came in, dressed for the day.

'Morning,' she yawned at Len. 'Do you need lunches?'

'Morning, Sara. If you wouldn't mind.' His hair was rumpled, he looked as tired as she felt.

'No problem.' There was cold meat and cheese, she thought, and pickle. That would do. She opened the fridge, then stiffened as an eerie whistling sounded. 'What on earth's that?'

'Curlew.' Jack had come in unseen. He dropped bread into the waiting toaster and pulled the pantry cupboard open. 'We got any dead horse?'

'What?'

'Red sauce. A curlew's a bird, by the way.'

'Well, I know that,' she said crossly. 'I'm warning you, Jack Ketch, I am not a morning person and you are starting to irritate me.'

'Can't have that.' He found the sauce and sat down. 'Not when you're looking so fetching.' He buttered his toast and winked. 'Great eggs too, just how I like 'em.'

Sara ignored him, dropping more bread into the toaster and then starting on the lunches. Twenty minutes later when the Toyota drove off, she cleared the table, left the dishes for later and returned to bed. She remembered the wink then, and smiled. Jack's cheerfulness could be irritating, but she had come to trust him. There had been no time yet for a private word, but that was scarcely his fault. She knew little enough about cattle country but water must obviously take precedence over all else, and even if he hadn't been called away, Beth's return today would leave her with little time alone. She would do a load of washing later, she thought, and some baking. Beth would be tired from the long drive; she'd appreciate an easy day tomorrow.

Sara yawned, snuggling luxuriously into her pillow. Life out here was certainly different. Who would have thought a month ago that she would find herself able to bake bread and entertain a child, and consider it all part of the job? The office and her previous life seemed like an old film she had once seen, her stalker no more than a stereotyped villain. She hadn't even suffered a migraine since coming to Redhill. Without quite knowing how, it seemed she had found the one place she truly wanted to be.

Mother and son arrived late in the afternoon, the station wagon coasting to a stop before the front gate. Jess promptly went mad, leaping at the passenger door, her tail beating a frenzy of welcome as Sam got out and fell to his knees to hug her. He looked thinner than ever, and dark rings below his eyes emphasised his pallor. Beth's weariness showed as she groaned and stretched, hands to the small of her back, before greeting Sara. She hugged Becky, but her eyes were on her son as he climbed the front steps.

'I've made tea,' Sara offered. 'It's all ready, if you'd like to go in.'

'Thanks, sounds lovely; I could do with something. Sam, too. You'd best have a bite now, Sam,' she called. 'Then rest till dinner. He's lost weight,' she explained. 'He always does. So, how's everything, Sara? Len told me they'd probably be late back tonight.'

'Yes. They're pulling a bore.' Sara felt satisfaction at having remembered the terminology.

'Mum, Mum,' Becky tugged at Beth's skirt, which she had teamed with another of her singlet tops. It was the first time Sara had seen her out of pants.

'Not just now, love,' Beth said. 'I need to get Sam settled first.'

'Yes, but see what I've made. It's my own book, all about us and the station. I did it all myself —'

'That's nice. You can show me later.' Beth was hauling bags out of the back of the vehicle as she spoke, so she didn't see her daughter's face fall, and when she turned with a bag in each hand, Becky had gone. Sara had reached a hand towards the child but Becky ignored it, running up the steps to vanish inside.

Sara bit her lip and said nothing, seizing the handle of Sam's bag instead. 'Look, I can get this. You go on. It's all set out in the kitchen.'

'You sure? Thanks.' Beth glanced at her watch. 'It's time for Sam's tablet, he's still on antibiotics. He's had a fever, which is worrying . . .' She rooted in her handbag, then hurried ahead, leaving Sara to follow. Sam was in the kitchen by the time she got there, a glass in his hand, and she smiled at him.

'Welcome home, Sam. We missed you, especially Becky. Where is she?'

'She went out. Do I have to eat that, Mum?' He eyed the food and milk Beth was setting before him.

'Just try, sweetie,' his mother coaxed, 'even a little bit.' She poured tea for herself and Sara and settled into her customary chair with a sigh, and a quick glance round the kitchen.

Sara smiled sympathetically. 'Good to be home?'

'Yeah. It's a tiring drive.'

Sara could see the palpable effort it took for Beth not to watch or badger Sam as he slowly consumed half a sandwich and drank some of the milk. 'The treatment really takes it out of him,' she said once the boy had left to lie on the daybed on the verandah. 'It makes him so sick, he barely eats for days after. And the chemo itself suppresses his immune system so he's wide open to infections. His temperature spiked the same evening, but we seem to have caught the bug in time. Or at least I hope so.' She sighed, rubbing absently at the tiny permanent crease between her brows. 'You've done a great job, by the way. How's the meat situation for dinner?'

'That's done. There's a casserole in the oven. Creamed rice and jelly for dessert,' Sara said. 'I didn't think you'd feel like cooking.'

'You're a treasure.' Beth sat back in her chair. 'I noticed the laundry basket was empty. Don't tell me you did the washing, too?'

Sara laughed. 'If you'd seen the men's clothes last night! It was wash them or have them walk out the door themselves. So Sam won't be up to school tomorrow?'

'Maybe Monday. Boy! I really needed that tea. Thank you, Sara. You've done wonders. Now.' She glanced around as if just now noting her daughter's absence. 'Where did Becky get to?'

'Gone after the goats, perhaps? I think,' Sara said carefully, 'that she really wanted you to see her book. She's worked very hard on it to surprise you.'

Beth looked stricken. 'Oh, God! I brushed her off, didn't I? Sometimes all I can think of is Sam. I don't mean to do it, but it happens and it's not right to expect someone her age to understand.' She got up as the clang of bells sounded, rattling rhythmically as their bearers cantered along. 'That sounds like the goats coming now, and rather too fast. She's angry, poor mite. I'll go and find her.'

11

The men were late returning again. Standing on the front verandah Sara watched the day die in an extravagance of gold and pink above the dark line of the mulga. The paddock beyond the garden fence had a melancholy cast at sunset, the shadows beneath the trees a place where loneliness lived. Sara turned her gaze to the darkening sky, amazed to see tiny bats darting on velvet wings as the stars pricked out above them. There must be insects to feed them, though what *they* would live on was a puzzle, when the parched earth and the very air crackled with dryness. The dim shapes of the scrub seemed to yearn towards the cloudless sky, seeking the moisture that never came. Sara wondered how long it took for mulga to die. What would the cattle do then – or Len and Bungy, and the rest of the people whose livelihood the mulga was? And she wondered too how the station people stood the endless deferment of hope. No doubt Jack could tell her. She frowned then at how often he seemed to creep into her thoughts – but then she looked quickly towards the track where a vehicle's lights were flashing through the trees.

'So did you get the bore fixed? Canteen, was it?' Sara asked once they were all at table. Len had greeted his son with a hug and spoken privately to Beth, and both the children were present, Becky subdued but Sam looking brighter than he had earlier. The fan was on, moving lazily in the warm air.

'Yep.' Jack ate hungrily, nudging Sam after his first mouthful.

'Dig in, mate. It's good. Besides, you don't wanna insult the cook, very bad move that.'

Sam gave a fleeting grin and obeyed. Sara was touched by his effort. He obviously adored his uncle, just as Becky did. The boy said, 'We had smoko at Mr Hammond's camp, Uncle Jack. He's building a new bridge over the Three Man. And I've got a new watch, see?' He held up a thin wrist to display it. 'What have you been doing?'

'Nice,' Jack said admiringly. 'You'll never be late for dinner now. It's about time Main Roads got off their butt and did something; that bridge was barely safe. The pump packed it in at Canteen so your Dad and I have been out there. It took us a day and a half to fix. Trough was bone dry for most of it.' He spoke as to another man. 'When we were done there we went onto Wintergreen to see the Kingco blokes about getting a hole put down on the Forty Mile – when they've finished their own drilling, that is.'

Sam looked eagerly at him, the fork halfway to his mouth. 'You gonna take your stick out there?'

'I'll have a look tomorrow. Wasn't time today. I'm not too hopeful, though. That's a dry strip of country, but your dad reckons it's worth a try.'

'I wish I could go with you.' Sam looked at his parents. 'Mum, I don't s'pose . . .'

Beth shook her head. 'I'm sorry, Sam. We have to be sensible. Later, when you're well, there'll be other trips.'

'It's okay,' he muttered, though his disappointment was plain.

Beth looked at her governess. 'Why don't you go, Sara? Would you be interested? You've certainly earned a day off and if you've never seen divining . . .'

'I haven't.' Sara hesitated. 'I thought it was, you know, side-show alley stuff, like tarot cards and fortune telling. But tomorrow's a school day anyhow.'

Her employer smiled. 'I can manage that. I've nothing else to do. You've baked, washed, cleaned – take a break and have a day out.'

'I want to go too,' Becky said. 'Can I, Uncle Jack?'

Diplomatically he left it to Beth to shake her head. 'Not this time, pet. You've got school.'

Becky's brown eyes flashed with remembered hurt. 'Then I want Sara to teach me, not you.'

'But Sara hasn't had a day off since she got here.'

'It's not fair!' Becky leapt to her feet, knocking her fork flying. 'I never get to do anything I want. I hate you! I hate everybody!' She ran from the room and a moment later the crash of her bedroom door echoed through the house.

Sara felt immensely uncomfortable, both from Becky's pointed retort and Beth's assumption that Jack would have no objection to her plan. She murmured, 'Perhaps I shouldn't, she's got used to my ways.'

'No,' Beth said firmly. 'I won't have her thinking that tantrums work. She's feeling hurt and insecure right now, but there have to be rules.'

Sara inwardly cursed Jack, who still hadn't spoken. 'Well, in that case I can open gates,' she offered after a moment, and was relieved to see him nod.

'Sounds like a deal, then.'

For once they had an unhurried morning. School had started before Sara finished cutting lunches for herself and Jack. She packed them into a cool-box along with a freezer brick, collected her hat and headed for the vehicle shed to find Jack fuelling up the Toyota at the bowser. The cool-box went into the middle seat, though first she had to pluck aside a Y-shaped stick. On the point of tossing it out, she waved it at Jack.

'What's this?'

'Hang on to that.' He hooked up the bowser hose. 'I just went and cut it.' He wiped his hands on a rag that he stuffed under his seat, then got into the cab. 'All set?'

'I think so.' Sara inspected the stick. 'What is it? Some special wood?'

'Nope, just a bit of mulga. Point is, there's precious few trees out on the Twelve Mile, that big plain where you felt crook. And before you ask, there are maybe a million Eight Miles, Six Miles and so on spread across the country and nobody is gonna change 'em into kilometres. Not even in fifty years' time when everyone's forgotten what a mile is.'

Sara laughed, a carefree burble of sound, suddenly glad of a day's freedom from chores. 'I see. Not just stubborn, but pigheaded too.'

'That's about the size of it.' His eyes went to her hair, which she was aware was sunlit and gleaming with coppery lights. Her hat was again on her lap, pushed off by the rifle behind her. 'Maybe you should think about getting some proper head gear?'

'What's wrong with this?' She picked up the straw covering.

He shrugged, lips twitching as he looked across at her. 'Mobs o' things. It'll blow off in the wind. Given the chance, the stock'll eat it. Rain'll ruin it —'

'Ha! Chance would be a fine thing.' She flung the words over her shoulder as she got out to open the horse-paddock gate.

Once they were underway again Jack asked, 'So what did you want to speak to me about?' The teasing note had dropped from his voice and his glance was serious, inviting her confidence.

'Oh.' Now that the moment had come, Sara hardly knew how to start. She stared fixedly at the dusty dash, feeling the judder of the vehicle moving over the corrugated road. From the corner of her eye she watched his left hand shifting the gearstick through quick changes in response to the dips and gutters in the track.

'Did you change your mind about it?' he wondered, as if prompting her.

Sara flushed. 'No, it's just – where to begin? The other day

71

when I told you I'd never fainted before? Well, I realised later that was a lie, because I did, once —' She stopped herself. 'Before I came here. It was a very hot day, probably a touch of the sun.' It sounded lame, but she was regretting the impulse to confide in him. He would think she was crazy. 'I just – well, I wanted to assure you that, despite that, I'm not ill or – or irresponsible. I thought you should know, that's all.' She bit her lip, cursing the heat she could feel in her face.

'Yes?' He sounded more puzzled than relieved. 'Well, that's good but I wasn't demanding an explanation, Sara. So why are you telling me this?'

'Because . . .' Sara pressed her hands to her hot cheeks, framing sentences and then discarding them. 'Because you're here,' she blurted. 'I'm sorry. This was a bad idea. I felt I needed to talk to someone and Beth has too much on her plate already. Look, can we please just forget it?'

'Obviously it's important to you. Whatever you choose to tell me won't go any further. If you have something to say, I'll listen. Maybe I won't be able to help, but often enough just setting out a problem – if that's what you have – helps to clarify it. And it'll be a damn sight cheaper than ringing your family from out here.'

'There's nobody I can ring,' Sara admitted. 'That's part of it, really. There's only my mother, and I can't talk to her, even if I knew where she was, which I don't.'

'Well, fire away,' Jack said comfortably. 'We've got all day.' When she didn't respond, he added encouragingly, 'A good trick is to start with a word. So in just one word, Sara, what's your main concern?'

And suddenly she wanted to tell him. The words spilled from her almost without volition, just pouring forth, and the relief of letting them go was immense.

'Memory,' Sara said. 'I've never been able to remember anything before the age of six – and now I think I'm starting to, and it terrifies me. That's why I fainted, both times, here and in Mildura. It wasn't the heat.' She gasped then. 'My God! I didn't mean –

I opened my mouth and it all rushed out.'

'Obviously you *did* need to talk,' he responded. 'Okay, that seems simple enough. Remembering makes you afraid. What of?'

'I don't know!' Sara gritted in frustration. 'Anyway it's not really remembering, because I *can't* – there are just teeny flashes now and then, like something seen at high speed. A glimpse from a bus window maybe – there and gone before I can make sense of it. It's the fear that comes with it that —' She stopped and tried again. 'It's like something bad happened back then when I was little, something so terrible that I shut my eyes so I wouldn't know about it. Not my real eyes.' She struggled to explain. 'I think I must've seen something I can't bear to remember.'

'So you think you blocked it out back then, shoved it into a dark cupboard, if you like, and locked the door?' Jack said slowly. 'And now that door's coming open?'

'Yes.' She was grateful for his quick comprehension.

'I see. Well, is there nobody you could ask about that time? Not your mother, you said. Your father, perhaps?'

'He died when I was a kid. I scarcely remember him. I only remember that he scared me. I have this picture of hiding from him; well, I think it was him, but I can't recall his face. Just somebody who shouted, a shadow on the wall that shouted.' She shivered. 'I think I made him angry going out. It was after the crash. I was supposed to stay in bed. Afterwards, Stella said he got sick. That's when he went away and I didn't see him again.'

'Hang on, you're losing me. Who's Stella, and what crash?'

'My mother. She said there was a car accident. I don't remember it so I can't say if I was in the car or hit by a car. I just recall a dark little room I had to stay in, and that my head hurt a lot.'

The vehicle had slowed to a crawl. Jack waited for a patch of shade on the road and pulled up in it. 'I seem to be missing something here. This was years and years ago, right? And you've never asked your mother about any of it – how this accident happened, or what you might've seen? Whereabouts did it occur, for instance, and was anybody killed? Questions like that.'

'Jack, you don't know my mother. I've never had a straight answer from her in my life about *anything* I've asked. She had no time for me as a kid and used to say so to my face. She never wanted me and couldn't wait to get me out of her life. Right now I don't even know where she's living.'

'Okay.' He tapped the steering wheel in thought. 'Family friends, then? Aunts, next-door neighbours?'

'I have no rellies,' Sara said simply. 'Not that I know of, anyway. And Stella always rented. She hopped – still hops around – like a flea on a dog. So, no neighbours, and as for friends . . .' These had only ever been male, men Stella met in the pub and brought home from time to time for companionship and casual sex. Sara had been a teenager before the true nature of their presence had dawned on her. With a teenager's righteousness she had made no secret of her disgust, disdaining the men with their fading hair and heavy bodies who littered the bathroom with their dirty clothing and filled the fridge with their beer. She had hated the way they treated the place as their own, sprawling on the couch, leaving their mess for others to clean up. Once, when she was fifteen, she had come home from school to find her own bed stripped back to the linen and a used condom on the sheet. Stella, when confronted with Sara's blazing green eyes, had been unrepentant, claiming that her own much prized waterbed had sprung a leak.

'It's *my* room,' Sara had yelled. 'How dare you and that hairy ape even go in there?'

Stella's eyes had narrowed. She said venomously, 'It's the room *I* let you have, and don't you forget it! What's your problem anyway? You can change a bed, can't you?'

'With that filthy thing in it?'

Her mother had laughed mockingly. 'Oh, grow up, Miss Priss. So Jerry's a careless sod. Men are, you'll find.'

Remembering the exchange, Sara pressed her lips together, reiterating, 'No, there's nobody. I never really thought about it before but my parents seem to have been rootless. Stella anyway, and all I know about my father is his name – well, not even that really. Stella called him Vic, so I suppose he was Victor, or even Vittoria. He could have been Italian, he had olive skin – at least, I think he did. I don't even know what he worked at. I asked Stella once and she just looked at me and said, "This and that. What business is it of yours?" He was my father and she wouldn't even tell me his occupation.'

'Not much help there, then,' Jack said. 'I haven't been either, I'm afraid.'

'You have,' Sara said. 'Maybe it hasn't solved anything but laying it out does help. If I'd only done it before, that man mightn't have driven me out of my job —' She swallowed the rest of the sentence.

Jack leaned back in his seat again, the key he had been reaching for left unturned.

'Which job, and what man was that?'

Sara told him. Part of her wondered if this was what she had wanted all along and that the slip of her tongue had been intentional, just an excuse to confide in him. Then halfway through the telling she had the unhappy thought that it all sounded too strange to be credible. Would he think she suffered from hysteria, or was simply seeking attention? He was frowning by the time she finished and her heart sank. However, his response surprised her.

'So this all began at the same time. I mean, you saw this man again in Mildura after he'd apparently followed you from Adelaide. You fainted in what, shock? And it was after that that the flashes of memory started?'

Sara goggled at him. She felt the blood begin to recede from her head, then rush back.

'I am such a fool,' she said faintly. 'I never put it together like that, but it's true. Does that mean . . . Do you think he's got something to do with . . . But surely he's too young to be involved? He looked to be about your age. And I never considered that the two events weren't separate. Him stalking me and me remembering things, I mean. I thought he just had some freakish fixation thing going. But if it's not that then how would he know who I was? And if it's to do with my past, then he must.'

'The electoral roll,' Jack said, 'the phone book, a private investigator – all you need's a name. People aren't hard to find. Vagrants might be, but not law-abiding folk. Of course, he might just have found you madly attractive.' He raised an eyebrow at her.

She shivered, unamused. 'Enough to break into my flat? Is that normal behaviour? Besides, why did I feel such terror at the sight of him, that first time I saw him on the beach?"

'No, none of that's normal,' Jack agreed. He leaned forward again and this time keyed the starter motor. 'You were wise to clear out. Dr Ketch's advice on the matter is to be patient, and wait for your subconscious to heave up whatever it's been hiding from you.' His glance was sympathetic. 'I'm sorry. That's not much comfort, but if it all gets on top of you again and you want to talk, I'm here.'

'Thank you. I appreciate it, Jack. It helps.' And it did; fresh viewpoints were always helpful. She wondered if her stalker was somehow connected to the crash that had stolen her memory. Was it possible that he had lost a relative in the accident and blamed her? Or could she have somehow been the cause of it? If so, might he have been tracking her down in revenge for the death of some family member – a parent, say, or a sibling? Nibbling her lip, Sara considered then dismissed the notion as fanciful, if not plain silly. No six-year-old could be held accountable for her actions. What sane person could think so? As for the alternative . . . She shivered, suddenly glad she was out here in the middle of desert country, where nobody would ever think to look for her.

12

So occupied had Sara been with her thoughts that the Twelve Mile plain burst upon her much sooner than she had expected. One moment dusty grey mulga filled her vision, then the trees peeled back to disclose the swimmy light across the wide plain. She felt a sudden vertiginous shift in ground and sky and swallowed at the immensity of space before her, the overarching blue touching the far reaches of the rolling pale-grassed land that seemed to stretch ahead forever. She had never felt so small and insignificant in her life.

Jack seemed unaffected by its vastness. Without slowing at all he turned the wheel and drove straight out across the open ground. It was no rougher than the road, and the occasional anthills were both easy to see and avoid. When he finally pulled up and switched off, the click of his door opening was the only sound, apart from the ever-present buzz of flies.

'Where do they all come from?' Sara waved her hands to keep them from her face.

'Beats me.' Jack held the stick he'd cut. 'There's nothing much to see, but if you want to grab a coupla those pegs and the tape there and bring 'em along.' He reached to pick up a hammer and thrust its handle through his belt. 'Right, let's see what the ground's like.'

'How?' she asked.

'We walk.' Holding the forked ends of the stick two-handed, with the stem pointing up like an inverted Y, he set off, pacing slowly across the ground. Sara followed curiously, waiting to see what would happen. Nothing did for quite a while, and then the tip of the stick quivered. Jack slowed down and the next moment the stick twisted in his hands until the stem was pointing to the earth. He grunted with satisfaction and gouged a mark in the dry soil with the heel of his boot.

'That's it?' Sara stared at the torn earth, examining the grass stems and the red soil from which it grew.

'Yep. You wanna pass me a peg?' He hammered it in and tied a streamer of tape to the top.

'So you bend the stick and that somehow makes this a likely place to drill?'

'Pretty much,' he agreed. 'Only the stick bends itself.'

'Of course it does.' The green eyes narrowed at him. 'How exactly?'

Jack shrugged. 'I dunno, just that it does. There's plenty of things I don't know but if they work, who's complaining? Here, have a try.' He handed her the stick. 'Hold it the way I did – tighter than that. Grab it like you mean it, girl! That's better. Feel anything?'

Was he having her on? Taking a firmer grip on the wood, Sara glanced suspiciously at him. Nothing happened, but she hadn't expected it to. 'Is this the bit where you fall about laughing at the city slicker? It's a forked stick, not a magical object.'

'You're forgetting the *galli-galli*.' He moved behind her and she jumped as his arms came round her to grip her wrists. He encircled them with ease, knuckles and fingers very brown against her own pale ones, crushing her bones with his grip. She was on the point of protesting when the stick came to sudden life. It twisted like a live thing hauling against her grip until the stem was pointing straight at the peg with its bright-red marker ribbon.

Sara gasped, astonished, but her hands were cramping; she loosened them and suddenly the living rod was an inert green branch again. Jack released her wrists and stepped back, lips twitching. 'Not a magical object, huh?'

'That was amazing. How *does* it work, Jack?'

'Like I said, I dunno. Plenty of people can divine, though.'

'So what's this *galli*-whatever?'

'Ah, that. Ketch family tradition. Anything different, that you can't explain, well, it's gotta be *galli-galli*. Covers the weather, women, divining. Useful sort of term, really.'

'I can imagine,' Sara responded dryly. 'Getting back to basics, though, does it guarantee you'll find water under that peg?'

He lifted the stick again and moved off. 'Oh, it's there all right, but getting it up – that's the gamble. It might be too deep, or unusable. Mightn't be good ground to drill. A dozen things could go wrong; all I know is the stick lessens the risk of a dry hole.'

'You've done it before, then?'

'The odd time or two,' he agreed, walking on.

'Amazing,' Sara was being left behind and hurried to catch up, her fascinated gaze on his hands. 'How many more will you peg?'

He squinted at the sun. 'A couple, ideally – if we get lucky. I've been south of the road, but it's as dry as a bone there. Truth? I'm not too hopeful.'

It took another hour but they finally pegged two more sites. A satisfied Jack tossed his stick aside and stuck the hammer handle back through his belt. Midday was behind them and the wind had picked up by then. Sara lost her hat to it twice before Jack bit off a length of tape and handed it to her. 'Here, tie it on. You gonna stay out here, you want to get yourself a decent hat.' His own shabby felt, she noticed, never shifted. He simply angled it down against the gusts, squinting even more to keep the dust from his eyes. He slipped the tape into his pocket and turned to her. 'That's that, then. You ready for lunch?'

'Yes, please.' Sara swept a look across the undulating grass-land, picking out the widely separated flashes of red tape. 'Which one will you choose to drill?'

'Ah, well, Len's decision. Let's hope the water's good and not too deep. This could save his breeders,' he said, waving a hand over the dry feed. 'Or he could stick with the mulga and agist it out, bring in a bit of cash. Either would work.'

'Like your place? Beth said you had it rented to someone.'

'Agisted,' he corrected. 'Yeah, I was dead lucky to get the rain. I was one of the few who did, so someone's looking out for me. Still, you've gotta win some of the time. You know what the definition of an optimist is in the mulga, Sara? It's any mug on the land.'

She didn't answer. He glanced across and saw her standing fro-zen, green eyes blank with shock.

'What's up? Are you okay?'

His voice penetrated slowly through the clamour of her racing heart. Sara blinked and swallowed; her hands were trembling, her face chalky white. She swallowed again dryly. 'God!' she said faintly. 'I think I need to sit down.'

'Something came back to you, a memory?'

'Yes, I —' But she couldn't talk about it yet. She felt him take her arm as the shock worked through her, leaving her pulse jumpy and her legs weak.

At the vehicle Jack yanked the driver's door open and helped her in, saying briefly, 'I'll get you some water.' Sara clutched the wheel, rested her head on her arms and closed her eyes until her heartbeat slowed. When she sat up he was waiting, the plastic water cup in his hand.

'Thank you.' She drank it down to the last few mouthfuls, then dabbled her fingers in them and trailed them across her face and throat. 'Sorry about that. It was just so strange.'

'You want to tell me?' The concern he showed was real and warming. He made a dismissive gesture with his hand as she hesitated. 'You don't have to if it's private.'

'It's not that. The truth is it didn't make sense. There was a vehicle that drove away and I knew I had to stop it or something terrible would happen. I didn't see anything, or – or do anything, except scream, but it drove off and my heart broke.' Her voice wavered as she transferred her gaze to his face, her eyes bright with unshed tears. 'I don't understand.'

'Neither do I, not right now, but if you remember more it might help. How old were you?'

'I don't know.' Sara stared at him. 'I was *me* and this awful, awful thing was going to happen and I couldn't stop it. It was like the world was ending —' She broke off, made an effort and drew a deep breath. 'Anyway, it was years ago now, water under the bridge, so . . .' Her voice trailed away, then she suddenly hit the wheel with a clenched fist, exclaiming, 'It doesn't make sense! And why now?'

Jack scratched his neck. 'Maybe it's time,' he suggested. 'What about this lunch?'

Today there was no billy tea; instead it was Jack pulling a steel-clad thermos from behind the driver's seat. The sun stood past the meridian but not far enough to cast sufficient shadow to sit in and the interior of the vehicle was unpleasantly warm.

'Tell you what.' He stayed Sara's hand as she was opening the lunchbox. 'Let's find ourselves some shade first.' He drove back to the line of mulga and parked, pushing his door wide. 'That's better. Make use of what nature provides, that's what my old man always told me. *She'll keep you cool and warm and fed and dry, son.* That's what he'd say. Course, you have to put in the effort to make it work, but it's the only way to handle this country. He grew up with the Aborigines, did Dad – there were still blacks' camps on the stations in his day – and you couldn't get better teachers. They were all gone into the missions by the time Beth and I were kids, though, so we learned from him.'

'He sounds an interesting man, your father,' Sara observed. 'What's your mother like?'

He grinned and bit into his sandwich. 'Ball of muscle. She had to be, of course. It's not easy battling on a small block. She kept the books, cooked for the station, taught us kids, made our clothes, grew half our food. She never seemed to stop, but she always made family time, you know? Special cakes for our birthdays when we were little, treats when we were sick; and she always barracked for us at our school sports.'

'I thought you said she taught you?'

'Yeah, she did, but School of the Air puts on sports days just like every other school. We always went and Mum'd be bouncing up and down at the finish line, yelling her head off for us. Embarrassed the pants off Dad but it never stopped her.'

'She sounds great.' Sara felt a stab of envy. She couldn't remember Stella ever turning up at her various seats of learning, not even the year she was dux of the school. 'Are they very old now?'

'No. Mum's only in her sixties, Dad's seventy-three, seventy-four – he's got a crook heart, supposed to take it easy. It's the main reason Mum wanted me to buy them out, so he wouldn't work himself to death. Well, that and to have a home for my wife.'

Sara kept the surprise from her voice. 'I didn't know you were married.'

He shrugged. 'I'm not; we split.'

'Oh, were there children?'

'No. Marilyn wasn't the maternal type. What about your –' he paused, searching for the right term – 'significant other? Isn't that what you call 'em these days? Can't believe there isn't somebody back in the big smoke.'

'There wasn't. Isn't,' Sara said, determined to keep it light. 'I'm divorced, but that was years ago. I married too young, so what was your excuse?'

He grimaced. 'A pretty face, and a failure to heed Mum's advice. She tried to warn me, but hey! When it comes to women, what man listens to his mother? Anything left in that box?'

Sara offered him the slice of fruit cake and watched him unwrap it, wondering about the woman his mother had warned him against, and what Beth had thought of her. Her own marriage had failed, she now knew, because she had entered it for the wrong reasons. She had needed emotional help and Roger had provided her with the crutch of his affection, to which she had clung like a drowning woman. There was no equality in their liaison, she had finally realised; she had taken and taken, giving nothing in return. He had idolised her, he'd been patient and long suffering, putting on hold his own desire for a move to the suburbs to start a family. He was admirable in every way, but she had gradually come to see that he would not always be gainsaid. Her own neediness had inevitably granted him control over decisions they would once have shared, and it had come as a salutary shock to Sara to realise she was in danger of being ensnared in a trap of her own making.

He was fair, Roger – fair-skinned, blond-haired, his open face a book in plain print. And far too easily hurt, a fact that had intensified her guilt.

'But I love you, Sara!' he had protested, in bewilderment and pain, when she told him she was leaving.

'You love the *idea* of me,' she had said sadly, 'but I was never what you thought. I needed you, Roger. I didn't love you. And I'm leaving you because I've done enough damage. I just hope you'll be able to forgive me. I'm seeing a therapist to sort myself out.'

'You don't need a therapist! We can fix it ourselves. If I made mistakes we can —'

'No, Roger.' She had wiped tears away. 'I'm sorry. You can't believe how sorry I am. It's all my fault.' She could cry because she pitied him, but shame consumed her. 'I've been a greedy, insensitive bitch. You have to find somebody better, somebody who really deserves you, who loves you. Because I've come to see that I never did.'

It had been a painful awakening, one that had led her to despise her past actions. It would have been easier if he had got angry, if he had yelled at her or punched the wall – anything but stare at her with heartbreak plain in his eyes. She had lowered her own gaze then, shame searing deeply through her, vowing in future to rely only on herself.

Eighteen months later she had learned through a mutual acquaintance that he was with somebody else, and four years after that Sara had glimpsed him in the street with a child riding on his shoulders, a little girl who had laughed and clutched at his thick blond hair. A shadow had lifted from Sara's heart that day and she was finally able to forgive herself for the harm she had wrought. She had dated since her divorce but never seriously, shying away from men whose overt admiration reminded her of Roger's infatuation with her looks. If love was out there, as the books and songs maintained, then it had yet to come her way, but it hadn't worried her. You can't miss what you've never known, Sara thought wryly now.

'Well!' She snapped the lid back on the box and tossed the dregs of her tea. 'Maybe we should found a club for the divorced? There's probably others like us out here, "in the mulga".'

'We'd get a few takers all right.'

'D'you know it's nearly three o'clock, Jack?'

He cast an eye at the sun. 'Christ, that late? I've got a bore to check yet. We'd best get going.'

13

The sun was low when they arrived back at the homestead. Sara collected her hat, lunchbox and the thermos while Jack emptied the water bottle out over the roots of the supplejack tree at the end of the shed. 'Waste not, want not,' he intoned. 'Thanks for your company today.'

'Thank *you* for taking me, Jack; it was most instructive. I can't wait for the driller to come now.'

'So I've converted you from thinking it's gypsy hokum?'

Sara laughed, mouth wide under her foolish hat. 'I can't deny what I felt.' The words hung between them, innocent though they were of any second meaning, as he walked to the front of the vehicle and felt for the bonnet catch.

'The proof'll be in what they find.' He triggered it as he spoke. 'See you later, then.'

The clang of the goat bells told Sara the flock was coming home. A tearing sound in the horse-paddock scrub made her stop to watch a willy-wind powering through the timber, its dust coils rising, like some monstrous red snake, from the parched earth to stain the sky. Sara had glimpsed her first one from the bus, a roiling spiral gathering in dry leaves and bits of old vegetation as it tore across a spinifex-dotted flat. She heard Jess bark and Becky's shrill yell at her to *'Come be'ind!'* Three galahs swung from the wireless aerial, crests erect and pink wings stretched wide as they surveyed their world upside down. They shrieked derisively at her as she passed beneath them.

'Show offs,' Sara murmured. The side gate clicked behind her and she ran up the kitchen steps, suddenly glad to be alive.

'Enjoy yourself?' Beth looked up from the vegetables she was chopping.

'Yes.' Sara pulled her hat off. 'I did. Very interesting.' She held the straw up, considering it. 'Beth, do *you* think this is a silly hat?'

'Well, it's not perhaps very durable.' Beth raised a single eyebrow, something her brother could also do. 'Why? Jack's been poking fun at it, has he?'

'He seems to think it's a joke,' Sara admitted. She filched a round of carrot and crunched it. 'How's Sam?'

The smile left Beth's face. 'His temp's gone up again. He's had almost a full course of antibiotics too. If it hasn't dropped by morning, I'll get onto the doctor.'

'I'm sorry,' Sara said. She looked at the preparations underway. 'Anything I can do here?'

'I'm right, thanks. But you could tell me about the divining. Did he get a hit?'

'He pegged three sites. It was the most amazing thing, Beth!' She looked down at her arms, remembering. 'He held my wrists and I felt the stick move. It was like trying to hold a tree up when the pull came. Anyway, he seemed pretty satisfied. Has he done many bores? I mean, where they've drilled and got water.'

'Oh, yes. The neighbours have used him, here and round Arkeela. There's an old chap in Charlotte Creek, a miner – used to scratch after tin – he does a bit of divining too. The stick works for different people.'

'For you?' Sara asked.

Beth shook her head. 'Mind, it's not foolproof but then you can't tell with a dry hole if they simply didn't go deep enough. It's an expensive business, drilling. It's charged by the metre, and at some stage you have to decide whether to stop or risk going on.'

'Yes, Jack said.' Sara hung her hat alongside Sam's and stood contemplating it. 'He's right. It is silly. He mentioned his wife today,' she said, turning back to the table. 'What happened there?'

Beth snorted. 'Marilyn was on the hunt for a husband, that's what. Everybody could see it but him. If ever there was a case of crossed wires! She was a city girl, cute as a kitten, and hell bent on having things her way. *He* thought she was going to settle down for life at Arkeela, and *she* thought she could get him to sell up for her sake and take a job in town. Only she didn't mention it till *after* the wedding. So it must have been quite a shock to them both once they realised neither was going to yield. Of course, she couldn't see why anybody wouldn't, but a team of draught horses couldn't get my brother out of the bush. Marilyn liked her comforts so when she realised what she'd let herself in for, she quit.' Beth scooped the chopped vegies into a basin. 'If you're quick, you'll have time for your shower before Becky gets in. Now I'd best go check on how Sam's doing.' At the door she looked back. 'By the way, you realise it's only a week till the school holidays start? Ten days of freedom. You could take a trip into the Alice if you wanted. Shop, get your hair cut, chill out.'

Sara patted her troublesome curls to hide her flinch at the thought of venturing back into the world. Of course, it was unlikely her stalker could know she had come through the Alice – only he had somehow found out about Mildura, hadn't he? She cut off the thought as she ran her hands over the hair bunched on her neck. 'Or I could just borrow some scrunchies from Becky. I'll think about it.'

Later, lying in bed, Sara stretched luxuriously and wondered about the upcoming holidays. She could fill the days quite adequately at Redhill: helping Beth, doing a bit in the garden, reading (there was a filled bookcase in the lounge), accompanying Jack and Becky on the bore runs. Len seemed to leave this task solely to his brother-in-law. Alternatively she could, she supposed, overcome her irrational fears and head for the roadhouse – Jack would probably take her – to catch the bus into the Alice. She had quite liked what she'd seen of the town and it would be easy to put in a few days there. She could indeed visit a salon, drink a cappuccino again, contact the city branch of her bank and have them forward her mail to the local branch . . . She could even have them send anything that came direct to Redhill. Sara had resisted leaving any other forwarding address at the post office, fearing that her stalker would uncover it. Now that seemed an unnecessary precaution. Where was the harm in having it sent to her? It was foolish to imagine that the man could still be looking for her. She turned her pillow, which had grown warm even with the fan churning away above her, thinking about the air conditioning in the Alice, and the swimming pools she'd find, if she chose the right accommodation . . .

Hours later Sara woke to the thunder of booted feet hurrying along the boards past the open French windows. As the boots clattered down the front steps, she sat up groggily and felt her way onto the verandah. Stars were visible and a faint wash of light from the front of the house. Whoever had gone out must have turned on the front floodlights in the yard.

Something was wrong. Sara, crossing back into the room, snapped on her own light and snatched her wrap from its hook behind the door. Beth was also up, her voice came faintly through the wall along with the sound of drawers sliding in Sam's room. Sara went hesitantly to tap on the open bedroom door, catching sight as she did so of the boy's pale, puffy face and bloodstained mouth. She gasped in shock and Beth met her horrified glance.

'He's ill,' she said tersely. 'I'm just packing. Len's rung the base and the doctor's on the way.' Her voice was steady though her face was tight and strained, and a nerve quivered at the corner of one eye.

'What can I do?' Sara tried to match her calm. There was a basin of discoloured water and a bloodstained towel on the floor. 'I'll get rid of that.' She scooped them up, saying gently to the boy whose lacklustre eyes seemed hardly to register her presence, 'You'll be fine, Sam.' He made no response but as Sara exited the room, she heard him speak, his voice alarmingly weak and thready-sounding.

'Mum?'

'I'm here, darling. Shhh now, everything's okay. Remember our practice? Just breathe slowly, that's it. I'm here and you're not going anywhere without me. I swear to you you're not!'

Sara grabbed a clean towel from the linen cupboard and slapped the kettle onto the gas. Outside, a vehicle roared away and another came towards the house. The kitchen clock showed three a.m. She wondered how the doctor's plane could possibly land in the dark. She hadn't even known there was an airstrip at Redhill; obviously there was, but what about lights? Pilots had to be able to see where the ground was. She couldn't bother Beth with questions, so returned to Sam's room with the towel and a fresh basin of warm water to clean his face.

'I'm filling a thermos for you,' she said quietly. 'Anything else?'

'The mattress from the daybed, and sheets.' Beth was stroking her son's face. 'Len's bringing the vehicle. We'll lay him on the back to carry him out to the strip. And I'll need you to look after Becky, Sara. We're both going with him, but Jack'll be here. You won't be alone. It might be –' her voice cracked – 'a little while till he's better.' In her eyes Sara read the knowledge that this time they might lose him and she shook her head, denying it.

'He'll make it, Beth. He will!'

It was as if she hadn't spoken, or dread had made Beth incapable of taking the words in. 'Do you think you can manage?'

'Of course I can. Becky will be fine. Will Len come to the front or the back?'

'The back. And thank you, Sara. I don't know how we'd manage without —'

'Jack would see to everything,' Sara said briskly. 'You know he would. I'll get the mattress. What have you forgotten to pack — toothbrush, money, shoes?' Beth was wearing her old house slippers. 'Better change those.' Sara pointed. 'Did you remember a nightie?'

'No.' Beth kicked off the slippers. Sam's breathing had evened and his eyes were closed. His mother stole from his side to snatch up her shoes, one of Len's shirts and the nightclothes from their disturbed bed. Five minutes later they were all outside in the dim wash of the kitchen lights where the vehicle waited. Len lifted his son onto the mattress while Beth scrambled over the tailboard to sit beside him. Sara thrust the thermos into the cab and handed the two bags up to Beth.

'All set?' Len called from behind the wheel.

'One moment. Is it far? I'd come too,' Sara said quickly, 'only I can't leave Becky. If she woke and found us all gone . . .'

'Stay,' Beth said. 'I'll ring when — Take care of my daughter, Sara.'

'I will, don't worry. Not about us, anyway.' Sara reached to touch the woman's shoulder. 'I'll be rooting for you all, especially you, Sam.' The boy's eyes were open. She saw the whites of them in the faint light, and that a trickle of blood had leaked from his mouth to stain his chin. 'Good luck! Okay, Len.'

Sara was not religious; the thought of praying was foreign to her, but as the vehicle pulled gently away she sent with it her desperate desire that all would be well, that the doctor would come in time and with the necessary skill to save the vehicle's precious cargo. And, she realised, she still had no idea how far it must travel to the airstrip.

It turned out to be no more than three kilometres. Sara made herself a coffee and waited for the sound of the plane. The ticking of the clock seemed to fill the kitchen as the hands crawled past four a.m. She rinsed out her mug and went to the front verandah to turn off the outside lights, then had second thoughts. What if they'd been left on to help the pilot locate the place? She switched them back on and checked Becky, who was sound asleep, then returned to her own room and made her bed. It would be dawn soon anyway and she was too wound up to even consider sleeping. Finally a hum in the air resolved into a drone and then the decelerating roar of a plane coming in to land.

'Thank God!' Sara said, the words an unconscious prayer. She went to the door to listen, hearing the small night sounds she had come to ignore – the creak of mill rods, a night bird's call, the scritch of the lemon tree branch against the side wall. For the hundredth time she resolved to trim it back, then with a shattering roar the plane engine came to life again and she heard it take off. Standing out in the garden, she watched the flashing wing lights until they vanished, noting that the star Becky had told her was Venus was at its apogee, meaning dawn was on its way. *When it goes down, it's coming up daylight,* the child had said. Sara hoped fervently that Sam would live to see it. She switched off the outside lights and returned to the kitchen to light the gas again to make tea for Jack.

He came at last, hatless up the kitchen steps, a rumpled shirt hanging over his jeans, face dark with stubble. 'You still up? And you've made tea. What a woman!' He yawned and sat down at the table.

'How was Sam when they left?'

Jack grimaced. 'Put it this way, I've never seen a stretcher loaded so quick. That take-off was damn near vertical. Poor bloody kid. Poor parents too. If they lose him . . .' He drank his tea, gave her a wry smile. 'Well, never a dull moment in the sticks, eh?'

'It seems not. Just for interest's sake, Jack, how did the pilot land in the dark?'

'He didn't. There're flares for night landing. In this case pots of dirt soaked in fuel. You string 'em along the flight path and light 'em up when you hear the plane. That's what I was doing. If you should ever need to do it, you'll find they live inside the marker tyres down the side of the strip.'

'I see.' Sara thought of the alternative, the long, bumpy drive to the bitumen with a couple of hundred kilometres to travel after that. 'Thank God for the flying doctor!'

'You're not the only one to say that, believe me.' He glanced at the clock as the first tentative rooster's crow sounded from the chook pen. 'I'll give it another hour, then ring Mum. She'll want to be there for Beth.'

'Of course. I'd forgotten your parents were in the Alice.' Sara felt vainly for the combs that she had forgotten to put in, pushed her curls back, then shrugged and let them flop back over her brow. 'That's a comfort; she and Len'll have somewhere to go for a shower and a meal. I imagine they'll offer to spell them at the hospital too – your mum and dad, I mean.'

'Yeah, and the minute Sam's out of danger, Dad'll be out here looking to take up the strain for Len. See if he isn't.'

'You know him best.' Sara collected their empty mugs. Beyond the window a faint greyness limned the horizon. She put the cups in the sink and heard the younger rooster give his uncertain crow. It sounded, as always, as if his tonsils needed oiling. 'Dawn's almost here.'

Jack yawned. 'Yeah. Whatever's happening, at least he's in hospital. Not much else to be thankful for right now, but there is that.'

Standing at the sink watching the stars die and the first tinge of colour steal into the east, feeling the drag of the night's experience and the weight of responsibility on her shoulders, Sara silently concurred.

14

It was past noon before Beth's promised call came through. Jack had stayed around the homestead trying to cheer up a subdued Becky while they waited for news. With no school to distract the child, Sara had set her the task of making a get-well card for her brother, then started her off on another page in her scrapbook.

'You could make it about the flying doctor,' she suggested. 'Draw some pictures of his plane, maybe write a little story about all the people he saves with it.' And may the Fates grant that Sam was among them. Sara couldn't bear to contemplate any other outcome.

When the phone finally rang it was Jack who answered it. Sara had flown from the sink, hands still dripping, to hang with bated breath in the office doorway, unashamedly listening to the one-sided conversation.

'Yeah,' Jack said. 'Uh-huh.' Then, 'Right, I'll tell – yeah, she's fine. Sara's keeping her busy.' The creases about Jack's eyes deepened as he frowned. 'Yeah, well, that's good, sis. I can do that. The main thing now – Yeah, yeah. Fingers crossed, eh? Okay, bye.'

'Well?' Sara couldn't restrain herself. 'What did she say? How is he?'

Jack blew out his cheeks in a long exhalation. 'Reading between the lines? Not too good. They've stabilised him and the official version is that he's holding his own. He's had a blood transfusion and some fancy drug for the infection. The doctors don't seem to know exactly what's causing that, but they're giving it their best shot with this drug. They've got him in intensive care and Mum's with them at the hospital. Dad –' he raised a brow at her – 'what did I tell you? Dad's gone home, for the moment. He's packing the car to head out here later on. If Sam improves overnight, chances are they'll both wind up coming.'

'Oh.' Sara's mind darted to sheets and the vacuum cleaner; she had best prepare the spare bedroom. 'How's Beth? She must be worried sick.'

'Holding it together. She's going to call tonight, wants to talk to you and Becky both. And there might be more news by then. Better news,' he amended.

It didn't seem terribly likely, Sara thought. People always glossed things, wanting to believe that *stable* meant *getting better*, when its meaning was actually closer to *still alive*. She sighed, and went to find Becky, wondering how to put a positive spin on the news that Sam was fighting for his life and wouldn't be home anytime soon.

They had roast mutton for tea with baked potatoes and pumpkin and a tin of green beans from the store. There was a fruit flan for dessert, the fruit also from a tin.

'Do you ever have fresh fruit?' Sara found that she missed apples most; she had seen packets of dried ones on the store shelves, but they were a poor substitute for the crunch and tangy juice of the real thing.

'There's a fig tree in the garden,' Jack said. 'Bit early yet for picking, though – that's usually round November. Beth always had a great winter vegie garden, before Sam got sick. Tomatoes, caulie, peas – if it had a seed, she grew it. You a gardener, Sara?'

She shook her head. 'A few flowers and herbs, but the only dirt I had was in tubs. The backyard had been asphalted over. My flat used to be a shop, you see, with a bit of a car park behind it. The front door opened onto the pavement. Eat your beans, Becky. They're good for you.'

'Who says?' the little girl muttered rebelliously.

'Well, let's see.' Sara pretended to think. 'I'll list them and you count. All the gardeners in the world, most of the doctors, every mother you can think of . . . Anyone else, Jack?'

'Heaps, woman,' he said loftily. 'Think of all the cows that'd eat 'em if they could. And goats, horses – also the people who make those fancy salads to photograph for magazines . . .'

'You're both weird, you know that?' But Becky looked a little happier for the fooling. 'When's Mum gonna ring?'

'Soon,' Sara promised. 'Then maybe you could show your uncle what you did today while I clear up.'

'Can we play a game after?'

'If we get finished in time.' Sara cast a meaningful glance at the uneaten beans. Becky sighed and demolished them.

The phone rang at half past seven. Beth spoke to her daughter and her brother, then Jack signalled and passed the handpiece to Sara. 'Beth?' she said, feeling the warmth of the plastic where his hand had rested. 'How is he?'

'The doctor thinks he's holding his own, thank God! The transfusion has helped and his temp's a little lower, but we're not out of the woods yet.' Her voice sounded thin and tired. 'Len's with him now, I'm at Mum's place while I shower and eat, then I'll go back. Look, what I wanted to tell you was that once Sam's out of intensive care, they'll be coming out to Redhill. Mum and Dad, I mean. Dad's bound to go and Mum's not easy unless she knows what he's getting up to. It's his heart, you see. There's no telling how soon till they leave – a few days, a week even. It depends on Sam, so if you wouldn't mind getting the spare room ready when you can. Mum'll relieve you of the cooking once she gets there, so don't be thinking it's more work for you. Okay?'

'Yes, of course. I've already done the room. Jack said they'd come. Don't worry about us, Beth. Everything's fine here. Just concentrate on Sam; give him my love and know we're thinking about you all, every minute of the day.'

'Thanks. Give Becky a hug for me. I've got to go.' She hung up and Sara was left listening to the empty line.

'He'll make it,' Jack assured her and she nodded as if there were no doubt.

'Of course he will. Here, I've made another pot of tea. Now, chicken – what game are we playing?'

'A short one,' Jack advised his niece. 'It's been a long day and we have a longer one coming up tomorrow.' He looked at Sara. 'Think you can hold the fort by yourself? I've got to get out to the boundary country so I'll be gone most of the day. I'll show you how to use the radio before I leave, just in case. You won't mind being alone?'

'I'll be fine – we'll be fine, won't we, Becky? We can keep each other company and if we get bored, I know there's a pile of Len's shirts needing their buttons sewn back on.'

'Well.' Jack shrugged, his lips twitching ever so slightly. 'I know how to feel redundant. Shirts, eh? You're quite a surprise packet, you know that? So where's this game, Squirt?'

Becky already had the dominoes out. She rattled the tiles onto the cleared table and climbed onto her chair, kneeling on the seat, brown plaits swinging over her shoulder. Jack narrowed his eyes at her. 'O-kaay. May the best man win, and seeing I'm the only one here, that'll be me.'

His niece grinned wickedly and snatched at a tile. 'Won't either!'

Later, with Becky in bed, Sara washed their cups and rinsed out the teapot. Jack lifted his hat from its hook and bade her goodnight as he went out the door. She heard him speak to Jess, then the squeak and click of the gate, which reminded her that she still hadn't trimmed back the branch on the lemon tree. Tomorrow, then. Suddenly inexpressibly weary, she gave vent to an eye-watering yawn and snapped off the kitchen light. It had been, as Jack had said, a very long day and she would be glad to fall into bed: after she had set the alarm, she reminded herself, or she'd never wake in the morning.

The sound that dragged her from slumber seemed to come only minutes after she had closed her eyes, but a glance at the alarm clock showed that it was closer to two hours. Sitting up, she listened and identified the noise as sobbing coming from Becky's room. Sighing, she pulled on her wrap and went to investigate. She found the child awake, the brown hair tangled on the pillow, the top sheet on the floor and Becky herself curled up in pink pyjamas, damp and disconsolate, her shoulders shaking.

'What is it, chicken?' Sara switched on the bedside lamp and sat down on the mattress, laying her hand on Becky's arm. 'Did you have a bad dream?'

'I want Mum,' the little girl choked. 'I want her to come home, and Sam too, and for him not to be sick.' Brown eyes, swimming with tears, looked up at Sara. 'What if he doesn't *ever* get better? What if he dies? Mum'll hate me and I'll n-never see him again.'

'Oh, no, no – you've got that all wrong.' Sara smoothed her hair and reached for a corner of the discarded sheet to wipe the wet cheeks. 'Goodness me, for a girl as smart as you are, Becky Calshot, you think some awfully silly things. First off, Sam *is* getting better. The doctor said so. Your brother is going to grow up to run Redhill, just like he told me. And your mum would never, ever hate you. She loves you to bits, even when you're naughty, which reminds me, she asked me to do something for her and, do you know, I clean forgot! It was while I was speaking to her on the phone tonight, but we started playing that game and it went out of my head.' She tsked to herself. 'Dear me! And it was a special request too.'

Becky stopped crying to look at her. 'What?'

'It's too bad of me,' Sara said and bit a finger pondering, looking doubtfully at her charge. 'Unless it's not too late? What do you think?'

'What was it?' Intrigued, Becky gave a final snuffle and sat up.

'This.' Sara folded her arms about the little pyjama-clad figure, speaking softly into her hair. 'She said I was to give you a big hug for her. Is it all right that it's a little bit late?'

Becky nodded wordlessly and clung as Sara rocked her, their fused shadows moving on the wall behind them. When she finally released her and made to rise, the girl caught at her arm. 'Don't go. Tell me a story like Mum does.'

'What sort of story?' Sara was practical and organised, she could run a house and – as she had just proved – comfort a child, but storytelling was not something she had ever tried her hand at.

'About her and Uncle Jack when they were little.' Becky wriggled onto her side, face expectant. 'Tell me about when you were little, Sara.'

'What about a fairy story instead? Cinderella maybe?'

'No, a real one. Please?'

She could tell her the dream, Sara thought, and add a bit – where was the harm? 'Well, let's see, then. When I was quite small I had a friend called . . . Ben. I dare say we used to quarrel sometimes, like you do with Sam, but if we did, I don't remember it. We always did things together. We used to go down to the creek – a big wide creek it was, with lots of gum trees and deep sand drifts – and dig there.'

'Why?' Becky asked, eyes intent on Sara's face.

'Because it was fun.' She *did* remember the sand, Sara was certain of it – the heat of it, the way it slid underfoot both hard and yielding. She raised her brows and sank her voice to a near whisper.

'Maybe we were looking for treasure, or,' she said, resuming her normal voice, 'making an underground cubby house. Sometimes . . .' She frowned, searching her imagination, almost seeing it, the way real storytellers must, she thought. 'Sometimes we played under a great thick bush with yellow flowers on it. We made tunnels through it where only we could fit. Oh, and the dog —' Her body jerked and she suddenly knew she was speaking truth, that both dog and bush had been real, and the name she had arbitrarily picked for her companion too. 'His name was –' she floundered – 'Oh dear, I've forgotten, but anyway, Ben and the dog and I had all sorts of games there in the bush. It was our secret place. Nobody else knew about it. *We're going to play in the bush,* we'd say, and our mum always thought we meant in the paddo—'

The shock of it stopped her. Sara rose, her smile mechanical. 'That's it, chicken. Maybe I'll think of something more later. Off to sleep now and I'll see you in the morning. If you want something nice to think about, remember that your gran and granddad are coming out soon. Won't that be lovely?'

'Yes, I forgot about Nan and Pop.' Becky's eyes were drooping, she yawned. ''S'a nice story, Sara. Thank you.'

'Sleep tight,' Sara switched off the light and returned in a daze to her own room, all hope of similar oblivion forgotten.

15

Sara woke from a fitful sleep broken by dreams whose content faded before the shrilling of the alarm. Jack, bringing the milk in, found her standing with a handful of cutlery before the half-set table while the kettle shrieked unnoticed behind her. He switched it off, heaved the bucket onto the bench and reached for the strainer.

'Morning, Sara. Sleep well?'

'Hmm? Oh, good morning, Jack.' She stared at the cutlery as if wondering how it had got there. Turning, she noticed the lack of flame. 'Have we run out of gas?'

'The kettle was boiling, I turned it off.' He narrowed his gaze. 'You okay? You seem a bit distracted.'

'I know, sorry.' She reached for the frying pan, then stopped. 'Jack, last night I was talking to Becky. I wasn't even thinking, and it just —' She stopped.

He lowered the strainer. 'You remembered something?'

'A brother,' Sara said baldly. 'I have a brother called Ben.' The electrifying knowledge still fizzed within her. *Our mum* . . . She had thought of nothing else since those words had escaped her mouth. She told him about the bush with the yellow flowers where they had played, and the nameless dog that had accompanied them.

'How old were you?'

Reaching again for the pan and this time setting it on the gas, she considered the question. 'Five or six? Old enough to be outside unsupervised if Stella really thought we were going to play in the house paddock. And that's another thing, she's a city woman, my mother. Where does a paddock come into it? And why has she never mentioned Ben?'

'Aren't you a city woman too?' Jack poured carefully, his gaze on the strainer. 'Your mother might have lived in the country, if only for a few weeks.'

'I suppose,' she said doubtfully. 'What about Ben, though? Why didn't she talk about him? She never did – not once!'

'Perhaps he died? If he did, it might just have been too hard. Grief –'

'No!' The protest was involuntary, then Sara shook her head, rebuking her reaction. 'That's silly. Just because I don't want to believe it.' She stared at nothing. Could it be that simple? Had her brother been the adored son and she the disregarded second child whose continued existence had been seen as unforgivable when the favoured one perished? She supposed it was possible. Besides, if Ben lived, then where was he? The pan was too hot; the chops she couldn't remember placing in it were jumping and spitting. Sara turned them and lowered the gas, working on automatic. Her breath caught suddenly. 'Jack, what if it was the car crash? I never thought of that before, whether anyone was killed in it. What if it was Ben?'

He had moved to the breadboard at the end of the table, and was cutting his lunch. 'That's a thought but isn't it a bit unlikely? Wouldn't there have been some proof that he'd died? Photos, belongings she'd have kept?'

'You don't know my mother! Stella doesn't have a sentimental bone in her body. She was bad tempered when my father died. Not sorry, not grieving – just cranky. Like he'd done it to spite her.'

'She certainly sounds a hard case. Not like someone who couldn't stand to face reality, which means he probably wasn't involved. I don't know if that helps – but there's no proof he *did* die.'

'So what's the alternative? I haven't seen him since I was six or seven. That I know. So she, what, abandoned him? Gave him away? I can't believe that, even of Stella. After all, there was no love lost between us, but she kept me.'

He was looking past her. 'Morning, Squirt. You missed the milking.'

'Becky.' Sara glanced at her. 'Wash your face, chicken, then bring your brush. I'll do your hair.' Becky mumbled a greeting to them both, yawned, and continued on her way to the bathroom.

'We could guess all day,' Jack said. 'But what has any of it got to do with the bloke who was stalking you? That's what really puzzles me.' He gestured at the pile of sandwiches he'd made and the box of cling film, as close to sheepish as Sara had seen him. 'You mind wrapping them for me? I'm all fingers and thumbs with that damn stuff, but you make it look easy. Thanks,' he said when she had done so. 'Okay if I start? Only I've got a long day ahead of me.'

'Of course. Go ahead.'

Becky was back with the brush. Sara gathered the child's hair up, split it and started to plait, her mind on what he had said. She had quite forgotten her stalker, but Jack was right in doubting that he could be connected to her past. Besides, his menace had insensibly dwindled with time and distance. If she had known Stella's whereabouts, Sara thought, whipping the band about the second plait, she would be tempted to return to Adelaide and demand the truth from her. The holidays started on Friday, after all. Only it would worry Beth if she left, however temporarily, and Stella could be literally anywhere.

Abandoning the idea with some reluctance, Sara sat down with Becky to eat breakfast.

Jack was gone before they finished. The day's routine took over and between dishes, teaching and cooking, Sara puzzled over the mystery of her missing brother. Logical though it was to assume he must have died, her heart rebelled against the thought. Perhaps, she theorised, he had been adopted for some reason by another family member? She could have innumerable relatives, from a complete set of grandparents down to third cousins, and be none the wiser. Never mind that she could think of no reason to support her idea. Ben *could* still be alive somewhere, unaware of her existence. But no, Sara frowned at the potato she was peeling, giving up that notion. She might have suffered amnesia but it beggared belief that he had too. All right – suppose somebody had told him she was dead? A kid would believe that. But why would anyone do so? Gouging at an eye on the spud, Sara sighed in frustration; whatever road her thoughts ran down they always reached the same dead end. Anything, admittedly, was possible, but it still had to make sense and none of this did.

The day was gone before she knew it, but then the silent unanswerable questions kept posing themselves throughout the week. She helped Becky make a collage for a school project and they did a simple cooking lesson together, making pancakes for lunch. Becky, tummy swathed in a large tea towel, insisted on tossing her first effort in the air and shot it into the sink, watching in open-mouthed horror as it sank into sudsy water. Sara tutted, trying not to laugh, and turned the next one, catching all but the edge of it, which fell onto the stove burner.

'Whoops! Not easy, is it?' She snatched up the spatula to scoop it from the flame and melted the edge of the plastic. 'Damn! Whose mad idea was this, Becky?'

'Mrs Murray's,' the girl said literally. 'I'll tell her you dropped one.'

'Well, *I'll* tell her you chucked yours in the sink,' Sara threatened and they both laughed. 'Just as well your mum's not here to see the mess we're making.'

Later, with school over, Becky took the feed to the horses while Sara walked through the brilliant light of mid-afternoon to the fowl house to collect the eggs. The station complex had become so familiar to her that it scarcely registered, but today for some reason it did. She stood outside the netting door watching the stick figure that was Becky walking slowly towards the horses. The sheds were rectangular blocks, rusty-roofed caves of darkness. The sparsely leafed tree at the end of the vehicle shed was a caricature of vegetation, the mill a skeleton of steel, enveloped by barren red sand. The sky glittered so brightly it forced her to squint.

Grateful for the thick, wide brim of her straw hat, Sara ducked her head and moved thankfully under the iron roof to the nest boxes. These were square plastic drums that had once held liquid of some sort – oil or chemicals, she supposed. One side had been cut from them and they were lined with a mixture of shredded paper and dried lawn clippings that gave off a musty smell. Sara reached for the three eggs visible in the first box, and glimpsed more in the others. The hens were still laying well, though Beth had said the supply would stop when they entered the moult in summer. She took off her hat, laid the first three gently in its crown and suffered an instance of deja vu so powerful that she knew it had to be another memory.

Somewhere long ago she had done this before. Standing rigid with closed eyes, Sara inhaled the smell of the grass and the ammoniac reek of the pen, and saw a smaller hand lifting the brown eggs carefully – oh, so carefully – and placing them singly in the hat clutched to her chest. Her smaller self was singing just below her breath: *Gentle, gentle, one at a time.* A mantra that somebody must have taught her before entrusting her with this very task. Opening her eyes, Sara gazed at the eggs, marvelling, as she had then, at their perfect ovoid shape and freckled shells. Stunned by the revelation, she moved down the row of nest boxes, transferring their offerings to her hat, then returned to the house not even feeling the burn of the sun on her uncovered head.

Beth continued to ring each evening, though the news on Sam hardly varied until Thursday when Jack, taking the call, had responded with a wild, 'Whackydoo, sis! Way to go!'

Both Sara and Becky had crowded into the office then, silently demanding the reason for his outburst. He'd held the receiver against his shirt, a wide grin on his face. 'He's outta ICU. They moved him to the ward today.'

Relief flooded Sara but Becky had looked confused. 'What's that mean?'

'That he's not so sick any more, chicken. He's really getting better now.'

'So he and Mum'll be home soon?'

'Well, it might be a while yet,' Sara cautioned. 'Maybe by the end of the holidays.'

'How long's that?'

'Not long. They start on Saturday.'

'That's *ages!*' Becky was not impressed.

'The time will soon go. It's mail day again tomorrow. You can show Harry your collage.'

Harry, however, wasn't their only arrival with the mail; when Becky scampered out to meet him, she checked her pace for an instant, then raced straight past the one-armed man to fling herself at the beloved figure alighting from the passenger-side door.

'Dad! You're back! You never said you were coming.'

'Hi, Becs.' Len swung her up in his arms, pendulous cheeks plumping with a fond smile as he kissed her. 'I didn't know myself till pretty late last night. How've you been? Mum said to give you a big hug from her.' He wrapped his arms about her wriggling body as he spoke. 'There, straight from her to you. We've been missing you.' He put her down and pulled out his bag. 'How's Sara? And your uncle?'

'She's making the tea. Uncle Jack's gone 'dozing today. Is Sam coming home soon?'

'We hope so. Come on. My belly feels like my throat's cut. Where's this tea?'

Holding his big hand, chattering excitedly, Becky led him to the house, leaving his side only at the steps, which she raced up before him to yell, 'Sara, you'll never guess! Dad's come home!'

16

There was no set date for Sam's return, Len told them that evening. He was very weak and would be in hospital for a while yet.

'How long for?' Becky demanded. 'He's been gone for*ever*.'

'Maybe a week or so,' Len said. 'Then he and Mum are going to stay at Nan and Pop's place for a while. When he's quite strong again, *that's* when he'll come home.'

'Good idea,' Jack agreed. 'He's had a bad time of it, poor kid. How're the old folks going?'

'They're coming out – tomorrow, actually.' Len grimaced. 'I wish he wouldn't but you know your father. Can't wait to make himself useful. 'Course he's only got that little car of his now, so I was wondering if you'd meet them at the roadhouse and bring them out?'

'You're not going in yourself?'

Len shook his head. 'I'd rather get round the run, see how the stock are holding up. There'll be a load of lick coming out in a bit. I talked to a cattle husbandry bloke in the DPI. He's advised upping the urea content from what we're currently feeding, so we'll try it. Which reminds me – the fuel truck's also due anytime soon. Have you heard anything from the drilling crew yet?'

'No. But I'll find out tomorrow. Bungy ought to be there.' Jack looked across at Sara. 'It's the flying doctor benefit tomorrow; the locals will all turn up for it. It's just smoko, and lunch, a few fundraisers and a chance to meet the neighbours. What d'you say to coming along?'

'Oh, yes, Uncle Jack!' Becky answered for her. 'We can go, can't we, Sara?'

'It sounds interesting,' Sara admitted cautiously. 'How does the catering work? Would Beth normally take a plate along for the lunch?'

'Nope. It's catered for. We pay for it, and the proceeds go to the doctors' fund. She'd take a cake along for smoko, but don't feel obliged. They won't expect it of you.'

'It'll be no trouble to make something,' Sara assured him. 'We'll do it for your mum, hey, Becky? Wouldn't want to let the side down. What time would you want to leave?'

'Say ten? That okay with you? It'll get us there in good time for lunch, and we can leave after the auction. That's always last on the agenda.'

'Casual dress?' Sara prodded. 'Will jeans and a shirt do?'

'Anything that keeps you cool and shaded.' He glanced at the hat pegs. 'That straw thingy of yours will be just fine. We eat in the hall so there's some shade, but you'll still need a hat.'

Sara wrinkled her brow. 'I don't remember a hall.'

He grinned. 'The concrete slab with the roof over it? The committee hasn't got round to the walls yet. Mind you, come winter and the race ball they'll all get keen again – except, of course, there *wasn't* a ball this year, or races either.'

'I see.' Sara wondered if there was time to put a load of washing through. She wanted to have the place spotless for Mrs Ketch's arrival, all chores done and the cake tins full. Well, she'd just have to fit in what she could. Perhaps a sultana cake would be the best one to take. Being solid, it would travel well. She could cream some rice in the bottom of the oven while it baked, which would take care of tomorrow night's sweets, and if she were to cook a shoulder of mutton – or better still, make a curry – it would be a quick and easy meal. Harry had brought out the usual bread order and there were plenty of eggs. She had better check the bedroom again and run the vacuum cleaner over the verandahs, which tended to get the most dust . . .

'You aren't listening,' Becky complained. 'I *said* can I take my collage with me to show to Nan?'

'Oh, sorry, chicken. I was thinking about tea for tomorrow night. It might be too crowded in the car with five of us, don't you think? Why not wait and surprise her with it when she gets here?'

'You're fussing,' Jack observed. 'I know the signs. Is there dust on the cupboard top? Is the sink clean enough? My mum's not a Tartar, you know. She'll be damn glad you're here. Just like we are, eh, Squirt?'

Becky nodded vigorously. 'Sara's my most fav'rite friend.'

Jack looked wounded. 'Hey! I thought that was me.'

'Both of you,' Becky amended and Len laughed.

'Very diplomatic. And Jack's right, Sara. You've been tremendous. With both of us away, I don't know how we'd have managed if you hadn't been here.'

'Thank you. I'm just glad I could help,' Sara said, but she was touched by his gratitude. It was nice to be appreciated even if none of what she was being thanked for had been a chore. It might be an alien world out there beyond the garden fence, but it was one she was coming to like.

The following day the three of them set off for the roadhouse in Len's station wagon. 'More room, more comfort,' Jack explained. 'Dad's little town job would never make it over this road.'

'Does it ever get graded?' Sara braced herself against the bumps as they hit a badly corrugated patch, noting how the red dust billowing behind them had completely obscured the back windows.

'Not as often as we'd like.'

'And what's that for you stoic mulga men, once a year?'

He snorted. 'Twice would be good, but the money'd be too short for that. With the drought there'll be a few places unable to cough up for their rates, and that's what pays for things like road-works.' Then without pause he asked, 'How's the memory coming on?'

'Slowly.' She told him what she had recalled collecting eggs, adding, 'It's strange that all the things I remember are country things, though Stella swore she'd spent her life in the city.'

'A country holiday?' Jack suggested. 'One of those rural shacks with a beach within coo-ee, and a grocery shop a coupla k away?'

'It's possible.' Sara frowned. 'You know what bugs me most about it? The dog. Stella wasn't one for pets, but I'm positive it was *our* dog – Ben's and mine. She went everywhere with us.'

Jack had caught her use of the pronoun too. 'So, a bitch.' He winked at her. 'Careful, you'll be remembering her name next.'

Sara smiled at him, thinking he looked quite handsome with his hair neatly combed, and the light bouncing off the plane of his closely shaven cheeks. She felt elated at having found another infini-tesimal piece of the puzzle. 'I just might, too.'

When they pulled in at the roadhouse Jack was forced to park at the end of a long line of cars.

'Heavens!' Sara eyed them. 'Where did they all come from? I thought nobody much lived out here.' She felt suddenly shy, which was ridiculous, but it was weeks since she had seen anyone outside of Redhill other than Harry the mailman. The isolation of the mulga was already changing her views, she thought. Since when had twenty people been a crowd? Why, she had worked with more than that in the office in Adelaide, and the queues of the unemployed and those on benefits must have been triple that. How distant and alien those days now seemed, a glaze of *Next please* and *If you could just fill out the form?* And at the other desks the faces of acquaintances that had somehow never become anything more than that. How could she ever have settled for so little? Donning her hat, Sara lifted the cake tin and glanced across at Jack, who was pushing his door open. Becky was already out.

'To whom should I give this?'

'Come on.' He settled his own hat. 'We'll locate Mavis in the mob, then I'll introduce you round. With that head gear you'll be easy to find again.'

'Will you please lay off my hat!' She touched it self-consciously, horribly aware that of the three closest women she could see, two wore standard felt hats and the third had a baseball cap with a flap sewn onto the back to cover her neck. The skin of their arms and faces was tanned, the oldest woman's badly sun damaged. They would probably despise her, she thought, her own pale epidermis evidence enough of the sheltered existence she had lived. At the very least they would find her attempts to fit into their lifestyle laughable.

But Mavis, serving at the bar, greeted her warmly. 'Sara! Hello – how are you finding things? Oh, and you've brought a cake. That was good of you. Thanks a lot! Harry tells me you're doing the cooking as well out at Redhill? Talk about being thrown in at the deep end.'

'Just while Beth's away,' she agreed.

'And how's young Sam today? I've been praying for him.' She seemed to mean it too. 'What's the news there?'

'Improving slowly,' Jack said. 'I dare say you saw Len yesterday? By the way, she's a fair cook, Mavis. That cake'll be worth a second look. Can I get you a drink, Sara?'

'Why, thank you, Jack. Something soft, please.' Sara was a little flustered by his praise of her cooking. What did that mean? She looked around for her charge. 'Where did Becky go?'

'Ah, don't worry. She'll be with the other kids.' Mavis put two cans on the bar and took Jack's money. 'You can pay for a lemonade for her too and I'll see she gets it. So, how do you like station living, Sara? Different to what you expected?'

'It's fascinating,' Sara said promptly. 'The homestead is comfortable, the children are great and I love the – the bigness of it all. I'm just sorry I didn't know about it years ago.'

'Sounds like you've found your calling.' Mavis moved to serve another customer. 'What'll it be, Reg?'

'Reg,' Jack interrupted. 'I'd like you to meet Sara Blake. She's new to the mulga, been helping Beth out with the kids.'

They shook hands, the first of many introductions, names and faces blurring into an overall impression – as far as the men went – of big hats, pale, squinty eyes and ropey, muscled arms burned by wind and sun. Most of them were middle-aged and awkward in their greetings, as if Sara were a new, little-known species, paler of skin and younger than their wives, her brilliant hair singling her out for notice.

The women seemed more individual, similar only in their frank curiosity about her. Clemmy Marshall from the national park was, Sara thought, closest to her own age. She was trim and blonde with soft wavy hair beneath a nylon hat shaped like the men's felts. She wore khaki shorts, a clingy blue polo shirt, and trainers streaked with red dust.

'Oh, yes,' Sara said, shaking hands. 'Harry mentioned you. From the park – Walkerville, is it? The ranger's wife.'

'Walkervale,' Clemmy corrected. 'And I'm a ranger too. Colin and I have worked there since the park was gazetted.'

'Sorry, my mistake. You have an unusual name – pretty, though,' Sara added. 'Is it short for Clementine?'

'I wish.' Clemmy's blue eyes lit with rueful laughter. 'It was my Dad. Not Clementine, but Clemency, would you believe? I have two sisters, Hope and Faith. Can you imagine a fourth? Mercy, Justice – the mind boggles.'

'Charity,' Sara suggested, smiling. 'Duty . . . I think you got off lightly, considering.'

'You're right. So what brings you out here, Sara?'

'Oh.' She hadn't expected to be asked straight out. 'I was looking for a change, I suppose.'

'What from?'

'An office job with the Commonwealth Employment Agency. Very boring.' It was a fair description, she realised suddenly. Life might be harder out here but no two days were the same. 'Also I've never been outside my comfort zone, or tried anything new.' She shrugged. 'I saw Beth's ad and contacted her, and here I am. So you must know everyone,' she said to forestall further questions. 'Tell me who they all are, and how they fit into the country.'

'Of course. You met Flo, didn't you? Flo Morgan, the big woman in pink? She's Bungy Morgan's sister; she never married.'

'Bungy from Wintergreen?'

'That's right. She's talking to her sister there, Rinky Hazlitt, from Munaroo, which is south of Redhill. There's another sister too, Maureen, but I haven't met her. She's up north somewhere on a property her husband manages. I hear her on the radio now and then.'

'Sounds like a real family affair,' Sara murmured. 'Does everybody out here marry onto the land?'

'This lot, pretty much,' Clemmy nodded. 'The Morgans are an old grazing family, been in the Territory forever. There're others the same. The Garritys, for instance – they're on Drumben Downs. And there're the Pinchens from Alanada. In the early days they had to marry each other because there was no one else much. Rinky's husband, Jim, is actually a Pinchen. He took the Hazlitt name when his mother married Sam Hazlitt after Harry Pinchen was killed. And going way back from that, one of the Pinchen wives was a Morgan.' Catching sight of Sara's face, she laughed. 'It doesn't matter. They were all just names to me at first, too. You'll like Rinky. Let's shift over there. Flo's nice too. Bossy, but she can't do enough for you.' Her eyes twinkled. 'They're all a bit shy, you know, but dying to talk to you. It's always lovely to have someone new in the district.'

Suddenly neither her hat nor her skin tone seemed to matter. If the women were so ready to accept her, Sara was eager to speak with them and learn what she could about their very different lives. 'Lead the way,' she told Clemmy. 'I'll try not to disappoint.'

17

The senior Ketches arrived, unnoticed by Sara, midway through the barbecue lunch. Jack brought them over to where she was sitting and she immediately rose to greet them, shake hands and enquire after their trip.

Frank Ketch was as tall as his son but shared his daughter's wiry build. He was dressed like the other men in worn but polished boots, now smudged with red dirt, cotton pants and shirt, and a wide-brimmed felt hat that covered silver hair. His face was splotched and scarred with past and present skin cancers, and the knuckles of his big hands were sharp and bony. The look of them denied the vigour of his grip. He had brown eyes, webbed in a mesh of fine wrinkles.

Helen, who only came to his shoulder, was plainly the younger of the pair. She had a brisk manner, iron-grey hair cut into a practical bob and her arms were tanned, their upper parts still firm. Her gaze was shrewd and assessing as Sara greeted her and asked about Sam, adding, 'I can see that Becky takes after you.'

'She's got the Ketch bones,' Helen agreed. 'Where is she?'

'Having her lunch with the other kids. Shall I fetch her?' Sara offered.

'No, they have little enough time together. I'll see her later. Now, Sam, he's all Calshot – and a bonny little fighter to boot. He's pulling round but he'll not be home for a bit. We've told Len to feel free to head back to town anytime he's worried. God knows Beth could use the support.'

'It must be hard for her.' Sara heard the criticism in Helen's voice and avoided outright agreement. 'What about some lunch? I could see if there're more chairs.' But Jack had anticipated the need and was already there, carrying two from the container behind the roadhouse, from which the tables, tea urns and cutlery had also come.

Helen, surveying the diners spread out beneath the roof, chairs crammed together to fit under the shade, shook her head and tutted. 'This place doesn't change. But I'm interrupting your lunch. You go. I'll sort something out for us. No, go on, I insist.'

Sara obeyed. She had been sitting with Clemmy and her husband. Colin's most striking aspect was the bushy black beard that covered half his face. Bungy Morgan, a big man who shared his elder sister's fleshiness, was seated beside Jack's now vacant place, alongside Rinky's husband, whose name Sara had forgotten. Everyone was talking, as though making up for weeks, or possibly months, of silence. The women's higher voices cut through the slow burr of the men's – save for Bungy's bull roar, which could be heard from one end of the table to the other. The abandoned barbecue smelled of onions and grease, and packets of salty chips littered the table. Sara took a handful and relaxed into the moment, lifting her hat to fan her sweating face. It was very warm. Everyone was as friendly as Jack had foretold, so she needn't have worried, she thought, listening to the talk, which was of drought and school and recipes. Rinky was poddying calves on the goats – poddying? She would have to ask Jack what it meant.

Lunch was a leisurely affair. When it was over they cleared the table and shifted their chairs around as the sun moved. The men formed themselves into teams for games of darts and horseshoes, with a cash forfeit for the worst effort in each round. For the women Mavis introduced an involved game of mnemonics where the players had to remember and repeat ever-lengthening descriptive passages to do with each other's appearance.

'You'd *think* it would be easy,' Clemmy said. 'I mean, it's not as if we can't all see each other.' The forfeits for forgetting were small but at the end of the day, and added to the funds taken for the food, they would produce a respectable sum.

'I know,' Sara agreed. 'But I've never actually thought of myself as either foxy or cucumberish.'

'You're right.' Clemmy eyed her critically. '*Fox red* is quite wrong. It should be, oh, *copper bright* – something like that. Your hair is lovely though, however you describe it.'

'Thank you,' Sara said. 'Still it's a pain being so thick. I'm sure yours is easier to manage. What about Mavis? Four words, remember?'

'Umm, *cushion soft* and . . . *cloud white*?'

It was a perfect description of their bosomy hostess with her white hair. 'Very good. Some are easier to see than others. Your husband?'

'Easy. *Earth brown, velvet black*. Your turn to try. So, let's see – Jack, then. What's he?'

Sara wrinkled her brow, thinking it would be less difficult if a list of the man's attributes were called for, rather than his appearance. He was patient, capable, tolerant, kind to children, protective of his sister. But how did he look?

'Well,' she said hesitantly, then laughed. 'Bother! It's harder than I thought. What about *mulga strong*? *Is* mulga noted for its strength? And – and *sharp-eyed*.'

'It'll do. You know he's married, don't you? Well, he was. I don't know where they're at now. Marilyn, I think her name was. Beth couldn't stand her; reckoned she was counting the cash from the moment she saw his land. Never occurred to her that she wouldn't get him to sell up.'

'I can't imagine him doing so.' Sara said, uncomfortable with the subject. 'Uh-oh, it's your turn again. I think we're both due for another forfeit.'

They paid up, after adding Clemmy's description of Mavis to the list.

'It's all for the doctor.' Clemmy was philosophical. 'And believe me there's no better cause.'

Sara nodded. 'I've already learned that.' She thought of the night he had come for Sam, of the tension and quiet desperation of his parents as they waited for the plane. 'I shall *never* forget the relief of hearing that engine in the sky.'

'Engines,' Clemmy corrected. 'The RFDS flies King Airs now, and they have two. Can you imagine what it must have been like for the women out here before the pedal radio and the first flying doctor? The children they lost! You see the little graves – nearly every station has at least one. There are three at Wintergreen, a set of twins and a third child. All Morgans.' She shivered. 'Much as I love the bush I don't think I could live out here without the mantle of safety – that's what they call it, you know, the flying doctor service. It's not just the children, though. The men have accidents too, get sick. Jim Hazlitt's appendix burst on him last year, nearly killed him. It's why everyone comes to these affairs and gives, despite the drought. There's hardly a soul here who hasn't at some stage had reason to call on the doctor.'

When the games were over, Flo Morgan went off with Mavis to organise afternoon tea. Sara was surprised at how quickly the time had flown. There was more shade beyond the concrete slab than on it.

Jack appeared suddenly at her shoulder. 'How's it going? You're looking blooming, Clemmy. They're laying on a cuppa, Sara, then they'll run the auction. Mum's getting a bit restive so I thought we'd push off straight after that.'

'Yes, of course. Whenever you're ready.' He left and she turned to her companion. 'What auction? What are they selling?'

'Cakes. Mavis keeps the best ones from those brought for

smoko and the men bid on them.' She grinned. 'It's a good fund-raiser. The wives naturally expect their husbands to buy theirs. Some of 'em'll have a bit to say on the trip home if they don't.'

Sara smiled. 'So will Colin buy yours?'

Clemmy's delightful laugh bubbled out of her. 'God, no! Nothing of mine's ever made the auction. Mavis used to judge the cakes at the Alice show so she knows her stuff. Bungy will be out of pocket again, though. Flo makes a fabulous sponge, and he'll get the rounds of the kitchen if he doesn't get to take it home.'

The auction, conducted by Mavis's husband, Alec, a short, heavily moustachioed man who was going bald but had a good line in blarney, was a lively affair. He named the provenance of each cake as he held it aloft, describing them in flamboyant terms.

'Yer sound like a flamin' cooking show,' somebody yelled from the back, occasioning a ripple of laughter.

'And some of our ladies could show 'em a thing or two,' Alec retorted, round face red from yelling. 'Here's a tea cake, gents, dusted with cinnamon, just cryin' out to be buttered. Soft, fragrant . . .' He sniffed appreciatively. 'Jim Hazlitt's a lucky man to be living with such talent. Now, if you can't get a slice of Flo's sponge, who wouldn't go for this? Somebody start me at twenty.'

The bidding ran up to thirty-five before Jim Hazlitt, mopping his brow in exaggerated relief, secured the cake. Sara, clapping along with the rest, leaned over to say something to Clemmy and was stunned to see her own sultana cake being displayed next.

'And here, last, but not least, baked by our newest import to the district, Miss Sara –' Mavis stretched up into Alec's hesitation and he bobbed his head in acknowledgement – 'Blake. It's a beauty, something different – a golden sultana cake, moist and scrumptious. And a big thank you, Sara, from all of us here today. We all heard about young Sam being taken crook and appreciate you pitching in to help the doctor's fund. Don't let her work be wasted, fellas. Bid 'er up.'

'Wow!' Clemmy looked impressed. 'You didn't say you were a cook. It's quite an honour, you know, to make the grade for the cake auction.'

Sara was embarrassed. 'It's a foolproof recipe. Anybody could make it. I enjoy cooking but it's not like I ever trained for it. Maybe I should've done a course, but I don't think I'd care for the pressure of restaurant work.'

'So what was it you said you did again before taking up governessing?'

'I was a clerk in a government office. A civil servant, I suppose.'

Clemmy wrinkled her nose. 'I trained as a hairdresser, then I met Colin. I couldn't go back to town life now. Oh, look – Jack's scored your cake. Forty dollars! That'll be top price for the day. You'll have Flo's nose out of joint, she usually gets it.' Everyone clapped and Clemmy raised her voice to speak over the applause. 'What d'you think? More fun than just handing over a cheque?'

'Definitely. It's been a great day. I hope we get to meet again soon.'

'I want to sit with Nan and Pop,' Becky announced as they all reached the station wagon, where Jack and his father were busy transferring the luggage and pulling a plastic tarp over Frank's little car.

'It'll cook under it,' Jack said critically, 'but it's some protection.'

'Alec needs a shed,' Frank agreed.

Helen made a sound like a snort. 'The whole place needs more than a shed. When are they going to finish that hall? And what happened to the tennis court they were talking about four years ago?'

'The drought, Mum,' Jack said mildly. 'Hop in, Squirt. You get the middle seat.'

Helen, however, was not to be gainsaid. 'You could make an

antbed court for nothing. All it takes is the labour to gather the termite mounds and flatten them. And there're grants to be had – the
Gaming Committee, for one. They'd fund the netting and equipment if you applied. You could cite isolation and the drought, the
smallness of the local population, the need to have a communal
focus with health benefits. Good God, the application practically
writes itself . . .'

Jack grinned fondly at her. 'Always said your talents were
wasted in the CWA. You ought to be in Canberra, Mum. Hop in,
Sara.'

Sara, who had been holding back, said, 'I'll ride in the back.
I thought Mr Ketch might like the front seat.'

Frank looked behind him. 'I dunno that fellow, but I'm riding
in the back. I'll get the gates.'

'Indeed you won't, Mr Ketch. I'll open them.'

'Righto.' He gave in easily. 'And my name's Frank.'

'Your first station job, Sara?' Helen asked.

'Yes, it is.' To forestall the next question she added, 'I'm really
enjoying it. I wish I'd tried it before.'

'Don't be too sure.' Helen's tone was dry. 'City bred, aren't
you? It can pall very quickly once the novelty's worn off. You
wouldn't be the first to learn that.'

Unsure how to respond, wondering if the woman was referring
to her daughter-in-law, Sara held silent, but Jack spoke for her.
'Don't discourage the help, Mum. She's been doing a great job,
despite her silly hat.' His closest eyelid dropped in a wink and,
unaware that the curve of her face was visible to Helen, Sara smiled
back, hoping her employer's mother wasn't going to take against
her. It would make things uncomfortable if she did, but if that was
to be the case, it was comforting to know that Jack at least was on
her side.

18

Once back at Redhill, the fact that their room was ready for them and the evening meal prepared seemed to soften Helen's attitude towards her daughter's employee. Or perhaps, Sara thought, she had misjudged her remarks and the woman was simply tired and worried. Both she and Frank must have spent wearying hours at their grandson's bedside and they'd had a long journey today as well. Not wishing to appear to be taking charge, Sara waited until their bags had been carried in then asked diffidently, 'Would you like a cup of tea? I could put the kettle on.'

'That's a grand idea,' Frank declared. Hands on hips, he stood on the verandah, looking about and sniffing the air. Jess had gone straight to him when they arrived. He brought his gaze back to Sara's face and grinned, stretching the thin, reddened skin of his cheeks. 'Maybe a slice of that expensive cake of yours too, eh?'

'Of course.' She found herself smiling back. 'I'll see to it.'

'Then will you come with me to get the goats, Pops?' Becky pressed.

''Course I will, kiddo.'

Helen joined Sara in the kitchen as she set sugar and milk on the table. 'Very nice.' She ran an approving eye over the room. 'You've obviously run a house before. Beth said you were very capable and I can see she was right.' She hoisted a carrier bag onto the bench. 'I brought a couple of extra loaves out. Beth said you'd been learning to bake?'

'A precaution – against Sam's treatment trips,' Sara agreed. 'But I like it. How do you take your tea, Mrs Ketch?'

Helen pulled a chair out. 'Just as it comes. And call me Helen, please.' She inspected the cake. 'Frank will enjoy that. I'll cook while I'm here, but if you like I could show you a few other yeast recipes. You'll have time during the holidays?'

'Oh, yes, I imagine so.' Sara added milk to her own tea, relieved that they would get on together. 'I'll look forward to it.' A faint murmur in the distance had her cocking her head. 'That could be Len coming home. I'll get down another cup.'

Over the next few days the five adults hung on the daily phone calls from the Alice, charting Sam's progress from his first full meal to his first shaky walk around his bed. Everything was finally going his way. His blood tests were improving, his strength slowly returning. The fact that he would be staying in town for a while meant that he could leave hospital sooner than if he had been returning immediately to the station. He was still ill, of course, but the immediate crisis was over. The concerned phone calls from far-flung neighbours dwindled and Len's lugubrious face seemed to relax a little as he came and went about the place. He was mostly in Frank's company. They had been to Wintergreen, where the drillers had pulled out of their first hole, and were now trying another site with Bungy in what Jack, who had also been over to the property, called baying attendance.

'You could hear him clear across the station,' he said. 'And not just when he realised it was a dud hole. Old Flo won't let him swear at home, so he makes up for it on the run.'

'They didn't get water, then?' Sara was surprised by the depth of her disappointment.

'Oh, yeah, but just a trace. Made it worse. Poor old Bungy

thought he had it, but no sooner did they get it up than it stopped. It happens sometimes.'

'Perhaps he'll have better luck with the next hole.' Sara put down the scissors she was using and knitted her brows. 'Something I meant to ask you . . . What does poddying mean? Rinky mentioned it at the fundraiser.'

'It just means she's raising orphan calves by hand. They've got quite a goat flock at Munaroo so there's milk to spare. Pregnancy weakens droughted cows. With a calf on 'em they soon die, so she's saving what she can on goat's milk.'

'Oh, poor things, that's awful! What about the calves here? Don't you —'

'Len shot 'em as they were born. Only way to save the cows.'

Shocked, Sara raised a hand to the base of her throat. 'That's – that's dreadful!'

'Yeah, well, it's drought. What are you doing?' Jack twisted his head to scan the scatter of papers spread across the trestle table on the verandah.

'Oh, Becky's making something for Sam.' She blinked, trying to match his matter-of-fact tone. 'A welcome-home gift for when he finally gets here,' she explained. 'I'm just helping her along. It's a bit hard to find the sorts of pictures she needs. And it's a lot of effort for little reward. Not easy for a nine-year-old, so I'm doing the dull bits.'

'I see. What's it going to be?'

'A map of the station. I'm looking for pictures of windmills, cattle, houses – *small* pictures, and therein lies the difficulty. Your father's going to build a frame for it, and Len's given me a pastoral map so I can make sure she has all the spelling right. So it's going to be a collaborative effort. She really misses him, you know. It's lonely being the only kid.'

Jack moved across to hitch a hip onto the corner of the trestle. 'Were you lonely growing up?'

'Yes, I was. It was hard for me to make friends; Stella never let any child come over to play, you see, so of course they palled up more easily with other kids. When I was in third grade a girl I was friends with wanted to come over, but she never even made it through the gate. After that I was always too scared and ashamed to ask anyone. So I wasn't asked either. And the older you get, the harder it becomes. I envy you and Beth, what you had as children.'

'She was your mother. Why would she be like that?'

'When it comes to Stella, why anything? She happened to be out the front of our house when we turned up and she just yelled that one brat was bad enough, and for Peggy – that was her name, Peggy Mansfield – to get off home before she set the dog on her. We didn't have a dog.' Sara picked up the scissors and turned them in her hands. 'She never talked to me again, Peggy. Nor any of the other girls in that class. They used to whisper about Stella being a witch.'

'Sounds more like a bitch to me.'

'Well, that was how she was.' Sara gave a rueful smile. 'Kids are amazingly resilient, though. I had an imaginary friend all through primary school. The funny thing is I was never sure if it was a boy or a girl – I guess its gender depended on my need at that moment. I called it You. It was someone to play with and talk to, even if it was all in my head.' She hesitated, laid the scissors down again and looked at Jack. 'These last few days I've been wondering . . . I suddenly remembered You, you see, for the first time in years, and I've been wondering if all the time it – he – was Ben? Do you think that's possible? That I had some sort of hidden, I don't know, memory or intuition that prompted the creation of him as an imaginary friend? It's quite common for children to have them.'

'Is it? I didn't know, but it sounds feasible. Have you remembered anything more?'

'It's hard to say. Nothing major anyway, but little things. Only I can't be sure they're really memories – lost ones, that is. What I mean is that last night when I was drying up I noticed the design on the handle of a fork and I remembered it – remembered rubbing it with a tea towel, the way kids do, and saying, *It's a rose!*' She shrugged. 'But, well, I could've said it as a ten-year-old too.' She moved restlessly. 'I'll never know unless I remember a whole lot more, or until I find my brother, and that seems unlikely.'

'I wouldn't pin my hopes on it,' Jack agreed, adding gruffly, 'but you're not alone now. You've got the Ketch family to root for you, and the Calshots too – that's something.'

'I'll remember it,' Sara said, touched by his concern. Later in the day, coming in from moving hoses, she was mulling over the conversation and spoke to Helen.

'How would you go about finding someone?' she asked. 'Any ideas? There's someone – I knew him as a child and then we lost each other. Now I have nothing but his name.'

'Hmm.' Helen pursed her lips. 'You could advertise, put a message in the agony column of a city paper with a box office number? People sometimes respond.'

'Yes, but which paper? It would depend which state he's in, and I don't know that.'

'Well, you might contact the Registry of Births, Deaths and Marriages where he was born. It would cost you but if his parents still lived there, you could get his address. It would probably be about thirty dollars for the certificate, but it mightn't help. How badly do you want to find him?' She emptied potatoes into the sink and picked up the peeler.

'Oh, quite a lot, actually,' Sara said lightly. 'We used to be great friends.'

'Ah, well, perhaps you should check the marriage section of the register too.'

'It's not like that,' Sara protested. 'I just want to get in touch, that's all.'

Helen smiled, a twinkle in her eye. 'My dear, in my experience, when it comes to men and women it's always like that. But have it your way.'

Sara forbore to argue; it hardly mattered and the registry was a good suggestion. Only, could you get somebody else's birth certificate? She doubted it, but she could at least get a copy of her own. Stella had one somewhere. She had produced it for Sara's wedding, but Sara had not seen it at the time. When she'd asked for it to keep with her marriage certificate, it had been misplaced. Stella was supposed to find it but that had never happened. No matter. She would send for a copy now and if Ben were older, he should surely be listed on it, if not named. If he was, then she could try to get hold of his. That way she would also learn where she had been born, and Stella's maiden name as well. Really, she might as well have been found under a cabbage leaf, for all the knowledge she had of her own beginnings.

Murmuring that she had ironing to do, Sara hurried off to her room. The ironing could wait but Harry was due tomorrow so she would write the letter now.

The evening phone call brought the news that Sam could leave hospital next week.

'That's wonderful!' Helen's face was wreathed in smiles as if her daughter could see her. 'I'm so glad. We all are. Wait on – yes, Len's just coming now. I heard the gate. I'll give you to Becky for a moment.' She handed the phone over and they listened to the child's disjointed gabble as she tried to report all her news at once – Sara, Pops and the goats receiving an equal mention. Len took the phone cautiously, his back to the room, listened for a little and visibly relaxed.

'Great,' he said. 'That's good, love. Yup, should do. Yeah, soon. I saw Bungy today – he got his hole. Yup, 'bout five thousand an hour, he reckons. Do ours next week. Yup, give the boy a kiss for me. Bye.'

He hung up, rolled his shoulders as though shedding a huge weight and turned to his mother-in-law. 'I hope you saved me a bite of dinner, Helen?'

'Of course I did. Isn't it wonderful news?' She beamed at him. 'He may not be coming home but it's a great step all the same.'

'Yup,' Len agreed placidly.

'Is that all you can say?' Helen said, sounding exasperated.

'Pretty well covers it,' Len said. 'Jack back yet?'

'He's in the kitchen,' Sara interposed. 'What you said – does that mean the driller got water at Wintergreen?'

'He did.' Jack had overheard. He stood in the doorway, tea mug in hand. 'Old Bungy was on the radio bellowing the news to Jim Hazlitt. They talk most nights – gives him a break from Flo, I guess. Good flow, and good water too. If he had it to spare, I reckon now'd be the time to ask him for a loan. *Pleased* doesn't come near his state of mind.'

Sara felt a surge of uncomplicated joy at the news. It was odd it should matter to her – she had met the man only once and then very briefly on the day of the fundraiser – but the thought went through her mind that the fierce triumph she felt at hearing of his success wasn't so much for Bungy Morgan as for the entire district. Like celebrating a battle won in an ongoing war. And drought was that war. She recalled Jack's unemotional tone speaking of the Redhill calves, *Len shot 'em as they were born.* What did that do to a man who raised stock for a living? Such hardiness had to be something the land bred into them, for no weakling, she sensed, could survive out here, could make such decisions and live with them, battling on, day after day, in the grim determination that, some day, the drought had to end, and when it did they would still be around, ready to pick up the pieces and start over.

19

The following week saw more visitors turn up than at any other time since Sara's arrival. The fuel tanker came first, diesel engine roaring as it powered through the horse paddock, throwing a plume of dust that must almost have been visible from the roadhouse. The rising red column was just settling behind the huge truck when a willy-wind tore out of the scrub, crossed its path and shot straight towards the homestead. Sara, watching from the verandah, gave a squawk of dismay and fled indoors, hearing the harsh rattle of the wind battering through the garden as she did so. The open louvres and latticework of the schoolroom were no barrier to the mini cyclone of dust and dead leaves contained within it. Becky's precious collage went flying and papers fluttered like bats until the centre abruptly collapsed, raining dust over everything.

Becky, bright-eyed, followed Sara in to survey the damage. 'It's a devil chasing you. That's what Uncle Jack says. An old blackfella told him that – willy-winds are devil men.'

'And the moon's made of green cheese,' Sara said affably, but the child's words had produced an instant picture of her stalker and her nape prickled. 'What a mess! Do you want to get the broom for me? Yuck!' She had touched her sweaty face and felt the grit transfer from her fingers. Her hair must be full of it too. Sweat beaded on her cheeks, itching its way downward to the point of her chin. It was so hot it *had* to rain, she thought, but when she looked hopefully across the paddock, the grey leaves of the mulga hung listlessly under the cloudless, dust-stained sky. Down near the sheds a motor was running – the pump on the truck, transferring fuel – and from the kitchen came the bump of the oven closing and Helen's tuneful humming. Just another day at Redhill.

Their second visitor was also a semitrailer, this one loaded with tonnes of cattle lick in white nylon bags. Sara added another mug to those on the table, next to Helen's date cake. Afterwards she went down to the sheds with Becky to watch Jack spin the forklift back and forth between truck and shed, unloading the heavy pallets. Frank was out on the bulldozer that day, pushing scrub. Helen later confided that it was a task she hated him doing.

'He's as stubborn as a donkey,' she said. 'He knows he should be taking it easy but men never really accept that they're mortal. Well, his heart is, and the doctor has told him so.'

True to her promise, Helen was giving Sara baking lessons and her pupil was rolling then folding dough into a long plaited loaf.

'Is there a history of heart disease in the family?'

'Not that I'm aware of. He's just worn his out with a lifetime's hard work, but he's too damn pigheaded to admit it. All he needs is long ears and a tail and you'd know him for an ass.'

Sara smiled at that. 'Are donkeys so stubborn, then?'

'Very. When the kids were young they had one for a pet. Nothing much under a tractor could shift it, unless it wanted to move, but they loved him anyway, stubborn old brute that he was.' She smiled faintly, remembering. 'I think both my kids were born with a death wish. They used to race him at the creek bank and then jump him over it, to see how long they could stay on. Bareback, of course – a recipe for a broken neck.'

Sara laughed. 'I can believe it. Beth told me about them catching snakes. Snakes! What else did they get up to?'

'Climbing the mill,' Helen said promptly. 'Jack was just six the first time Frank hauled him down from the homestead mill. It had a thirty-foot tower.' She shook her head. 'They were so naughty. I couldn't take my eyes off them. They both got into the stock tank one summer – to cool off, Beth said. If the station hand we had working for us hadn't heard them, they'd have drowned. There was no way they could have got themselves out again. And they were forever wandering off, following the goats.'

'Getting lost, you mean? Should I tuck the ends under or press them into the loaf?'

'Tuck them under. Luckily they never did – get lost, that is. We told them to always look for the mill head to find their way home, but people have died in the bush, even with roads to follow. Did you ever hear of Elizabeth Darcy and her son?'

'What about them?'

'They vanished from Malapunyah Station, oh, years back. In the forties, it would've been. Bred to the bush, but they just disappeared one day and were never seen again. Elizabeth's husband searched for them for over a month with every man he could raise, including trackers. It's a puzzle that's never been solved.'

Sara paused, fingers poised over the beaten egg. 'But – what – how?'

'Nobody knows. It's not the only mystery, though. The bush holds many secrets. People vanish, perish, are murdered – like the Bowman family. They were travelling down to Adelaide. They camped by the side of the road one night and some nutter shot them. Back in the fifties, that was. Or those kids who disappeared from Kings Canyon a dozen or more years later. Their parents were station folk but it didn't help. They found one boy dead, the other was never seen again.'

Sara was thoughtful as she spread the glaze over her loaf. 'I suppose that sort of thing happens more often these days. People killed or taken, I mean, but in the forties? Could somebody really have spirited the Darcys away? The country seems awfully empty to me now, so what must it have been like back then when travel was so much slower and more difficult?'

'I don't believe anyone else was involved,' Helen agreed. 'Something happened to them – snakebite, an injury, perhaps, and somehow the search missed them. It's rough country up there and there's plenty of it.'

'And the children at . . . Where did you say it was?'

'Kings Canyon. It's a holiday spot the tourists visit. The children were quite young and at first they were thought to have drowned. It was only later that they widened the search to beyond the canyon, but it was far too late by then to recover them alive and everyone knew it. A child can perish in a day out here, even in early summer, which at the time, it was. The media blamed the parents for the children's disappearance, which was unfair. I'd like to have seen those journalists keep up with my two! There was a huge turnout of searchers – police, army, station people. Months later, it might even have been a year or more, they found the boy's body, then the mother took her own life. It was all very sad, but it can happen. It pays to remember that.'

'But that's so awful! The poor parents,' Sara exclaimed.

'Yes, dreadful.' Helen went to the window. 'I wonder where that child is?'

'I sent her to the chook pen,' Sara offered. 'We've been experimenting with dyes made from grass and stuff. I thought we'd hard-boil an egg and paint it.'

Helen's face softened. 'You're good for Becky, Sara. Beth said you were and I've seen for myself how much time and thought you put into her day. A nice change, I must say, from some of the young women who come out to the stations. Come out here to work, they claim, but they're just looking for husbands.'

Sara rinsed her hands, then whisked the bread bowl under the tap, hardly knowing how to answer.

'Well,' she said, 'I've had one husband and I'm not in a hurry to find another.' A burr of sound beat against her eardrum, growing rapidly louder, and she raised her brows at the older woman. 'It's not Friday, is it? No, of course not. Then I wonder who that could be?'

It was Clemmy Marshall driving a green Land Rover with a canvas back. The canvas was red with dust, but Clemmy looked fresh and attractive in short blue shorts and a patterned top. She waved from the gate, then looked down to unlatch it. A baseball cap covered her hair and wraparound sunglasses obscured her eyes, but neither concealed her wide smile.

'Hello, Helen. Hi, Sara. I'm heading into the Alice. Thought I'd stop by and see if there's something I can take in for Beth, or if there's anything you need brought out?'

'That's good of you,' Helen said. 'We'll think about it. Come in and have a cuppa while we do.'

'Love to.' Clemmy negotiated the steps, fluttering her fingers at Becky who had popped her head out to see who the visitor was. 'Hello, ducky. How's your brother doing?'

'Getting better, Mum says.' The girl stared curiously. 'What's a ducky?'

'Just a name. Like pinhead, only nicer. It means you're sort of cute.' Clemmy wrinkled her nose at her.

'Sara calls me chicken,' Becky revealed.

'Does she? Do you like it?'

Becky thought about it. 'It's okay. We're gonna paint an egg.'

'After we've had some tea,' Sara said. 'You want to wash your hands, and maybe ask your nan if you can put a pretty cloth on the table for our visitor?'

Becky shot off as though galvanised.

'I'll put the kettle on,' Helen said to the young women. 'Sara will show you the loo if you need it.'

Clemmy grinned. 'I do, thanks.'

Sara meanwhile was working out distances. 'You didn't drive all the way in here from the bitumen?'

'No, I came the back route. Rougher but miles shorter. The

road comes due south from Walkervale to Kileys bore. Used to be the main track, about a hundred years back. So, how are you passing the holidays?'

'I hardly know. Here you are.' There was a pause but when Clemmy emerged to wash her hands, Sara continued, 'The time's gone by so fast. Helen's teaching me to bake all sorts of fancy bread, she's a real master at it. There's the garden, I just hose things but it's not quick, and there're little jobs about the place I do. Becky and I have a project going too. The drillers are coming in next week. Did you hear that they found good water for Bu– Mr Morgan?'

Clemmy was smiling and nodding. 'I'll bet you never knew so much went on out in the backblocks.'

'I didn't. Nor that it led to gossip! Here's a man I barely know and I'm tattling his news as if I had a back fence to lean over.'

'Don't worry about it. News is currency out here. There's poor value in people who don't listen and pass on what they hear.'

When they reached the kitchen the table had been spread with an embroidered cloth and Becky was carefully creasing paper napkins. Helen had put down cups and saucers in place of the regular mugs, and had found something better than the breadboard to hold the slices of fruit cake.

'Wow!' Sara surveyed the table. 'The napkins are a great touch, Becky. Do you remember the pretty table you made for me on my first night? It was so nice. It made me feel special, like you really wanted me here.'

Clemmy stroked the cloth. 'I know what you mean. I feel special now too. How long is it since you've seen your mum, Becky?'

'I dunno.' Becky wriggled, looking to Sara for the answer. 'Ages an' ages. She's not coming home when Sam gets out of hospital neither 'cause they're gonna stay at Nan's house.'

'Well, what if I was to take you into town to see her, and bring you back Sunday? Would that be all right, Helen?'

The child's face lit up as she swung to face her grandmother.

'Could I, Nan? That would be so cool! Oh, please say yes. Please!'

Too late, Clemmy realised the quandary she had placed the older woman in. She bit her lip. 'I should've rung you, given you time to – but I just thought of it. She would be safe with me but of course it's for you to decide.'

'I don't know.' Helen hesitated. Len was out for the day and in his absence responsibility devolved upon her. 'It's been almost a month but what would Beth . . . I mean, she spends all her time at the hospital.'

'Why not ring her and ask?' Sara interposed.

She nodded decisively. 'We'll ask your mum, pet, and if she says you can, then you may.' She looked at Clemmy. 'I'm sorry, what's your surname again? And it's in today and back Sunday?'

'Yes, and it's Marshall, Clemmy Marshall. Beth and I are old friends.'

When Helen went to make the phone call Sara pointed Clemmy to a chair. 'Have a seat. I'd pour but —'

'Let's wait.' Clemmy agreed, biting her lip. 'I hope I haven't offended her, only it's such a long time to be away from your child.'

'It's a kind thought.' Sara's own thoughts were on clothes for Becky. She could go in what she had on, but would need better out-fits for Friday and Saturday, as well as a toilet bag, pyjamas, hair clips . . . She glanced down at the familiar, daggy trainers dangling from the child's chair. Something more respectable for her feet too, and a hat? Did her wardrobe run to a town hat at all? Then Helen was back, smiling. Becky's eyes flew straight to her face.

'Mum said yes?'

'Better than that! Sam's going home today. She was getting him ready when they called her to the phone.' She beamed at Clemmy. 'She said to thank you, she'd love to have a visit from Becky and you. I'll give you the address – oh, haven't you started yet? Let's have a cuppa first, then I'll write it down for you.'

'I could find your house, Nan,' Becky burst out.

'I'm sure you could, pet,' Helen said tactfully. 'But Mrs Marshall might forget how to get back to pick you up. So I'll write it out anyway.'

'And I'll pack her clothes,' Sara volunteered. 'If there's anything special you want to take, run and get it out, chicken. We mustn't hold Mrs Marshall up too long.'

A bag was soon packed, Sara sorting quickly through the clothes Becky pulled from the drawers in her room. There was a cloth hat, and an almost new pair of red sneakers. Sara tucked a hairbrush into the bag and said, 'Run and wash your face. Oops, nearly forgot your PJs. Tell Sam hello from me, won't you? And have a great time with your mum.'

'I will. I wish you were coming too.' Becky danced from the room to hug her grandmother, the dog and, at the last moment, to rush back and enfold Sara's waist in a bony embrace. 'Bye, Sara.'

'Bye, chicken.'

Clemmy climbed behind the wheel and waved. 'See you Sunday,' she called as the vehicle drove off.

'Well.' Helen dropped her hand. 'Two days isn't much of a holiday, but they'll all enjoy it.'

Sara didn't reply. It was the word *holiday* that did it. It had flashed fully formed into her head, the picture of herself and Ben with buckets and spades at the beach. They wore bathers and were building a sandcastle in the shade of a huge umbrella, digging at the sand with more enthusiasm than skill. Their father was helping them. On the edge of her vision were big shoulders and hairy forearms that steadied the buckets – bright red and yellow to match their spades – and somewhere, she knew, was the caravan with the striped awning. They were on holiday, she and her parents and Ben, and his cloth hat fell back on its string from his ginger hair.

Here was another piece of the puzzle. Sara had no idea where it fitted but hugged to herself the happy feeling that the memory imparted. She was smiling when she went back into the house.

20

Helen was waiting for her in the kitchen doorway. 'I like that young woman. Her timing is pure serendipity for Beth and the kids.'

'Yes.' Sara looked past her. The cups had been cleared into the sink and the bread bowl was out on the table. 'What are you making now?'

'Depends. Would you like to try your hand at croissants?'

'Why not? Did you bake professionally, Helen? You seem to have endless recipes in your head.'

'That's because I worked for a boulanger in France when I was young. That's a baker. I was only there for twelve months, not enough time to become a master baker, but I enjoyed it. It was long before I was married, of course, but when I came back home, I kept it up. I love working dough. Just as well really, as all the stations baked their own bread back then. There were no freezers on the properties, and in some places no electricity either.'

'So what were you doing in France? This much?' Waiting for Helen's nod, Sara mixed the yeast with the sugar and warm water.

'Seeing the world, which in those days was Europe. My generation did that. The next lot raced off to India and Egypt to find themselves, but we did Britain and the continent. I went to stay with an old battleaxe of an aunt in Yorkshire, but she was too eighteenth century for words. So I cleared out and travelled around a bit. I did maid work in Spain, washed bottles in Italy, picked grapes in Malta.

France was the best, though. I was broke. Monsieur Lesseur didn't pay much but the job had lunch thrown in, so I stayed and then got interested. I'd always liked cooking.'

'How wonderful! I wish now that I'd travelled more. This is only the second time I've been out of my home state. So how did you find Frank? Was he in France too?'

Helen laughed. 'Fat chance! Victoria's a foreign country to him. Sift the flour twice. No, I got a job in the Alice. It was like coming out to a frontier back then. I was still looking for adventure, you see. I met him at the races there.'

There was a hint of a smile in Sara's eyes. 'Love at first sight?'

'No. I was twenty-five, a bit old for teenage flights of fancy. But I liked him so when he asked me out I agreed and it grew from there. Quite a few young things come out to the bush looking for romance, but it's a tougher life than it may seem before the shine wears off. I was older, and up for the isolation and the drudgery – not like Jack's wife. She thought that having land, even if it's desert, meant piles of money.'

Sara covered the dough with a cloth and turned to the sink. 'So, where is she now?'

'Gone.' Helen set the timer. 'It won't take long to prove. You'll need a baking tray, butter and a sharp knife for the next bit. And an egg for the glaze.'

The two women passed a quiet day. Sara, shifting hoses around and carrying the feed bucket early to the horses, was surprised by how much she missed having Becky chattering away beside her. Seeing Sara approach, Star and Lancer nickered a greeting and thrust eager muzzles into their feed tins. She had largely lost her fear of them and stood patting their necks and combing her fingers through their coarse mane hair as their lips gathered in the feed. If it ever rained – no, *when* it rained, she corrected herself – she would take up Sam's offer of riding lessons. If he was ever well enough to give them. Sara was aware that his recent victory was only part of an ongoing war. Standing there in the heat, eyes pinched against the brilliant light and breathing in the smell of dust and powdered dung, her heart ached for the young boy.

The day dragged on. It was odd how much difference Becky's absence made; the men were out and Helen was busy in the office, sorting through the accumulated mail for the bills marked as requiring immediate attention. Sara drifted through the house, bereft of purpose, and finally settled on the daybed on the side verandah. Here a late fitful breeze stirred the foliage of the lemon tree and set up the annoying scritching from the still-untrimmed branch. She would fix that this very day, she thought drowsily, but later, when it cooled off. The book fell from her fingers and with the sweat pooling in the hollow of her throat, she dreamed of parched paddocks layered over with carcasses, like the one she had seen on the day she arrived. Under a pitiless sun the mulga stood bare-branched like dark skeletons, and the only sound was the thin bleating of calves and the raucous cacophony of crows. Sara twisted and moaned unhappily, but a thin thread of awareness penetrated the dream. *It's not Redhill. Len shot the calves.* Beside her head the branch dragged against the wall and suddenly, in the manner of dreams, she was back in her flat, standing at her bedroom door with the hair prickling on her neck, knowing that her stalker was somewhere downstairs.

Sara woke with a gasp, her back bolting off the bed before she remembered and relaxed. *God!* Lifting the hem of her shirt, she wiped her face as her racing heart slowed. That, at least, hadn't happened. Yes, the man had broken into her flat and searched it but she hadn't been there at the time. It was just a dream. And she was safe now – Adelaide was hundreds of kilometres behind her. The break-in and getting the flowers afterwards had been the final straws that had pushed her into taking the temporary posting in Mildura as well as that last attempt at contacting Stella.

Recalling it now renewed the baffled fury of discovering that her mother had again eluded her. She had meant to demand answers of her, because whatever reason the man had for following her about, if it wasn't sexually motivated, had to lie in the past. Or did she only think that now that her memories had begun to return? Stella was the only key to her childhood. Sara's stalker's sudden appearance had seemed just a coincidence at the time but Jack was right – somehow the man's obsessive pursuit of her was connected to those lost years, as was the fear he generated in her. But Stella was insanely secretive, always had been, and forewarned by Sara's foolish phone call to her two days beforehand she had simply decamped, leaving no clue to her whereabouts.

Sara breathed out in exasperation; the wind had risen while she slept and now it dragged the lemon branch against the wall in a long ear-piercing scritch. It was too much! She rose on a flame of frustrated urgency and went looking for the secateurs.

The men returned just on dark, full of good spirits. In Len's case this was enhanced by the news, delivered as he reached the kitchen door, that Sam was out of hospital. 'Great! I'll give them a call now.' He tossed his hat at the peg above the cupboard and glanced about. 'Where's Becky? She'll want to talk to him too.'

'She already is, if I know Becs,' Helen said. 'The young woman from the park came through and she's taken her into town. I rang Beth first, of course.'

'Ah, good thinking, Helen. I wish I was in there myself.'

'You know you can go at anytime. We can manage here,' Helen began, but he was already striding for the office.

Jack, appearing next with Frank at his heels, hung his own hat. 'You won't get rid of him now, Mum,' he announced. 'Not with the driller on site.'

'Already?' Sara jerked her head out of the cupboard where the plates lived. 'I thought he was coming next week?'

'Nope, he shifted camp today. He had a bit of trouble with his load – a chain broke on the rig and he never noticed. Scattered casing over ten k of country before he realised.' Jack filled a glass at the sink and drank it down. 'Damn hard to spot white casing in dry grass, we've been chasing it all afternoon.'

'It's why we're late, love,' Frank told Helen. 'He'll be setting up in the morning. We could have water there come midday.'

'So soon?' Sara stared. 'But doesn't it take days, weeks even? I thought —'

Frank shook his head. 'It's a rotary rig. Barring trouble, they'll punch a hole down in a coupla hours. Not like the old mud thumpers, they went at about the pace of a good man with a crowbar. This one's all hydraulic. There's something to be said for progress after all. Sometimes, that is.' He spoke more slowly than was usual and raised a hand to rub his brow, his face flushed with excitement – or perhaps relief, Sara thought.

'Oh, I hope you get it,' she exclaimed. 'I'll keep all my fingers crossed that the water's there.'

'Why don't you come out with us tomorrow?' Jack asked. 'You too, Mum. There's nothing here that won't wait half a day. Pack some lunch and if the luck's with us, we'll boil the billy from the new bore. How's that sound?'

'Very Ketch,' Helen said dryly. 'I trust you're planning on taking water out as well. You can't be too careful in this country.'

Jack gave an exaggerated sigh. 'I know, Mum, I know. You've been telling me so since I was six. So that means you'll come? What about you, Sara?'

'I wouldn't miss it for quids.' She smiled happily, but the words echoed in her head. What had made her say that? It wasn't a phrase she normally used. It must be something she had picked up from Frank, who still thought in quids and gallons and miles. He had confessed to her he couldn't get his head around litres. To his mind it was like measuring in pannikins – and where was the sense in chopping up miles just to call them kilometres?

'It'll be hot,' Frank warned. He glanced at the ceiling fan as he walked towards his usual chair. 'Doesn't this damn thing go any faster?'

'It's on high,' Jack said. 'You're getting soft in your old age, Dad.'

'Age be blowed. It's hot – ask Sara. She hasn't had the brains baked out of her yet like the rest of you lot.' He reached for the chair back but staggered and missed it, fetching up against the table. 'Clumsy,' he muttered and abruptly sat down. 'Bit dizzy all of a sudden.'

Helen dropped the pot of beans she was draining into the sink and came to him, wiping her hands. 'Frank Ketch,' she exclaimed wrathfully. 'What have you been doing?' She laid her palm against his brow and then his face. 'You're red as a tomato and burning up. Has he been in the sun?' she demanded, her glance skewering Jack.

'Well, of course he has. We all have, Mum. There's not much shade on the Twelve Mile,' Jack protested.

'Don't be dumb. I mean without a hat?'

'No – well, yes, but only while the derrick was going up. Hard to look up without losing it. He took it off then, but only —'

'Men! Let's hope it's just a touch of sun and not a full sunstroke. Come on, get him into the shower, Jack, and I'll make up an icepack. Have you a headache, Frank?'

'Now you mention it, yeah. God, I don't feel too clever, and that's a fact.' Leaning heavily on the table, he pushed himself to his feet, his ruddy face noticeably paler. 'I think I'll lie down for a bit.'

'After you've cooled off,' Helen said. 'Do as I say, please. If I must, I'll get the thermometer to prove I'm right.'

'Better listen to her, Dad,' Jack advised. He shook his head in exasperated reproof as they passed through the doorway. 'Why didn't you say something? We could've come straight back if we'd known you were crook.'

'It was just a bit of a headache . . .' Frank's voice faded and Sara turned a concerned face to his wife.

'Is there something I can do?'

'Put the beans back to keep warm, there's a love.' Helen was decanting ice blocks into a plastic bag, which she wrapped in a tea towel. 'I'll put the fan on in the bedroom and wet a sheet. With the icepack and a cold shower that should do the trick. He'll be right once his temperature comes down.'

'Should – I mean, will you call the doctor?'

'I'll check in with him,' Helen said. 'He might suggest something else to try. Bad sunstroke can kill, but Frank's symptoms would be far worse if it was that. He'll need rehydration. Perhaps you could make up a jug of lemon drink?'

'Yes, of course.' Taking a bowl, Sara switched on the yard lights and went out into the garden.

At breakfast the following morning Frank pronounced himself as fit as a mallee bull, which cut no ice with his wife.

'You needn't think you're going anywhere today,' she said, layering cold meat and pickles on bread destined for sandwiches. 'The doctor said to take it easy and that's exactly what you're going to do. I'll make sure of it. Honestly, Frank, you're not safe to be let out alone.'

He scowled half-heartedly, then changed it to a leer. 'So with the place to ourselves, what shall we get up to? Any ideas, wife of mine?'

Sara giggled involuntarily and he winked at her. Helen cast him a withering look, then smiled. 'Daft old goat,' she said, but her tone was fond and she touched his grey hair in passing.

'I love the way your parents act with each other,' Sara

commented to Jack as they drove off. She sat in the middle seat, wedged between the two men. 'I didn't get to ask last night, Len – was Becky enjoying herself?'

'Most fun she's had since Christmas, Beth reckons. Said we missed an opportunity. You should've gone too. Bit of a break for you.'

'I don't mind,' Sara replied truthfully. 'Town's just town, but how often can you see a driller strike water?'

Len's ebullient mood seemed to have collapsed overnight. He massaged his rubbery cheeks, pushing the flesh about, his tone pessimistic. 'Yeah, well, that's if we do.'

21

Long before they reached the Forty Mile block Sara saw a column of dust rising above the mulga and pointed. 'What's that up ahead?'

'Vehicle coming,' Len said. 'Probably the mail.'

'Of course. It's Friday.'

'Shoulda brought the mailbag with us,' Jack said. 'I never gave it a thought.'

The Toyota was in sight now and slowing as it saw them. Len pulled over to one side and Jack hastily wound his window up as Harry approached, the dust cloud catching them both up. Once it had settled, the men got out and Sara followed, knowing it would be cooler in the mulga shade than in the cab of the vehicle.

Harry nodded at them. 'G'day, Len, Jack, Sara. How's it going?' He had a passenger, a tall youngster who looked scarcely out of his teens. He stood uncertainly in the background while the men gathered to talk and when Sara took pity on him and asked him his name, he blushed. The youth pushed back a felt hat to disclose fair hair and an open face where one or two acne spots still lingered.

'I'm Nick.' He was clutching a camera and was togged out like the other men, but in newer clothes. He offered his hand. 'Are you from round here, er, Miss?'

Sara shook it, reflecting that his skin was nearly as pale as her own. 'Sara Blake. I'm the governess at Redhill. And you? Where are you going?'

'Walkervale National Park.' He sounded grateful for the attention, his gaze lingering admiringly upon her. 'I'm gonna help build a fence there.'

'Really? Have you done that sort of work before?'

He didn't reply. She prompted, 'Nick?' and he blushed fierily again.

'Oh, sorry. I just – well, no, but it's a job.' He hefted his camera. 'And I hope it'll help my real work. I'm training to be a photographer. I wanna get on a paper, see, be their regular photographer, but you've got to have, like, a portfolio first. So the editor knows you can deliver the goods, see? I was stuck in Stepney, nothing but buildings and street pics there. Not my scene. I want the wild stuff, you know? Big pics. Nature, animals, storms, that sort of thing, so, well, here I am.' He smiled in uncomplicated pleasure and leant confidentially towards her, jerking his head at the three men. 'You reckon those blokes'd let me take their pictures?'

Sara shrugged. 'You could ask.' She nodded at the camera. 'Have you had many of your photos published?'

'I won a competition last year,' he disclosed proudly. 'They printed that one. And about a month later I was down at the port the day that yacht pitch poled. You mighta heard about it? Bit of luck really. I already had the long lens on and the tripod set up. Sheer fluke, but lotsa great pics happen 'cause you're on the spot. I was trying for a shot of the seabirds over the breakers and caught her just as she dug in and flipped. It made the front page. That's when I thought about getting on the staff . . .' He paused for breath.

'I was wondering, Miss, er, Sara, if I could get a coupla shots of you? Would you mind? It'd be great – you and the sky and the trees. I like shooting black and white for portraits, but yours should have colour. I'd send you a copy, of course.'

He reminded Sara forcefully of a pup, a gangly deerhound, perhaps. He was plainly smitten but she'd likely never see him again, so where was the harm in a photo? She smiled for him while he clicked away, asking her to turn or lift her chin while he muttered fervently behind the camera.

'Beautiful! Oh, man, the light! Now turn a bit to the right. Stop! That's it, that's perfect. And smile . . . Thanks, thanks a lot. They'll be the best pics I ever take.'

'I hope not,' she said gently. 'Look, the men are making a move, best ask them now. And in a year or two, Nick, I'll be watching out for your work.'

He ducked his head, looking absurdly pleased. 'Thanks. If it works out I might even get overseas. That'd be great, wouldn't it?' He flushed when she smiled at his enthusiasm, and capped the camera, then had to remove it again to snap a couple of shots of the two station men, then one of Harry leaning against the mail truck, before they all climbed back into their respective vehicles and departed.

'Well, you certainly made a hit with the kid,' Jack said as they drove on then, echoing her own thought. 'For a minute there I thought he was gonna roll over so you could rub his tummy.'

'He's young, that's all. He said he's going out to the national park to build a fence. Why would they have paddocks in a park?'

'Doesn't have to be a paddock,' Len said.

'What, then?'

Jack shrugged. 'Could be anything. Fencing in a parking compound, stringing cables to keep the tourists where they want 'em, enlarging the garden at the ranger station. Something small any road.'

'Because?'

'The kid's casual labour, so the work force will probably be just him and Colin. They'd hire a contractor for a real job.'

It made sense, Sara thought, impressed anew by the way these bushmen could weave a probable story from the merest threads of fact picked up from a few sentences.

She smiled. 'You're just jealous they didn't get you.'

He snorted. 'Fat chance. The government makes a great boss.

Muck you around for a month before you can start, then wait another three to get paid. I'd sooner chew nails.'

Sara was still laughing at his vehemence when Len slowed the vehicle and swung off the road onto the open plain, heading for the drilling truck beneath its towering derrick.

The driller's name was Sean. He wore a scruffy beard and filthy clothes, and his mate, a midget-sized man called Terry, looked no cleaner. A camp trailer, shrouded in red bull-dust, stood a little to one side, its door open, a heap of miscellaneous objects including boots and tools piled near the foot of its steps. A thin aerial swooped down from the top of the derrick but if the radio was on, she couldn't hear it for the plant that was already working. Grimacing, she covered her ears, waiting in the Toyota's shade as the two men walked across to join the drillers. She could make nothing of the drill itself, a moving mass festooned with hydraulic hoses, but instantly saw the reason for the men's filthy clothing. At first she had imagined they had already struck water but the liquid mud spewing from the hole was, she realised, generated by the water the drillers added. It splashed messily about over everything. Len shouted something and the taller man spread one hand twice. What did that mean? Had they been drilling for ten minutes, ten hours? Would they take a smoko break in ten?

Jack shouted something, tapped his wrist and came back to her. 'Noisy,' he commented. 'Not much to see, either. You want to come over to the van? Terry's gonna swing the billy for us. They're about ready for smoko.'

'How is it going? Any sign of water?'

He grimaced. 'They blew a hose then they had to change a bit, so no – not yet.' Seeing her incomprehension, he added, 'The bit's what does the cutting, and they wear and break, like anything else. So the pair of 'em aren't too happy but a cuppa will improve things.'

'I see.' Reluctantly following Jack, she was pleasantly surprised to find the inside of the dusty van as neat and clean as she could wish. The little man was standing in his bare feet on a box, scrubbing his hands in the sink. The seats, she saw, had heavy-duty plastic taped over them, and the table was covered in newspaper.

Terry, it transpired, was the cook. He produced a credible brownie to go with the strong tea that the three of them drank while seated on the covered bench seats. Terry was an articulate, well-travelled man, despite his appearance, and the fact that he didn't remove his hat, which both looked and smelled like a dead animal.

'It's a filthy job,' he observed, reading Sara's thoughts. 'If I take my hat off, I'd have to chuck it outside.' He laughed, a surprisingly deep sound for such a little body. 'Chances are the damn thing'd take off if I did. This gets hosed down each evening.' He tapped the plastic under him. 'It's the only way, if you don't want to live in a sty.'

'I never realised mud could be so messy,' Sara confessed.

'Yeah, well, chuck in some grease, oil and hydraulic fluid. There's all the gunk in the world on a rig. Now . . .' He slid short legs to the floor and stood. 'I'd better go. Feel free to wait in here if you want, Miss. Sean and Len'll be in, in a bit.'

'Thank you, but it's Sara, Terry.'

'Miss Sara, then.' He touched his hat and went out followed by Jack. The floor of the van, Sara realised belatedly, was also sheathed in plastic. Keeping it so clean must require quite an effort. She could see bunks at the opposite end. There was a gas stove and fridge beside the sink, but no bathroom. They must bathe outside, which given the state of their working clothes was probably just as well.

Sean and Len appeared in the doorway and Sara turned automatically to relight the gas for their tea. Sean stamped his boots and grabbed at the doorjamb, leaving a dirty smear behind. A sharp odour she couldn't place accompanied him. He swore, 'Bastard of a job this is.' Catching sight of Sara he stopped and grunted an apology for his language, looking ruefully at the mark on the door. 'Terry'll be after me for that. Likes the place clean, he does.' He sat where Terry had, as Sara freshened the pot. 'Well, you got this one well trained, Len.'

Sara stiffened at the remark and was glad when Len ignored it, murmuring instead, 'You're down the best part of thirty metres, you say. Most of the bores we've got are round the fifty mark. Fifty-five's the cut-off at any rate.'

'Twenty metres – easy to say,' Sean groused. 'The state of the rig, we could be lucky to get another three before somethin' else blows. I've said it before but I swear this is me last season in the bloody desert. More chance of gettin' service and spares under a six month, on the back side of the moon. Man's an idiot,' he grumbled, slurping tea. 'Gotta be easier ways to make a quid.'

'Try mine,' Len said dryly. 'At least a rig's not dependent on the seasons.'

'Yer think?' Sean lowered his mug and jerked his head at the door. 'You fancy digging that lot outta black soil after five inches of rain? I done it up on the Barkly year b'fore last. Bloody thing ended up buried to the top of the wheels on the off side. Miracle she never tipped over. Took me and the little fella a week to get her out. Mud to our arses. Damn near smothered young Terry.' He grinned as if the memory had cheered him, his dark face suddenly lightening. 'Well, that's life. No point bitching, eh?'

'Nobody listens.' Len nodded. In amicable silence they finished their tea and went out.

Sara put the milk back in the fridge and the cups and empty plate in the sink. Then, because she had nothing else to occupy her, she washed them up and found a rag in the cupboard with which to scrub away the greasy handprint on the doorjamb: it exuded the same sharp smell as Sean had, and she wrinkled her nose in distaste. It wasn't just mud. Something oily had been added and she had to really scrub to shift it. That done, she prowled the length of the van, looking at the fixtures. There was a screened skylight, she discovered, and windows, also screened, above the bunks. These had linen on them and one, which she presumed to be Terry's, had an old towel spread over the pillow. There was a magazine on the other bunk. Sara flipped it open, gave a little gasp of surprise, then dropped it again. *That,* she thought, was probably Sean's. Not that it was any of her business. It served her right for snooping. She took herself back to the kitchen end and sat down, wondering if Roger had ever possessed magazines like that. She could not believe it of him, there had been nothing concealed in his life, which had been as wholesome and open for inspection as the gym he had managed. But didn't most men read them? What about Jack, then? The thought made her flush and she instantly wished it had never occurred to her. That was definitely none of her business!

Seated at the table, chin cupped in one hand, the brief images she had glimpsed replayed in Sara's mind and she shifted uncomfortably, wishing she hadn't seen them – or at least had not linked them, however fleetingly, with Jack.

I wish I never, whimpered a tiny voice in the back of her head and like an echo came a tearful answer, *Oh, I wish I never, too.*

Sara froze to perfect stillness, as if movement of any sort would banish the memory. It was such a fragile thing. Concentrating hard, she whispered the words and the picture seemed to grow – the two of them, terrified, somewhere in the dark. From the tearful litany she had heard, Sara knew they had done something very wrong. Were they hiding from parental displeasure and, if so, where? She squeezed her eyes shut, willing the picture to expand, but only darkness and the muffled sobs came to her, and the fear, stark and formless. She rocked in her seat, reaching, reaching – and the door flew open, dispersing the picture as wind does mist.

'Sara!' Jack called. 'We hit it! We've got water.'

22

The water turned out to be of dubious quality. Not that it mattered, Len said, the relief of the gamble having paid off plain to read in his face. There was a sort of buoyancy too in the way he moved, as if a weight had been eased from his shoulders. By then the drillers had hauled the rotary drill from the hole and were casing it, slotting and lowering the lengths of poly-piping until the last one stood proud of the muddied surface. They ran a pump down it and the water came gushing up.

'Bit under fifty metres in depth.' Len beamed. 'Couldn't ask for better'n that.' He cupped his hands beneath the flow they were measuring and lifted the water to his mouth, drank and spat. 'Bit of mineral there, touch of salt too. Still, the stock won't mind.'

Jack, rolling a mouthful around, also spat. 'You're right about that. I've tasted better.'

'And worse,' Len reminded him. 'It's water.'

Terry fetched a mug from the van and filled it for Sara. 'Want to try it?'

'Thanks.' She took it with a smile, which quickly changed to a grimace. 'Aargh! That's awful.' Warned by the others' reactions, she'd taken only the tiniest sip and now dumped the rest. 'Is it normal for bore water to be so nasty? Can cows really drink that?'

Terry scooped up a handful and pulled a face. 'The quality varies from good to bad. The best is soft enough you can wash your hair in it. The worst'll keep stock alive. I'd say that's about mid-dling. Luck of the draw, Miss Sara.'

They kept the pump running for an hour. Sara, watching the water soak away into the red soil, spoke quietly to Jack. 'Isn't that wasting it?'

'Just testing the supply. Has to be enough there to make it worth the expense of equipping.'

The liquid glittered briefly silver, then sank into the thirsty ground leaving a little trail of debris, composed of grass stems and dead leaves, about its edges. The red earth's appetite seemed insatiable. 'How much is enough?'

He rubbed a thumb against his jaw. 'Twelve, fifteen hundred gallons an hour – anything over's a bonus.'

'I see. Congratulations, by the way. That stick of yours *is* magic.'

'Well, shucks, Miss Sara,' he drawled. 'I was only exercising the gift God gave me.'

'Of course you were.' She smiled in sudden, uncomplicated delight. 'It's wonderful though, isn't it? Len, and Beth too, of course, it'll mean such a lot to them.'

He looked at her. 'You really ride for the brand, don't you?'

'I beg your pardon?'

His look was quizzical. 'It means you care about the place you work for. It matters more than just another job.'

'Oh, well.' Sara flushed a little. 'Of course I care! I *like* Beth, and her family. Even I can see that this is important to them – so yes, it matters. Do you think because I'm from the city I don't care about people?'

'Nope. You've proved that. What *I* think,' he added, lips bent into the suggestion of a smile, 'is that you were a country gal once. Maybe only for a bit, but you said yourself that what you're remembering isn't city based.'

Sara nodded thoughtfully. 'True enough.' She snapped her

fingers. 'And there's another bit that came back while I was in the van. It doesn't make much sense yet, but it's a memory.' She sniffed suddenly, a waft of the sharp odour she had previously noted on Sean's clothes reaching her. 'What *is* that smell, Jack?'

'Hydraulic fluid. One of the hoses burst earlier. Drenched Sean. Well, looks like the hour's up.' The pump had stopped. 'Now we'll see what we've got.'

It turned out to be better than expected. The bore's capacity was two thousand gallons an hour. 'Roughly speaking,' Sean cleared his throat and spat. 'Wouldn't wanna live on it, but.'

'It'll do me.' Len was exuberant. 'That'll water more stock than the grass'll support. A great day's work, boys. If there was a pub, I'd be shouting, but as there isn't we might as well have lunch instead.'

It was after two when they left the drillers' camp but they still had bores to check on the way home. 'You don't mind, Sara?' Len asked. 'No sense wasting the fuel, seeing we're already out here.'

'Of course not. Helen must've expected something like it because she packed extra cake. Smoko, I presume.'

'That'd be Mum,' Jack agreed, settling into his seat. 'She's got this boy scout thing about always being prepared.'

Little was said after that; the vehicle was too noisy and Len's driving was of the bull-at-a-gate kind. The primary road out to the bitumen was one thing – not particularly good, Sara had thought – until she experienced the narrow tracks that served the bores. Len had a tendency to crash through the holes and gutters and speed through the deep sand drifts, which sent the back end of the Toyota fishtailing wildly. Jack swore as his elbow made violent contact with the door, saying pointedly, 'This old bomb does have a brake pedal, you know.'

Len ignored his remark, but when they made their first stop Jack replaced his brother-in-law behind the wheel. Len didn't seem to mind, simply remarking, 'It'll add an hour to our time.'

'Be more than that if you wrap us round a tree,' Jack retorted tartly. 'I dunno how you ever got a licence.'

It was a long and sobering drive for Sara. It was her first close look at the stock, and even her untutored eye could see the effect of the drought in the bony frames of the cows. Their bodies had shrunk to skeletons wrapped in hide, their ribs prominent enough to count. They looked as tired and worn as the country around the bores, which was denuded of grass and leaves alike.

'They lick up the fallen leaves,' Jack explained as she stared at the barren ground. 'It's that and the stock supplements keeping 'em alive.'

Sadly, this wasn't true for all of them. There were three dead at one bore, one dead and another incapable of rising at their second stop. Sara sat silent in the middle seat while Len shot it, then hooked a chain about its horns – as he had done with each of the others – and towed it away from the trough. Plainly an all too familiar practice, as the odoriferous pile of hide and bones already gathered there showed.

There was a *clank* from the back as Len unhooked the chain and tossed it onto the tray.

'Lick's running low again.' He got in and slammed the door. 'Rate they're going through it, we'll need another truckload. The overdraft's gonna kill us.' He spoke as if he had forgotten Sara's presence. Jack grunted – in assent or commiseration – as a willy-wind started across the flat and whirled towards the trough, sucking the red dirt into a huge column that grew exponentially as Sara watched. It tore past the mill, rattling the wheel blades, and the cockies drinking from the tank rim fled squawking. The cows, she noticed, didn't even lift their heads, or alter their slow, wobbling pace as they left the bore.

She remembered Sam's words then, that there were always droughts out here, and spoke with sudden passion. 'It *has* to get better though, doesn't it?'

'Oh, yeah,' Len agreed. 'Eventually. Just a question, really, of how much worse it's gonna get first.'

His weary acceptance silenced her easy optimism. What did she know of the struggle and heartache that comprised the weeks and months and years of the battle for men like Len? Beth would understand the toll it took, she thought humbly, as would Helen. All she could see was the ugliness and waste. The knowledge silenced her and certainly helped to put her own problems into perspective. So she was missing a few details of her childhood? Big deal. Out here people were fighting for their very existence.

At the next bore a cow lay drowned in the trough. A mass of crows took flight at the vehicle's approach and Jack wheeled the Toyota about, backing up towards the trough. Sara looked away after one quick glance, sickened by the holes where the animal's eyes had been. In a small voice she asked, 'How did it get in there?'

'Something stronger pushed her.' Jack's eyes were on the mirror watching Len attach the chain. 'It happens. They have to walk long distances for feed. Leaves 'em dry, so they rush the trough when they come in. Something bigger – a bullock, maybe a bull – gave her a shove and she went arse over teakettle into it. Happens. We're gonna be here a while because the seal's cracked and the trough's leaking. Might be a good time, if you're up to it, to swing the billy?'

Sara looked blankly about. 'Start a fire? With what?'

'Okay,' he said, engaging low range as Len gave a shout. 'I'll do the fire.'

The bore had good, soft water, but the taste of it was spoiled, for Sara anyway, by the faint smell of corruption in the air from the dead cow's body. The carcass had joined others near the scrub-line and should have been distant enough for its stench to be undetectable, so perhaps she was imagining it. The stock had gone from the bore and only a faint, hot breeze stirred the dust about the tank. The men had turned the water off, then knocked the end right out of the trough, flooding the ground about it. Sara breathed in the scent of wet earth and glanced at the sun, which had drawn long shadows across the land.

'Home in the dark again,' Len said resignedly, tossing the dregs of his tea.

'Have you much more to do?' Sara asked.

'Nah.' Jack was standing. 'Bit of extra packing should see it tight.'

They had beaten the buckled metal straight and used wide strips cut from an old grader tube to pack between the trough's edge and its end. The tube came from a medley of items on the back of the Toyota. It seemed a strange thing to carry and Sara wondered if it was there by design or happy accident. She emptied the billy and gathered up the gear as the men walked back to their task.

The lights were on when they reached the homestead, shining a welcome through the drab grey trees that looked black in the head-lights. Sara was tired, her body numb from the jarring of the road. Jack pulled up near the shed and switched off, and they all sat for a moment, absorbing the quiet, broken by the tick of the cooling engine and Jess's tail thumping against the vehicle's metal. The smell of dust and diesel overrode the scent of water and blossom which, Sara realised, must be the oleanders along the front fence.

'Well.' Jack shoved his door open, the cab light affording a glimpse of his tired grin. 'We know how to show a girl a good time, eh, Len? Enjoy your day off, Sara?'

'Bits of it.' It was almost a shock to remember the drillers and their news. 'What will you call the new bore, Len?'

'I'll think of something.' He smacked his hand against his hat, raising dust, then refitted it, bending to pat Jess. 'I've got a phone call to make first.'

Helen was hovering near the kitchen door, tea towel in hand, as Len pushed it open. 'Well?' she demanded.

His lugubrious face broke into a smile. 'We got it! Two

thousand an hour, bit under fifty, not the best water in the world.'
He continued through to the office, heading for the phone to tell
Beth.

'That's wonderful!' Helen beamed at Sara and Jack. 'Where are
you, Frank? They got the bore!' she called. 'That's a good quantity.
Why, back home, Trinity only tested out at twelve hundred and it
hasn't forked in thirty years. Harry said he saw you. So where have
you been all day, apart from the Twelve Mile?'

'Bore run.' Sara answered, disregarding the rest. What in heav-
en's name was *forking*? She was too tired to care. She hung her hat
and pressed her hands to her face where the skin felt tight and drawn
despite her hat. 'Oooh, I could do with a wash. The water's really
horrible, Helen. You couldn't drink it. But the drill went down so
fast. They hit water before we had lunch.'

'It was a latish lunch and a later smoko,' Jack reminded her. He
looked to his father. 'There was a dead beast in the trough at Potshot. We had to reshape and refit the end of the trough.'

'These things happen,' the older man said. 'Did you see the
young hopeful riding the mail? Going fencing, he told us. Dear God!
What's the country coming to?'

'Well, he's shown initiative in taking the job,' Sara defended
him. 'He wants to be a photographer. Did he take pictures of anything here?' Her eyes crinkled in a smile. 'I can see one of you
turning up somewhere, captioned *Cattleman*.'

'Did he take pictures? Only of everything he saw! The house,
the sheds, the mill. He must've taken at least a dozen of the old forge
out behind the shed, and he had to ask me what it was!'

'So would I. You make things with it, don't you?'

'Yep. Back in the day blacksmiths used it to forge metal into
stuff – horse shoes, wheel rims, that sort of thing. Now it's just
junk.'

Sara tsked and mock frowned. 'It's nothing of the sort, Frank.
It's heritage. Glossy magazines love that sort of pic – falling down

sheds and milk churns and quaint old mailboxes. He'll probably sell it for more than his job'll pay.' She grinned mischievously. 'You could find yourself on the same page.'

Helen laughed. 'Watch it, dear. She's got your number. Use-by date all used up. Right, who's ready to eat?'

On Sunday afternoon Clemmy and Becky returned. Sara, who had heard the vehicle coming, lingered in the garden, prudently not approaching the gate until the dust cloud had dispersed. Becky tumbled out clutching a little bag, beaming at Sara.

'Did you have a good time, chicken? I missed you.'

'It was great. Mrs Marshall got me this.' She displayed the bag, which contained a Barbie doll and a spare outfit. 'And Mum bought me this.' She tugged breathlessly at a new headband that sported a red plastic flower.

Sara admired both and, as the child ran up the steps, moved to greet Clemmy, then to collect Becky's gear from the back.

'Careful! There's dust everywhere.' Clemmy ducked ineffectually and snorted as drifts of it puffed over her from the lifted canvas. 'Oh, well,' she looked down at herself. 'What's it matter how I look? It's just dust.'

Even coated in dust she looked pretty darn good. She must have had a haircut while in town. The short blonde strands capped her head like a golden helmet, and her skin positively glowed with health as if the long drive had no power to weary her. 'Come in,' Sara said. 'Helen will have the kettle on. How was your trip?'

'Great.' Clemmy stretched. 'Ooh, that feels good. Becky's a nice little kid. Beth sent her regards, by the way. She's happy with Sam's progress, though he's still quite pale and thin, poor little chap. How have things been here?'

'We got the bore,' Sara said. 'Everyone's thrilled, as you can imagine.'

'That's wonderful.' Clemmy's eyes sparkled with uncomplicated pleasure. 'It's about time the Calshots caught a break! I'm so
pleased for them. Hello, Helen. Here's your granddaughter safely
back.'

'So I see. And she enjoyed herself. Thank you for that. Come in
and sit down. Have some tea. You must be parched.'

Clemmy nodded. 'I could certainly assault a good cuppa. Tell
me all about the bore.'

The time flew by and too soon Clemmy rose, stacking cup and
plate.

'Just leave them.' Helen handed her a parcel. 'A nut loaf. Your
cake tins will be empty if I know men. And there's not just you and
Colin to feed now.'

Clemmy's gaze flew to the older woman's face but there was
real gratitude in her smiling look. 'That's sweet of you, thanks a lot,
Helen.'

'I'll walk you out.' Sara eyed her, a question in her mind. When
they reached the gate she said, 'Um, if you don't mind my asking,
you wouldn't be pregnant, would you?'

Clemmy laughed, white teeth flashing, blue eyes alight. 'I've
been *dying* to tell someone my news, but I was waiting for it to be
Colin. How did you guess?'

Sara laughed too. 'Your face, when Helen said that about not
just having you and Colin to feed. Of course she meant young Nick.
Congratulations. How far along are you?'

'Eight weeks. Colin will be so thrilled!'

'He hasn't guessed about the reason for your trip?'

'I told him I was going in for a breast screen. I didn't want to
get his hopes up in case . . . We've been trying for so long, we both
thought it was never going to happen. I'm so happy, Sara!'

'I'm glad. Better news than the bore, then?'

Clemmy smiled happily. 'As good, anyway,' she said. 'Horses
for courses.' She kissed Sara's cheek. 'Our secret for the time being?'

'Yes, of course. Take care.' Sara waved her off and stood watching the ribbon of dust spiral up behind the vehicle as it vanished down the paddock.

23

Getting back into the discipline of the school day after the holidays proved hard for Becky. After a morning of sighs and inattention Sara began to wonder if her pupil's visit to town had been such a good idea. It seemed to have unsettled the girl and even made her envious of her brother's situation.

'Sam doesn't have to do school,' she muttered resentfully.

'Sam is sick. I'm sure he wishes he was well enough to be home and at school,' Sara said. 'Some things we just have to do, Becky, and school is one of them.'

'Well, I hate it. It's not fair! How come nobody makes *you* do things you don't want to?' She had been copying out her spelling list, and suddenly scribbled all over her work, the pencil point scoring through the sheet. Her face flamed in rebellion as she glared defiantly at her teacher. 'I don't care if I never learn the stupid words.'

Sara kept her voice calm. 'That's a pity. You'll have to do it again now and I was hoping we'd have time for a story this afternoon, but it seems we won't. You had better get a clean sheet of paper and start over.'

Becky's face darkened and her bottom lip stuck out but Sara saw that she didn't quite dare to openly refuse. She scowled at the paper pile instead but curiosity was eating at her and after a brief struggle it won.

'What story?'

'Oh, just one about some kids who find a magic tree in the forest,' Sara said. 'Harry brought it out on Friday. It's quite a long story. I thought I'd read you a bit each day after your lessons, but if you're not going to do them . . .'

The ploy worked and then it was time for the on-air lesson. When that was finished Becky had resigned herself to the inevitability of schoolwork for the rest of the day. Sara read her the first chapter of *The Magic Faraway Tree* as both a reward and an incentive, and wished she had a library to draw from. She resolved to thoroughly investigate the bookshelves in the dining room, but doubted there would be much in the way of children's books among them.

Becky, however, settled back into routine and got through the week without further problems, working eagerly towards the fifteen-minute story time each afternoon. Helen, consulted on the topic of children's books, frowned thoughtfully at the china cupboard she was in the act of cleaning out.

'I think – yes, I'm pretty certain that I did keep a box of my kids' books. They were on the bottom shelf of the bookcase on the verandah at Arkeela for years, and when we packed up I remember putting them aside. I wasn't sure that Becky and Sam would read them. It's another generation, after all . . .'

'I loved Enid Blyton,' Sara pointed out, 'and Becky does too. I'm sure there'd be something suitable in them.'

'Well, the box is stashed in the garage. I'll ask Len to grab it. He'll be going in over the weekend to pick up the bore equipment. He's taking Becky with him.' She raised an enquiring eyebrow. 'If you wanted a trip to town, I'm sure it would be fine, as long as you don't mind travelling in the truck.'

'I'll think about it,' Sara promised. The truck in question looked a dreadful old bomb and she couldn't imagine it would be a comfortable ride, particularly with Len at the wheel.

Helen misread her hesitation. 'Of course, you'd stay at our place with the family. They could move Sam's bed into the lounge and Becky could sleep there too, so you'd have your own room. No need for it to cost you.' Her eyes twinkled. 'You wouldn't even get a chance at the shops, he'd be loading and heading back Sunday afternoon.'

Sara smiled at her. 'Thank you. That's very kind. I'll see how I feel about it on Friday.'

Friday came, a still, hot morning that had Frank pinching the folds of his shirt between his fingers as he set down his tea mug at morning smoko, his face running with sweat.

'I reckon that's it for spring,' he said, flapping the folds of cloth to cool himself. 'Summer's here.'

'It's certainly hot,' Sara said faintly. 'It feels like midday already. It's so still!'

'A perisher,' Jack agreed. 'You want to drink plenty today, Sara. The heat's got a way of sneaking up on you.'

'Let's hope tomorrow's cooler,' Len said. 'We'll get away early in any case. That truck's a hot ride at the best of times.'

'It's not air-conditioned?' Sara asked horrified. Even Jack's battered Toyota had air conditioning.

'Nup.' Len shook his head. 'Doubt they'd invented it when it was built.'

It was enough to decide Sara against the trip, a decision that Harry's tardy arrival only underscored. He arrived pale and sweaty-looking with a dirty rag twisted about his hand, and the mailbag clamped between arm and body.

'Gawd! It's hotter'n the hinges of hell,' he declared and slumped into a chair. Belatedly he remembered his hat and pulled it off, allowing Helen a sight of the wrapping on his hand.

'What have you done to yourself, Harry?'

'This?' He held his wrist and grimaced. 'Bastard puncture. Sorry, ladies. There was so much bloody sweat in me eyes I didn't get the jack centred proper. Damn thing slipped orf and caught me thumb.'

'Let me see.' Helen was eyeing him. 'Sara, would you get that jug of lemon juice from the fridge, please? And a glass. Thanks.' She pinched the skin of his arm, assessed the result and said sharply, 'You should know better, man, you're dehydrated. Drink that, then I'll look at your hand.'

Helen, arms akimbo and eyes flashing at male stupidity, was a formidable sight. Harry was forced to down two more glassfuls of the cool juice before he was permitted tea. His hand was a mess, the point of his thumb flattened, the nail split in its bed and the rest swollen to twice its size. Blood crusted the rag that covered it.

'Well,' Helen said, 'I dare say a painkiller or two wouldn't go amiss, then I'll clean it up for you. But you realise that you're not going anywhere, don't you?'

'I gotta,' Harry protested. 'The mail —'

'It can wait,' Helen retorted. 'Len's heading into the Alice early tomorrow. You can ride in with him. He'll be back Sunday so if you want to find somebody to take over while you mend, he can bring him out. Can't you, Len?'

'Yeah, 'course.' Her son-in-law squinted at the injured hand. 'That's gonna swell up so much you'll never hold the wheel, let alone change gears. And what about the gates?'

'Or,' Helen pursued remorselessly, 'I can call the flying doctor. Suit yourself. And sip a bit more lemon.'

Harry groaned, whether from pain or frustration Sara couldn't tell. Jack said cheerfully, 'Bulldozers have nothing on my mum, mate. I get a minute, I'll mend that tyre for you. Seriously, it's not a good day for anyone to be driving.'

That comment sparked a reminiscence from Frank about a day back in the sixties when the temperature was over fifty and the heat had burst the tyre on a semitrailer. Sara shuddered at the thought and cleared away the tea things while Helen collected basin, disinfectant and bandages to treat her patient. Just as well she hadn't fancied the trip after all, Sara reflected. If tomorrow was anything like today, she would spend the weekend comatose under a fan.

Later, with the men dispersed back to their jobs and Becky returned to school, Helen brought in a letter for Sara. She had forgotten all about the mailbag. Harry was dozing on the daybed on the verandah, his socked feet visible through the lattice of the schoolroom. Taking the envelope, Sara nodded towards him. 'Is he all right?'

'He'll be fine now he's seen sense,' Helen said. 'But it could have been serious. The shock and the heat – it's why he forgot to drink and once you dehydrate it's a downward spiral. I can't emphasise it too much, Sara – days like this are dangerous. And he ought to know it.'

'Is it safe for Len to be taking Becky then? I mean, if the truck's not air-conditioned . . .'

'They'll be fine. It'll be cooler tomorrow; this sort of freakish heat never lasts more than a day. I've seen birds drop dead out of the sky. You just have to stay out of the sun and keep drinking – but men being what they are . . .' She left with the sentence unfinished and Becky looked up, sucking thoughtfully on her pencil end.

'Does Nan mean ladies are cleverer, Sara?'

'Well, maybe not cleverer. Just smarter at being sensible. That's nice writing, Becky. Mrs Murray will be really pleased with that page.'

'D'you think I'll get a star?'

'Mmnn, maybe.'

Sara's letter was from the registry office. She opened it and looked blankly at the single page to which the cheque she had sent was attached. The short paragraph danced before her eyes. She read it through and then, uncomprehendingly, read it again before mechanically folding it back into its envelope.

'What's your letter say, Sara?' Becky asked. 'Is it from Mum?'

'No, it's not.' Sara frowned at nothing and Becky persisted.

'Well, who? *I* don't get letters.'

'You know, mail is private. It's not really polite to ask people about it. And you can't expect to get letters unless you write them. You could write one to Sam.'

'That's silly. I'll see him tomorrow.'

'Yes, of course. I forgot. Well, never mind.' Sara made an effort, stuffing the letter into the pocket of her shorts as she took up the timetable. 'What's next today?'

Alone in her room on break after lunch she read the brief paragraph again. Her cheque was being returned because the office was unable to comply with her request. No child bearing her name or parentage was listed in the state's registry. Sara stared at the words as if doing so might rearrange their meaning. It simply wasn't right. Stella had obtained a copy of her birth certificate, so it had to exist. Had the book – she imagined a humungous ledger – been lost? Or, if the records were computerised, had there been some sort of glitch, a mistake in the spelling? But how many ways could you spell Blake? Unless, she suddenly thought, Stella had lied about spending her life in Adelaide and Sara had been born in some other state – Queensland, say, or Western Australia. Did that mean writing to all the capital cities, then? Sara groaned and lay back on the bed, limp from heat and the futility of trying to pierce the fog enshrouding her early life.

Helen was right. Saturday was marginally cooler with a hot wind out of the south that tinged the morning sky a pale pink. There was nothing refreshing about it but it kept the air moving, drying the sweat as it sprang on the skin. Len's party had got away before daylight, Becky stumbling sleepily to the table where her father and

Harry already sat, the latter with a piece of toast jammed between his fingers. He had looked better than yesterday, Sara decided, but the hand was obviously painful.

'Here, these will help,' Helen said, snapping two Panadol from their foil casing. 'You'd best go straight to the emergency room when you get in. I can fix a sling for you if you like, that'll take the pressure off a bit.'

Harry swallowed the pills dry, the look he gave her one of both gratitude and exasperation.

'How's a man gonna manage then? I only got one bloody 'and.'

'Poor man,' Sara said when they'd gone. 'But he's got a point. I mean, how will he even undo his zip without his thumb?'

Jack snorted. 'Just as well you didn't ask him. Right, I'm off. You ready, Dad? We'll be home about five, Mum. Anything for Munaroo? We might drop in on our way back.'

'No, well, unless you think you could take a rooster across? It's about time ours were changed. Beth mentioned it, said she'd arranged a swap with . . . Rinky, is it?'

'Yeah, it is, but not today. When it's cooler or when I'm going straight there. Today all she'd get is roast chook with his feathers on.'

'Why would you do that?' Sara asked as the men left. 'Isn't one rooster the same as another?'

'Fresh blood. Means you don't get two-headed chicks.' Helen poured herself another cup of tea and eyed the rattling window frame. 'What a thoroughly awful day. I was going to wash but I think I'll save myself the trouble. The same with the cleaning. Perhaps you could start the hoses a little later? After yesterday the garden could do with a proper soaking.'

The hot wind that day was freighted with grit and as the morning progressed, despite the tightly shuttered windows, it found its way into the house. The still air within was oppressively dry and hot, but outside was worse. By midday the sky to the south had darkened from its earlier pink tinge and Sara, blinking at it from behind her sunglasses, called excitedly to Helen to come and see.

'It's so dark way back there. Is that cloud? Is it going to storm?'

The older woman shook her head. 'In a sense, but that's dust, not rain. We'll be shovelling the stuff out of the house tomorrow. You know,' she said crossly, 'there are times when this country could get you down if you let it. Well, there's nothing we can do about it. It'll be a cold dinner tonight, if we have one, so we'd best make a good lunch. No point in trying to cook once it gets here.'

By three o'clock the wind was blowing in earnest and the air was full of flying sand. The mill moaned, its blades a blur before the force of the wind, and the birds fled down the sky, their strength no match for the force that drove them. With a scarf wrapped about her hair and her eyes half-shut, Sara fought her way to the shed where the poultry was sheltering and wrestled the lid off the drum in which the wheat was kept. She scattered it within the shed but even so the wind found the hens, buffeting them until their feathers stood on end as they staggered about. The rooster with his greater volume of plumage was blown over and struggled squawking to his feet, tail feathers inside out. Sara clanged the lid shut on the wheat drum, then measured out the horse feed, and set off into the blast again but there was no sign of Star or Lancer in their yard. She debated briefly before sharing the feed out, then wished she hadn't, for the wind instantly lifted the lighter chaff from the drums and blew it away. Well, it couldn't be helped. She wondered where the horses had got to. They were always waiting for their feed when school ended. Perhaps they were sheltering in the scrub and would come in later and eat their grain? She was turning to leave when she heard the rattle of bells and remembered the goats.

It was early to pen them but they were coming home and she had no desire to seek them out, not with the visibility fading as it was. Where was the harm in yarding them early for once? Casting an uneasy look at the mill, still plainly visible through the flying dust, Sara dropped the feed bucket and jogged towards the sound of the bells. She'd just hurry them all into the yard and shut the gate. It shouldn't take more than ten minutes. She'd worry about separating and penning the kids when the storm ended, by which time Jack should be home anyway to take charge of things.

The bells were further off than Sara had first thought. She dithered, wondering if she was being foolish, but they were in a paddock and the mill head would guide her home, after all. Turning to check on its whereabouts, she felt the scarf lift from her head and swore as it sailed off into the bush. She chased it, grabbing at its folds and missing a half-dozen times before finally snatching it back. Sara was tying it firmly in place when she came suddenly upon the goats. The flock, as startled as she was by their sudden meeting, bolted, bleating wildly, the bells bongling dully as they fled.

Of all the stupid animals! She called to them, trotting in their wake as their scattered parts slowly coalesced back into a whole. They were still wary, snorting warningly, heads high and yellow eyes skittish. 'Good goats,' she encouraged. 'It's horrid, I know, but it's just a bit further.' Sara's own head was bent and she pulled the ends of the scarf across her mouth and nose. The dust was so thick she could only see parts of the flock, which, like her, seemed driven forward by the gale. All around her the sky had turned a solid ochre colour and grit and bits of leaves and sticks pelted her back. The mill and homestead had vanished, together with the sun. Her vision was down to the last half-dozen goats, but it was all right, she told herself, because the animals knew where they were going. She only had to follow them and they'd bring her to the yard. She hoped it would be soon. Helen would be wondering what had become of her. Bent against the gale, eyes screwed almost shut, she stumbled on, blundering through the skeletons of bushes stripped bare by the howling storm, and once almost falling when her foot met with a log her eyes had missed.

At long last the goats halted. Sara paused and peered ahead, wondering if the storm had swung the gate shut. The wind howled and now she could actually feel the fine sand settling as it met the resistance of her body, building up in the folds of her shirt and scarf, and sifting inside her clothes. The flock was jammed together, unmoving, rumps to the storm, heads lowered into the protection of their collective bodies. No post or netting was visible, nor was the tramped and darkened ground of the goat yard. And, twist and peer how she liked, she could find neither sign nor sound of the mill. The realisation was slow but inescapable. She was lost, like the woman Helen had told her about, the one who had gone out with her son and was never seen again.

24

Mouth dry, Sara swallowed as fear clawed at her. She stood rigid, wondering what to do. Surely if they had missed the yard, they would have blundered into the sheds or the stockyards instead? Unless they had slipped somehow between the two? But weren't animals supposed to have a fine-tuned homing instinct? Perhaps not, or perhaps the ferocity of flying sand had addled it. Should she wait out the storm, or try to retrace her steps? But just turning to face the screaming wind was enough to decide her.

Crouching, Sara shuffled closer to the nearest goat and bent her head, fighting the instinct to get up and run before the wind, fleeing the terror pressing upon her. Her throat and mouth were parched and Helen's accusing words rang in her head. *You should know better. You're dehydrated.* How could she have been so stupid as to wander into the cloaking storm and expect the animals to guide her? They would think her a fool, a city ninny without the sense to come in out of the rain. She welcomed the stream of reproach and remorse her brain was manufacturing because behind it all, as she huddled there with her fingers dug into her arms with force enough to mark them, another terror pushed at her.

You can't, you can't! She was screaming, kicking, tiny fists bruising as she beat and struggled, weeping and raging against the dreadful truth, her small face smeared with snot and tears. *Nooo! Benny!* What was it? What were they doing to him?

Grimly Sara forced her wailing younger self away, shutting her back into the shadows from whence she had come, and with her the unreasoning terror that threatened to engulf her grown self. She would think of that later. For now there was fear enough of a purely visceral kind. She must remain calm. Panic, she knew, would only make a bad situation worse.

Afterwards Sara never knew how long she huddled there among the goats, head and back bowed to the blast. Long enough for the sand to have covered her feet and built little hills against her legs. Her mouth and eyes felt gritty, and the heated, dusty air had dried her nasal passages until it seemed that even through the veiling scarf she had breathed pure sand. She could feel it in her hair and down the back of her neck where the formerly protected skin felt flayed by the wind's force. Her mind had been blank for so long, set to endure the violent pelting and threnody of the storm that it was some while before she registered that the unholy force was abating.

The goats knew it first. They were lying down by then, still huddled one against the other, and it was the soft bleat of the nearest nanny that roused Sara from her trance-like state. A kid's voice answered as the goat rose to her feet, shaking sand from her coat, then the youngster was on its knees, under its dam's belly, tugging at her udder. Sara watched bemused, aware that the sky was lightening around her, pulling nearer objects into view. The sun was still hidden but she saw they were in the corner of a paddock where an old yard must once have stood, for the rusty barbed wire was netted on two sides. Jolted by her alien surroundings she swung her head, searching for the mill, but the fog of dust hid all save the closest trees. The sight was disorienting and a bolt of pure panic shot through her as she tried to reconcile the perceived geography of her whereabouts with the facts.

The goats must not have been making for their yard after all. Sara tried to reconstruct her movements and was shaken to realise that she couldn't. She had been so certain. Now all she positively knew was that she must still be within the home paddock so if she followed the fence it would, eventually, take her back. But which way? One must be shorter than the other, but if she chose wrong, how far must she walk? Would it be one kilometre or ten? Had she veered so far off course? She was seriously thirsty but she would walk ten if she had to, she told herself. From somewhere else within her a little voice whispered, *And if it's twenty? Can you do that?* Sara swallowed, afraid. Because it might twenty. The distances to anywhere out here were enormous – at least to her city mind.

Well, she had best start before the absent sun sank somewhere beyond the dust cloud and left her in the dark. Sara glanced at her watch, amazed it still worked, and saw that it was a quarter to five. Jack would be home soon. Her frightened heart lifted. If she couldn't get back herself, he would surely find her. Chiming with that thought, Sara heard the faint surge of a motor somewhere in the distance and a minute later saw the battered motorbike burst from the screening dust to come to a halt before her, scattering the goats as it did so.

'There you are,' Jack said, as if they had met in the street. He propped the bike and dismounted, the brim of his hat flattened back against the crown, his face and shoulders powdered with dust. 'All right?' The concern in his glance belied his casual tone.

'I – yes.' Sara fought the desire to burst into tears. She swallowed to ease her dry throat. 'I was about to follow the fence back, only I couldn't decide which way.'

'Either would've done,' he said. 'Here, I brought you some water.' He pulled a plastic bottle from the leather bag buckled to the carrier and handed it to her. 'Some blow, eh? Half Munaroo's topsoil is decorating Len's paddocks, which'd be good except half of his has shifted onto the National Park.'

Sara strove to match his tone. 'It certainly felt like it.' Behind Jack a dim glow showed, the sun coming back through the thinning dust as she drank deeply, the water like nectar to her parched tissues. 'I was trying to get the goats in,' she explained, looking away. 'Only they weren't headed for the yard after all.' She damped the end of her scarf and wiped her face, scrubbing at her eyes to remove the threat of tears.

'No,' he said gently. 'Goats, any stock, they turn their rumps to the storm. You couldn't have driven them into it and that's what you'd have to have done to get them back. You're fine, that's the main thing. Hop on the back and I'll run you home.'

Seated behind him, her hands clutching his body, Sara let the silent tears course down her cheeks. The sweet relief of his presence and the comfort of being close to his sturdy frame after the ordeal of the storm was overwhelming. She tucked her head into the shelter of his shoulders and clung to him as to a lifeline, knowing that her tears would dry before the ride ended and no one would ever know just how frightened she had really been.

Later, standing in the shower shampooing her hair, Sara could feel the sand washing away beneath her feet. There had been a layer of it on the soap, she had been forced to shake the towels before entering the shower stall, and a small pile of soil lay beneath her discarded clothing. Turning her face up, she let the cool flow spill over her, resolutely shutting her mind to everything but the blessedness of water. The rest she would think of later – both her foolishness, and the screaming child struggling back there in the darkness of her shuttered mind. It was a good thing her memories had hidden from her for so long. Imagine bearing that terror through adolescence!

Helen had been kind, uttering no word of reproach for the worry Sara had caused her.

'Thank heavens you're safe,' she had said briskly, her thoughts on the havoc the sandstorm had created. 'My lord, even the fan's covered with dirt and I'll have to turn out every cupboard . . . You'll want a nice long shower. Take your time, Sara. Nobody's getting fed until I get this mess cleared away. Will you look at the stove for heaven's sake! Ten to one the jets are clogged solid.'

Talk over the evening meal was of the dust storm. It had been widespread, according to Frank, forcing them to turn back before they even reached the Munaroo boundary.

'Really?' Sara pretended interest. 'Will it have done much damage?'

'If there had been feed to lose, yeah,' Jack said. 'It'd all be buried. Take a squiz at the lawn tomorrow and you'll see what I mean. The mulga will have had a pounding too.'

'The horses didn't come in.' Sara remembered suddenly. 'I suppose I shouldn't have put their feed out?' She looked questioningly at Jack.

'Don't worry about it,' he said. 'Animals shift for 'emselves. They'll come back soon enough.' He yawned, setting his mug aside. 'Dunno about you, Dad, but I'm for an early night. We're gonna have to check all those damn mills again tomorrow or they'll be seizing up on us. I dare say there's a few will have lost vanes as well. There's no end to it.'

'Not till the rain comes,' his father agreed placidly. 'Some things just are, boy. That's the way of it, and we don't get much say in the matter.'

Sara helped Helen clean up and agreed that there was no point in making a start on the house that night.

'Frankly I'm too tired.' Helen hung up her apron. 'It's years since I've seen a blow like that. God!' She scratched her head. 'My hair's filthy, I must shower. Everything else can wait till the morning.' Abruptly she said, 'You showed good sense sticking with the goats, but I was worried about you when you disappeared. You're a bit too precious to lose, you know.'

Tears pricked Sara's eyes at the words. If Stella had only ever told her that, just once.

'I was stupid, but it's a lesson well learned, I assure you. As for the house, the pair of us will have it to rights in no time. Just think of it as a late spring clean. Now, I'm off to bed. I feel as if I could sleep for a week.'

First, however, her bed had to be remade. The white counterpane was red. Sara folded in the edges of it and lifted the whole thing carefully, but the sand from the pillowcase had slipped down into the sheets, so she stripped the lot, carried the linen onto the verandah and shook it all out. The night air was cooler and the stars shone brightly. The last of the dust must have cleared – well, either that or it was all underfoot, she thought, feeling the crunch beneath her sandals. Every ledge and shelf and louvre would be coated with the stuff. It would have infiltrated the wardrobes and drawers, and the books and papers in the schoolroom. She sighed. She and Helen had busy days ahead of them.

Once in bed with the French doors set wide and the fan whirling, Sara could no longer suppress the memory that had come to her in the storm. Her skin prickled and she shivered, drawing the sheet closer. What could it mean? Children made and received wild threats all the time, didn't they? *Touch that and you'll die!* How many kids said that to siblings? How many teenage girls husked breathlessly to friends' extravagant statements? *If he looks at me I'll just die!* But there had been nothing of threat or delighted anticipation in that memory. The awful terror behind the words went deeper than that: she had been frantic for her brother's safety, hysterical over the danger she had perceived him to be in. Had she been mistaken then? Could a six-year-old actually judge such things? And if so, could this explain the mystery of Ben's apparent disappearance? Had the young Sara witnessed what had happened? Might it have been something so dreadful it had caused her to forget everything about it?

It was no good. There were too many questions and no answers she could trust. Sara wondered if she would ever know the truth.

She smoothed her hand over her face where the skin felt dry and abraded; she should have creamed it, the back of her neck too – everywhere the flying grit had stung – but she had been too tired to bother. Who could have imagined the country could turn on one so suddenly? It was the impersonal nature of the storm that had made it so frightening. Now that she was safe, she could admit to the terror of being lost in that howling cacophony, of the unspeakable relief of seeing Jack coming for her on the bike. Sara had been afraid to let herself realise the full extent of her fear, afraid that she would snap and run heedlessly, as her feet had wanted to, until reason itself was lost.

Staying in control had saved her. If she had left the goats or climbed through the fence, she might still be wandering out there. Sara shuddered at the thought. Next time she would know better, would remember for instance that the storm had come from what Sam had identified all that time ago as the south. *How can you tell?* Sara had asked and he'd looked at her as if her wits were lacking. *From where the sun is, of course.* If she had only remembered that it would have helped her get her position in the paddock.

Jack had said the flock turned their rumps to the storm so that must mean she had followed them north. So if the goat yard was south of the homestead, it meant that the road to it came in from the west. If she had walked to the left, she would have reached, and perhaps recognised, the corner of the fence paralleled by the track to Kileys bore. From there it was just a matter of following it home.

So simple, once you thought about it. Sara yawned. Most puzzles were, in the end, save for all the bewildering questions she had around her own beginnings, such as the fact that her name wasn't on the registry. In the press of other events she had almost forgotten the letter. She would write again, then, to the Victorian registry and the one in New South Wales and, if need be, to Queensland.

Her thoughts drifted and she found sleep, dreaming of a garden with a bright flowering bush near a broad stone wall upon which she and her brother sprawled. They hung face down across the sun-warmed stones, flicking a carefully gathered hoard of gumnuts at a big goanna that was gorging himself on a nest of eggs in the grass below. The sight of the long-clawed lizard entertained but didn't alarm them. High on the wall, rendered safe by each other's presence, they laughed and shot their puny ammunition at the monster, as untouchable as a knight in some magic fairytale.

25

Cleaning up after the sandstorm took the best part of two days. It was no good just sweeping, Helen said; they would have to start at the ceiling and work down. Sara tied a scarf about her unruly curls and went to the shed for a ladder, which Frank insisted on carrying back. Sand lapped to the very steps of the homestead. The lawns, Sara was astonished to see, had completely vanished, buried by the sand, and the area between the sheds was like a bare page marked by minimal poultry tracks, and Jack and Frank's boot prints.

The mail truck's load was heaped with sand, as was the cabin, for the windows had been left open to the storm. All the birds had vanished. The usual crows were absent, no galahs shrieked above the sheds and the magpies had gone. Sara remembered the corella she had seen, helpless in the grip of the wind, and wasn't surprised. But most amazing of all was the lack of flies. She mentioned the fact to Frank.

'Blown to hell.' He nodded. 'They'll be back. You'll see.'

'What should we do about the lawn?'

'Call it top dressing.' He smiled wryly. 'Don't worry about it. I'll get the sprays going.'

Jack had left early on a bore run to inspect the mills for damage and was still away when Len and Becky turned up with a hipless stranger in a big hat who introduced himself as Pearly. He was Harry's replacement and at the sight of Frank a grin split his face, displaying a tombstone-like row of teeth.

'Frank, yer old bastard! Thought you was dead and buried long since.'

'Nope, still hanging in there.' They shook hands and Sara, who had come out to greet the travellers, was introduced. Pearly lifted the bonnet of the mail truck, which he then circled accompanied by Frank, kicking at the tyres. He tutted and swept an armload of sand from the cab, cast a jaundiced eye over the load, and nodded.

'Looks like she's fit ter go. Know what 'e's done with the spare?'

Frank glanced around then jerked his thumb at a sand covered hump a few metres distant. 'That'll be it. We mended her, and propped her against the back wheel. Wind musta rolled her off. Here, I'll give you a lift on with it.' That task accomplished, he dusted his hands. 'Coming in for a cuppa before you leave?'

'Thanks, might as well,' Pearly said. 'What yer doing out here, anyway? Heard they'd turned you into the pensioners' paddock.'

'Just helping out. Len's my son-in-law.'

In the kitchen the newcomer doffed his hat to Helen, greeting her as Missus. Becky was talking nonstop about Sam and her mother and the effects of the dust storm, which had apparently started just north of Alice.

'Did you know the grid at the boundary's been filled in, Sara? Dad says it's gotta be dug out again. And somebody hit a cow on the bitumen. It was lying there all swelled up, right in the middle of the road with bits of glass and metal all around it. Dad towed it off to make it safe. Can I have some cake, Nan?'

'When you've washed your hands and put your gear in your room,' Helen answered.

Sara went with her as Becky, still chattering, rummaged through her holdall. She had bought a sparkly plastic bracelet for Sara. 'They had stalls near the big church with all sorts of stuff. Balloons and toffees and a lady painting faces on kids. Cats and butterflies and things. It was great. Me and Sam went with Mum.'

'Like a church fete, you mean?'

'Yeah. Mum tried on your bangle so we'd know it would fit. Do you like it?' she asked anxiously.

'It's lovely.' Touched, Sara stooped to hug her pupil, turning her wrist to admire the iridescent band. 'Thank you, Becky. How was Sam?'

'He's skinny, but good. He's gotta do school too,' she revealed. 'Just a bit every day, Mum says. He goes into the school and sits at a desk in the radio room with Mrs Murray, and gets to listen to all the kids.'

'Does he like it?'

Becky shrugged. 'He just wants to come home.'

'Well, he will soon. Come on. Let's get your cake. I heard a vehicle come in just now – I bet that's your uncle.'

Becky ran, and Sara followed more slowly, smiling at the garish bracelet. She touched it gently. Save for flowers from various men, nobody, except Roger, had ever really bought her gifts. His had been things like chocolates and china kittens, and once a frilly apron: gifts reflective, she thought now, of the person he had believed her to be. Stella's idea of birthday presents had been new shoes or essential clothing, although one Christmas she remembered she had got a doll and a little bag of balloons she had not had the lung power to blow up. Sara had loved the doll to bits. Even learning she had simply benefited from an unwanted prize Stella had won in a pub had not lessened the intensity of her feelings for it. She wondered now what had happened to it, and decided it had probably been lost in one of their many moves sometime in her fourteenth year, when books had replaced her passion for other things.

Jack had just come in and was pouring himself tea. Frank introduced the stranger, saying, 'He's one of your lot, son – good with tools.'

'We could do with you, then,' Jack said, shaking hands. 'Half the bloody mills are wrecked.' He sounded unwontedly discouraged.

Then, as if hearing himself, he sat down and shook his head. 'It's not really that bad, Len. There's vanes missing from two of them and one of the tails is buckled, but both those tanks are full. A couple more dead 'uns at Potshot bore too. Blown over, I'd reckon, and too weak to get back to their feet. So how're things in town? You get all the gear?'

'Yeah. The boy's doing well. And I checked through the equipment when I took delivery. For a wonder it's all there.'

'I'd best be getting on.' Pearly got to his feet. 'Thanks for the cuppa, Missus. Good to see yer again, Frank.' They shook hands and Frank accompanied him out. Presently they heard the mail truck's engine turn over, misfire, and then catch.

'Isn't Pearly an odd sort of a name for a man?' Sara asked.

'It's a nickname,' Helen said. 'He's really Sid White. He got the name for his teeth. You know, White – pearly whites.'

'Well, you can hardly miss them. I've never seen such a dreadful set of dentures,' Sara agreed. 'What happened to his real ones?'

'A horse kicked him in the mouth.'

Sara flinched and Helen said, 'It happens. So now they call him Pearly. He and Frank go way back.' She shifted her attention to Len. 'If Sam's doing okay, any idea when they'll be home?'

'About a fortnight now, Beth thinks. His next lot of chemo's due next week, so they've decided to give him a bit of extra time to recover before he comes out.'

'That's good. We might even have the lawns showing through again by then. There's hardly a leaf left on the lemon tree though *and* it's dropped all its fruit.'

The garden was a mess, Sara thought, and so were the sheds, though she'd been too busy to check them thoroughly. Certainly the house had never been cleaner, save for the verandahs and the schoolroom, which were still to do. Reminded of the fact, she got to her feet, saying, 'Lessons tomorrow. I'd best get back to it.'

'Isn't it your day off?' Jack asked.

'Mmnn, only I've got a beach to deal with.'

'A *beach*?'

'Well, it's red, but it's still sand.' Sara rotated her wrist, making the bangle flash, and looked at Becky. 'You can come help if you like while you tell me what else you did in town.'

Becky jumped eagerly to her feet. 'I can skip,' she said proudly. 'There was a skipping rope on the jumbo table and Mum bought it for me.'

'Jumble,' Sara corrected. 'That'll be fun. You can show me when we're finished. I used to skip – I wonder if I still can?'

Smiling, Helen watched them go. 'Beth was certainly lucky with that ad. Becky's really going to miss her when she leaves.'

Jack looked startled. 'Is she going? First I've heard of it.'

'Well, of course she is – eventually.' Helen slid plates and mugs together. 'This isn't her country. She's like all the rest, just passing through. Finished, Frank? Good. Let me have your mug.'

Len was eager to get the new bore equipped and cattle shifted onto it. His first task, however, was to repair the damaged mills. He and Jack took off at daylight in the loaded truck leaving Frank to do a service on the dozer, which had been brought home for that purpose.

'You know it's my bore,' Becky said complacently as she pondered over sums. 'Dad said he's gonna call it Rebecca after me.'

'Is he? That's quite an honour.' Sara was going through the box of books from the Ketchs' garage, putting aside those she thought might interest her charge. She rose from the floor, wiping her hands on the cloth she had been using to dust off the books. 'Have you nearly finished?'

'Yeah. Can we have some more story today?'

'When you've tidied your desk.' Sara glanced at her watch. 'I think we have just enough time before afternoon tea. You know, you could read some of these new ones yourself if you tried. They're not very big.'

'But I like listening to you make the different voices,' Becky objected, just as the hiss of the wireless in the office, left on out of habit, was broken by the station call-sign.

'Eight Oscar Whisky, Eight Oscar Whisky, do you read me?'

'That's Uncle Jack!' Becky was off her chair in an instant, running to answer him. Sara, following, heard her breathless tone as she unclipped the mike and spoke. 'Hello, Uncle Jack – it's me.'

'Hi Becky. Is your grandpa there?'

Sara reached to take the mike, depressed the button as she'd been shown and spoke carefully. 'Sara, Jack. What do you need?'

'Hello, Sara. I'm after Dad. Could you tell him I need to speak with him?'

'I'll find him.' She handed the mike back to Becky's reaching hand and, hurrying to the shed, delivered the message, then called Becky back to the schoolroom and managed ten minutes of further adventures in the lands at the top of the Faraway Tree before the bell rang for smoko.

'Can't you read some more?' Becky begged, as she laid the book aside.

Sara shook her head. 'Tea,' she said firmly. 'Then I'm going to wash my hair.' She pulled the slipping combs free, scooped the mass of curls that now reached her shoulders into a knot and pinned them up off her sweaty neck.

'How would you feel about a quick trip across to the National Park?' Helen asked, setting the teapot down on its stand. 'Frank has to pick up some cable from there for the boys. Would you mind? I suppose I could –' she cast a flurried glance at the stove – 'but it would mean you cooking dinner, and I've just set some yeast . . .'

The kitchen held no appeal for Sara just then and she spoke quickly. 'No, that's fine. I'd love to see Clemmy again. Is it very far?'

'A bit over an hour,' Frank replied. 'It's all nonsense. That damn doctor's got my wife hypnotised into thinking I can't be let out alone without keeling over, but if you'd like to come for the run . . .'

'And me,' Becky clamoured. 'It's not fair to take Sara and not me.'

So in the end all three of them went, spinning down the road towards Kileys, with the mulga shadows flicking across the narrow track and the sun like a blazing ball in the sky. Glancing at Frank's reddened profile and bony hands gripping the wheel, Sara asked, 'So is Helen really being over-cautious about your health, Frank? Because I'm almost sure Jack said something about your heart being weak or damaged.'

'Ah, women!' He shook his head. 'I had a bit of a turn a year or two back, wound up in hospital. If I listened to her and the damn quacks, I'd be good for nothing.'

'Nan said the doctor gave you surgy,' Becky announced. 'That means they cut you open. Sam's sick but he never had it.'

'You mean surgery, chicken.' Sara hid a smile, adding, 'It sounds like a bit more than a turn, Frank. Did you have a bypass operation?'

'Yeah,' he grunted, and cast her a quick look. 'Now, don't you start!'

'Wouldn't dream of it. Why are we chasing cable, what does Jack want it for?'

'Lifting stuff. There's only bits of slings at Redhill, they need more length. See, they've rigged a tripod over the hole and they'll run the pump and rods down with a block and tackle rig.'

Sara let his incomprehensible explanation flow over her as they rattled onwards. The sand in the wheel ruts cushioned the ride somewhat but every now and then the vehicle slammed into a gutter that jarred her teeth. The only tracks to be seen were those of the mail truck and once they had to get out and shift an uprooted tree that had fallen across the road. The flies had returned but there were few birds, only a pair of crows cawing their way westward. The mulga foliage seemed thinner than usual and, here and there, trees that stood alone or in small groups were completely stripped of leaves.

'As droughts go, Frank, how bad is this really?'

'You wouldn't want to strike a worse one.' He swung round a final bend and trod on the brake. 'When it's over, the land will come back, it always does. Anyone's guess though how many of the owners will make it. Here we are, then.'

There was a gate, newer than the fence supporting it. It must have been the station horse paddock in the days before the property became a national park. A short distance beyond it a professionally made sign proclaimed the location and beyond that the road forked. A smaller sign read *Car park* while its opposite end pointed to *Office* – obviously an extension of the ranger's home, which sat gardenless on a stretch of unfenced lawn.

'Do many tourists visit?' Sara wondered.

'Must do if they run to a car park.' Frank pulled up, just as Clemmy stepped onto the verandah, shading her eyes.

'You've made good time,' she called. 'Come in. How are you, Sara? And Becky, well, how nice to see you. I think Colin's round the back, Mr Ketch. He'll be here shortly, unless you want to take the vehicle round? You'll find him at the compound. It's where the cable is.'

'Sounds like a plan.' Frank drove off and Sara crossed the ragged-looking grass, smiling at her hostess. 'You're looking well, Clemmy.'

'I feel great.' Her lips made a comical little moue. 'Right now, anyway. Might be a different story in a month or two. But come on up and have a seat. I've got cold lemonade, unless you'd rather have tea?'

'Lemonade sounds perfect, and the more so because the storm just about wrecked our lemon tree. How was it here?'

'Dreadful! It took the three of us a full day to clean up. We wound up sweeping the lawn.' She turned her head to the corner and yelled, startling her guests. 'Nick, drink!'

An indistinct, 'Coming,' answered her as she excused herself to fetch a covered jug, tinkling with ice, and a tray of glasses. The table wobbled a little as she set them down, and Sara saw that the floorboards were sunken and holed.

'It's a dreadful old dump,' Clemmy said cheerfully. 'It's the original station homestead and about forty years older, I believe, than anything in the district. But at least we're finally getting it painted.'

Painted by Nick, it seemed, for he appeared just then in a paint-spattered T-shirt and shorts, scrubbing at his hands with a much-stained cloth. He smiled at Sara. 'Hello. I didn't expect to see you.'

'Hello, Nick,' Sara said. 'This is Becky. I thought you were building fences?'

Nick greeted the child. 'Yeah, I was. Only a small one, though. Out back, round the vegie garden.'

'What will be the vegie garden if it ever rains,' Clemmy corrected. 'He's also helped re-roof the shed, and now he's painting the house, starting from the back. National park green, as you can see from his shirt.' She grinned. 'Some of it makes it onto the walls.'

'Not fair.' But he didn't seem to mind her teasing.

'How's the photography coming?' she asked, accepting the chilled glass. She took a sip, and settled back into the wooden chair with a sigh. 'Wonderful. Thanks, Clemmy.'

Nick beamed at her. 'Yeah, great! I got some beauties of the dust storm rolling in behind the mill. And some moonscapes. I went out one night when the moon was full – you coulda read a newspaper by it it was that bright – and there were these horses. Brumbies, Colin said. Man, it was lovely. He's great, Colin! He's got an SLR too and some terrific slides. He's got his own darkroom! I never expected to find that out here.'

Sara was amused by his enthusiasm. 'So all your wages will be going on developing costs?'

'Pretty much,' Clemmy agreed. 'But go on, Nick – don't be shy. Tell her about winning the competition.'

'With one of your snaps? Congratulations. That's wonderful, Nick! What was the shot?' Sara asked.

He blushed and mumbled, 'Oh, just a themed thing – they do that sometimes. I guess it makes it easier to judge, if all the entrants have to, you know, shoot on one subject. I won a hundred bucks anyway. And they published it.' Despite his embarrassment, the fact obviously pleased him.

'Well done!' Sara said sincerely. 'And what was the winning pic?'

Nick ducked his head to Clemmy's peal of laughter. 'It was you, Sara! For a contest entitled *The Girl of My Dreams*. Maybe you ought to think about modelling as a career – the camera obviously likes you.'

It was Sara's turn to blush. Nick, scarlet cheeked, said hurriedly, 'Of course, I never thought such a – I mean, well, it had to be a pic of a girl, didn't it, with a title like that? And you *are* very pretty,' he finished miserably. 'You aren't mad at me, are you?' he asked, eyes on his paint-splattered sneakers.

'I think you've paid me a great compliment,' Sara said, frowning at Clemmy's gleeful face. 'But I'm sure winning was more about your talent than my looks. Did you hear about old Harry?'

'Yes.' Clemmy nodded. 'The new chap said something about him hurting his hand?'

Sara grimaced. 'He was changing a tyre and the jack slipped. It was an awful mess. Len took him into town and brought Pearly out. Becky went in too.'

'Yeah, and guess what, Mrs Marshall? Sam's coming home soon.' Becky stuck her tongue into the glass trying to capture the ice.

'He's as skinny as a stick.'

'But at least he's getting better,' Clemmy said. 'That's really good news.' She reached for the jug. 'Here come the men.'

'I'd better get back to it.' Nick crunched ice and set his glass down on the tray. 'Nice seeing you again and – and thanks for being nice about it, Miss, er, Sara.'

'I'm glad you won, Nick.' Then Colin was there, nodding to her, black beard like a defensive hedge through which his grey eyes peered. Frank accepted a glass and drank it off with gusty appreciation.

'That sure hit the spot, thanks. We'd better get going. Helen'll worry if we don't beat the dark home.'

'I'll give her a ring, tell her you've left,' Clemmy offered. Colin had moved to stand beside her, and Sara, turning to wave goodbye from the lawn, saw how her body leant towards his until they touched. He'd placed a protective hand on her shoulder, his dark beard brushing her blonde head. Seeing them like that gave Sara a momentary pang, making her wonder if she would ever feel that degree of closeness to another person.

26

It took most of the following week to get the bore equipped. A truck came out to deliver the stock tank and trough at the site, both of which had to be assembled once the pump-jack and diesel motor had been installed. Tanks, Sara learned, needed a mound ring before they could be bolted together, a process that seemed insane to her.

'Won't it leak?'

'No. There're rubber strips between the panels and you coat the join with a sealant,' Frank explained. 'It'll hold. Just takes time, that's all. Then there's the pipes to the trough, and the trough itself'll need cementing in. We'll get there, just not tomorrow.'

The men camped out on the job and came home late Friday, to report the bore now equipped and working. They would start shifting stock across on Saturday, which would be another slow undertaking. The cattle were too weak to bustle and would walk better in the cool of the night. So they would leave late in the day, muster them as they came off the water and walk them as far as they could travel before pulling up. They would rest and feed them on the scrub already knocked down, then complete the trip – hopefully before the full heat of the following day struck.

'That's the plan, anyway.' Len left the table to make his nightly call to Beth and Sam, and Frank wandered off to watch the news. Once the last plate was dried Helen joined him, while Sara chose a cane chair on the verandah where it was cooler and she could lie back and watch the stars. Becky was working on another scrapbook page. Tomorrow Sara would have to get her motivated again to finish Sam's map in time for his return. She gathered her hair off her neck and sighed with relief as the breeze touched her sweaty skin.

'Hot?' Jack dropped into the chair beside her, his profile dimly outlined in the light leaking from the inner room.

'When isn't it?' Sara sighed. 'Nice out here, though. I'm getting to like the stars.'

'They tend to keep things in proportion,' Jack agreed, glancing up. Dark stubble covered his jaw. He looked tired, she thought, but it was brutal work wrestling metal under the full power of the desert sun. Like Len's, Jack's shirt was stiff with dried sweat. 'Makes you realise how insignificant we really are. At the end of the day, what's it all matter?'

Sara frowned. 'But it has to, doesn't it? Life would be pointless otherwise.'

'Maybe it's only humans that think it has to have a point.'

'I'd like to believe it does. It's not like you to be pessimistic, Jack. What's up?' Sara enquired.

'Ah, I dunno. Fed up, I suppose. Don't mind me. It's been a long few days and the drought . . . Jesus.' He ran a hand over his face, rasping the bristles. 'This country makes you pay to the last ounce of sweat. I guess we all need our heads read or we wouldn't be out here. What about you? How's the memory coming?'

'In bits and pieces.' She didn't want to talk about the flashback she had experienced during the dust storm. 'Something else, though. I had another letter back today, from the registrar in Melbourne, and they've never heard of me either. Just like the Adelaide one. I'm beginning to wonder if Stella ever registered my birth.'

He turned his head, eyes in shadow, but she could feel his gaze 'That might've been possible once but now, what, twenty-odd years back? It seems unlikely.'

'Twenty-seven,' Sara corrected, 'but thank you, sir.' She

shrugged. 'I still have a few states to go but I don't know . . . There was *some* sort of document. I saw her with it when I was married. She was supposed to give it to me then, but she never did.'

Jack grunted softly. 'There's an obvious answer, not that it will help much. Would she have changed your name, and hers? Perhaps your father wasn't called Blake?'

'I suppose it's possible, but why?'

'Any number of reasons. Maybe he didn't die but left her. Maybe he, I dunno, robbed a bank or something, and she did it to protect you?'

'Ha! Chance would be a fine thing,' Sara snorted. 'Stella never thought of anyone but herself.'

'Maybe she was protecting herself then, but a kid with a different name would be a dead giveaway.'

'If that's the case, I'm never going to know.' Sara said, discouraged. 'If the other letters draw a blank too, it's a better than even bet that you're right.'

'There is another possibility,' Jack said slowly. 'This car crash you remember —'

'The one I *don't* remember, you mean,' she said. 'But yes, what of it?'

'Well, what if, apart from causing your amnesia, your brother died in it and your father, say, was driving? If that happened and your parents split up over it – and God knows the guilt he'd have to feel would be terrible – mightn't that warrant a name change? I mean, something like that's bound to end up in court and in the media.'

'I suppose it's possible,' Sara admitted. 'But it just doesn't sound like Stella. For one thing she'd have to have cared about us – and she didn't. Not me, anyway. And if she *did* love Ben, well, why didn't I ever hear about it? Believe me, Jack, if there'd been a stick like that to beat me with she'd have used it.'

He fell silent and she let her breath out in a soft sigh, turning her head to study his profile. 'Enough about my problems. What's really wrong?'

He gave what might have been a wry laugh. 'You know me so well already, eh? After what, a month?'

'A bit over two.' Alarm touched her, making her heart thump. 'There's not – is it something about Sam? They aren't stopping his treatment, are they?' That, she knew, was shorthand for sending incurable patients home to die.

'No – no, of course not. Does Len act like that's the case? It's nothing. Well, only Marilyn. My wife,' he qualified. 'I had a letter from her solicitor. She wants a divorce.'

'I see,' Sara said slowly. 'Then you still love her?'

'No. What we had, it's long over. In fact, I dunno why I care, only I see Beth and Len together, and with all their troubles they're happy. And even after forty years of struggle Mum and Dad still love each other. But I couldn't . . . ' He sighed. 'It just makes things a bit clearer than you like, that's all.'

'What sort of things?'

'That you've failed,' he said roughly. 'That instead of the wife and family you thought you'd have by now, you're still living out of a swag with no one to come home to. It's a lonely life out here when you're on your own. It's one of the reasons there're so many grog artists in the bush.'

'It's grief, Jack. I felt the same when I left Roger, only I carried a bucket of guilt for it too. We grieve for all sorts of things other than death, you know. I think it's healthy, something you have to do before you can move on. Yes, it's failure of a kind, but we all make mistakes. Don't you see? If you *didn't* feel anything now, it would make a complete sham of your marriage. Even if you were only briefly happy, you have to care that it's over.'

'Obviously you did,' he said to the stars beyond the roof edge.

'Oh, yes, desperately. Because it was all my fault. I married Roger not for love but because I needed him. I married him from pure self-interest to have somebody, anybody really, of my own. That's the truth of it. He was my emotional life raft. I didn't care what his needs were, he was just there to fulfil mine. When I finally realised, I walked away and it broke his heart. It was a wicked thing to do. He was such a boy! Such an open-hearted, decent person. You know that saying, as honest as the day? That was Roger, not a mean bone in his body. He really loved me, you see, but I couldn't love him back. I was too selfish for that.'

'He didn't know about your past, then?'

'No more than I could help,' Sara admitted. 'He met Stella once, at the registry office. I always made excuses for not taking him home. She was working, we didn't do family dinners, we didn't get on. It was my fault he didn't know how screwed up I was.'

'He didn't want to know,' Jack corrected. 'I was the same. Looking back I ask myself why I couldn't see what was so plain to Beth and Mum. Even Len tried to tell me Marilyn wasn't the type to settle in the bush, but would I listen? Like hell! I truly believed I was the luckiest man alive. It was only when I learned she'd married me to get me to sell up that the blinkers came off.'

Sara laughed a little sadly. 'Love blinds, they say. Well, the poets tell us so. Maybe we should protect ourselves by reading more poetry?'

Jack levered himself up and yawned, arms doubled, stance wide against the stars. 'Maybe I should go to bed. It's not a chance I'm likely to get tomorrow night. Goodnight, Sara, and thanks. It was good to talk to you.'

'Goodnight, Jack. Sleep well.'

Sara waited till the echo of his boots had faded, then sought her own bed, to spend a night broken by restless dreams of Roger that morphed into a search through an impenetrable garden. It was bounded by a high wall, over which thorny brambles spread. There was no way out and its growth made progress in any direction all but impossible. She woke warm and unrested in the grey light, at the rooster's first crow, to find that the fan had stopped moving because the station's electricity had failed.

In the kitchen Helen was philosophical. 'Lighting plants break down,' she said. 'First things first: don't, on *any* account, open the freezer. The washing will have to wait and Becky won't have her on-air lesson. I'll ask Len what we can do about lights. Maybe there's an old pressure lamp somewhere, or candles.'

'But Jack will have it fixed before tonight, won't he?' Sara asked.

'That depends on the problem.' Helen tipped chops into the pan. 'If it's a matter of parts, maybe not. Frank's filling the canvas cooler with drinking water, and we can shift a table onto the verandah for meals. You can phone the school, explain about Becky's lesson.'

'Yes.' Sara, having put out the cutlery, moved automatically towards the fridge for butter, milk and jam, just stopping herself before she touched the door. 'What can I do to help now?'

'The eggs should be ready. Maybe you could drain them?' Helen suggested. 'I've boiled all we had. They'll do for lunches. Then you could have a look in the linen chest. I'm sure I saw a length of flannel among Beth's sewing material. It'll do to make a cooler for the butter. Come midday the inside of that fridge will be hotter than the kitchen.'

'Okay.' With the eggs seen to, Sara was halfway to the door when she halted. 'I've just thought, what about Len? Won't he need Jack to go with the cattle?'

Filling the teapot, Helen paused to nod. 'The best laid plans . . . Let's see what the problem is first. Oh, God, there's the milk too.'

Sara glimpsed Jack and Becky coming through the garden gate with the milk as Helen spoke. 'I'd forgotten that. Well, if it goes sour

I suppose the chooks will just have to benefit.'

Breakfast was a hasty meal, the men eager to get into the engine shed and the two women to finish up in the kitchen. Early as it was, with the sun's rays just laying long fingers of shadow across the lawn – already grown through its involuntary top-dressing – the air was quite warm. Sara fiddled with the louvres in the window above the sink, dismayed to think what midday would be like. It had been hot from the day she arrived but the constantly turning fans in the house had taken the edge off it. Without them the place would be an oven.

By smoko, taken at a table on the front verandah, the worst was known. The problem, Jack explained, lay with the generator not the diesel. It needed a new part, which a phone call to the Alice had ascertained would have to be ordered. Their best estimate for getting it in was two days if they could locate it in Adelaide and longer if they had to send to Melbourne for it. In the meantime he would have to strip the genny back and check over the rest of it to find out if the solar array had been affected.

'Might've blown the lot,' he warned. 'Something shorts out, everything can go.'

Len looked glum. 'How long's that gonna take?'

'Might be done by tomorrow.' He hesitated. 'Thing is, I do it now, and save time, or when the part gets here. Either way it's got to be checked. You reckon you and Dad can handle the stock job without me?'

'Looks like we'll have to. 'Is there much in the freezer, Helen?'

'It's a little over half full. It should hold a couple of days if it's not opened. No longer, though.'

'Right.' He wiped sweat from his face. 'We'll have to forget the vehicle then and use the bikes. Means we can't carry much, unless . . .' His gaze dwelled on his mother-in-law. 'I don't suppose you could come out with us?'

'No,' she said firmly. 'It's not fair to leave Sara to manage here without power. And I'm not at all sure, Len, that I want Frank out in the heat on a bike. Certainly not without a back-up vehicle. Can't you borrow somebody from Wintergreen to give you a hand?'

He frowned. 'There's nobody but Bungy. Besides —'

'I can drive,' Sara said.

All four of them looked at her and she coloured self-consciously. 'Of course I don't know anything about cows, but if you just want a driver, and someone to boil the billy, then I'm your man – girl – woman,' she finished.

Jack said, 'What's your car, an automatic?'

Sara put up her chin. 'It's a manual. I *can* change gears, you know.'

Len's frown had vanished. 'And you wouldn't mind? Then thanks, Sara. It would truly be a big help.'

Becky, who had been listening, fixed the table's occupants with a challenging stare. 'If Sara's going, then I am too.'

'Well.' Len looked to Helen. 'What do you think?'

She flung up her hands. 'Oh, why not? She'll only be hot and crabby here. She can help keep an eye on her grandfather – for all the good that'll do.'

'He'll be careful,' Sara promised. 'Won't you, Frank?'

He grinned penitently and patted his wife's hand. 'Looks like I don't get a choice. 'Course I will.'

27

Becky, to her disgust, still had to do schoolwork.

'We're not leaving until this afternoon,' Sara pointed out. 'And you know you'll only have to catch up later.'

'But it's so hot in the schoolroom when the fan isn't on!'

'We can take it outside under the trees. You bring your chair and I'll get the little table from the verandah.'

It was so much cooler that they all ate lunch out there too. Copious watering since the previous week's dust storm had brought the lawn through in a greener state than before, and new leaf buds, Sara noticed, were already showing on the lemon. Jack had put in a brief appearance at the meal, wolfed down egg sandwiches, and left again. The knuckles on his right hand were barked from where a spanner had slipped against metal casing. He had found further damage to the wiring that morning.

'Isn't it dangerous to mess with?' Sara asked worriedly. 'I mean, you aren't a proper – a trained electrician, are you?'

'No, but Blind Freddy could stick a finger in it now and nothing would happen. And I'm not sure I appreciate my work being called *messing*, thanks very much.'

'You know what I mean.' Sara tossed her curls and bit into her sandwich. 'I know you fixed Mavis's fridge but that's a bit different to a generator.'

'Yeah. It was gas,' he agreed. The skin about his eyes crinkled in private amusement. 'Don't worry, I know what I'm doing. And while I think of it, Len, you'd best chuck my swag on. Give the girls somewhere to stretch out when you take a break.'

It was on the load next to a roped-down agricultural bike when they were ready to leave. Sara had pulled on jeans, sneakers and long-sleeved shirt; she then took up her hat and left her stifling room to check on Becky and tell Helen they were off. The child's hair was a sweaty tangle, her face scarlet.

'It's *boiling* in here, Sara. Can you plait me, please?'

'What about a ponytail for now and plaits later?'

'Okay. Dad already loaded Pop's bike. He's gonna ride the other one out to Canteen bore. Can you ride a motorbike, Sara?'

'No, I can't, chicken.'

'Sam can. Dad was learning him before he got sick.'

'You mean teaching. There. Where are your spare scrunchies?' She pocketed a couple and was ready. 'Let's go.'

Outside the sun hit them like a blow. Sara could feel the burn of it through her shirt and was grateful for her sunglasses and the heavy straw brim of her hat. Frank was a better driver than his son-in-law, who had roared away before them, raising a thin plume of dust that hung, reddish brown above the mulga, until caught and absorbed by their own.

At Canteen bore they pulled into the sparse shade and waited while Frank's bike was unloaded, then the two men collected the camped cattle and drove them slowly away in a nor-westerly direction towards the new bore. She and Becky sat on in the Toyota, both doors wide open for coolness, watching the slowly weaving backs and the bony rumps of the cattle disappear. They were travelling across country, whereas the vehicle would go by the road, the start of which Sara could see heading off into the scrub. Her directions were to follow it for five kilometres, then pull up and wait until the cattle caught up.

'Don't be anxious,' Frank had cautioned. 'It'll take a while.

You can boil the billy if you want when you hear us coming.'

'We'll be fine,' Sara said. And now here she was, alone in the bush with a child, desperately hoping that she would be able to follow the track that served as a road, and not wind up lost. A little breeze rose, carrying the smell of dust and the faint odour of dead flesh that seemed to hang over all the bores. It touched her face, as dry and hot as the bare ground where the desiccated cow pats, almost ground to dust, darkened the soil. She was suddenly glad of the water drum lashed to the headboards of the vehicle. There was a full container in the footwell besides, even if it was lukewarm. The knowledge comforted her in a way she would once not have considered possible. The mill moaned as the tail swung about, turning it out of the wind, and Sara realised that the shade had inched its way off the cab and long shadows now lay across the dusty ground. Her watch told her it was after five.

'Well.' She leaned forward to turn the key, winking at her now be-plaited charge. 'Here we go, then.'

They drove and waited. The vehicle was heavier than Sara was accustomed to, the steering stiffer. At first she crept along, uncomfortable with the narrowness and inequalities of the track, but as her confidence increased her body relaxed and she drove more easily. Becky chattered and bounced in her seat, then sneezed explosively when the front wheel sank into a hole, sending a shower of dust in through the open window. The gear on the back would be smothered, Sara thought, hoping the tucker-box was firmly sealed.

The five-kilometre limit put them on an open space that Becky called a clay pan. It was a wide red surface, hard as marble, fringed at the edge with mulga. The moment the vehicle stopped Becky bustled off to collect sticks for a fire, then scraped up the narrow grey leaves from under the trees to serve as kindling. Sara was impressed.

'You know quite a bit,' she said admiringly. Becky wriggled with pleasure at the praise.

'Me and Sam go out sometimes when the muster's on. Mum

comes too. It's fun.'

'I can see it would be.'

'Only we didn't muster this year.' Becky spoke wistfully. 'And Dad sent all the horses down to Uncle Jack's place, 'cept for Star and Lancer. I *wish* it would rain, Sara. Mrs Murray says it will, in God's good time, but when's that?'

'I don't know, chicken. Do you think we should fill the billy now so it's ready for later?'

Time passed and the light slowly died, the sky leaching to lavender, then grey. The tops of the mulga were silhouetted briefly against it, their branches like pencil strokes, until they merged with their background. The stars shone palely and for the first time Sara noticed the almost-full moon. It cast shadows about the vehicle as she lit the fire, stood the billy beside it and investigated the food supply, wondering if it had gone off in the heat. But Helen would have thought of that.

Becky was up on the load, tugging at the canvas rolled bedding. 'We have to get the swags off, Sara. Dad always says only cavemen squat. What's a caveman?'

'Does he? It means when people lived in caves because they didn't have houses, or furniture,' Sara explained. 'A long time ago.' She helped tumble the two swags off the vehicle and discovered they did make excellent seats. Becky, wriggling herself comfortable, tipped her face to the stars, and sighed contentedly.

'This is nice. Tell me a story, Sara?'

'I've got a better idea. Suppose you tell *me* one. All about how you muster – and don't leave anything out.'

The ploy kept Becky amused until the arrival of the cattle, heralded by the faint popping purr of the motorbikes. The mob itself made very little sound, only the click of their hooves as they filed onto the clay pan, black humps in the moonlight with the occasional pale flash of a horn. Once the cattle settled and had begun to lie down, the men switched their bikes off and came to the fire. Helen had made a curry, which Sara reheated, and there were bread rolls but no butter. Frank's first action had been to rig the trouble light, a bulb with a long cord that plugged into the cigarette lighter and cast a brilliant glow over the cutlery, plates and sugar tin that Sara had arranged beside the tucker-box.

'No problems?' he'd asked, and she shook her head and looked at Len.

'How far should I go this time?'

'The next stage is to the fence. They won't walk much further without a spell. Well, just through the fence to where the dozer is. Wait there until we catch up. We'll be a while, past midnight, I'd reckon, so roll a swag out and have a camp. With luck we'll pick up a few more head on the way.'

Once the cattle had gone Sara packed up and prepared to set out again. The night air had cooled and with a bit of imagination, she thought, you could make the clay pan and surrounding scrub into a silver-stippled glade in some forest. She unplugged the light, brushing away the amazing quantity of insects that had flocked to it. No wonder there were bats! An owl called from the darkness and she jumped.

'What's that?'

'A boobook. They're like little night birds. I saw one once, all fluffy with big eyes. He was so cute. We shoulda brought a torch.'

'You're right,' Sara said. 'Hop in.'

The fence when they reached it glittered silver in the headlights, but the wire gate flummoxed Sara. She stood pulling vainly at the double loop holding it shut until Becky got grumpily out to advise her.

'You have to lift the lever. On the other side.'

'Oh, I see.' Sara climbed through the wires and tugged without result.

'You have to take the pin out first!'

Between them they got it open and in a moment of inspiration Sara, instead of closing it, pulled it wide. 'For the cattle,' she said. 'Now, where's this bulldozer?'

The dozer stood beside a wide swath of pushed mulga, lapped by a sea of billowing grey bush. They used the headlights to find firewood, then Sara tipped the swags over the side and unrolled one beside the vehicle. Becky's grumpiness had changed to yawns and in three minutes she was asleep, face pillowed on a grey blanket and one hand curled into her neck. Sara readied the billy and pannikins, found the sugar tin and block of fruit cake Helen had provided, then built up the fire before lying down beside her. It was a little after ten so she had two hours, at least, to wait. She looked for the stars that Becky had shown her, and wondered how Jack's repairs were going. Her bedroom would be stifling and she was glad to be in the cool night air, even if the blanket she lay on smelled faintly of dust. Well, everything did. It would be so wonderful to see this barren land transformed by rain, but there wasn't a cloud in the sky. Just stars, millions and millions of them, and the white, impassive face of the moon . . .

Sara slept, unaware of the little mob of cattle that came to feed on the mulga, or later the ululating cry of a dingo hunting through the scrub. Becky moved in her sleep, her top arm coming to rest across her companion's shoulders, and at some level Sara felt it there and smiled in her sleep, her throat making a little sound of content.

Len woke her, opening the cab door to find the trouble light.

'It's on the seat,' she said, sitting up sleepily and yawning. 'What time is it?'

'Half one. They've done well. Thanks for opening the gate.'

Frank made coffee and the adults drank and ate slices of the cake, leaving Becky to sleep. The cattle were shoulder deep in the mulga, branches cracking as they moved and fed. Len yawned and leaned back against his rolled swag, long legs thrust out before him.

'We'll give 'em a coupla hours. We've picked up another fifty-odd. What do you reckon, Frank? Bit under three hundred all up?'

''Bout that. Maybe two seventy. They fill their bellies here, they'll be ready for a drink by the time we arrive.'

'And that's good?' Sara asked.

'Yeah. Cattle remember water. If they don't drink they'll want to be heading back to where they came from.'

'I'll stay on with 'em, any road,' Len said. 'Turn 'em back to the bore in the afternoon. Is there gonna be anything left in the tucker-box, Sara – once we've had breakfast, I mean?'

She got up to look. 'Plenty of tins. Baked beans, peaches . . .' She moved a can towards the light to read the label. 'And camp pie. There's sauce and more buns, they'll be getting stale, though.'

He nodded, then slid lower on the swag, tipping his hat over his eyes as he did so. Sara pushed the ends of the fire together and covered the cake. 'You should rest too, Frank.'

'I'm good. You sleep less as you get older. Dunno why. You'd think you'd need more.'

His face looked bonier in the moonlight, cheekbones accentuated by the deep shadow his hat cast across his eyes. His voice though sounded strangely young, at odds with the loose skin of his neck and the bony hands clasped over one knee. 'It's good of you to help out like this. So what do you reckon about bush life now?'

Sara's face lifted towards the stars as she pondered the question. 'It's satisfying,' she said slowly. 'I suppose I've got involved with things in a way I never have before. And I'm learning stuff I hadn't even thought about – mainly from your granddaughter.' She watched a star streak across the heavens and vanish. 'Sometimes it feels like it's what I'm meant to be doing, but that's crazy. At any rate I'm very glad that Beth needed help. This place beats an office job hands down.'

'Ah, there's all sorts take to the life,' Frank said. 'One of the best bushmen I ever met – apart from blackfellas, that is – was a Pommie bloke. Grew up in London if you can believe it. Either you

take to the country or you don't. Helen did and she was city bred.'
He gave a wheezy, old man's chuckle. 'Turn either of 'em up and
you'll find *Made in the Mulga* stamped on the soles of their feet.'

Sara smiled at him. 'So it grows on Arkeela too?'

'Yeah, anywhere there's desert. The country there isn't so flat as
this, mind. We've got a few ridges and that means spinifex, but say
what you like about rubbish country, that's useful too.' He talked on
and Sara listened, absorbed, to tales of early struggles, and the hard
years he and Helen had endured as they established themselves on
the property. There had been no electricity in their first home, which
sounded more like a dirt-floored shed than a proper house. There
was only a single tap and the windows had been gaps in the walls.

'Cool in summer,' Frank told her, then shivered. 'Cold as bug-
gery in winter, though.'

'That's hard to imagine.' The fire had died to embers and the
night was very still. If she listened hard, Sara could just hear the cattle in the darkness: the occasional gusty sigh, the creak of trodden
branches and once a low sound, more like a murmur than a bellow,
that seemed to hang in the air before fading to silence. Frank cocked
his head, listening too.

'Old girls are getting their bellies full.' He glanced at the stars.
'Be time to get 'em moving again soon.'

'When do you think you'll get there?'

'After sunrise, I'd reckon. We'll all be tired tomorrow.'

Frank's estimate proved accurate. It was an hour after sun-up when
Sara blinked awake from a doze behind the wheel to see the cattle
stringing onto the trough at the new bore. They came in long, dusty
files, trotting the last few paces to jostle for space along the trough's
length. She yawned and got out to stir up the fire on which the billy
already simmered and wedge the saucepan of baked beans onto the
coals. Becky, one plait undone, came to join her.

'I've been up *all* night,' she announced. 'I bet Sam never has.'

'Except for a bit of a sleep in the middle.'

'It was only a *little* sleep, and Dad had one too. It was nearly all night.'

'Nearly,' Sara said diplomatically. In the dust behind the last of the mob she could see the two riders peeling off and puttering towards them. She stooped to stir the pot. 'I hope you like baked beans. We seem to have plenty.'

28

They met up with Jack on the road home. Frank was driving, Len having stayed behind at the bore with his bike and the remaining tucker to patrol the fence again that afternoon, turning any cattle with a penchant for straying back onto their new water. Becky, bouncing between the adults, was the first to spot the glint of sunlight on chrome.

'There's a car coming. It's Uncle Jack.' Frank stopped, letting the other Toyota pull level. 'Know what, Uncle Jack? I stayed up all night,' Becky shouted.

He grinned. 'Hi, Becs. Did you? Hello, Sara. How'd it go, Dad?'

'Good. Wound up with about two hundred and seventy head. They poked along easy enough. Len's gonna turn 'em back onto the water this arvo before coming home. Where're you heading?'

'The roadhouse. Miracle really. The electrical mob flew the part up from Adelaide and the bloke in Alice managed to get it onto the bus this morning. Fingers crossed we should have the power back on sometime this arvo. Enjoy yourself, Sara?'

'Very educational.' She gave him a wink. 'Can't wait for a shower though.'

'Right, I'll let you get on, then.' He drove off, sending a gust of red dirt all over them before Frank could get his window up.

Back at the homestead Sara shampooed her hair, revelling in the sluice of cool water on her skin. She kept forgetting about the lack of power, her fingers automatically pressing the light switch, or reaching for the fridge door. It stood open now, and a large lidded tin, swathed in wet flannelette, rested on the sink in front of the louvres where it could catch the breeze.

'Butter,' Helen said. 'Wet it anytime it's dry.'

'And that stops it melting?'

'Stops it turning to oil anyhow,' Helen assured her. 'There was life before refrigeration, you know.'

'Yes. Frank was telling me last night about the early days on Arkeela, how your first house had dirt floors and no window glass.'

'Ant bed, not dirt,' Helen corrected. 'It's like cement. Made of pounded up termite mounds. All the bush tennis courts were built from ant bed. Damp it down before you sweep and it lasts for years, just like the mounds do. It's one thing we had plenty of on Arkeela.' Her gaze drifted to the window and she smiled reminiscently. 'Yes, it was hard, but those were good years. If I'd known how hard it would all get . . . but that's the thing about life. You can never see what's ahead. And a good thing, I dare say, otherwise this country would never have been settled. So, what are your plans for today?'

'Oh, excuse me.' Sara covered her mouth, yawning until her eyes watered. 'I think we should do a little school after lunch, and the rest tomorrow. That way we'll be caught up for next week. Have you heard from Beth about her travel plans?'

'They're catching Monday's bus.'

Sara rubbed her hands. 'Great! Just the incentive I need. Now all I have to do is convince Becky.'

On Monday morning Len left straight after breakfast to meet the bus. Becky was in the schoolroom, only half her attention on her lessons as she wriggled on her chair, sighing over sums.

'Guess what, Mrs Murray?' she blurted, when her on-air lesson began. 'Mum and Sam're coming home today. And last week I stayed up all night!'

'That must have been exciting, Rebecca, and it's wonderful about Sam. We'll hope to hear him back on school soon. Now, write down these words, please . . .'

When the lesson was over Becky pouted. 'I wanted to tell her about the map, but there wasn't time.'

'Never mind.' Sara lifted her face to the blessed coolness of the fan whirring above the desk. She vowed to never take electricity for granted again.

Thanks to a Herculean effort on Sunday, Sam's welcome home gift from his sister was finished, the framed article wrapped and waiting for him. Some of the inscribed fences were less than straight, but Becky had printed the names of the various bores and paddocks in her best handwriting, and the pictures, tedious as they had been to gather, enlivened the plain background. There was a photo of Jess to mark the homestead and a compass rose in one corner that Sara herself had constructed from photocopied mulga leaves. Jack had been impressed with that touch.

'Nice,' he'd said. 'You're quite the artist.' Sara had blushed and immediately praised his father's work, pointing to the pine frame that Frank had made from an old packing case, sanding the timber smooth and staining it with wood oil. Now they had only to wait for the travellers' arrival. The house positively shone, Jack had cut the lawn, and the buds on the lemon tree had burst into tiny leaves. Helen, who had filled every biscuit and cake tin in the house and had a week's supply of bread in the freezer, was making plans to leave, though Frank was more reluctant.

'What's the hurry, love?' he had protested.

'I don't want our house standing empty,' she had said. 'A fine thing to get home and find we've been burgled. Besides, the garden will need work. I doubt Beth's had much time for it. And have you forgotten you've an appointment with your specialist this week?'

He had grimaced and sighed, plainly preferring the station to suburbia. She would miss him, Sara realised, as she corrected her inattentive charge's work, and found herself wondering how different her life might have been with someone like Frank for a father. Then Becky, who had momentarily escaped to the kitchen on the pretext of being thirsty, gave a sudden yell.

'They're coming!'

Something clanged into the sink, footsteps raced through the house and Sara heard the front door bang. She switched off the fan and now she could hear it too, the low growl of an engine coming up the paddock. That night, filled with Beth's palpable terror and the agonising wait for the doctor's plane, seemed something that had happened six months rather than six weeks ago. But Sam was finally coming home. Well, it was for his family to greet him first. She lingered in the schoolroom, tidying papers and looking at the afternoon's work, doubting that much more would get done today. When it seemed unreasonable to wait any longer, she went out to join the family at the gate.

Becky was with Jess in the forefront, with Frank and Helen expectant behind and Jack propped against the gate post. Len slowed to let the dust drift away, then came to a stop and Sara saw Sam's face grinning through the shaded glass from the back seat. He was pale and as bald as ever. Beth, unbuckling herself in the front, was less brown than she had been. Jess was barking madly, then her hackles rose just as Jack spoke.

'Who's the bloke?'

There was a fourth person in the vehicle, a man. Sam's door opened and he tumbled out to grab Jess, who licked him, her whole body wriggling with excitement though her hackles stayed up and she growled low in her throat.

'Knock it off, girl,' Sam commanded, himself almost flattened by her exuberant welcome. 'Hi, Nan, and Pops. Hello, Uncle Jack.

We brought a friend to see you, Sara. He was on the bus too.'

All three adults were getting out. Beth said something but the words were lost on Sara, whose whole attention was riveted on the man levering himself out the far door. She saw his face first, the dark head covered with a cloth hat, and then, as he turned towards her, the olive skin and brown eyes.

'Hello, Sara,' he said, the dark hairs along his arm glinting as he raised it to the vehicle's roof. 'You've certainly taken some finding.'

The day seemed to freeze as the blood left her face. Sara stepped backwards on shaking legs until she came up against the gate and cowered there, her arms lifting to shield her face. She cried, 'No!' Her voice a strangled gasp of horror.

Becky's voice piped, 'What's wrong, Sara?' Her mouth had opened in surprise; everybody's head swung about, as if pulled by a single string, to stare.

All but one.

'Hold it!' Jack stepped into the stranger's path as he came round behind the vehicle, and glanced quickly back at her. 'Who is he, Sara? What's up?'

'It's him.' She was utterly terrified. 'The one who stalked me.'

'Hey, hey! I wasn't —' The man got no further. Jack shoved him hard in the chest, sending him stumbling away. 'Clear off.' He bit the words short, voice flat and hard. 'And don't bother coming back. Got that?'

'Who the hell do you think you are, you big ox?' the stranger snarled. 'It's nothing to do with you.' He tried to sidestep his challenger and Jack said grimly, 'I warned you,' and socked him in the jaw. The man staggered again and sat down in the dirt, and Jess lunged at him.

'Jess!' Jack's voice stopped her. Len shook his head. 'Does somebody want to tell me what's going on?' And Becky, eyes like saucers, shut her mouth, then opened it again to state the obvious.

'You hit him, Uncle Jack!'

Sara remembered suddenly and grabbed his arm. 'He's a copper, Jack.'

'Funny bloody copper that goes in for breaking and entering.'

Half the stranger's face was hidden by a hand pressed to his jaw, but the skin around it flushed. He glared murderously at Jack. 'I wasn't,' he protested, his eyes on Sara. 'I went inside your place but I had my reasons, which, if you'll call off this bloody nutcase I'll explain. God almighty!' His anger suddenly broke through. 'I've chased you all over Australia – surely you can spare me five minutes to tell you why?'

'Why would she?' Jack demanded. 'You stalk her, you break into her home, you frighten Christ out of her – cop or not, you oughta be locked up. And if you come near her again, you will be. I'll see to that.'

'All right, all right.' His hat had come off when he fell. He looked about for it and stood up, a red splotch on his jaw where Jack's fist had landed. He rubbed it, scowling. 'I owe you one for that, you bastard! And I'm not actually a cop. I said that because – look, can we talk about this somewhere out of the sun? I never meant to alarm you, Miss Blake. And I certainly wasn't stalking you. If you would just give me a chance to explain.' He glared at Jack. 'I'll settle with you later.'

'Anytime.' Jack rubbed his knuckles. 'You want me to chuck him off the place, Sara?'

Before she could answer Beth spoke, her eyes narrowing. 'Did he really stalk you, Sara? He said he knew you – that he'd come a long way to see you. Do you want to speak with him? If so we should go inside, or out of the sun at least. But only if that's what you want,' she added. 'Otherwise he leaves.'

Jack turned an enquiring glance on her. 'Your decision, Sara. He might know something.'

'All right.' Her breathing had steadied and her fear was

subsiding. Nothing could happen to her while Jack was near. The knowledge emboldened her and her composure returned. She studied the man – he was ordinary-looking enough – then frowned in recollection, addressing him directly for the first time. 'You said, that time on the beach, that your name was Mike.'

'It is. I'm Michael Paul Markham, but I use Paul professionally because my father was Mike too. I'm a journalist. *He* was the cop.'

'So why tell lies, and pretend to be him?' she demanded, green eyes stony.

The stranger said ruefully, 'Okay, I admit that was dumb but I thought you might be more amenable if I called myself a cop, that you might talk to me, answer a few questions. So I could find out what I needed, without revealing who I was. Not everybody's happy to talk to a journalist.'

They had negotiated the steps by then and she turned at the top, nostrils flaring. 'So, the gutter press, then. You must have been desperate if you really thought there was anything to write about me.'

He was stung on the raw. 'Nothing of the sort. I'm an investigative journalist. I don't do tits and bums and sex scandals.'

'What's that mean?' Becky asked interestedly, and was ignored by all.

'So what, then? You deliberately knocked me down!'

'No – yes – well, it wasn't – I meant to bump you, that's all, not knock you over. Look, I just wanted a chance to speak to you. I thought I could apologise, introduce myself. But you shrieked your head off and I knew I'd blown it. Then afterwards you wouldn't let me near you . . .'

Jack took a step towards him. 'Give me one good reason why she should.' He looked furious, his protective instincts obviously roused. His hands had hardened into fists, which he clearly yearned to bury in Markham's face.

The journalist saw it too and took a prudent step backwards, which brought him up against the verandah railing. 'Because,' he said rapidly, 'I know who she is. I wasn't sure then but I suspected, and I was trying to learn what *she* knew first to put it all together. It's my job, for God's sake.' Sara stared, incomprehension and amazement warring on her face. 'Interviewing people, following leads, that's what I do —'

'Wha—' Her voice failed. She swallowed and tried again. 'What do you mean, who I am? I'm Sara Blake.'

'No,' Markham said, 'you're not. That's why I've been chasing you all round the country. If I'm right, and I'm about 98 per cent certain of it, your real name is Christine Randall. Now, Miss Blake, Miss Randall, will you *please* talk to me?'

29

Jack was the first to recover. 'Supposing we all sit down for a minute?' Taking Sara's arm, he led her to the collection of cane chairs on the side verandah. Helen had returned to the kitchen to make tea but Beth, with one ear on the children – Sam appeared to be receiving his welcome home present in the schoolroom – was an interested spectator, along with Frank and Len.

The latter spoke with restrained patience. 'Is anyone going to tell me what's going on here? Are you okay, Sara? He said he was your friend.'

Jack waved him off and cocked an eyebrow at his sister. 'Do you mind? We – Sara – could do with a bit of privacy here.'

'No, of course not.' Her brown gaze was speculative as it shifted between the two of them. 'We'll leave you to it.'

Sara sat stiffly, ignoring them all, her attention on the man called Paul Markham.

Her arms felt heavy and uncoordinated, just like her mind, which seemed weighted in treacle. Unaware of the others' departure, she said, 'You've found Stella, then? What exactly are you saying? That I was adopted? But that can't be right! She would never —'

'No.' Markham leaned forward in his chair, eyes on her face, ignoring Jack. 'I did find her but she told me nothing. As good as spat in my eye. Miss Blake – Sara – I need you to tell me about your childhood, anything you remember.'

'She can't. She lost her memory way back,' Jack snapped.

The man continued as if he hadn't heard Jack. 'Because I'm pretty certain your so-called parents kidnapped you.'

She stared at him, speechless.

'Kidnapped,' Jack said, eyes narrowing. 'Why?'

'Because JC Randall is among the hundred wealthiest businessmen in this country. Now, that is. But he wasn't too badly off in the early seventies either. I'm betting it was enough that the Blakes expected to make a killing when they snatched his kids.' He grimaced at the unfortunate pun. 'Well, they did kill – the boy died. I'm sorry. That sounded terrible but it's the truth. Once his body was found, everyone figured his twin sister had perished too, and the actual investigation sort of lost focus, then gradually folded for lack of evidence.'

Startled, Jack said, 'They were twins?'

Sara's hand closed over his forearm, her nails scoring his skin.

'Benny's dead, then? You're sure?' Her face was paper white, her green eyes enormous.

'I can show you Bennett Randall's grave,' Paul Markham replied softly. 'And the spot on the map where the cairn is that his – your – father had erected where his body was found. Look, I expect this is upsetting for you, and I apologise but I've been over every inch of the ground in this story, from the family home at Vinibel Downs to plotting every campsite they visited on that last holiday when the snatch occurred. I've been working on it, doing the research, putting the bits together for over a year, most of it in my holiday time.'

'What's in it for you?' Jack demanded roughly. 'Is this Randall bloke paying you?'

'JC – the transport man,' Markham said equably and watched Jack's eyes widen. 'I see you recognise the name now. And no, he isn't. He knows nothing about it. I told you, I'm an investigative journalist. It's what I do. Turning up the stones to find the truth people would prefer to keep hidden. Getting the story. You did have a brother called Bennett, Miss Blake?'

'I – he was Ben.' She cleared her throat. 'I don't – I can't remember much about – about that time. Just little bits that have come back to me. I remember a dog, and playing with Ben. There was a garden and a creek bed and a stone wall. Once we were at the beach. My dad swung me up on his shoulders, and the sea was all frothy when it came in. We dug sandcastles. I had a yellow bucket and I think there was a caravan too.' She had removed her hand from Jack's arm, both lay in her lap now, her right index finger flicking agitatedly against her thumb. 'Was it from – I mean, where did it happen? At the beach?'

'It happened here in the Territory at a tourist spot called Kings Canyon. It's west of the Alice – a full day's drive, maybe even two, the way the roads must have been back then. JC and your mother went off for a day's hike. They were into all that nature stuff apparently. Anyhow, they left you kids with your governess, a young woman named Lana, whom they'd included in the trip. When your parents got back you were gone and she was hysterical – she was seventeen, only a kid herself. There were other campers at the canyon and they'd already started looking, but it took a day and a half for a copper to get out there and start a proper search. The Blakes – and you with them – were long gone by then.'

Jack straightened suddenly. 'Of course! The Randall children. I remember that. It was on the news, in the papers . . . I was about nine or ten at the time.'

'It made headlines worldwide,' Markham said. 'Like the disappearance of the Beaumont children in Adelaide. That was earlier, of course. Randall owned a couple of properties then but it was long before he really started amassing his wealth, so it's a puzzle why the kidnappers picked his kids to snatch. But as I said it was headline news. Searchers covered the country. Even the army was brought in at one point and all to no avail.'

Sara stirred. 'Kings Canyon.' She frowned. It didn't mean any-thing except – she shook her head, losing whatever she had almost remembered. 'Yes, Helen told me about it, some station owner who lost his children, but I thought they were boys. *They found one boy dead, the other was never seen again . . .* That's what she said. How do you know that I was kidnapped?' she demanded. 'What's your proof? There must have been hundreds, thousands of little boys called Ben and many of them would have had sisters. Was a ransom demand ever made, for instance? Anyway, it couldn't have been him, Vic Blake, because he was hospitalised soon after and died. I was seven when Stella told me.' She remembered her naive ques-tion, *Does that mean he's never coming back?* And her relief at Stella's answer.

Markham shook his head. 'He was arrested about a month after the kidnapping, and tried and jailed on charges of grievous bodily harm against a bank guard in a botched robbery. The guard was bashed so badly he turned into a vegetable, spent the rest of his life drooling in a wheelchair. Blake got a twelve-year stretch with no parole. He died seven years later, still inside.'

A hundred conflicting thoughts and questions warred in Sara's head and it ached from the pressure of trying to think.

Could any of this be true? Should she trust this man? He was plausible but he hadn't yet said how he came by his information. Indeed how had he, if Stella had refused to talk and Vic Blake was dead? And why, on that first meeting, had her reaction to this man been so overwhelmingly visceral?

There had been no time for thought. She had seen him looming above her on the beach and reacted. What if it was true, only it was *he* who had . . . No, that was patently ridiculous. He was too young to have been involved. Well, what if he was running a scam, pre-tending to find a long-lost daughter for a grieving old man, and had hit on her because he knew about her amnesia? But again, how could *anyone* know about her amnesia? Jack was the only one she'd ever told. Stella knew, of course. He'd said she wouldn't talk. Had he lied? He was pressing her again with questions, bending forward eagerly in his seat.

'Think, Sara! Is it all right if I call you Sara? Do you recall anything at all about that last trip where you camped? No, put it this way, what's the last thing you *do* remember?'

She turned her head, shielding her eyes from his hungry gaze, her face white and distressed. 'I can't.' Abruptly she stood, Jack rising beside her. 'It's too much, Jack. I can't do this. If Ben's really . . .' Her voice wavered, she turned blindly and hurried down the verandah to her room, shutting the French doors behind her.

'That's it,' Jack said angrily to the reporter. 'Just leave her alone now, you hear me? God almighty, are you witless? You tell her the brother she's only just remembered exists is dead, and then expect her to answer a slew of questions?'

'Come on,' Markham said disdainfully. 'It's history. It's twenty-one years since he died.'

'Not to her. To her it's like you just killed him.' His face screwed into an expression of disgust. 'Muckrakers, that's what you journos are.' A thought struck him and his eyes narrowed. 'How did you know she was here, anyway?'

'I saw her pic in the paper. Some dopey competition for amateur photographers. I couldn't believe my luck! They didn't publish her name but there couldn't be two like her in the entire country. *Territory beauty winner,* that was the caption. So I got myself to Alice with a copy of the pic and showed it round the motels. It only took half an hour to pick up her trail. As for muckraking, mate,' he said, leaning on the last word with heavy irony. 'You ever hear of justice? Or do you reckon kidnappers and murderers should get off scot free?'

'Thought you said the bloke you're blaming was dead?'

'Well, then, you don't think Sara's got a right to know her real family? Or JC Randall to know his child?'

Jack rubbed the back of his neck and sighed. 'I suppose. Just leave her be for now – orright? Give her some time.' Grudgingly he added, 'Come into the kitchen and have some tea.'

'Thanks.' Markham eyed him as if he distrusted the truce but followed Jack down the verandah and through the doorway. The moment they entered, the conversation about the table ceased and all eyes turned their way.

'Sit down, Paul,' Beth said, her face full of questions, and glanced at Jack. 'Is Sara around?'

'Not at the moment. Could I have a word, Mum?' With a jerk of his head he drew her towards the office.

Whatever request Jack made was lost in Becky's loud and immediate question. 'How come Uncle Jack hit you, Mister? Did you do something bad?' Between reprimanding her daughter and pouring tea for her guest, Beth had taken her eyes off her brother and when she next glanced up it was to find both him and Helen gone.

The knock on the French door, some twenty minutes later, roused Sara from the trance of indecision that gripped her. Her mind could not settle to any one thought beyond the grey finality of Ben's death. A rebellious flicker of hope reminded her that it wasn't necessarily true. But of course it must be, if there was a cairn and a grave to prove it. Only why did she find that part of the journalist's story so compellingly believable, yet was still able to dismiss the rest?

Why would kidnappers keep their victims and raise them as their own? It didn't make sense. Desperate childless women might snatch babies from their parents; political victims might be taken and murdered; but in some parts of the world, Italy and Latin America for instance, kidnapping was a business. You took someone, named a price, the family paid a ransom and they got them back.

However crude, it was a business. Things went wrong and victims sometimes died, as in the tragic affair of the young boy who'd been left trussed in the airless boot of a car and perished. It was a famous case, Australia's first kidnapping, that was periodically revisited by the media. As were the Chandler killings and the Beaumont mystery, baffling cases that had caught the public interest, but Sara had never heard of kidnappers keeping their victims indefinitely – unless it was for sexual purposes.

'Sara?' It was Jack at the door. He tapped again, then inched it open; she saw he was holding her hat.

'I don't want to, Jack. Not now. I can't —'

'I know,' he said. 'Come on. There's no need to talk to anyone. We're going for a drive.'

'What?' She rose from the chair, her undisciplined hair blowing wildly in the fan's draft, and repeated stupidly, 'A drive?'

'Yes. A bit of peace and quiet. That's what you need.' He handed her the hat and switched off the fan. 'Come on.'

Sara was in the cab of the Toyota before she thought to ask where they were going. The usual water bottle was in the footwell and there was a foam cool-box on the seat. She sat back and the bulk of the rifle pushed against the brim of her hat, toppling it forward.

'That *bloody* gun!' She snatched at the straw as it slid from her lap. 'Where are we going?'

'Kileys.'

'Why can't you carry it somewhere else? What do you want a gun for anyway?' she demanded peevishly.

'To shoot dingoes and dying stock.' His voice was patient. 'If a weak beast goes down, or a horse, it can take 'em a coupla days to die. Rifle's kinder.'

'There aren't any horses,' she snapped. 'Becky told me Len sent them down to your place.' Then she heard her tone and stopped, appalled. 'I'm sorry. You're trying to help and I'm being h-horrible.'

Her voice wavered and she blinked determinedly, staring out at the passing scrub as they followed the track down the horse-paddock fence.

'It's okay. If it'll make you feel any better, I'll go back and flatten that little squirt again. What do you say, hey?'

'Thank you.' Her smile was tremulous. 'You're a good friend, Jack. I suppose it's not his fault – if what he says is true. But I don't know what to believe. One minute I'm sure that Ben is dead and the next that the whole story is totally unconnected to me. I've never even heard of JC Randall! If that was really my name, shouldn't it sound just a little bit familiar?'

'Let it go for now,' he said. 'You need a bit of space to get your head round it. Mum made us some lunch; we'll check out the bore and boil the billy and eat, then see where we're at. I always reckon new ideas are like stirred-up water. You've just gotta wait and let it settle, and everything becomes clear.'

'It or them?' Sara asked bewilderedly. 'What are you talking about, Jack? Water or ideas?'

The grey eyes glinted in the light as he turned his head, the skin about them creasing in the half smile she had come to love. 'Both,' he said.

30

There was cattle on Kileys, their dark shapes standing and lying in the shade of the bloodwoods about the bore. They watched apathetically as the vehicle nosed past to halt on the creek bank under the white-trunked gums. The little copse of bright-green trees broke the drabness of the bare earth and Sara pointed to them. 'What are they?'

'Whitewood. You find them in soft country.'

She cast a bemused look about at the brazen sky and barren ground. 'You call this soft?'

He shrugged. 'Softer, then. It's sand country. Grows wattle, whitewood, eucalypt. Not solid mulga. You'll see wild hibiscus here when it rains, and a little desert rose too. Not exactly fern habitat but still.'

He built a fire with quick, economical movements and when the tea was made they sat on the same log as on her first visit to the bore and ate the sandwiches Helen had prepared. It was very peaceful: a pair of finches, their twittering tiny in the stillness, hopped and fluttered along the trough's edge, and were presently joined by another pair. The jaws of the cattle moved as they chewed the cud. The occasional flap of their ears, dislodging attendant flies, sounded plainly in the silence. Sara sipped her tea and let go a long breath that she seemed to have been holding since that moment at the gate when her stalker got out of the car.

'Am I imagining it, or is it cooler today?'

'Nope. It's being under the trees. They lose moisture through their leaves and the breeze moves it about. Nature's air conditioning.'

'Of course. God, I just thought, Jack! It's a school day and I walked out without a word – and Beth's only just got home. I hardly said more than hello to Sam. We should get back.' She would have jumped to her feet save that his hand had closed over her wrist.

'Relax, Sara. You've had a big day today. Besides, the station owes you more than a couple of hours off. Beth's not a tyrant, you know.'

'Of course not, but —'

'She and Mum will manage. And you can catch up with Sam later, he's too excited to be home again to miss your attention just now. Meanwhile, what do you want to do about Markham? I'll dump him back to the roadhouse, if that's your pleasure. Or you can hear him out – trust me, he'll have a proposition to put to you or he wouldn't have come all the way out here.'

Sara looked distressed. 'He wants to splash my name and picture all over the papers,' she said. 'What if it's not true, any of it? I don't want to feature in a media scrum.'

'Yeah, but think about it for a minute. If you don't talk to him, chances are he's still going to write something. *Is this the missing twin? Could this woman hold the clue to a decades-old mystery?* That type of stuff. You heard him say he's been chasing the story down for twelve months. So one way or another he'll write it, factual or speculative. With Blake dead he doesn't even have to worry about libel. If it comes to that, can you defame a criminal? He hasn't got a good name to worry about.'

Sara frowned, green eyes troubled, and he shook her wrist lightly. 'Look, it's okay. You've got the Ketches in your corner, remember, and the Calshots. Whatever you decide, we're here for you. You're the best damn governess the mulga's ever seen. Nobody will care what the papers print. Not out here.'

Her smile was grateful. 'Thank you, Jack. I love your family, all of them – and Marilyn is a fool.' Hurriedly, cheeks pinkening a little for the last phrase had slipped out, she added, 'You think I should talk to him, then?'

'Only if you want to, but it does seem possible that he knows something. If we find out, for instance, what put him onto you, how he connected the dots – if indeed he has.' He raised a hand to stop her interrupting. 'Yeah, I know, why no ransom? Why hang on to you? All of that. But maybe he's got answers. I just think it won't hurt to find out. And maybe –' he gently tapped her forehead, dislodging her hat as he did so – 'talking to him might shake something loose in here, so that you can definitely say that yes, that happened or no, it didn't.'

She heaved a sigh. 'All right, then. I will.' She glanced at him. 'I don't know whether he's right but a bad thing did happen to Ben. Something came back to me just for a second or two when I was lost in the dust storm.' She bit her lip, remembering.

'Hey, you weren't lost,' Jack assured her. 'You showed good judgement turning your back on the storm and sticking with the animals.'

'Okay, so when I wasn't lost,' she amended. 'It was just the briefest flash of recall that didn't make any sense at all. We were in a dark place, Ben and I, and scared stupid, and somehow I knew I was losing him. I was screaming my head off. And that was it.'

'You mean literally dark?'

'Yes, everything was black. We were crying and wishing we hadn't done whatever it was. And then I knew . . .' She swallowed. 'I'm sure of that much. Benny *is* dead, even if the grave and the cairn aren't his.'

This time Jack put his arm round her and gave her a hug, her hair a soft cloud under his chin. 'We'll find out,' he promised. 'It has to be better to know, Sara.' He patted her back before glancing at the angle of the sun. 'Come on, let's go home and make a start.'

Driving back Sara spoke out of the silence that had fallen between them. 'If we were twins . . .' She trailed off, unaware of the scrub flashing by or of the unfinished sentence. She was in a state of turmoil, caught up in surmise and sadness. Was Ben the shadowy presence she had subconsciously missed all these years? Could their being twins be the reason she felt, deep down, they had been closer than most siblings? Or did all young children feel that way about the brothers and sisters nearest in age to them?

'Paul said, didn't he, that we – they – lived on a station.'

'Yeah,' Jack agreed. 'Vin-something. I'd never heard of the property name, so it's not in the Centre. Might be in Queensland I suppose, or Western Australia – anywhere really. Your father, if he *is* your father, owned a couple according to Markham.'

Sara frowned, saying reluctantly, 'That would fit with some of what I've remembered.' Her memories of collecting eggs and of the dog. At that moment the name slipped smoothly into her head. Astonished, she spoke the name aloud. 'Bindy. Our dog was called Bindy. She was red, with a thick coat and a dark patch over one eye.'

'Sounds like a cattle dog,' Jack mused.

'She was the same age as us.' Sara's eyes widened as the implication of the words struck her. 'We *must* have been twins, then!' She hardly knew how to feel about it and sat silent for the rest of the trip, her index finger tapping repetitively against her thumb.

At Redhill Paul Markham paced aimlessly about the homestead garden, thinking that he had never seen a drearier, more isolated place in his life. It was like some tiny outpost stuck down in the middle of the Gobi Desert, supposing they had scrub there. The women were inside, and the men off somewhere amid the collection of rusty-looking sheds.

None of them knew anything useful. Sara Blake had been a complete stranger, it seemed, who had simply answered an advertisement for a governess. They were full of praise for her abilities, and knew damn-all about her past or where she presently was. While the rest of them were drinking tea, the bolshy bastard had shanghaied her out of the place and driven off to God only knew where.

Paul cursed himself again for taking the Greyhound. He should have dealt with the expense and hired an off-road vehicle. He had taken his own car only as far as Alice Springs, having been warned it wouldn't manage station tracks. He would have to rely on getting a lift back to the roadhouse before he could leave, which he had no intention of doing until he'd obtained the confirmation that he'd come for.

He didn't hear the Toyota's return and started in surprise when Jack spoke from a few feet behind him. He was flanked by Sara.

'Seeing you've come all this way, we'll hear what you've got to say. Give us a hand to get some chairs off the verandah first.'

'Okay.' Paul brightened, not prepared to challenge Jack's use of *we*. He flicked a look at Sara and smiled. 'Thanks, and I want to apologise for entering your flat. I feel bad about that. How did you know I'd been there?'

'I saw you. I had a migraine and came home early.'

'Christ!' He banged the heel of his hand against his forehead. 'Then I sent you flowers. You must've thought I was the worst sort of creep.'

'The jury's still out on that, mate,' Jack said coldly. 'You gonna gimme a hand or not?'

Seated in the garden as the sun westered and the evening breeze rose to bring the sound of the goat bells coming home, the journalist took Sara carefully through the evidence he had compiled. A call had come in to the paper the November previous, which by good luck he'd happened to take. The man on the phone had a story to sell and wanted to meet him. Markham had demurred. The caller's speech was a little slurred, making him hard to understand; he suspected he'd been drinking or was high on some drug. He was, he admitted to his listeners, brushing him off, and the man must have known it for he suddenly blurted, *Yous'll wanna hear this. I know what 'appened ter the Randall kids.*

Well, of course that changed things. The story might have been a couple of decades old but every journalist knew the background to JC Randall's financial rise. How, following the loss and presumed death of his abducted children and his wife's subsequent suicide, he had turned his back on his grazing interests and moved first into trucking and then commodities. The pundits had said that the country boy would be out of his depth in the big end of town but he had proven them wrong, rising above tragedy to conquer in the boardroom. His bid to bury the past was less successful: reporters regularly disinterred his history as a footnote to every column in which his name featured.

'So you met him,' Jack cut in. 'What did he claim to know? And where did he get his information?'

'You should be a journo yourself,' Paul said sourly. 'I'm telling you, all right?'

The man was a deadbeat with a record. He and Blake had been in prison together and he claimed to have learned it from him in the last year of his life.

'Blake just up and confessed?' Jack was sceptical. 'He admitted to a capital crime that coulda got him another, I dunno, twenty years? And all this to another crook?'

'Not exactly. According to my informant, who shared a ward with him in the prison hospital, Blake wasn't aware of what he was saying. It happened when he was dosed up on painkillers. Blake had prostate cancer that metastasised to his bones. That's what killed him. He rambled a bit when he was drugged, apparently. Ordinarily he was a cagey bastard, my caller told me. Mind you, so was he. I never got his real name and he wanted five hundred for the information.'

Jack was incredulous. 'You paid him? For that, a yarn anyone could spin?'

'I gave him a fifty,' Markham said curtly, 'then I started digging, and the more data I amassed the more it fit together. Blake pulled that bank job, which was a bust, by the way. Blake and his mate got away with less than three hundred bucks to show for it. Anyway, Blake lit out for the Territory till things cooled off, which puts him in the right state when the kidnapping went down. The way I'm thinking, he needed to score again and he lucks onto JC and his family, and follows them out into the bush.'

'And you know Blake was in the Territory at that time because . . .'

'Because I trawled through the old registration books in half the pubs in Alice Springs until I found his name. So yes, he was there all right.'

Sara spoke for the first time. 'But how could he have known that Randall had money?'

'That I don't know,' the journalist admitted. 'Somebody might have mentioned he was a grazier. That automatically makes him wealthy in most people's eyes. Or he might have just looked well to do. An expensive vehicle, a fancy camp rig – your regular middle-class bloke. Blake might've reasoned that he'd have savings, a house to mortgage, who knows. You're not gonna argue with someone holding your kids, are you?'

'If he was in the area, how come the police never put two and two together?'

'Because he shot through back to Adelaide, then got banged up for the bank robbery. They were hunting him all right, but for another crime altogether. The state and territory armed robbery squads wouldn't have been searching for kidnappers. Blake wasn't given bail so he was on remand until he was sentenced, which happened just after young Bennett's body was found. The police weren't looking in jail for their kidnapper, either.'

Jack pulled abstractedly on a knuckle until it cracked. 'There's an awful lot of *mights* and *maybes* in that lot. How'd you come to latch on to Sara? Weren't both kids supposed to be dead?'

'Not according to Blake. Well, Blake's alleged ramblings. He claimed his old woman had her.' He looked at Sara. 'I tracked you through the electoral rolls. Lucky for me you were still single. I figured they must've changed your name to match theirs and when I had a list I went looking for redheads of the right age and found you.'

So if she had kept Roger's name instead of reverting to her old one, he would never have found her. 'How did you know my hair was red?'

'It seemed likely. Your mother's was,' he said, and she felt a strange frisson at the words.

If he was right, she had a mother other than Stella. But also, if he was right, that mother was dead and she had further grief to face. Sara swallowed and pushed her hair back, catching Jack's concerned glance as she did so. It steadied her.

'I still don't know what you want from me. If I can't remember, then I'm afraid I can't help you.'

Paul leaned towards her. 'You can,' he said earnestly. 'I want you to come back to Kings Canyon, to the scene of your abduction. It's the only way to get to the truth. If you see it again, the memories of what happened might return. Surely you want to know how your twin died? Everything I've told you I believe to be true, but it's all circumstantial. You were the only witness – or you will be, if you can just remember what happened.'

31

Sara's first instinct was to refuse. She had opened her mouth to say so but her own words gave her pause. *How did you know my hair was red?* It wasn't anything like proof. There were redheads everywhere, but if the woman Paul claimed was her mother had been among them, then surely, however tenuous, it was a link. She was on the verge of saying no but instead found herself asking, 'Does Mr Randall know about this?'

'Absolutely not. Even my editor doesn't know. I've taken a couple of weeks' holiday to finish this last bit, if I can. My reputation's on the line here. I'm not going to break a story I can't prove.'

'Well, I'm not on holiday,' Sara reminded him. 'So I can't just take off. And, no offence, Paul, but even if I could I'm not heading out to a remote location with a man I've only just met. And have no reason to trust.'

He bowed his head. 'I guess I deserved that.'

Jack looked at him with dislike. 'You did. No way is she going with you alone. If you want to do this, Sara, and I think you probably should, I'll drive you.'

The look she flashed him was grateful. 'Thank you, Jack. But Helen and Frank are leaving tomorrow or the next day. Frank's got that appointment with his specialist, remember? Beth will need me here.'

'Leave it with me.' He rose from his chair. 'We'll work something out.' He waved a hand at the corner of the house where the children, who had obviously been told to leave the three adults undisturbed, had bobbed into view. 'Okay, kids,' he called. 'We're all done. Sam, why don't you take Paul over to the quarters and find him a place to sleep? Get a towel from your mum and some sheets for him first. Becky, Sara's finished now. She's all yours.'

Picking up his chair, he headed for the steps. Sara lifted her own seat. 'Can you get the door for me, Becky? Then perhaps you can fill me in on all the news from town. Sam must have had heaps to tell you.'

'When he talked on the wireless at school he had headphones,' Becky revealed. 'He said you don't have to hold the mike, and you hear everything straight in your ears. It's not out loud at all.'

'Well.' Sara hoped she sounded impressed. 'That's sort of special, isn't it? Did you show him the new kiddy goats? They're special too.' But she could see from Becky's face that in this instance nature ran a poor second to technology.

Given his way, Paul Markham would have left for Kings Canyon the following morning – when it *was* morning, he thought sourly as Jack rousted him from sleep at some godforsaken hour. The roosters might have been crowing but there wasn't much daylight about.

'Shake a leg,' the hatted figure in the doorway said brusquely. 'Breakfast in five, then I'll take you back to the roadhouse. The bus runs down to the Alice later today.'

Yawning, Paul tried to gather his wits. 'But – what about our trip?'

'Your trip, mate. Sara and I will go under our own steam. We'll meet you in town three days from now. You'll need a four-wheel drive,' he warned and left, leaving Paul to scramble into shirt and pants without time to shave.

At the house even the children were up so the hour must have been normal for them. Jack ate with concentration, which Paul felt obliged to match. He made his goodbyes, thanking Beth for her hospitality and Len for the ride out, saying to a preoccupied-looking Sara, 'I'll see you in three days, then?' He made it a half question.

'Maybe,' she said unhelpfully in the face of his expectation, and turned back to the little girl.

Jack picked up a cut lunch, touched his nephew lightly on his bony skull and jerked his head at Paul. 'Let's get moving, then.'

When they had gone and the children were cleaning their teeth, Sara spoke apologetically to Beth. 'I feel really bad about this, leaving you in the lurch this way.'

'Don't,' Beth said. 'Of course you must go.' She and Helen had heard the full story from Sara and her brown eyes were warm with sympathy. 'It must be terrible for you, not knowing what happened to your brother. Not remembering *anything*. And with a horrible mother too – if she *is* your mother. You must've felt so insecure, not anchored to anything.'

'Yes.' Beth's observation surprised her for its accuracy. Sara rested her chin on her hand and sighed. 'What Paul believes, I'm still not sure it's true. I mean, there're bits of it that don't really add up, like Stella keeping me. Why?'

'But what else could she do with you?' Helen asked. 'Was she going to murder you, or turn you onto the street when Blake was arrested? You weren't a baby to be left at a church door. Dumping you somewhere would have led to the police getting involved and what then? And supposing you had started to remember? Keeping you must have seemed the safest bet. And your amnesia a positive miracle.'

Sara considered her words. They made sense – as much sense as anything about her situation did. 'But why wouldn't she just ransom me?'

'Perhaps the kidnapping was his plan, not hers.' Beth chimed in. 'She mightn't have known how to set it up or was too scared to carry it through without him. Can't be easy making that sort of handover without getting caught.' Her eyes crinkled. 'It must've come as a hell of a shock to them both when the cops turned up for him with you under the same roof.'

'I suppose . . .' Sara reverted to her earlier thoughts. 'How will you manage with Helen gone?'

Helen patted her hand. 'I'm staying on for a bit. Don't worry about it.' She began stacking dishes and Sara automatically rose to help.

'But Frank's appointment?'

'Oh, he's going into the Alice with you. He can look after himself for a few days while you get what you've got to do done. I just hope you'll come back, after.'

'Of course I will,' Sara said fervently. 'Where else would I go?'

The eyes of mother and daughter met. 'Well,' Beth said, 'if it turns out this man Randall is your father you'll want to meet him.'

'Yes, of course I would.' Warmth came with the thought and a giddy speculation as to what life would be like if it contained somebody of her own blood. 'I'm not counting on it though. And in any case,' she said firmly, 'I wouldn't leave before the summer holidays. So you can depend upon me coming back.'

At breakfast the following morning Becky was disconsolate about Sara's departure.

'I'll only be gone a few days, chicken,' Sara said. 'Your grand-dad and uncle and I are just going to town.'

'But I'll be so bored!' Becky wailed.

'You won't because you've got Sam now. Besides, you haven't finished your scrapbook yet. Why don't you do another page while I'm gone? I'm sure Mum'll help you. Let's see.' Sara pursed her lips in thought. 'What about a grandparents' page? You've got pictures of your nan, haven't you? You could write out the recipe for your favourite cake of hers. Which one would that be?' She lifted an interrogative eyebrow.

'Um, sponge . . . No.' Becky wavered, frowning, then her face lit up. 'I know! The chocolate one with the cream in the middle.'

'Good choice. That one's really scrummy,' Sara agreed.

'But what about Pops? What could I write about him?'

'You could make a list of his sayings,' Beth suggested. 'How he calls you *kiddo* or what he says every time he finishes smoko. Things like that.'

'You mean like *Sitting round here won't pay the rent*? What rent, Mum?'

Leaving her employer to explain, Sara went to clean her teeth and retrieve the bag she had packed for the trip. They left shortly afterwards, the three of them packed into Jack's Toyota. The water bottle and lunch esky were in a crate up the back with the luggage and camping gear. Jack had removed the rifle but out of habit Sara held her hat on her lap. She saw with some dismay that recent wear had shredded part of the brim.

'Bit of a squeeze.' Frank fumbled for the seatbelt catch, his elbow nudging Sara's ribs. 'Still, it's only to the roadhouse.' He would take his own car in and return with it to pick up his wife later in the week.

'You reckon on being back by then, son?'

Jack shrugged. 'I dunno, Dad. But it's also a while since I've been home, so I might take a run into Arkeela while I'm down that way. See how the feed's holding up. If that's okay, Sara? It wouldn't add more than a day to the trip.'

'Whatever suits. I'm just grateful for your help. I really didn't want to travel with Paul.' She tried to be fair. 'It's not that I don't trust him, only, well, perhaps I don't. It's mainly that I can't work out why he frightened me so much when I first saw him. And until I know that, I'd rather not be alone with him. It sounds ridiculous, I know. Put it down to city paranoia.'

'Makes sense to me,' Frank said. 'Always trust a gut feeling. If you're undecided, go with it every time. At least he is who he claims to be.'

Surprised, Sara looked at him. 'How do you know?'

'I rang his paper and asked. We only had his word for it, after all.' His near eye dropped in a wink. 'We can be paranoid too, you know. We get all sorts out here, not all of 'em harmless.'

Sara's heart was warmed by his care for her. Slipping her hand through his arm, she hugged it to her. 'You're an old sweetie! Thank you, Frank.'

'Think nothing of it, girl.'

On the edge of her vision Jack's lips quirked upwards. 'I told you you had the Ketches in your corner, Sara.'

'Yes,' she said with a heartfelt smile for them both. 'I have, and you did.'

At the Charlotte Creek roadhouse the two men uncovered and fuelled Frank's car. He'd worried about it starting, fearing a flat battery after standing so long. Sara left them to it and went inside in search of Mavis, pulling off her hat as she entered the blessedly dim room where a fan was spinning above the bar. Sighing with relief she pushed the curls off her neck and went to stand beneath it.

'Morning, love.' Mavis bobbed up into view. She had been restocking the bottom shelf of the coldroom, Sara saw, and now came to lean on the bar, wiping her damp hands on a towel. 'How's it going? Did you drive yourself in?'

'No, Jack brought me. He and his father are making a quick trip into the Alice. I thought I'd get my hair cut,' Sara improvised. 'Could I have something cold, please?' She fumbled in her bag, eyeing the bottles through the sweating glass doors. 'A lemon squash would be nice.'

'Coming right up. I wondered if you were here for the doctor, that's all.'

'The doctor?'

'Clinic day.' Mavis unscrewed the lid, tipped ice cubes into a glass and poured. 'The flying doctor comes out once a month on a clinic run. Rinky's bringing Jim in – he dropped some part of a grader on his foot, can't get his boot on. Clemmy's booked in too, plus Kev from across the way.' She jerked her head at the dusty blue police sign on the building beyond the hall roof. 'Poor sod's got boils. Comes of living on tinned stuff, if you ask me. There'll be a couple from the road camp most likely too, and the old blackfella from down the creek always comes up to see the doc. How's young Sam?'

'He seems fine, thanks. Glad to be home. A pity I'll miss out seeing Clemmy, but it can't be helped.'

'As to that.' Mavis smiled and lowered her voice. 'She'll have other things on her mind. She hasn't said but I'm thinking maybe she's pregnant. Not that you heard it here, mind.'

'Ah.' Sara sipped gratefully at her drink. 'Do you and Alec have children?'

'I have two. Alec doesn't. He's my second, not that we're married. My boys are grown and gone.' She folded the hand towel and straightened the cloth on the bar top. 'Pity you're not staying. There'll be a barbecue lunch, bit of a chance to socialise. I'll tell the girls I saw you, shall I?'

'Please. And give Clemmy my best. I'd love to visit her, but without a vehicle . . . Maybe she could come to Redhill one day. I could ask Beth when it would suit. Oh, it looks like they're about ready.' Glimpsing Jack's approach she drained her glass just as he parted the plastic streamers guarding the entrance. 'I'm coming. Thanks, Mavis. Bye.'

It was less cramped without Frank's presence. Sara watched the little red car scurry down the bitumen before them and fretted about the days ahead. She scarcely noticed the crows and wedgetails on the roadkill, or the beaten-looking countryside where willy-winds grew out of nothing and died again as mysteriously as they had come. Ochre and lavender ranges swam in the distance, insubstantial as dreams, and the red car floated on phantom lakes across the bitumen. She sheltered her hands beneath her hat and was grateful she had worn long sleeves, for the sun striking through the windscreen was fiercely hot. Jack had moved the water bottle back into the footwell and she sipped from the plastic cup, amazed at how quickly her thirst, once quenched, returned.

Jack broke the long silence that Sara was unaware had fallen. 'You are okay with this, Sara? I wouldn't like to think I'd pushed you into it.'

'You didn't.' She shook her head. 'It's something I had to do. And when it's over I'll know something. I was just wondering, Jack, do we have any sort of a plan? Like how long it will take to get there, and where we'll stay once we do?'

'Oh, that sort of plan. Well, kind of. We'll sleep at Dad's tonight. He's lending you his swag, by the way, because there's no accommodation out at the canyon. There might be a bush dunny, and a tank if we're lucky. I believe it's a national park but I doubt they've got a ranger station there. Will that be a problem camping out with me?' he asked bluntly.

'No.' She didn't hesitate.

'Okay, so we'll carry our tucker and water. It's a bit over three hundred k but the road'll be crap so I reckon it'll take most of the day. I've been looking at the map, the canyon's actually a bit southwest of the Alice. There're two roads in – one goes south, the other west. I think we'll take the western route, and a drum of water to be on the safe side. If we pick up some food in town, and pack up tonight, we should get away a bit after daybreak.'

'And Paul?'

Jack shrugged. 'He can follow us if he's ready, or make his own way if he's not.'

Sara said mildly, 'He did apologise, you know. Maybe all

reporters go a bit overboard when they think they're onto something. I noticed he had quite a bruise coming where you punched
him, too.'

'He had,' Jack said without apology. 'It'll remind him not to try
anything.'

'Like what?'

Jack shrugged. 'JC Randall is a very rich man, Sara. Something
to remember if he should turn out to be your father. Do you think
our journalist friend hasn't thought of that too? Maybe he's planning to sell information about you to Randall? We only have his
word for it that he's never spoken to the man.'

'That's true, but —'

'I know. We can argue ourselves into knots over it. Let's just
wait and see, eh? And if you could pour me a drink – I'm as dry as
chips.'

32

The following morning the two vehicles crossed the bridge over the Todd River, heading out of town just as the sun touched the rocky surface of the range looming behind them. Paul Markham had arrived earlier at the Ketch home driving a beige-coloured Pajero, while Jack was snugging down the last rope over the Toyota's load. Sara greeted him, kissed Frank's cheek as he held the vehicle door open for her, then slid her legs into the footwell, arranging them around the water bottle.

'Good trip.' The old man patted the hand she was resting on the window frame. 'Take care, my dear. I hope you find what you're looking for.'

Sara nodded gratefully, fussing with her hat. 'Yes, me too.' She had slept poorly, her mind a-churn with apprehension, and now felt unready to face the day. Everything was happening too quickly. Yesterday, standing by the vehicle's side in the late afternoon as they finished their shopping, Jack had asked if she wished to visit the cemetery. His shadow had stretched behind him across the car park as he rubbed thoughtfully at his bristly jaw.

'We'd just about have time before they lock up. They'll have a plan of the layout if you wanted to find your – the Randall boy's grave.'

'Not yet. Maybe when we come back.'

'Okay.' He'd left the subject there, sliding in behind the wheel and swearing as his hand inadvertently touched the hot metal of the cab. 'Phew! I'm here to tell you officially, as a Territorian, that it's middling hot today. You can quote me if you wish.'

Sara had laughed at that. 'Know what? I'd already figured it out myself. Let's get back before the butter melts.'

Jack started the vehicle, wincing from the heat trapped in the steering wheel. The cab was like a furnace; Sara felt momentarily faint and cracked her window open, letting the trapped air escape. She was afraid, she realised, and for a treacherous moment wished she had never set eyes on Markham. The man was a human vulture, like all his type, feeding on misery. Surely it would have been better never to know the truth, only it was too late now for that option. Markham with his unproven surmises had seen to that. He had left her no choice but to take this path to possible knowledge. Jack, thank God, had seemed to understand that and her heart lifted at the thought. She could never have faced it without him, but she didn't have to.

Paul caught up with them just short of Hermannsburg, a Lutheran mission, where they pulled up for lunch. The mission was started sometime back in the eighteen hundreds, Jack told her, as he cracked sticks over his knee to feed the fire he'd coaxed into life. Sara, unpacking food from the esky, looked around at the endless red flatness broken by low scrub and the distant ochre ranges. Paul was the only other living thing in view.

'Wasn't it an awfully long way from anywhere back then? How did they live?'

'They were tough men, the brothers. Made their way overland from somewhere near Adelaide, I believe. But the Aboriginals they'd come to Australia to Christianise were here, or hereabouts anyway, so I suppose they had no choice.' Jack set the billy against the flames and waved a hand southwards. 'The Finke River's in there, and

Palm Valley. We won't see either on this road; further along it takes a big loop around the end of the Gardiner Range.' He drew it with a stick in the dust. 'There's the Mereenie gas field, 'bout there, then it heads straight south to Kings Canyon.'

'Across Dare Plain,' Paul, who had come to stand at his shoulder, interjected. He cleared his throat, the sound loud in the silence. 'That's where the cairn is. I've got the coordinates, but there's supposed to be a track in to it. One of the station owners looks after it apparently.'

'Well,' Sara said, turning away for fear the fluttering in her stomach would be visible on her face. 'That's for later. Come and eat, both of you, before the butter melts entirely.' She had put out salami and cheese, and hard little red apples that turned out not to have much flavour. None of them had any inclination to linger in the sparse shade the low desert trees provided, so they packed quickly and drove on, Paul's Pajero now leading the way.

'Randall can't have towed a caravan out here,' Jack said, as they jounced over gutters and slewed through heavy sand drifts that gripped the tyres causing the vehicle to slew violently about. 'Not twenty years ago. So he must've just had a camping rig on his vehicle, or maybe he towed a trailer and put up tents. It would've been fairly warm too. Didn't it happen about this time?'

'That does seem a bit odd. So it wasn't school holidays, then?' Sara's lips felt stiff. 'Maybe he thought the twins were young enough to miss a few lessons. You'd think the June holidays would've been a better choice though.'

'Not for him. That's the middle of the cattle season. Anyway, he had a governess along, according to Markham.' Jack was assessing the country. 'This must be crown land because there's plenty of feed, and I haven't seen a single track – well, beyond camel and emu. No stock, I mean.'

Sara pointed in mute answer and he slowed to watch a little mob of camels with their curious undulating stride trot through a low patch of wattle. Their dun-coloured hides blended into the scenery, wide pads raising little dust, identical woolly tufts on their humps and necks.

'They're such funny-looking animals,' she mused. 'Do you have any on your place?'

'We saw them occasionally when we were kids. Dad hadn't finished fencing the boundary back then and they'd drift in from the desert further south. The Simpson's full of 'em. When the season's good they can stay down there living on the parakeelya. Supposed to be a million or more of 'em in the Territory, all wild.'

'And parakeelya is?'

'It's a native succulent, full of moisture. The blackfellas used it too, Dad says.' He glanced at the sun. 'Sing out if you'd like a break, we're making good time. We can afford to pull up for a bit if you want.'

'No,' she said starkly, and after a moment, as if to soften her refusal, 'We'd lose Paul.' The Pajero was a dust cloud dwindling into the mirage dancing before them. Abruptly she said, 'Tell me about yourself, Jack. Did you always want to work a property? And how did you come to meet Marilyn?'

'As to that, it's in the blood. Think of young Sam now and you've got me at the same age, cracking my neck to grow up and run the place. I never imagined any other sort of life. When I was about sixteen Dad tried, not very hard, mind you, to point out that I didn't *have* to follow him into the business. I could do an apprenticeship, get a trade. But I was like, why would I want to do that? Funny thing is I did in the end. Mum was responsible. She reckoned I should get away, sample a bit of what life had to offer and learn something at the same time. So I wound up apprenticed to a workshop. I only agreed because I fancied myself in love.'

'Oh, yes.'

He was glad to see her smile.

'Who with, then?'

He sighed dramatically, corners of his eyes creasing. 'Fittingly enough, a Juliet – Juliet Marani, my boss's daughter. An Italian family and hotshot Catholics, so she was guarded like Fort Knox. I thought it only right at first, but it was damn frustrating. Took me eighteen months before I even managed to kiss her. Just as well, I suppose, because it dragged the whole thing out and kept me going in the garage till it didn't make sense to stop. Teenagers, eh? What about you? Anyone you broke your heart over?'

'Not really. I couldn't take boys home and I didn't have the clothes or the confidence to attract them anyway.' Sara shook her head, dismissing the matter. 'A bit of necking at the movies – all spit and sweaty hands – and that was it until Roger. So you forgot about Juliet and went back to Arkeela with your ticket, I presume. What then?'

'I pretty much stayed. Mum was right about the trade though. When the seasons weren't so good or the work was slack, I took jobs at neighbouring properties sorting out broken-down machinery. Then when the government introduced the campaign to test the national herds for TB and brucellosis, I became a fencing contractor. There was good money in it. That's when I met Marilyn.'

'When was this?'

'Let's see. I was twenty-eight when we married, back in eighty-seven. I met her the year before at a dance in Katherine. She'd come down from Darwin with the friends she'd been holidaying with. I was working on a property near Adelaide River and she was the prettiest thing I'd ever seen.' His voice hardened. 'And that's about all she was – pretty. Mum didn't like her, or Beth. That shoulda told me something, but it didn't.' He shrugged. 'We lasted three years, then she lit out for the city. Four years ago now. I suppose the notice that she's started divorce proceedings means she's found somebody else.'

'I'm sorry,' Sara said. 'Marriage break-ups are messy things.'

He glanced across at her. 'Was yours?'

'Yes. Roger was difficult. He kept wanting us to try to mend things. As if it were that simple, like, we could just try harder when . . . Never mind. He's happy now, so some good has come out of it. I think that he was first attracted to me because I was so vulnerable, walking wounded, if you like. Only I didn't know I was because I thought my life was normal. Well, not normal, but within the range.' She looked down, pleating the hem of her shirt. 'I'm not explaining this very well but you see I never knew what real family life was, until I met yours. Then I could see the gaps in mine. Whacking great holes, really. And when I started to remember, I realised that I'd once known happiness and trust. It only really came to me then what Roger had taken on, when he decided to love me. It made me glad that I'd freed him when I did, because eventually he would've come to hate me. And he deserved better.'

'But we don't, do we? Decide, I mean. It happens for whatever reason – a man sees a pretty face or, in your ex-husband's case, someone in need of help – and that's it. At a thinking level we have little say in it, so you're not really at fault. Do you know that old song, "Que Sera, Sera"? Mum used to sing it all the time, *Whatever will be, will be*. Just about sums it all up. I – what's he playing at now?'

'He's stopped, I think.' It was hard to tell. Sara pulled off her sunglasses and squinted hard into the splintering light, but between the shimmering air and the elongated effects of the constant mirage, it was impossible to tell if the distant blob of Paul's vehicle was stationary or not. The uncompromising solidity of the range rose to the left and a little behind them, and elsewhere the earth stretched away, flat and apparently water strewn.

'Maybe it's the turn-off,' Jack said. 'We should be getting close.'

Sara didn't reply. She had replaced her glasses and was staring at the landscape as they neared the Pajero. It was definitely stopped, driver's door open and Paul standing beside it with map in hand as they pulled up. She caught her breath and Jack glanced at her.

'You okay?'

'I – yes. Is it much further to the canyon?' she asked faintly.

'Depends on the road. Maybe an hour.' The dark lenses veiled her eyes but her cheeks looked pale. 'Keep drinking; it's hotter than you think.'

That brought a brief, ironic laugh. 'I doubt it.' She turned the fan up a notch as Paul came to the window, red-faced and sweating.

'Christ! What a climate. This is the turn-off. The cairn is about half a k in. Shall we?'

Jack jerked his head. 'You go ahead.'

'Right then.' Paul re-entered his vehicle and they set off, following the wheel tracks – for they could see little more than that – that wound across the plain. It was as flat as the Twelve Mile, its red quilt of soil sewn over with dried desert grasses and the tangled balls of roly-poly. Something gleamed ahead and Jack was suddenly aware that both of Sara's hands were pressed flat against the dashboard and she was breathing in heaving gasps. His foot slammed onto the brake and the Toyota came to a shuddering halt.

'What's wrong?'

She swallowed, face ashen, and he reached to pull the sunglasses off, exposing her features to his alarmed gaze. 'It was here!' she gasped. 'I – it's coming back. The man – the bad man – Benny said we had to run. He said he'd make them stop and when we got out, we had to run.'

She rocked forward, face buried in her hands, a wild keening sound coming from her. Jack reached for her but the gearstick and esky were in the way. He tore his door open and ran to hers, yanking on the handle, and went to pull her towards him, then swore and wrestled the seatbelt free. He eased down the hands she had curled over her face.

'It's all right,' he said firmly, placing an arm around her. 'You're not back there any more, Sara. You're here with me, you're safe. Shhh now, just take it easy. Breathe, that's it, in and out. It's old stuff, remember, it happened years ago. You're safe here with me.' Her heart was racing, and he could see a pulse hammering under the pale skin of her throat. His ears told him that the Pajero had pulled up; its engine note fell to an idle and then switched off. The sun was a blade against his neck as he bent his head to peer at Sara. 'Okay now?'

'Yes. Sorry.' She wiped a shaky hand beneath her nose, green eyes wide and blurred, saying, 'It was him, Vic Blake, the man I thought was my father. He left him here to die. He must have *known* he would, but he —'

'Shhh.' Jack caught the hands she was wringing and held them firmly. 'From the beginning. I take it you and Ben were put in a vehicle and you both tried to get away?'

'Benny said – it was all dark and Benny whispered we had to get out.'

Jack's skin prickled into goosebumps for her gaze had gone blank and wide, and her voice had softened to a childlike pitch, with nothing of its normal timbre.

'He was going to pretend to be sick. They'd have to stop, and then we'd run. We did run. Only –' her voice trembled and rose in anguish – 'I fell over and he caught me. I screamed and kicked, but Ben didn't hear. And then he said to the lady, *One's as good as two and I don't fancy running.* And they left Benny behind.' Tears brimmed over her lower lids and slid down her cheeks and her voice was a desolate wail. 'I *told* him, I said he couldn't, he had to stop, but he wouldn't.'

'I'm so sorry, Sara.' Jack didn't have a handkerchief. He patted his pockets then unrolled a shirtsleeve to dab gently at her face. 'Come on, now, shhh. I know it feels raw and new but it happened a long time ago. You were just a little girl then. Here.' He settled her against the backrest of the seat and fumbled with the water bottle. 'Drink this. It seems Markham was right after all. You're the missing twin and that bastard did kidnap you.' He should have been glad for her, he thought, but his belly twisted icily at the words. Turning his head, he saw the journalist walking across from his own vehicle and waved him angrily off.

Sara drank obediently, then wet her hands and wiped them over her face. 'Sorry,' she said again. Her voice was back to normal as she frowned. 'The first time I saw that big plain at Redhill . . .' She paused, fiddling with her hat.

'The Twelve Mile, yes?' Jack nodded encouragingly, relieved that her tears had stopped.

'I was sick, remember?' Sara wiped her fingers under her eyes and pushed back her curls. 'Do you suppose that was because of this?' She made an abrupt gesture at the emptiness around them, not looking at him to hide her sudden embarrassment.

Jack took a pace back as if also touched by it, though he kept his voice even. 'It could be, or maybe it was the road. But this track's a good deal rougher, so I think the emptiness may have foreshadowed this memory. I'm sorry, Sara,' he said, spreading his hands helplessly. 'All this way to discover something like this. I wish I could help you with it, but I can't.'

She lifted wet eyes to his face. 'Don't say that, Jack. You are helping just by being here. I couldn't do this alone.'

'Well, remember we can stop anytime. You know about your brother now. You needn't see the cairn, or the canyon. We can go home whenever you want to.'

Sara hesitated then shook her head. 'I've come this far,' she said. 'And there must have been other happy days before – before Vic Blake, I mean. I want to remember them too, if I can. So now we're here I might as well finish what we've started.'

'If that's what you want.' Jack carefully shut her door and resumed his place behind the wheel.

33

The cairn John Randall had caused to be erected was a simple block of concrete inset with a bronze plaque and enclosed within a chain strung from four low concrete posts. The inscription was simple, a commemoration of the lives and tragic deaths of Bennett H Randall and his twin sister Christine M Randall, born 17 April 1967, died 3 November 1973.

The three of them read it in silence. It was Jack who said softly, 'When's your birthday, Sara?'

'July twelfth. That's a lie too. My whole life is a lie built by those two monsters. What if I hadn't lost my memory? Would they have murdered me, do you think? I was a witness to them abandoning Benny to die.'

'Do you remember your brother's middle name?' Paul asked. 'And has this,' he waved at the cairn, 'jogged anything loose?'

She ignored all but the first part of this. 'I don't know my middle name. M, it says there. Mary, Maxine . . . it's anybody's guess. I find it hard to believe my real name isn't Sara. I certainly don't *feel* like a Christine.'

'You'll always be Sara to me.' Jack had one eye on Paul, who had pulled out a camera and was now photographing her standing by the cairn. Of course, he would want pictures for the story he'd write.

'It was Hamish,' Paul said. 'Bennett Hamish. It's your father's middle name. Yours is Mary – for your mother, I assume.' He eyed her pale face. 'You were a witness, you just said. Does that mean you've remembered what happened?'

'Yes.' She swallowed. 'I know how Benny died. I don't want to talk about it now.'

'Let's get on,' Jack said abruptly. He was fed up with the man's single-minded focus. Sara's distress meant nothing to him, he thought savagely. All he wanted was a good story for his damned paper.

The two vehicles came to Kings Canyon late in the afternoon across undulating, lightly wooded country. Sara sat forward in her seat, straining to recognise something, anything, but she couldn't. The long line of the range towered over the scene: it was almost flat on top, its sheer-looking sides deeply indented with shadowed hollows where the duns and ochres of the rock were touched with purple. It seemed to run on for miles and she might never have set eyes on it before, for all her memory told her. 'It's like I've never seen it before,' she said despairingly.

'You were six,' Jack answered comfortingly. 'Probably cranky and tired and just wanting to stop. How many little kids notice their surroundings?'

'It's hard-looking country, and beautiful in a way.' She shivered. 'But a tough beauty. Does anybody live out here, apart from the men at the gas field, I mean?'

'Yeah, there're stations. Kings Creek is up the road a bit. I don't know about back in the seventies though. It musta been pretty empty country then.' He slowed down, squinting from the range to a worn set of wheel tracks. 'That could be the road in. I dare say it gets a fair bit of traffic these days now everyone's got a four-wheel drive – though not lately, by the look of it.'

'Too hot,' Sara suggested and heard him grunt agreement.

'There's a sign.'

It led them to the campground, deserted at this time of the year. Paul booked them in and they pulled up at length in the shade of a cluster of kurrajong that Jack named as bean trees. The area had been graded flat and was delineated by a line of half posts sunk into the ground. There were fireplaces, a big overhead tank at the ablutions block, and beyond that a screen of scrubby growth that hid the simple corrugated iron dwelling where the ranger lived.

Jack looked about and addressed the journalist. 'It'll be dark soon. We'd better get set up. You wanna fetch some wood, I'll start a meal.'

The ice in the cool-box had melted. Jack removed the fresh food – the remaining apples, cheese, salami, bread and butter – and drained the box. There were dry supplies in the tucker-box; he rooted among them to produce rice, onions, a tin of sausages and another of whole tomatoes. Then he found a lidded tin to decant the melting butter into, and a jute sugar bag behind the seat to wrap around it for a butter cooler.

Observing his preparations, Sara peeled and chopped the onion, then searched for a pot to cook in. Paul had started the fire. It flared golden against its stone windbreak as the night closed softly around them, pulling a cloak of dusky velvet over the range that blotted out the shapes of trees. The stars glittered out of the darkness as the day's heat fled and it seemed to Sara that the very earth sighed in relief.

Jack stood the filled billy against the flames and dropped into an easy squat beside her while Paul laboriously rolled a rock towards the fire to serve as his seat.

'Did you bring a swag?' Sara asked him.

'I'll sleep in the vehicle. I borrowed a blanket from the motel.' He fidgeted, trying to get comfortable. 'Should have grabbed one of their chairs too,' he said ruefully.

'Tell me,' she said abruptly, ignoring his remark. 'That day at the beach. Was that the first time you saw me? Or did you follow me there?'

His eyes shifted from hers. 'Yeah, I did, follow you, that is. I'd just pulled up at your place when you came out and drove off. I was using a phone book and you were the fourth Blake I investigated. A redhead and about the right age. Of course, I couldn't be sure about the hair colour but that and your skin tone seemed to fit. I was right behind you when that beach ball came over us. Bumping you seemed the easiest way to make acquaintance.'

'I see.' She searched his face, frowning in thought. 'It still doesn't explain why the sight of you freaked me out.'

'About tomorrow,' Jack interrupted. 'Are we all done here now we know who Sara is?'

'Well, I sorta hoped, if you don't object, Sara, we could take a walk up the canyon first. See if anything else comes back to you. So far we've got nothing about the actual kidnapping. We know that JC and your mother did the rim walk.' He waved an arm at the towering cliffs. 'There's a track round the top apparently, and whatever happened occurred in their absence. The governess said she went to speak to neighbouring campers – she told the police that she was only away for five or ten minutes and that you were gone when she returned. The campers were a family group, parents and two kids, up from Port Augusta. The police tore into them, of course, treated 'em as suspects at first, but they all told the same story. And no previous connection could be established between them. The only conclusion one can draw is that you must've been snatched during that ten-minute window.'

'How could anyone plan that?' Jack demanded. 'It had to have been a spur of the moment thing. Which raises another question, how did the kidnappers know whose children you were?'

'Unless they weren't after a ransom? There are other uses for kids, and the younger the better,' Paul said levelly, poking a stick end into the flame.

'Except that it didn't happen,' Sara objected. She fetched bread and the butter and enamel plates to the fire and they ate in its glow. Jack reached for the billy, pouring for himself and Sara, whose fingers tingled as their hands brushed. Paul seemed to sense the current between them. She saw his hand lift to touch the yellowing bruise on his jaw, as if he had just understood the reason behind Jack's aggressiveness. When the meal was over he collected a much-scuffed briefcase from his vehicle. From it he took an exercise book and handed it to Sara. 'Here. It's all the clippings I've managed to find. Most are photocopied. It hasn't done much for the pictures, I'm afraid.'

Sara held it for a moment, almost afraid to open it. Her fingers felt the slickness of the thin, brightly patterned cover that showed a cartoon character. Jack said, 'Let's get you some light,' and she followed him dazedly over to the trouble lamp in the Toyota's cab. Taking a deep breath, she bent her head into the white glare and opened the book. *Missing Twins* screamed the headlines and *Lost in the Bush*, then in huge black type *Randall Children Feared Kidnapped*. The print was smudged in places and her brain seemed incapable of taking in all of it. Much was repetition and surmise – reporters hundreds of miles away from the tragedy building stories from the little that was known, which was basically nothing. The children had vanished, nobody knew where, why or even how it had happened. The kidnapping headline was premature. The police were still treating the twins as lost rather than taken. They had wandered into the bush. Perhaps they had tried to climb the canyon in imitation of their parents, an officer was quoted as saying. Grave fears were held for their safety. Only the year previous a man had fallen to his death from the walls of Kings Canyon.

There was a photograph of the parents. Sara stared and stared, straining to recognise some detail she could relate to in the picture, which was obviously taken at some function at an earlier date. She moved a finger gently over the faces but they remained unreal to her, just two strangers she would never have recognised had they met. Perhaps the picture had been taken at the races, for JC Randall wore a tie and a broad-brimmed hat that shadowed the top half of his face. Beside him Mary Randall, a head shorter than her husband, smiled into bright sunlight. Her hair, or the bit visible from under a close-fitting hat, was curly, but it could well have been permed. It was impossible to tell its colour. She was probably pretty, Sara thought, for her features were even, but the photo was too grainy to show much more than that.

Disappointed, Sara turned to a picture of the missing children that had been superimposed over a wide shot of the canyon. The original image must have been a studio portrait and showed the two seated side by side on a padded bench backed by dark drapes. The young faces staring out at her were solemn, caught in a sudden shyness. Sara's heart ached to see the way the hands between their two bodies were gripped together as they faced the ordeal of the picture shoot. She saw and recognised herself – her nose, her chin, the neatly pinned riot of curls. She wore ankle socks and a dress with a patterned yoke and little capped sleeves, but it meant nothing. No memory of the occasion existed, or at least none she could access. Sara stared hungrily at the image of her twin. They were very alike but only in a familial way. His hair had been curly too but there were differences in the shape of his face. Sitting he was a little taller, his knees knobby below the shorts, his neck looking thin within the collar of his shirt. She touched his image tenderly, mourning for the boy who had never grown up.

Back at the fire she returned the book to Paul. 'Did it bring anything back?' he asked hopefully.

Sara shook her head.

'Never mind. Tomorrow's another day.' Jack yawned and tapped his head. 'It's all in there somewhere, just give it a chance to assemble. Meanwhile I suggest an early night if we're walking tomorrow. We'll need to be moving by daylight.'

'Then I'll say goodnight.' Paul stood and stretched. 'You better give us a call in the morning.'

Jack grunted assent and picking up Sara's swag carried it to the far side of the vehicle. 'There you go. Sleep well, and don't worry,' he added gently. 'It'll work out. Things mostly do.'

'Says the man facing divorce, who has a sick nephew and is caught in the middle of a drought,' she responded wryly. 'But thanks, Jack.'

'I'm not taking your problems lightly,' he protested, hurt by the implication. 'Just trying to put the best face on things.'

'I know. You were being kind. You are kind, Jack – to everyone, and I appreciate it. I really do. Goodnight.'

It was a dismissal.

'Goodnight,' he said. Then his tall frame, black in the moonlight, retreated into darkness, leaving her alone under the stars.

34

Sara unrolled the familiar swag and pulled off her footwear. She wriggled her toes and lay back, facing the stars and the white curve of the moon. The evenings at Redhill had been hot, for the day's accumulated heat had clung to the building and necessitated fans, but here, under the bare sky, the heat vanished with the sun. Frank's swag was comfortable. A thin foam mattress and several blankets softened the ground and she had a pillow as well. After the long hours of travel with muscles tensed against the lurches and bumps of the vehicle it was bliss to stretch out and relax.

She thought of Paul with his single, borrowed blanket. Unless Jack relented towards him and gave him the tarp to sleep on, he was in for an uncomfortable night. He would be disappointed too that she hadn't remembered more. *She* certainly was. Sara had believed that seeing a picture of her parents would bring their faces back to her, but the sight had woken nothing in her mind. Perhaps she would never remember.

Jack with his endless optimism would encourage her to think otherwise, of course. He had hope enough for three men, and spent it unstintingly on others. He'd lavished it on her and the thought of his goodness, mixed in with her own uncertainty and despair, made her eyes suddenly well and tears roll down her cheeks. Sniffing, Sara wiped them away. Even if she couldn't recognise her mother, the woman was dead and had been for twenty years, as was her twin.

Instead of feeling sorry for herself she should be thankful that her father still lived.

The moon blurred in her vision and she heard a curlew call, the sudden sound startling, emphasising the emptiness of the silent land. Sara tried to imagine how she and her father would meet, what they would say to each other. He'd had her image to remember through the years, whereas she had never guessed at his existence. It was like looking across a gulf so vast she couldn't guess where it ended. Would he welcome her return from the dead? Or had his life moved on and did he no longer care? How could she love somebody she didn't even remember? Jack would tell her . . . Jack . . .

Sara slept, her brow twitching in a little frown and a sigh escaping her parted lips. She dreamed vividly.

The tent ropes were fluttering and the papers they'd been colouring in slid from the little wooden table at which she and Ben ate. They did their lessons there, too.

Lana scolded them, bossing them into tidying up. She was plump, with untidy yellow hair and a big pimple on her chin. Fat Lana, *Benny yelled and she went red.* I'll tell your dad, *she threatened, and Benny scowled. They weren't supposed to be cheeky to the governess.* Fat Lana, *he mouthed at Christine the moment the governess turned her back, and she grinned and waggled her little finger, their secret signal of accord.*

Outside the birds were calling, and the gum leaves tapped against the taut canvas of the tent. Dad had rolled up two sides of it to let the breeze through and the twins could see the other tent where their parents slept at night, and hear the clear voices of the big kids in the next camp. They were too old to be interesting to them, but Lana kept walking to the tent opening and looking across. She gave them both ruled pages to practise their letters on and shook a minatory finger. Mind now, I'll just be a minute so you had better not muck up while I'm gone.

Fat Lana, Benny chanted softly, watching her plump legs hurry *away from them. She wore shorts that stretched tightly over her bottom. They saw her stop near a sprawl of conkaberry to smooth her hair. She glanced back once, then hurried on, and soon the sound of her shrill giggle joined the deeper tones of the big boy that she seemed to like so much. Neither twin could work out why – after all, they had only met the previous day.*

They sneaked out the front of the tent, jumped down into the dry creek bed and ran.

'Where are we going?' Chrissy panted.

'We'll just look. No –' he'd decided – 'Dad says there's a spring. We'll find it. She'll be mad when she gets back,' Benny predicted. 'Maybe so mad she'll squeeze her pimple!'

The idea was delicious. 'Fat Lana's got a pimple,' Chrissy yelled, but her voice was swallowed by the rising stone around them. Then her elation was tempered by caution. 'Will she be really mad, Benny?' Lana could be unpleasant; she grabbed their arms sometimes and twisted them in Chinese burns, then pretended she'd only been holding them. 'What if she tells Dad?'

'She won't. 'Cause we'll say we'll tell on her for leaving us. She won't dare,' he said complacently.

Chrissy laughed happily. It was true. Benny always knew what to do.

It was very still in the gorge. The sun beat down out of the relentless blue of the sky, striking blinding colours from the high rock walls. The twins barely noticed the heat. Lost in their own world and a rising wonder for the sheer magnitude of their surroundings, they wandered and stared: at the rock-strewn creek bed they were following, at the gnarled, familiar trunks of gums, and at the slabs of stone that in ages past had crashed to the floor of the canyon. They detoured on their search for the spring to climb a couple of slabs and stare around from the top. 'Where's the camp?' Chrissy asked.

Benny pointed. 'Back there. Nobody can see us now. Watch

this! I bet I can slide all the way to the bottom.' He did so, ripping the cuff of his jeans and putting a rock smear all down the back of them. He bounced happily to his feet. 'Now you.'

Chrissy shot down the same path with a shriek composed equally of fear and delight and they went on until suddenly the lady was there at the base of the largest rock yet, a vast square of stone as big as their tent. The moment she saw them she put a finger to her lips and beckoned them closer. It was impossible not to obey. The twins crept near, wild speculation in their hearts.

'Do you want to see?' the lady whispered. 'They're down through there, the sweetest little babies! Only you have to be very quiet or we won't get close enough. Can you walk very quickly and very quietly?'

They nodded, eyes alight. 'What is it?' Chrissy breathed, but the lady's finger was back at her lips.

'You'll see. Quick. Come with me.'

Their guide turned back, not on the path they had taken but at right angles to it. She was thin and athletic with dark hair pulled back on a sunburned neck. There was no collar on her shirt. She wore pants and sneakers and a cloth hat with a chin tie, and kept turning her head to smile at them, the tension in her eyes inviting them to hurry before they missed their chance. When Chrissy stumbled over a root because she was trying to peer ahead, the lady took her hand. 'Come, I'll help you.' And after a while all three of them were hustling through the low bushes, Ben on the other side of the woman, his hand also in hers. Then the bad man stepped into their path from where he'd been waiting behind a jumble of boulders. He blocked their passage, menacing in his bigness, and the children unconsciously shrank closer to the lady.

'How'd you find 'em?' he asked.

'They just walked up to me.' A shrug. 'Seemed too good a chance to pass up.'

'The parents?'

She shrugged. 'No sign of them. The kids were on their own.'

'Bewdy! Let's get outta here.' He grabbed Benny round the waist, like an awkward parcel, and as the boy yelled in protest, lifted him and clapped his free hand over his mouth. Chrissy's heart lurched in fright as the happy day dissolved around her. She yelled, 'No!' and pulled back, but the lady's grip was suddenly like steel and she clouted the girl hard enough to make her ears ring. 'Shut it!' she hissed and now she looked like a witch, dark eyes daggering at her, the mouth hard and thin.

In her swag Sara moaned and thrashed weakly as the dream children struggled. She was Ben, kicking furiously, arching his body, helpless in the man's grip; and she was Chrissy too, with a heavy fore-weight of knowledge and the blind terror of a little girl whose world has suddenly turned against her.

She bit the hand clamped over her mouth and received a stinging slap in return; she kicked frantically at the legs braced to hold her and her captor coolly punched her in the stomach. The breath and the fight went out of her and the man grinned.

'Good one, Kitty.' He punched his own struggling captive with the same result. Ben collapsed, whooping, and in a daze of tears and terror the two were carried off.

It was dark under the blanket and hot, stiflingly so. The twins held hands, feeling each other's tears leak onto them. The lady's feet were pressed into their backs as they lay on the floor that sped and bumped beneath them. The man was driving fast and had been for a long time. Chrissy was thirsty, but she badly wanted to wee too. And she wanted her mum. She knew that Benny felt the same, and she was sorry, so sorry, that they had been bad and run off from Lana. 'Oh, I wish we never —' she whispered, and Benny's teary voice answered like the echo it always was, 'I wish we never too.' He sniffed, getting some fight back, and she knew without needing to see that he was scowling. Benny hated giving up even when it was sensible to do so. He moved so his mouth was against her ear, his *breath making the words hard to understand. He had lost his hat somewhere and his curls tickled her eye. 'We gotta get out, Chrissy. I'm gonna be sick. When they let us out, we'll run. Run real hard, an' don't stop.' His little finger moved against her hand, and she understood and moved her own back. Then he heaved his back against the restraining feet holding him down and began to retch.*

Benny could make himself sick whenever he wanted to. He didn't seem to mind the horrid rush of it the way Chrissy did. Vomiting made her cry but Benny could pretend so well that even when he didn't sick up, everyone thought he was going to. It worked with the lady. The moment he started she snatched her feet away and yelled, 'Stop, Vic! Stop!'

'What the hell?'

'The little bugger's gonna spew. I'm not riding in a car stinking of vomit. Let 'em out. We've come far enough now.'

Sara moaned in her sleep, knowing what was coming. Her heart pounded as if it would tear itself loose. 'Don't,' she tried to shout. 'Don't, Benny, don't!' But the words fell weakly from her lips, indistinguishable, no more than a sigh.

It was happening. Benny had made them stop. The lady whipped the blanket off them, one rough corner catching Chrissy painfully in the eye. Her hands were hard and strong as she thrust them out the opened door onto hard red dirt. They scrambled to their feet, Chrissy all but blinded by the blaze of light and the hurt in her eye. 'Run!' Benny shrilled and was off like a rabbit, but his twin was behind him and took a fraction longer to start, and with a wild roar the man leapt from his seat and took after her. Her legs plaited and he caught her as she went down, his hand like a cruel claw digging into her shoulder. He whirled her about, backhanding her twice across the face and she fell, losing her hat. Nobody before today had ever hit her, nor had anybody ever shouted such bad words at her. Sobs choked her and Chrissy cowered in the dirt, screaming hysterically as he reached for her again.

'Right, I've got her.' The lady's hand was gripped about her wrist as she bent to retrieve the fallen hat. 'You gonna get after the other brat?'

'Ah, stuff him. Get the little bitch into the car. All said and done, one's as good as two.' The man wiped sweat from his face and spat. 'Christ, what a country! No worries, he won't last the day out. Let's get going.'

She hesitated, squinting in the cruel light. 'If somebody picks him up, what then?'

He laughed harshly. 'It ain't exactly Rundle Street, Kitty. Leave the planning to me.'

For a few blessed moments Chrissy didn't know what was happening. The woman dragged her into the vehicle but not under the blanket. This time the lady sat beside her holding her wrist, but every movement Chrissy made was punished by a vicious yank that bruised her flesh. It wasn't until the engine fired that she realised they were leaving Benny behind. Her body jerked as she jacked her legs into the back of the driver's seat and flung back her head, screaming in terror and outrage. 'No, no – I want Benny! You can't leave him! Benny . . .'

The cry, thin and distant, woke Jack, who bolted up in his swag, head cocked to isolate and identify the sound. The night wind brushed his face then he heard it – not another scream, but the desolate sound of weeping coming from Sara's swag. Instantly he sprang to his feet.

She slept, her body hiccupping with sobs, the moonlight making tracks of the tears on her cheeks. He shook her gently.

'Sara, wake up. It's okay, it's just a dream.'

Her body stiffened and her eyes jerked open. Her face was full of loss and terror and the tears continued to flow. 'Oh, Jack.' Her hand clutched his arm. 'It was – I was – and Benny.'

'Hush,' he said. 'It was a dream, Sara.' He took her in his arms, one hand cradling her head as he smoothed the unruly curls. 'Just a bad dream, dear heart. None of it's real.'

'But it is! It was,' she choked out as the tears poured forth to soak the skin of his neck. 'It's a nightmare – the real one. Because I know now how they killed him. They left him to perish. He was only six, Jack, and he died out there all alone.'

'I know,' he soothed. 'I'm sorry. He's gone, but not really, you know, because now you remember him and he'll always be with you.'

In the midst of her wild grief, it was an oddly comforting thought.

35

Jack rocked her against him and let her weep. He kissed her hair, murmuring soothing nothings until she quieted and when she separated herself from him, he rose wordlessly and led her to the fire to stir the fading embers to life and make a billy of coffee. The moon had moved, Sara saw. The night looked late, past midnight. The only sound was the tiny whisper of the flames and the muted snores coming from inside the Pajero. Paul, despite his lack of bedding, slept. The thought reminded her and she looked at Jack, who had not yet asked about her dream.

'I've worked out why he frightened me. At least I think so.' She told him how that day at the beach their relative positions – herself on the ground, his shadow falling across her – had mimicked the moments before Vic Blake had thrown her six-year-old self into the car and driven off, leaving her twin to die. Then, holding the enamelled mug close for comfort, she recounted the rest.

'He called her Kitty,' she said. 'She was different, younger of course, but even then she had this mean way of looking at me – I'd know her at any age. I wonder if Stella was even her real name?'

'The police will find out,' Jack said. 'If Paul could locate her then so can they.' It was the first time he'd used the journalist's Christian name.

'But would they consider a recovered amnesiac who was six years old when the crime was committed a credible witness? I can just imagine the response you'd get from a judge if you tried present-ing a dream as evidence.'

'A dream that answers many puzzling questions,' Jack reminded her. 'A grown man couldn't have walked to Dare's Plain from the canyon, let alone a child, not in November. So, dead or alive, Ben had to have been taken there. Which immediately proves the crime, if there was any doubt of it. That's a start. What about after, do you remember where they took you, or – shit, how stupid am I? That's when it happened, that's when you lost your memory, wasn't it?

'No.' Her face looked blank in the soft light of the moon and the dying flames, the green eyes shadowed. 'The details are there now, how we drove and drove . . .' She had cried until her eyes were swollen almost shut and her throat too sore to speak, and had then fallen asleep exhausted.

It had been only the start of the road trip, the rest a jumbled memory of strange rooms, odd meals and lukewarm water taken from a big blue barrel in the back of the station wagon in which they had travelled. She had wet herself once and Stella had slapped her again and called her dirty. She had made her wear the pants all day because she had no clothes to change into. Stella never left her side except to shop for food. When that happened Chrissie had stayed in the car with the man, but she had been so scared of him that she'd always scrooched back into the seat against the door, as far from him as she could get.

'Bastard,' Jack muttered at this point of the telling. 'I'd like to break his neck.' There was a grim line to his jaw and his shoulders were tense. It wasn't hard to imagine that it was Becky he saw in her place, hopeless and lost, all the bounce and shining innocence torn from her. Sara had paid a high cost for a moment's disobedience.

So they had arrived at last, Chrissy didn't know how many days later, at the ugly little clapboard house with its neglected yard. Most of the adults' conversations had gone over her head but one bit of it had stuck.

'When do we call her father?' Stella had asked.

'We'll give it a week,' the man said. 'Let him sweat for a few days. The more he worries about his brats, the readier he'll be to pay to get 'em back.'

'Just don't wait too long,' the woman snapped. 'I'm not a bleeding nursemaid.'

All Chrissy took from this was that they were going to tell her dad where she was, and the horrid lady didn't want her to stay. Benny had been right when he'd tried to get away from them, but he wasn't there to help so this time she would have to go by herself. The immensity of the city and the sheer number of houses she had seen as they drove in daunted her, but she had faith in her father. If she just got away from the bad people, he would come and find her.

They had locked her up in a room bare of anything but a bed with an iron frame and an empty wardrobe. The floor was covered in sticky vinyl, and there was a window that wouldn't open overlooking a street full of other houses. The window was set quite high from the ground, because there had been steps where they came in. The bed had a thin mattress, a blanket and only one sheet. And there was a ratty pillow without any cover, and it smelled. The lack of a second sheet bothered Chrissy most because she hated the touch of the scratchy blanket against her skin when it got cold towards morning. Stella gave her a grown-up's shirt to wear in bed, and once she had to wear it all day too when her clothes were taken away. That was the only time they were washed. She initially had to bang on the door when she needed the toilet but on the second day the woman brought a big china bowl, like a giant potty, and told her to use that. It was probably the day following that that Chrissy took the knife from the tray and hid it under the mattress. She didn't usually get cutlery, but Stella had been distracted. It wasn't a proper lunch, just dry biscuits and some peanut butter that was lumpy and hard to spread. It scared her, taking the knife, and she nearly wet herself again when Stella came back, but she was in a hurry and had just grabbed the tray and walked out, leaving a bottle of water behind.

'You were a game little kid,' Jack said. 'Six years old, for Christ's sake! What were you going to do with a knife?'

'I needed it for the window.' A smile trembled briefly on Sara's lips. 'We were naughty little brats, my twin and I. We used to climb and dig and get into all sorts of stuff. We were always in trouble. I suppose you would say that, young as he was, Benny had a very analytical mind. He could take things apart and I guess I learned from him. I had nothing to break glass with but the window had a catch on the sill. I wasn't strong enough to shift it but I thought I could prise it open. And I did.'

She had kept her head, waiting until she saw the bad man drive off in the car that had brought her there. It had taken a long time to move the catch because of her height in relation to the sill: she had to stand on tiptoes to reach, which quickly made her arms tired. Luckily the chamber pot got emptied when her breakfast came and she hadn't used it again yet, so she'd turned it upside down and stood on it. It helped a lot but the catch was very stiff and had, besides, been painted over. Every time she heard footsteps pass her door she had to stop and retreat to the bed in case Stella came in. But in the end the knife had done its job.

When the last bit of paint was chipped off, she had been able to wedge the tip of the blade in the catch and exert her strength against it. It took three goes and when she finally felt it move Sara could hardly believe she had done it, but there was no time to waste. She pushed the window pane up, then only a thin screen remained between her and freedom. Benny, she knew, would punch it out, so she would too. Balanced on the sill, she butted it with her head and it tore like tissue paper, so that she had to grab the window frame with both hands to stop herself falling. Only that was silly because she wanted to jump. So she had let herself go, tumbling into a drop twice her own height just as Vic Blake's vehicle had swept in off the street onto the short, weed-grown drive.

Sara drew a breath and picking up a piece of charred mulga stick poked the dying embers. 'There never was a car accident,' she said, 'just me falling. I must've landed on my head and knocked myself out. I was unconscious anyway – that's when my memory went. Stella must have realised and I suppose gave me the name Sara and told me that they were my parents. And the rest all grew from that.'

Jack nodded. 'They saw the opportunity and grabbed it. How much simpler to keep a stolen kid that didn't know she *was* stolen? And I suppose they waited a bit before sending the ransom demand, to inch up the asking price and perhaps see if your memory came back – and while they were waiting the cops arrested Vic for the bank robbery. So your real father never learned you still lived and Stella was stuck with you.'

'Some of it's very plain.' Sara's face twisted. 'I *believed*, I really did, that Stella was my mother. Inside I must have known that something was amiss. At first, I mean, because I used to run to her for hugs and I never got them. After a while I stopped, but it always seemed unfair – as if some part of me knew that I should blindly expect to find comfort with my mother. The rest is a bit blurred. We moved from that house, but I don't remember if it was before or after Christmas. I don't remember having Christmas, but I do remember starting school. It was all new to me and I hated it. Everyone else had friends and the kids teased me about my hair.' She sighed. 'It didn't get any better. I'm sorry, I sound like a real wimp but children can be quite cruel. Later on in high school it wasn't just being a redhead, it was the wrong clothes and not fitting in. I was a late bloomer so my hair always got me teased —'

'I think your hair is beautiful,' Jack said. 'The boys in your high school must've been blind.'

'That's nice, Jack, but honestly it didn't look so great with a pimply chin under it and a daggy dress from St Vinnies. Stella kept shifting us around the city, which didn't help me make friends. Of course initially she must've been waiting for Vic to serve out his sentence. I expect they saw me as an ace up their sleeve – like a bank draft waiting to be cashed.'

'She'd have been pretty pissed off when he died, then,' Jack agreed. 'No money and suddenly, should your memory ever return, you're a real liability to her and her only. But it was a bit difficult to get shot of a daughter everybody knows you've got. And she already had your brother on her conscience.'

Sara's expression darkened. 'I really hope so. He didn't even have a hat, I remember that clearly. It was lost in the canyon when the man took us.' She could see it now, a billed cap with the cotton neck guard their mother had stitched across the back. Red for him, yellow for her – to make them more visible, she now supposed.

As if divining her thought, Jack asked, 'Your parents – how's your memory of them?'

'Sort of patchy,' she admitted. 'I can't see their faces. Maybe kids don't look at actual faces so much? I don't know. It's more aspects of them. Like he's big with gold hairs on his arms and he whistled a lot. And Mum was – she was cuddly and smelled of cigarettes and talc. And at night when she was going out our bedroom door she'd look back and blow kisses to us. Paul said her hair was red too, but I don't remember that.' She fell silent. The fire had died to white ash and the moon lay far over to the west, thin and white in the sky. She heard Jack yawn, the hinge of his jaw cracking, and she straightened. 'I'm sorry. I must've been talking for hours. What time is it?'

'Pretty late. After four, by the stars. There's Venus rising now. We should sleep for a bit.'

'Yes.' She stood and he rose beside her. 'Thanks for being here for me, Jack, and for listening. It's been a – well, a strange journey.

I'm glad I wasn't alone on it.'

His arm slipped round her shoulder and he gave her a deep hug. For a breathless moment she thought he might kiss her and her heart quickened. It seemed an age that she waited, feeling the rise of sexual tension between them, but he did nothing. His arm slipped back to his side. 'You're never alone, kiddo,' he said. 'That's the thing to remember. Get your head down. We'll be up again in an hour.'

Sara was hurt by his rejection then mortified by her own expectations. Well, scarcely expectations. Yes, she had fallen for him; she had known weeks ago that her body desired him though her heart warred with her head about her feelings. It was one thing for her to love him, quite another for him to reciprocate, already entangled as he was with one city woman. Why would he even look at another? His hug had been the sort of embrace he would have given Beth along with the same words of assurance. He was just being kind and – what did they call it in the mulga? – riding for the brand. She was his sister's governess, part of the station to which he temporarily belonged. Flushing, thankful that he couldn't see her face, she slipped away to bed.

36

The sun was still behind the range when the Pajero, carrying the three of them, left the campground to travel the six kilometres to Kings Canyon. Sara was heavy-eyed; her mind had been too busy for further sleep. Jack had watched her as she came to the fire for breakfast.

'Are you sure you want to go on with this? There's no real need after all.'

'We've come this far.' She drew a long breath. 'I may as well see it. Benny and I – we never got to the spring, you know.'

Paul, who was trying to pour from the billy, swore as it spilled, and jerked his head up. 'You've remembered?'

'Everything, yes. Well, so far as I know,' she admitted. 'Which is another reason for going. I'll fill you in later. How did you sleep?'

'What? Oh, fine. A few aches this morning. So your memory's come back, that's great!'

'The memory of a six-year-old. It's not proof,' she said shortly, and was immediately sorry she had snapped at him. Relenting, she added, 'I know why I reacted as I did at the beach though. I'll explain that too, once we're there.'

They parked where the track into the canyon ended, in a space where the wattle scrub had been cleared away for the purpose. As briefly as she could Sara spoke of what she'd learned. Paul listened carefully, his dark face thoughtful. When she had finished he nodded. 'It covers all the points for me. It'll make a hell of a story but whether it's good enough for an arrest, or to convince your father, remains to be seen.'

Sara was stunned into silence and it was Jack who said roughly, 'What the hell's that supposed to mean? Chris'sake, man! Why wouldn't he believe his own daughter?'

Paul flicked him a look. 'Wake up, cowboy.' His tone was unfriendly. Either he hadn't forgiven the punch, or he didn't like being questioned about his own world. 'Old JC is a multimillionaire and his history's well known. How many conmen do you think, through the years, have tried to sell him news of his daughter? Or even his actual daughter? You want my best guess? At least a dozen. It's why he's so hostile to the press. Only a DNA test will convince him. Give me the exclusive on this, Sara, and I'll do my damnedest to get my paper to pay for the test. They're not cheap. They take a while to process, too.'

Sara said, 'I'm not baring my life again for anyone else.'

'Good.' He hesitated. 'We should get the test started, I think, before I contact JC.'

'Whatever.' Until now Sara had not considered the reality of having a father. Not the actual man who had once underpinned her world. He would have changed, of course he would have, from the strong god-like figure she remembered, the one who had swung her up in his arms and ridden her on his shoulders. The one whose stern voice had let her and her twin know it when they had done something wrong. He had been the kingpin of their young worlds and if she'd had time since Jack had woken her last night to think beyond the events of childhood, she'd have assumed he would still be the same. It shocked her to think that he might doubt her, might demand proof of the legitimacy of her claim. Troubled, she put the thought from her mind and turned to Paul. 'So, where were we camped back then, do you know?'

'Not exactly, but probably somewhere close to here. The ground's pretty uneven further in. You don't —'

'No.' She didn't wait for his question. 'There was a little creek, like that one. That's all I'd be sure of.'

'Let's follow it up, then,' Jack said.

This early the canyon was in shadow, only the tops of the western side touched to red by the sun. Compared with the surrounding flatness its walls looked incredibly high, the upper reaches formed from sheer slabs of rock that towered above the eucalyptus foliage like an island rising from a sea of green. Jack took the lead, tramping through scrubby wattle and then a band of silvery grey shrub that he identified as holly grevillea. Its leaves bore the spikes to prove its name. Sara recognised spinifex and the clumpy growth that Jack had said was kangaroo grass. The creek widened and shallowed; the pad they were following clung to the gradually rising near wall, which was fractured and worn by weather and time.

Sara, using her arms to fend off branches and steadying her steps against boulders and tree trunks, wondered if it ever rained out here. The low scrub-covered sand drifts in the creek bed and the depth of bark and debris littered along its bank showed that it was an infrequent occurrence. Some of the wattle was in bloom, lending its fragrance to the morning air, and it was cool enough still for the birds to be active. There were honeyeaters in the grevillea, the bold flashes of parrots among the gum tops and myriad other smaller birds she couldn't name. Above, in the brilliant sky, kites rode the updrafts on outspread wings.

Sara tried to reconcile it with her dream, but her recollections focused more on herself and Benny than the actual area. Besides, she had been smaller then. The scrub that now she could see through and sometimes over would have completely engulfed children. The boulders that were chest high must have been well above their heads. She looked in vain for the one they had climbed and slid down. There were so many possibilities and twenty years, even allowing for the slowness of desert growth, must have changed the look of the country.

Jack had stopped to pluck a switch for the ever-present flies. He cocked a brow at her. 'Are you getting anything from it?'

She shook her head in frustration. 'I'm not looking at it from the same viewpoint, that's the trouble. They were half my height.' In her mind's eye she could see them trotting easily beneath the branches she was pushing her way through, the two bobbing heads with their billed hats and nape protectors, one red, one yellow. 'It's like returning to your primary school years later – everything's so small and crowded, even the playground you used to think was enormous.'

'It's quite a sight anyway.' Jack was gazing around. Paul was scribbling on a pad. 'What're you doing?'

'Getting down a sense of the place. Who would ever think a crime could be committed somewhere this wild and remote? Though I suppose,' he added thoughtfully, 'that fact makes it the ideal venue.'

'Not if the locals hadn't buggered the kids' chances from the outset,' Jack argued. 'The droves of people that came in to help with the search put paid to any hope of ever finding anything useful. The cops should immediately have cordoned the place off and got a tracker in, but I suppose by the time they got out here it was already too late. Randall might've been a property owner but he wasn't desert-bred. Tracks last out here – sometimes for years, if there's no rain or five hundred volunteers tramping 'em to death. I'd lay odds that, given a clear field, a tracker would've known —'

'Jack,' Sara said, an odd edge to her voice. They were deep in the gorge now and she was pointing ahead at a massive block of stone, the size of a room and so even that it almost looked square. 'There! That's where she was, by that rock – Kitty. That's where she led us back from. Down to the creek first, then that way.' Sara was moving as she spoke, going up close enough to touch the red solidity of the huge stone, then following its edge to the creek side. 'We went down here.' She trod unerringly as if in a trance through rocks and tangles of dead hop bush, angling across the shallow creek bed and, arrested by her sudden certainty, the men followed unquestioning.

Sara led them by degrees, stopping occasionally to turn aside where it was impossible to push through the scrub, but always veering back to her original line as if she could actually see the two little phantom figures before her. Her gaze was fixed ahead. Jack, exchanging a glance with Paul, wondered if there was some point on the canyon wall by which she unconsciously navigated. They were more than halfway back to the mouth of the canyon, the rock on the eastern side sinking so that the cliff became a steep buttress, when she abruptly stopped.

'Here.' Sara was casting about her as if suddenly lost. 'I think it was somewhere here that he was waiting, or perhaps coming to meet her.' The purpose seemed to leave her. 'It's where – at least, I think – where we started to struggle. But she was dragging me then and I – he carried Benny. He screamed and hit him and kicked. His face was so red from temper and from being held upside down, I expect.'

She moved aimlessly around the rocks as if she had lost her way, then sank down onto one, without regard for its position in the sun. Markham, Jack saw, had his camera out again.

'It was twenty years back,' Jack reminded her. 'What is it that makes you think this is it?'

'What?' Her thoughts had been far away. 'Oh.' She blinked as if suddenly waking, the dazed look clearing from her green eyes. 'I – I'm not sure. Did I say that? I'm sorry, Jack. Half the time it seems like yesterday and then there's a sort of gap and I hardly know who I am or how old I am. The double timelines are doing my head in.'

'I'm not surprised.' He poured a drink from the water bottle. 'Here, it's heating up and you're sitting in the sun. Come over into the shade. Have you had enough bush bashing, or do you want to go onto the spring? Could be a way off.' He swung the heavy water container onto a rock and waved the cup at the journalist. 'You wanna drink?'

'Thanks.' Paul took the container and Sara followed Jack into the shade. His quick eyes caught the movement of a small lizard that had been sunbaking on the stone as it whisked out of sight into a crack. 'Keep an eye open for snakes,' he cautioned her, then bent suddenly to a patch of faded colour half-hidden by red gravel and the siftings of old grey leaf litter.

It was his stillness, Sara thought, that caused her to notice. 'What is it?'

He turned to her then, dumbly proffering the object he'd found, faded and half rotted but still recognisable as a child's hat. The bill had peeled and the crown was missing but the red nape flap was still attached to the remnants, the once-bright colour faded now to an anaemic pink.

Sara took the rag in trembling fingers.

'Oh, God. It's Benny's hat.' She looked wildly about, tears starting to her eyes. 'I was right, then. This *is* where —' Overcome, she sank to the earth, cradling the pathetic relic to her breast, the tears rolling down her pale cheeks. 'He didn't have a chance,' she cried. 'They *murdered* him. He was a little child, Jack, younger even than Becky and they killed him.'

'I know.' His hand, warm and solid, patted her shoulder. Sara didn't see his face twist in pain for her own suffering or the inimical look he cast at the journalist, as if fearing the man would breach her privacy by choosing to photograph the moment.

There was no further talk of finding the spring. Returned again to the campsite, Paul looked at Jack. 'I've got all I need. So we'll head straight back to Alice?'

'The old mission for starters. Then we'll see how we're travelling. We've used up a fair bit of the day and I'm not driving that road in the dark.'

'It'd be cooler,' Paul protested. 'And the track's plain enough if you're worried about losing it. We could be in town by midnight.'

'We could do an axle too,' Jack retorted. 'This is the desert; you don't take chances with it. You're free to suit yourself of course but if it comes to it, we'll be camping.'

Sara left them talking and packing up and got into the Toyota. She had said little since her display of grief. She placed the hat she was still clutching in the glove box. Her father might want it, either as proof of her story or as the last tangible link with his son. It was odd to think that she couldn't guess how he would feel about it – about her. Did he still grieve for his twins or was his memory of them no more than an old regret? She hadn't even thought to ask Paul if he had remarried. It seemed highly likely. It was more than twenty years since Mary Randall had killed herself. Which meant that Sara probably had half-brothers or -sisters. How would they feel to suddenly find themselves with an older sibling, supposedly long dead, who'd come miraculously back to life?

Muttering something uncomplimentary under his breath about the journalist, Jack slammed his door shut and glanced across at her. 'You okay?'

'I'm fine,' Sara said and realised that it was true. Yes, she was exhausted and sad, bereft in a way that she suspected only another twin would understand, but the storm of tears seemed to have drained a weight from her chest, as if a bladder of hurt somewhere inside her had burst, leaving her freer and lighter. 'Jack, I was just wondering, do you happen to know if JC Randall is married?' It seemed too strange as yet to call him *my father*.

He started the motor and thought about it. 'I dunno. Maybe. All I know about the man is that he owns a trucking company and he's a venture capitalist – whatever the hell that is. I've never paid any attention, and any road it's the sort of wealthy blokes that have racehorses and buy football teams, or go in for politics that make the news. He doesn't. Markham would know though.'

'I'll ask him.'

She settled into her seat, tucking her hands under her hat as he swung away from the campground, the red dust the vehicle raised visible for miles across the flat stretch of desert that ran from the range to the far horizon.

37

The Pajero suffered a puncture just short of Hermannsburg and the vehicle proved to have neither jack nor wheel brace included with its spare. Jack spoke his mind pithily on the subject while providing the missing equipment, but the delay meant they had no hope of completing the journey in daylight. They camped near a stock bore where cattle trickled in as the sun set across a flat shadowed plain, and Sara woke in the night to the drumming of shoeless hooves. The loud snorts of the brumby stallions approaching the trough seemed to tear the night apart. Sitting up in her swag, she watched them, black silhouettes in the moonlight, until some sound or scent alarmed them and they were off in a rush of tossing heads and lifted tails, the thunder of their going drifting back to her on the breeze. Sara lay down again, breathing the scent of dust and distance, oddly comforted as the silence closed round her again, and slept until dawn.

It was good to be back at Frank and Helen's neat suburban home. Showered and shampooed, with her wet curls tamed into a knot on top of her head – she still hadn't found time for a hairdresser – Sara shared a pot of tea at the kitchen table with Jack and his father.

Paul Markham had returned to his motel. 'Are you going to contact my father, tell him about me?' she had asked on the return journey.

'Not yet.' Paul had been definite. 'Tried that. He won't listen. We need the DNA results first. He's a pretty formidable bloke, Randall. I tried to meet with him, I flew to Sydney especially for that purpose right after I'd spoken to Blake's cellmate. I couldn't get near him. Tried the phone, with the same result. That's when I learned from that toffee-voiced woman that guards his door about all the other guys who'd tried it on over the years. Saying they'd found you or had information to sell. The only way it's gonna work is to mail the test results, *then* contact him.'

'I see.'

Thinking about Paul's words later, Sara supposed that she couldn't blame her father, however cold his behaviour seemed. Wealthy men were the targets of the unscrupulous and he believed her dead. Her name on the memorial out on Dare's Plain proved that. She found that she wanted him to have gone on hoping, vain though the years had shown that to be. Perhaps if her mother had lived – weren't women supposed to be more constant in their devotion? Sara brought herself back to the present, to the cheerful room with its bright curtains and scarlet kettle.

'So what now? You heading for Redhill?' Frank asked Jack.

'Maybe tomorrow. I'll give Len a ring first, see if they need anything picked up. And Markham's finding out where Sara can get her mouth swabbed for these tests. It's got to be done with proper supervision so it can't be doubted. What about you, Dad? You seen this quack of yours yet?'

'Yesterday. He says I'm fine. I'll give you a day's start then before I head on up the bitumen and pick up your mum.' He glanced through the window at the patchy lawn. 'I've had the sprays on but the grass has suffered a bit while we were gone. Might get it cut tomorrow.' He wagged his head at Sara. 'Damn woman sets quite a store by her garden but at least while she's fussing with it she's not pestering me.'

'Oh, yes?' Sara said. 'You know you'd miss it if she wasn't, Frank.'

'Yeah,' he agreed dolefully. 'Just shows what habit reduces a man to.'

'You're a pathetic old faker.' Sara smiled at him and rose to clear the table.

The following morning, her hair still uncut – she'd bought two big plastic grips instead – Sara and Jack left for Arkeela. It would add roughly three hours to the overall trip, Jack told her. The track into the station was, luckily for him, one of the better roads, as it served as a main link into Queensland. 'One of these days we'll get it bituminised,' he said optimistically. 'Tourism's a growing force in the Territory.'

'I get that.' Sara gazed out at the country slipping past. The gravel under their wheels kept the dust down and there was actual grass along the table drains, which spread to the red, lightly forested flats. White-trunked gum trees grew in abundance and together with the distant purple ranges they gave the scene the slightly unreal look of a Namatjira painting. 'It's beautiful. Not as hard-looking as the country around Charlotte Creek.'

'It's the feed makes you think so. Like I said, we had a band of storms. They fell in a narrow strip but it's made a world of difference. And don't be fooled, Sara – this country's pretty but it's unforgiving of mistakes. All desert country is.'

She glanced across at him. He'd wedged his hat in the gap between the seats, and she could see the clean curve of his skull beneath the newly shortened dark hair – he at least had found time for a barber – and the flush of sunlight on the tanned skin of his cheek. 'You sound like you're warning me off.'

His eyes crinkled. 'Nope, a reminder, that's all. What was the likeliest outcome for Markham's flat tyre if he'd been travelling alone? Carelessness costs out here. We met nobody, coming or going, so he'd have been on his own. That's why you travel with a full complement of gear, and check it before you leave.'

'Mmm.' Sara eased one of the new grips that was pulling on her scalp as they rattled over a cattle grid. 'The kids said you had the Redhill horses on Arkeela. How did you bring them down?'

'Len trucked 'em. Took a while. I was holding the gate, as it were, for a week. He had to wait on a single decker, you can't use doubles for horses. Come to think of it, it was a Randall truck. Well, Randall-James, which is one of your father's companies. They're not just interstate hauliers. They run stock transports too. You see 'em all over.'

'I hadn't realised —' Sara halted the thought and stared out at a patch of feeding galahs that were exploding from the grass in a cloud of pink and silver. 'It's strange enough to suddenly have a father, let alone a wealthy one. I wonder what he'll be like.' Panic touched her. 'It sounds crazy, Jack, but I'm almost scared of meeting him. He's my dad but he's a complete stranger.'

'It'll be okay. You forget. By the time he learns about you, he'll know you really are his daughter. And that's got to matter to him.'

'After so long? He has another family now.' Paul had confirmed that. She had a stepmother and three half-siblings – a brother and two younger sisters. The boy was seventeen. If he had been ten or even fourteen it would be different, Sara told herself. Her father, it seemed, had scarcely paused after Benny's and his wife's death before marrying again. She tried to recall the remembered warmth of his presence, the strength of his arm, the solidity of his broad shoulders, but all she could conjure was a faceless seventeen-year-old boy who signalled to her how quickly her father had moved on. If his first family had meant so little to him, why, after believing her dead for so long, would he wish to have her back?

Arkeela homestead was tucked into a small flat between two ridges covered with spinifex and low scrub. The complex was surrounded by a horse paddock boasting a blue gate. There was a mill and tank, a stockyard at the foot of the furthest ridge and a scatter of out-buildings. *Arkeela* was painted across the roof of the largest shed, and a fenced garden edged with shade trees enclosed the house. The garden growth was lush, the lawn vividly green, the whole dominated by an exuberant burst of colour from a magenta bougainvillea growing in one corner.

'It's beautiful,' Sara exclaimed, feasting her eyes on the green. 'All Helen's work?'

'Yep. She's got two green thumbs. Well, you'll have seen that in town. Stuff'll grow here if you've got the water and are willing to put in the work. Wonder where old Eddie is? He's been caretaking the agisted stock. Camps in the quarters but he uses the kitchen. Might be out checking the waters, I suppose. Ready for a cuppa?'

'Always,' Sara assured him.

'Right. I'll show you where stuff is, then have a quick check around. We can't take long though. I was hoping he'd be here to tell me about the paddocks.'

The house, which faced south, was set on low stumps. It was a solidly built steel construction with ventilation spaces between ceiling and walls, and banks of louvres that started at floor level. A verandah ran across the front with some sort of scented climber growing over the lattice at one end. Inhaling its sweetness, Sara saw the table and chairs it sheltered and knew it would be the perfect place for summer smokos. She wondered if it was Helen or Marilyn who had placed the furniture there. The kitchen was airy and modern with a gas stove, a fridge and a huge walk-in coldroom. The cupboards were pine with bronzed knobs and the benchtops ochre. A heavily marked calendar, with progressive days crossed off, hung beside the sink where a dish mop and soap saver were upended in a drinking glass. Jack ran water into the kettle, started the gas and rummaged in the cupboard for tea and sugar.

'Can I leave you with it?' He looked around. 'There could be a bit of cake somewhere. Try the coldroom.'

'You go on. I'll find it.' Sara set her hat on the table and rinsed her hands, looking around as she did so. The missing Eddie was a tidy man; everything in the room was spotless and even the tea towel was folded. He cooked too. She found a tin of rock cakes in the fridge, next to the remains of a rice pudding and a plate of cold potatoes, tidily covered with cling film. Sara set out the mugs and the milk next to the cakes and, as the kettle boiled, went to explore the house.

A light film of dust shrouded the living room and in the tiled bathroom dead insects had fallen into the unused bath. Eddie plainly didn't intrude beyond the kitchen. Sara fingered a shelf of books, peered into the laundry, opened the door of the office, and examined a large framed photograph of the Ketch family taken when Beth and Jack had been teenagers. She looked quickly through the bedrooms. There were three of them, and a long sleep-out, screened and louvred, which ran across the back of the house. One end was taken up with storage and a ping-pong table. Two bunk beds and a wardrobe filled the remaining space at the opposite end.

The main bedroom contained a king-sized bed, wardrobe and a dresser, the last heavily filmed with dust that lay over a clutter of leather straps, ripped packaging, a holed sock and bits of metal that could have been engine parts. Pushed to the back was a photograph face down in an elaborate silver frame. Feeling like a voyeur, Sara picked it up. It showed Jack and his bride, their heads together, laughing into the lens. Marilyn had perfect teeth and beautiful skin. She was really very pretty, with pearls and flowers caught up into her dark hair. She wasn't tall. Her head was on a level with Jack's shoulder. That was sprinkled with confetti and he looked almost fatuously happy, his face relaxed into a beaming smile, his dark hair tidier than Sara had ever seen it.

The kettle shrilled, dragging Sara back into the moment. She replaced the photo as she'd found it and hurried to the kitchen. Sipping her tea as she waited for Jack to return, she wondered how much of the house had been changed for, or by, Marilyn. If the woman had been set upon selling from the get-go, as Frank had said, surely she wouldn't have bothered changing anything? It was none of Sara's business, of course, but looking around at the relaxed and colourful kitchen she couldn't help but feel glad that her conclusion was probably right.

Eddie not having returned, Jack scribbled a note to him and left it propped against the teapot. On their way out, Jack collected a handful of mail from the kitchen bench, most of which he then dropped unopened into a bin by the back step. He detoured to tug at the lock on the petrol pump.

'We're a bit close to the Plenty Highway,' he explained. 'Tourists are always looking for fuel – and some of 'em aren't above helping themselves.'

'It's lovely,' Sara said, looking back at the receding homestead as they drove off. 'It must've been hard for Helen to leave. The house is perfect and that garden! When I think of the couple of tubs I used to have at my flat! I'd like to have a proper garden some day, though when you're working . . .' Her voice trailed off. 'Helen was though, wasn't she? She raised a family, cooked for a property, taught school. How could I think she wasn't working? And she still grew that.'

'Nature helps,' Jack said, 'and time. As for what you'd like, I expect you can have pretty much anything now, your old man being who he is. So work shouldn't come into it.'

Sara's immediate response to this was dismay. 'Of course I'll work,' she said. 'And I never for a moment thought otherwise! I want – no, I hope to find my father. I mean, I know he's *found* but it's not who he is, we already know that. It's the man I remember him being that I want. The money is nothing, it won't make any difference to me.'

Jack flicked the gearstick and slowed for the horse-paddock gate, ignoring her protestations. 'It will,' he said quietly, 'and you're kidding yourself if you think otherwise.'

38

It was late afternoon when they pulled up at the gate of the Redhill homestead, the western sun raying in behind them to light the dusty oleander bushes and the spectacle of Becky rushing down the front steps, arms and improvised pinny flying.

'Hello, Sara! Hi, Uncle Jack! You'll never guess what I'm doing! Mum's helping me fix Nan's cake up. It's a special thank you cake 'cause she's going home tomorrow. Pops is coming to pick her up. Come and see, Sara.'

'Yeah, I know, Squirt,' Jack interposed. 'Has your mum got the kettle on? We're dry as lizards.' He reached into the back to swing Sara's bag down, belting off the dust in a red cloud.

Sara nodded. 'Okay, chicken, I'm coming. I'm grateful for all the driving and your company, Jack. I don't think I could have done it alone. Certainly not the driving.'

'Well, you were wise not to head off with that twit Markham. He might be a good journo but he's a damned liability in the bush. It's been a rough coupla days for you, but at least you know now.'

'Yes.' The hat wouldn't fit over the hair grip so she stood with her head angled to keep her face from the sun, which lit coppery gold lights amid her curls. She drew a breath. 'For better or worse, I know. And heaps of little things have come back to me since. Feeding the lambs with bottles, and playing under a hose somewhere in a garden, stuff like that. Come on then, Becky. How's Sam?'

Sam was doing well. *Making strides* was how Beth described it as she turned from making tea to hug Sara. 'The kids are just off to get the goats,' she reminded Becky. 'Go on then. I'm just making a cuppa for the travellers, you won't be getting anything to eat this late in the day.'

Helen greeted Sara with a hand laid against her cheek. 'How are you, my dear? And how's Frank doing?'

'He's okay, Helen. And so am I, thanks.'

'But I've got *heaps* of things to tell Sara —' Becky complained.

'You can tell her later. Off you go,' Beth said firmly. Pouring tea and reverting to Sam, she added, 'I really think he might have turned a corner, you know? It's just little things I've noticed since we got home. The reading glasses seem to be helping him. He hasn't had a headache since he got them, so he can do more and it seems to tire him less. His appetite's better too. But enough of Sam. We want to hear what the outcome of your trip was, don't we, Mum?'

'We do,' the older woman asserted. 'Frank rang, but all he'd say was that you were back and had remembered it all, which left us no wiser. So,' she folded her hands on the tabletop, 'we're listening.'

The goats had been yarded by the time Sara finished speaking. She pressed her lips together for a long moment and sighed. 'So that's it, and right now I honestly can't tell if knowing is better or worse. But I'll always be grateful for Jack's help in finding out.' She turned to look at him where he stood sipping tea by the door. He made a dismissive gesture. 'No, I mean it, Jack. It's been scary but having a Ketch in my corner throughout has meant a lot. A Ketch in each corner really, and I thank you all for it.'

Helen patted her hand. 'To have to relive all that! You poor thing. There are parts of life we'd all love to revisit but once through the mill with all that is quite enough.'

'So you're really Christine?' Beth shook her head, bemused.

'I'd rather stick with Sara,' Sara said quickly.

'Well, of course – but JC Randall! He could buy Redhill with his loose change and it turns out his daughter is here, slaving away for us on a governess's wage.' She looked suddenly glum. 'I expect you'll be going now though. I'm really, really going to miss you, Sara. And Becky will be heartbroken.'

'She won't, because I'm not leaving until school ends. I'm not making any plans before then.' Sara hesitated. 'If you don't mind, I'd rather you didn't mention any of this to anyone.'

'Of course not,' Beth said. 'You want to meet him first, don't you? It must be a daunting prospect after so long. I imagine adopted children feel the same way about their biological parents.'

'Yes.' Sara stood. 'Well, it's what, Thursday? I'd better have a quick look in the schoolroom before I shower.'

'Don't bother, and it's Friday. You've lost a day.' Beth began clearing the cups. 'There's a cricket match and a barbecue on at the roadhouse tomorrow. We thought we'd all go in with Mum, have a day out. Could you bear to face the road again so soon?'

'Oh, why not? The road's pretty good really, compared to the one out to Kings Canyon. But two kids and five adults, are we all going to fit?'

'We'll take two vehicles; the kids can ride with me,' Jack said. His smile was wry. 'That's gotta be a first for the mulga. A city gal who thinks the road's not bad.'

'Well, it isn't.' Sara was stung by the appellation. Since she'd arrived she had made it a point of honour not to complain about anything, so the remark was unfair. Did he think she secretly scorned his country now that life might take her from it? Could that be what he had meant when he said her father's wealth would change her? Ignoring him she turned to Helen. 'We went into Arkeela this morning. I just loved your garden. It's like a little oasis when you come upon it. And it was a treat to see so much grass everywhere. Oh, and I must remember to tell the kids – I saw some wild camels and brumbies too.'

Helen's brows rose. 'Not on Arkeela, I hope?'

'No. The camels we saw on the way out to the canyon, the brumbies coming back. I was so thrilled.'

'They're a pest,' Helen observed. 'Still, I'm glad you had the chance to see them. There've been so many changes out here over the last few years. Who knows? There might well be no wildlife left for Sam's kids to look at. Even the pest kind.'

'I doubt there's much danger of that,' Jack observed darkly and headed off.

The cricket match was kicking off at mid-morning, according to Beth. 'Though that's just a sort of early warning call,' she explained, twisting around to look at Sara and Helen, who were seated in the back of the station wagon. 'Not everybody will have turned up by then but they'll be right to kick off around eleven.'

'Surely there aren't enough players for two teams?' Sara tried to count the number of men she had previously met. 'Does old Bungy play too?'

Beth grinned. 'You bet. And numbers aren't important. Anything over five a side is good. Dad'll be there too, so that's an extra. And Clemmy said something about a lad working at the park – there's another.'

'Nick,' Sara remembered. 'Yes, I'd forgotten he was still there. Though he'll probably want to photograph the game, not play it.'

Beth ignored the comment. 'She's pregnant, you know. Clemmy. Colin must be thrilled.'

'She told me. Actually I guessed and she confirmed it. Are the Hazlitts coming, and what about old Harry? Is he driving the mail again yet?'

'He is, silly old sod,' Len answered. 'He went through yesterday. The bone in his thumb was smashed but he reckons he can handle it. He's carrying an extra spare tyre as insurance.'

'Will Sam play?' Sara asked.

Beth shook her head. 'Maybe a bit of fielding, ten minutes or so. I don't want him exhausted and I hope to God nobody turns up with a cold. I can't remember when we took him out last. So we might be leaving early, Sara, but if you want to stay on you can always come home with Jack.'

Sara nodded. 'I'm just glad nobody expects me to join in. It's November, you know. And something about *mad dogs and Englishmen* springs irresistibly to mind.'

'They're playing in Adelaide,' Len put in unexpectedly, 'and Darwin. Summer's the time for cricket.'

'I know, Len.' Smiling, Sara met his eyes in the mirror. 'But they invented it in England too, didn't they? That's okay. Every match needs its barrackers. I'll sit in the shade and clap for you.'

It was extraordinary, Sara thought, getting out of the car at the roadhouse, how much and how little had changed since she first set eyes on Charlotte Creek. The barren flat and sun-blistered houses were the same and nothing about the roadhouse had changed – perhaps a little more red dust had accumulated on the fuel sign – but it no longer felt alien, only welcoming. Mavis, serving Sara's drink, asked how she'd enjoyed her trip into the Alice, and Bungy, a beer stubby in his large fist, bellowed a greeting. Rinky and her sister Flo had their heads together but paused to ask how she had been, and Clemmy, eyes sparkling, waved her over to a corner table near the fan. Colin was with her and sprang up to get another chair, insisting that his wife keep her feet up on the only empty one at the table.

'Go and have a drink with Len, why don't you, Colin?' Clemmy said. 'Go on, I'm fine. Honestly.' She whipped her feet down the moment he turned away. 'He's driving me crazy! You'd think I was made of porcelain and due to give birth tomorrow.'

Sara laughed. 'You look very fit to me. How's the whole baby thing going?'

'I've never felt better, except for Colin's fussing. So you had a trip to town, I hear. Have you decided to grow your hair, then?'

'Not as such.' She had gathered it into a ponytail, low on her neck, to accommodate her hat. 'Short notice and a quick trip. I couldn't get an appointment.'

'Well.' Clemmy observed her, head on one side. 'I like it and judging by the notice when you came in the blokes do too. You haven't done any modelling, have you? I know I kidded you about it the other day, but seriously? You've got the looks and the height for it, and your hair does make you stand out.'

Sara grimaced. 'You could say so, especially when I was at school. So, have you been thinking about baby names at all, or is it too early yet?'

The red herring worked and they fell into an animated discussion that was broken into by Colin returning to tell his wife that the match was about to start, but she would be more comfortable inside with the fan than out in the dust.

'I'm fine, dear.' She waved him off and lifted a brow at Sara. 'You want to come out and watch? It's not far, just this side of the racecourse. Alec will have put the chairs out and there's a bit of a bough shed for shade.'

'If you want to,' Sara said.

Clemmy rose with alacrity. 'Come on, then. I've done my stint as a hothouse flower for today. How long till school breaks up?'

'Just a few weeks now.'

'Then you leave – will you come back next year?'

'I suppose it depends,' Sara said slowly.

'On the drought, you mean?'

'There's that.' If it hadn't rained by the end of January, would the Calshots still be able to afford to pay wages? 'But there's Sam too. Maybe he'll be well enough soon, to stop the chemo. That would be wonderful, only Beth could manage without me then.' Sara shrugged. 'I'll just have to wait and see.'

They found chairs under the bough-covered shed, which, Sara saw, was a timber framework layered with netting and freshly cut gum foliage – from the banks of Charlotte Creek, presumably. A fitful breeze blew through the wilting leaves and wafted the refreshing scent of eucalyptus over the little group of onlookers.

'This is the life.' Clemmy wriggled toes free of their sandals, then brought her hands together for a fielder. 'Oh, good catch, Nick! Who's in next?'

'It's Bungy,' Flo said. 'I hope one of the kids is going to run for him. The old fool'll drop dead if he tries it.'

'The team could use the runs,' Sara observed. Jack was bowling and they had already lost three of their five players. 'Can he use a bat?'

Flo snorted with sisterly contempt. '*He* thinks so. Ah!' A ball soared like an eagle from the bat. 'Young Joey's going to do it. I see Sam's out there, Beth. So he's doing okay for the moment?'

'I'm just about to call him in,' Beth said. 'But yes, thank you, he is. This is his first outing in more than a year.'

Flo reached a work-roughened hand to pat the younger woman's thigh. 'He'll make it, love. Don't you fret. He's a tough little kid. Well, colour me purple!' Another ball flew off her brother's bat. 'There's another six. The old boy *is* in good form today.'

Bungy's run of luck, which owed as much to a steady hand as an obvious arrangement with his runner not to leave his partner exposed to Jack's arm, lasted until Alec declared the barbecue ready. Bungy had half-a-dozen boundaries to his credit by then and was the toast of his side as the crowd milled around serving themselves from the long table set under the hall roof. It was much hotter there than the bough shed had been, and Clemmy and Sara carried their plates into the roadhouse to join Sam, who was spread out on the floor in front of the fan, reading a dog-eared comic.

They had finished eating when Helen came in to say goodbye, competent and unfussed as ever, hazel eyes warm with concern for Sara. 'Frank's just finishing a beer,' she explained, 'then we'll be off. Now, let us know, won't you, how you get on with everything? And remember, anytime you're in the Alice you're to come and stay. Beth'll bring the kids down for the school break-up, but you'll be very welcome when you're heading off south too.'

'Thank you, Helen. I'll miss you – and Frank. I'll come and say goodbye to him. And I'll be back if I can. I'm going to miss you both so much. And Redhill when I leave at the end of term.'

Helen's glance was shrewd. 'There's always next year. We'll have to wait and see how things pan out. I hope it's how you want it to. We'll be thinking of you anyway.' Her arms enfolded the younger woman. Sara felt the warmth of her embrace, caught the scent of her talc and hugged her back fiercely.

Frank, when they found him in the throng, said, 'Come 'ere, you skinny thing,' and hugged her too. The kiss he planted on her cheek was flavoured with his beery breath. She stood with Beth and Jack to wave them off, watching the little red car dwindle in size down the straight stretch of bitumen.

Jack blew out a breath. 'Well, we've still got a match to win. Not that I like our chances much.'

'Neither do I,' Sara said frankly. 'I wonder if the Australian Cricket Board knows about Bungy? He could be their new secret weapon for the next international match.'

Jack laughed. 'Anybody can be bowled out. Just not always soon enough. But that's life.'

39

Jack's prophecy proved correct. Bungy's side had stacked too many runs for the other team, whose batsmen were quickly taken out. Jack himself scored five and Rinky's husband Jim was out for a duck. With the game over, the Calshots took their leave mid-afternoon, Sara riding in the back of the station wagon with the children. Jack, who always carried his tools, remained behind to take a look at the diesel motor on the roadhouse bore, which Alec had been unable to start. 'Probably nothing major,' he told them. 'Christ, that bloke's so useless with engines he couldn't tell a right-hand thread from a left. If it's nothing much, I'll be home later tonight. Otherwise they'll find me a bed and I'll be back when I am.'

The Marshalls followed them home, peeling off with a fanfare on the horn at the horse-paddock gate for the back road past Kileys bore. Sara waved at the departing car and settled back in her seat with a yawn.

'It was lovely to see Clemmy again. She looks so well. Colin is really sweet with her, though I hate to think what he'll be like in the delivery room.'

'Why?' Becky predictably asked.

'Mrs Marshall's going to have a baby,' Beth said. 'Sometime next year.'

'Cool. Can we go and see it when it's born?'

'We'll see. How are you doing there, Sam?'

'I'm okay, a bit tired. Did you know, Mum, that Joey's raising five poddies all by himself? Three of them are bull calves and if they make it through the drought, Mr Hazlitt said when they get sold Joey can keep the money for himself. He's gonna buy a new saddle with it.'

'Is he? Well, he'll have earned it.' Beth twisted in her seat to look at him. 'You do look a bit washed out. No more activity for you today, my lad. Becky will have to get the goats in alone.'

'I'll go with her,' Sara volunteered. 'Unless you want a hand with something?'

'No, that's fine. But only if you want to, Sara.'

'I do.' She smiled at Becky and gave the hand the girl had slipped into hers a little squeeze. 'I won't be able to much longer, so I'd best make the most of it while I'm still here.'

Becky looked dismayed. 'You aren't leaving us?'

'Not right away, chicken, but the holidays are coming. I'll have to go then. You don't want to be doing sums still at Christmas, do you?'

'No, but you could stay – can't she, Mum? I thought you were gonna be here always! I thought we'd have Christmas together. If it doesn't rain first, Uncle Jack's gonna build a special shed out at Kileys for us, and he said we'll make a tree out there, and tie wishes on it –' Her voice broke, she battled for a moment with a trembling lip, then burst into tears. 'I don't want you to go, Sara! You're my bestest friend.'

'And I still will be.' Sara met Beth's eyes in the mirror and raised helpless brows as Len slowed at the front gate. 'We'll always be friends and maybe I'll come back next year if your mum still needs me. Besides, I'm not leaving tomorrow. There's plenty of school time yet, and there's the break-up party and everything.'

'You mustn't be selfish, Becs,' Beth admonished gently. 'Sara has her own family, you know –' she caught Sara's urgent shake of the head and changed tack mid-sentence – 'and I'm sure she has other friends she'll want to see. And *they'll* want to see her too.'

Becky glared at her mother. 'She hasn't got any family either! Only her mum – and she doesn't like her. I heard her tell Nan so. So why would she want to stop with her?'

'Yes, but she might have found her father now.' Beth cast an apologetic look Sara's way. 'So you should try to be glad for her and hope that it's true. I know you're upset but Sara's life is hers to order.'

'How?' Becky ignored this and turned a demanding gaze on her governess. 'I'm not stupid! You can't just find fathers like that.'

'No, you can't,' Sara agreed, getting out. 'It's a strange story and I don't really know if he wants me yet, because it's a long time since he's seen me. Not since I was younger than you. Look, the sun's behind the mill already. Let's get after the goats and I'll tell you all about it, but you can't tell anyone else. Not Harry or Mrs Murray. You have to promise that first.'

'Okay. Does Uncle Jack know?' The lure of a story drove her tears away. 'Is it like the one about the dog and the little boy that you told me?'

'Uncle Jack does know. And it is, a bit. I forgot him for a long time, then I remembered, and it was the same with my dad. But get your hat first.'

Inexorably, more swiftly than Sara wished, her remaining time at Redhill flew by. The magpies' song marked off each dawn and the hot red line of the sunset each dusk. Jack, back from the roadhouse, worked with Len either bulldozing scrub, checking waters or doing the lick run about the bores. Both men came home with the smell of the drought on them – of dust and diesel and the sour whiff of smoke and death when there had been carcasses to handle. A week after the cricket match Jack and Sara sat together on the verandah, the first time they had been alone since their return from Arkeela. She suspected that he was deliberately avoiding her and the knowledge hurt. Silent and awkward for the first time in his company, she watched the lightning slash across the darkened sky. There was no rain, just the distant crackle and tear as jagged white lines zipped across the heavens.

'Dry storm,' he said abruptly as the last flicker died away.

'Yes.' Sara couldn't keep the disappointment from her voice.

'The rain'll come. One day.'

'I'm sure, but it's like the bowling now, isn't it? A matter of time.'

He sighed, neither agreeing nor arguing, and changed the subject. 'Have you thought about what you'll do when your story breaks? It can't be long now. Markham said they'd print it the moment your DNA results were known. You'll have reporters swarming all over.'

Sara frowned. 'What's the point? The story will already be out there. I should think they'd be more likely to chase my father than me.'

He grunted sardonically. 'They call it human interest, Sara. *How does it feel to know you're the daughter of a multimillionaire?* That sort of thing. We can lock the horse-paddock gate but the media are like vultures. A padlock won't stop them.'

'I don't know. Hide inside, I suppose. There's no law says I have to talk to them.'

'They don't give up that easy. What about when you leave? Becky said you are.'

'Well, obviously I must; another fortnight and school will finish and with it my job. I suppose I'll go and see him. My father,' she said slowly. 'He'll know by then. Paul must be able to tell me how to find him.'

'He might come to you, once he has proof. Why would he wait?'

She swallowed. 'I'm hoping he will but it's a big thing to do, isn't it? For him and for me. I'm scared he'll . . .'

'What?' Jack finally asked as the silence stretched.

In a small voice Sara said, 'Not want me.' He started to protest and she cut him off. 'Jack, he's already mourned and buried us – me, Benny, my mother. He's an old man. Why would he want it all back now? He's moved on, made another family. He's left the bush and all the memories behind. He must have wanted it so or why sell the stations? Paul said he had two but now he's into transport and commodities and other things. What if I'm just an unwelcome reminder of all the stuff he's left behind him?'

'He won't think that! And just supposing for a single moment that he did, he's still human, which makes him curious. Of *course* he'll want to see you, Sara. You're his flesh and blood.'

'I don't know.'

He said roughly, 'I thought you were smarter than that. How long have you been thinking this rubbish?'

Sara shrugged in the darkness, which made it easy to lie. 'It just occurred to me today.'

She had grappled with it every night since her memory returned, her emotions on a roller-coaster of dread, excitement and apprehension, because what if the golden-armed man she remembered had turned into an indifferent stranger who, at best, found her presence tiresome? It was why she hadn't wanted Beth to assume, as she had, that Sara would be flying home to family life once she left Redhill. You might wish that loved ones hadn't died, and cry for their return, but time had a way of stitching closed the holes they left in life. What if this was the case with her father when they met? Her half-siblings too – could they be expected to welcome a cuckoo in the nest? What would the son think; he must consider himself heir to the Randall business empire. Not that she had the least expectation or interest, but would a seventeen-year-old believe that? She sighed and lied again. 'I expect you're right. It was just a thought. Which reminds me – are you coming in for the school break-up? We've been practising all week for the concert.'

'No.' He sounded indifferent. 'The kids'll have to give me a private show sometime. I'll be needed here to run the waters while you're all gone.'

'Unless it rains first.' Her disappointment at Jack's words bit deeply. Sara turned her gaze to the starry, cloud-free night where a mopoke was making its distinctive call. She heard him snort as he rose.

'I don't believe in the tooth fairy. 'Night, Sara.'

'Goodnight, Jack.'

She didn't believe in much that was magical either, right at the moment. She could feel the closeness, the bond that had been between them, loosening and slipping away. It was her background, of course. She had been hopelessly naive to think that he would ever overlook it. It was just too much to expect after his experience with Marilyn. Men seemed to be universally stupid once they got an idea into their heads. Dynamite wouldn't shift it. Roger had been living proof of that in the way he'd determinedly clung to the unrealistic image of herself he'd created. Jack, it seemed, was prone to the same failing. He was fond of her but he wouldn't allow himself to take it further. City-bred Marilyn, damn her avaricious soul, had seen to that.

Sighing – it seemed to be the night for it – Sara turned away from the stars she had come to watch and went to her room to lie wakeful under the fan's cooling breath. It was ironic to feel this restless yearning for change when she actually dreaded leaving the secure cocoon that Redhill had become. As she must, and very soon, too. She was, she realised, sick of being alone, sick of sleeping alone, of having no one but herself to think of.

Once she had believed that regaining her memory would free her from the shadows of the past but it had only compounded them, introducing new worries of rejection. And soon, if Jack was right – and if Jack had a strength, it was his steadiness of vision and purpose, so he probably was right – soon she would be the object of a media scrum as well. Misery flooded Sara; she almost wished she were Becky and could relieve her feelings in a storm of tears. Better to think productively instead, about finding another job, for instance. Because whatever happened with her father, she was going to need one. Perhaps there would be something for her in the Alice? Then if Beth should still need her after the holidays she would be only a bus ride away . . .

Sara dreamed of a faceless horde of people who chased her down narrow streets past shuttered houses whose doors, when she banged on them for admittance, were all barred. Her pursuers shouted questions she couldn't understand and Paul seemed to be leading the pack. She ran desperately, bursting out through the graffiti-covered walls of an alley into a park that became a paddock as she ran. There was a creek and the grey swathes of mulga, then the oleanders and the blessed sanctuary of the front gate. Sara ran up the steps into her bedroom and the rain blossomed behind her, greying out the paddock and the pursuing hordes, who melted away, their shouted questions lost in the whirr of the fan.

Heart thumping, gasping for breath, Sara sat up in bed and fumbled for the light. A sweet, heady fragrance filled the room, then as understanding broke upon her she jumped up to switch off the fan and listen. Surely not? But it was. There came a pattering on the iron roof, and the smell filling the night air was that of rain. She stumbled through the French doors onto the verandah and saw that the stars had vanished behind a layer of thin cloud through which a crescent moon glowed, thin as a nail paring. She caught her breath, willing the rain to fall.

'Please, oh please!' It was a prayer, but even as the words formed, the light spatter of drops ceased, leaving only the aching of hope deferred. The clouds parted fully about the moon and the night seemed to sigh its hopelessness and defeat. Then the wind came whooshing out of the west and half an hour later the sky was clear again.

'I dreamed it rained,' Sara said at breakfast. 'Then I woke up and it was, about five spots' worth.'

'Six,' Jack said. 'I counted. You musta missed one.'

'It's a start,' Len observed. 'There might've been more to the north. I'll give Dumben Downs a call later. God, it smelled good for a moment there.' The phone rang as he spoke and he went to answer it.

'Somebody with the same idea,' Beth said, hearing him greet the caller by name. 'That's Munaroo. Everybody will be phoning round to see who got lucky.'

The next ring, however, had him popping his head out the office door. 'It's for you, Sara.'

Swallowing a sudden trepidation, Sara took the handpiece. 'Hello? Sara here.'

It was Paul Markham, his voice brisk. 'Sara. How are you? Just to let you know the test results are back. I faxed them to Randall last night and the story's in today's paper. He'll have to have his own DNA tested for comparison but you can expect to hear from him pretty soon. I imagine he won't be queuing at the lab.'

So now it would begin. On the plus side, Sara thought, pulling her thoughts into order as she hung up, her father knew that his eldest daughter existed. The test results would surely stall any immediate repudiation of the claim. Where did he live anyway? Melbourne? Sydney? She should have asked Paul. Sara relied on television for her information; she had seldom read more of the daily news than the headlines displayed in the cage outside the newsagents'. Tonight it would all be on the telly, she thought, and then the whole world would know. She said as much to the others as she clattered her cup and plate together, her appetite wholly gone.

Beth glanced up, brown eyes bright. 'Right then, we'd best prepare to repel borders. I'll ring Clemmy to prepare her in case the place really does come under siege. I'm sure she'd have you stay until they clear off again. Hopefully he won't actually have written that you're here.'

'He promised he wouldn't, but there'll be pictures of me. Not much chance the locals won't see or recognise them.'

'Doesn't mean they'll tell,' Jack said. 'People like you, Sara, and nothing gets up bush folks' noses quicker than pushy city types.'

Whether he was right or not the day passed without visitors. The midday news carried the story but in an understated fashion. There had been an unverified claim that a woman said to be the lost daughter of the business tycoon JC Randall had regained her memory, purportedly lost during the abduction believed to have cost herself and her twin brother their lives twenty-one years earlier. Mr Randall had been unavailable for comment but an insider had brushed the claim aside. It wasn't the first time it had been made, she had said, and given the scurrilous nature of certain elements of the press, it probably wouldn't be the last.

Beth turned the switch and raised a brow at Sara. 'So far so good.'

'What does it mean, Mum? Who are they talking about?' Becky asked. 'You didn't get the weather. Dad always does.'

'Well, I expect he'll listen on the Toyota wireless, then.'

'Did you really forget *everything*?' Sam asked curiously. 'Wouldn't that be sorta weird?'

'It was. And very –' Sara searched for a way to describe it – 'dislocating. Like not being able to find bits of yourself. You don't know who you are, you see.'

His eyes, so like his mother's, regarded her seriously. 'I'm glad you found out, then. Is that man they were talking about your father?'

'Yes, he is. But he doesn't know me and I don't know him – not yet anyway.'

'Will you go and see him?'

'When the holidays get here, if he wants to see me.'

'Well, if he doesn't,' he said firmly, 'you can come back here, can't she, Mum?'

'Of course she can, Sara knows that, I hope,' Beth said. 'But he will, just wait and see.'

Sara's eyes suddenly filled at both her kindness and her certainty. Seeing it, her employer patted her hand, adding, 'Now, come on, kids, eat up. You've got to get your acts perfect this arvo. Uncle Jack said he wants to hear them, seeing he won't be with us for the concert.'

40

Their first visitor after the news broke was Harry, stumping up the kitchen steps, mailbag in hand. He nodded to Sara saying, 'Nobody found yer yet, then?'

'You're our first visitor in a week,' Beth answered. 'Why?'

'Just wondered. Had a city bloke round my place askin' questions. How many stations did I go ter on me run? Were there any redheaded women on 'em? He wanted ter book a ride for today but I told him I was full up.'

'Thank you, Harry.' Sara poured his tea. 'A reporter, you think?'

'Well, he had one of them little recordin' things sticking outta his pocket. 'Course it won't stop him hirin' a car if he's fair dinkum about findin' yer.' He nodded, chewing on a biscuit. 'I remember when yer went missin', you know. Fact is I carted a load of horse feed out for the copper's nags when the search was on. And now here you are.'

Sara turned her cup about and studied him afresh. 'That's amazing!' A thought occurred to her. 'Did you see my parents at all?'

His faded eyes were kindly. 'Forgotten them, have yer? No, lass, I never set eyes on 'em. Musta been near a hundred people out there by then. They'd dragged the army in to help. So I expect you'll be headin' orf to the big smoke to see your dad, now?'

'After next week,' she agreed, unwilling to pursue further a subject on which her decision changed at least twice a day.

'Which reminds me,' Beth broke in. 'There'll be nobody home next Friday, so you can leave the bag on the verandah. Jack'll be here but probably out. The rest of us will be in town, it's school break-up.'

'And me and Sam are gonna sing, Harry,' Becky said, adding with satisfaction, 'Uncle Jack said we're really good. You wanna hear us?'

'Perhaps not right now,' Sara said hastily. 'If you don't run and feed the chickens, you'll be late for lessons.' A broody hen had hatched out a clutch of eggs, much to Becky's delight, and she leapt to her feet at the reminder.

'Glass in the sink, please,' Beth said but the door banged and she spoke to the empty air.

The weekend was spent packing and making lists. They would do their usual Christmas shopping and store order while they were in town, Beth said. They were to travel on Monday. School events would occupy the following three days, culminating in the concert on Thursday evening, and on Friday Sam would have his next hospital visit. Sara and the other governesses would be in attendance at the school activities, leaving Beth three days to get through her list of things to buy and do.

'It's always a marathon job,' she confided. 'Other years I've left the kids with Rinky on alternate days, and then she's left hers with me, to give us both time up town. It'll be a boon having you there.' She paused before asking, 'No word from your father yet?'

'No.' The mail had brought a copy of Paul's story spread over two pages with pictures and black headlines that announced: *Decades-old Mystery Solved. Millionaire's Kidnapped Daughter Found.* Paul had written a coherent and detailed story of the kidnapping of the twins. The only speculation it contained was that they had been taken for ransom – a safe enough assumption, she thought, lacking evidence to the contrary. He had described Benny's abandonment by Vic Blake just as Sara had remembered it, together with a graphic description of the desolate country in which the little boy had died. There was no mention of Paul's part in Sara's recovery of her memory or of her present whereabouts, beyond briefly noting that in an ironic twist she had unknowingly returned to her outback roots, and was currently employed on a remote cattle property in the Northern Territory. A side bar to the piece added that South Australian police were currently seeking Stella Blake in connection with an alleged kidnapping in the seventies.

'It's a good pic of you,' Beth had observed, studying it.

'Nick took it. Colin's offsider at the park. He wants to be a professional photographer.'

'Well, he's got the talent.' Beth laid the paper aside and returned to checking cupboards.

Monday morning Jack left before them, carrying his lunch. He patted Sam's shoulder and staggered a little from Becky's exuberant clutch as she hugged him round the waist. 'Bye, Uncle Jack. I wish you were coming too.'

'Can't be helped, Squirt. What's Jess gonna do without me? And your nags and the goats and the chooks? This place is a flaming zoo. Have fun. Goodbye, Sara. I hope it all turns out for you. If a message comes for you, I'll ring it through to Mum.'

'Thank you, Jack.' The sun was touching the back steps where he had paused on his way out, lighting one side of his face, casting brow line and nose in stern relief. He didn't smile and the grey eyes were inscrutable.

Every fibre of Sara's being cried out for her to embrace him but his stance subtly forbade it. It was as if a stranger stood there in his boots, somebody she didn't know at all, and certainly not the man in whose arms she had wept for her brother. After the slightest hesitation she offered her hand.

'And thank you for all your help; I'll never forget you – any of you,' she hastened, feeling panic overwhelm her. Couldn't he at least smile or say something? Once they had shared companionable silences but there was no sense of sharing now, just an awful feeling of constraint. As they shook hands she felt as embarrassed as a gauche schoolgirl with a crush on the new teacher.

'Safe journey,' he said, and like that, with an abrupt turn, he was gone.

Beth, already clearing the table, sent a puzzled look after his retreating form and shot a swift glance at Sara. 'Something wrong?'

'Of course not,' she said hastily, picking up the nearest dish. 'Look, leave the cleaning up to me, I'm already packed so I've nothing else to do.' And it gave her an excuse to hide her face over the sink.

Jack couldn't, she thought miserably, have made it much plainer that her leaving meant nothing to him at all. She was just another governess to him, one of several who had worked at Redhill.

'Well, if you're sure . . .' Unconvinced but too distracted to pursue the subject, Beth clapped her hands. 'Right, kids, we've no time to waste. I want your rooms tidied first. Then you can fill the horses' feed buckets, Becky, and Sam, you might put the hoses away. Let's make things as easy as we can for your uncle. He'll have heaps to do while we're gone.'

The road trip passed for Sara in a waking dream. She gazed upon the barren landscape, remembering how alien and unwelcoming it had once seemed. Would she ever see it softened by the benison of rain, with water in the table drains and the bare bones of the land cloaked by a coverlet of green? Would she ever know the fullness of the vision that Jack had once painted for her – of whirling flocks of budgies rising from grassy plains; of the ducks that came to the filled claypans that for a week or two after rain reflected the sky; of paper daisies flowering through the mulga? She would miss it all, and the hardy people with whom she had shared the past few months. And it wasn't just Jack, she realised. She really wanted to know how they would all fare – whether Sam's quiet courage would prevail over his illness, what the gender of Clemmy's baby would be, whether the walls of the Charlotte Creek hall would ever be built . . .

'You're very quiet, Sara.' Beth caught her eye in the driving mirror. 'You're not a bad traveller, are you?'

'Just thinking, that's all.'

'Of course.' She nodded understandingly. 'He knows where you are, though. He'll call soon.'

'Who, Mum?' It was Becky, of course – always with the questions.

'Sara's dad.'

'Cool.' The child turned a rapt gaze upon Sara. 'Can I meet him? I want to tell him I'm sorry about his little boy dying – the one you used to play with.'

'Do you, chicken? That's nice of you.' Sara gave her a hug and herself a mental shake. Life went on regardless of heartbreak. 'What about I-spy? Only with proper rules, mind. Because we can't guess about something that's already fifty k behind us.'

'She does that all the time,' Sam agreed smugly.

'Do not!'

'Okay, I'll start,' Beth interposed peaceably. 'I spy with my little eye . . .'

In the Alice they stayed with Helen and Frank, the former overriding Sara's feeble objection that she was one too many and could easily go to a hotel.

'The kids are here,' Beth pointed out. 'So this way's simpler, and cheaper because as your employer I'd be responsible for your accommodation.'

Sara was horrified. 'Of course I'd pay for myself! I didn't mean —'

'That's all right. I know you didn't. Do stay. We'll be losing you soon enough as it is.'

Sara gave in. 'Okay. Thank you. I'd love to.'

It wasn't Beth's intention, however tempting, to expose Sam to the communal school life of the next three days.

'Too much danger of infection. He's sure to pick up something from one of the kids,' Beth said. 'We'll chance the concert and Mum'll take him out when she can. Dad said he'll drop you and Becky off wherever – the school or the swimming pool – and collect you again. You'll be home by three p.m. each day, so if you want to make a salon appointment, or do some shopping, Dad can drive you there, too. You just have to say.'

'That's great.' Sara eyed her now shabby hat. 'I think a haircut for starters; a new hat wouldn't go amiss either. And I'll have to check up on the job possibilities here. It seems like a nice little town. I might stay, if there's work.'

'Oh, but won't your fath–' Beth bit her lip. 'Sorry, not really my business.'

'I don't know,' Sara replied to the half-spoken assumption. 'But I can't assume anything at this stage. And that being so, it seems best to carry on as if nothing has changed. So I'll need a job.'

'Of course. Well, Mum's got a cuppa going. Let's have that and then get settled in.'

Tuesday was busy but Sara made an appointment at The Hair Place and duly emerged feeling much lighter. She ruffled her clipped curls for Frank, who was waiting for her outside, and struck a pose. 'What do you think?'

'Pretty damn stunning, young lady. Shows off your neck. You've got a very elegant neck, if you don't mind my saying so.'

She smiled at him. 'Why, thank you, Frank. You can compliment me as much as you like.'

He harrumphed, hunching his shoulder. 'Somebody with sense oughta. That son of mine's a damn fool.'

Sara flushed, didn't pretend to misunderstand him. She said sadly, 'From what I understand he was warned against making one mistake and still went ahead and did it. The way that turned out, you can hardly expect him to repeat it.'

He snorted. 'Well, that makes as much sense as nothing. You mean if a brown mare kicks me, I should only ride chestnuts after that? She was a mean-spirited woman, Marilyn, out for what she could get. Wouldn'ta mattered where she'd been raised, that's how she was. She couldn't come within a hundred miles of you.'

'It's his decision to make, Frank. Let's talk about something else. Like, could you bear it if I looked at the shops for a bit?'

'You take your time. In fact, what if you start and I shoot home and get young Bec? She's got a bit of pocket money to spend on Christmas presents. Maybe you could help each other decide.'

Sara grinned. 'So you don't get dragged in, you mean?'

'Something like that. I get enough of that with my wife.'

Wednesday was sports day, with the children divided into houses and then age groups. Becky was in yellow house, identified with a sash of that colour, and milled about excitedly with her peers while the events unfolded. Sara found Rinky and Flo Morgan amid the parents and was surprised to see Clemmy as well, ensconced in a chair amid the spectators.

'I didn't expect to see you here,' she said, taking the seat beside her. 'Are you well?'

'Blooming, thanks. We're doing our Christmas shop like everybody else. I ran into the Garritys at the supermarket, and the Pinchens are in the next unit to ours at the motel. So is it true, Sara, all that stuff on the news? They're all talking about it – you being the lost heiress the papers are on about?'

Sara grimaced at the media's latest description of her. She had been recognised in the hair salon, and forced to rehash the story of her memory loss and upbringing when Beth had introduced her to both Mrs Murray and the principal of the School of the Air, both of them Territorians who remembered the kidnapping. The one aspect of her history that had the greatest grip on the public imagination, she had discovered, was the fact that she had been raised by one of her kidnappers. 'I wish they wouldn't call me that, but yes, the basics are true. I fell and hit my head after I was kidnapped and that caused amnesia. I only began to remember things after I got to Redhill, but it took an investigative journalist to put it all together. I grew up believing that my kidnappers were my parents. I seem to have been explaining that ever since the story broke.'

'And your twin brother died,' Clemmy said sympathetically, ignoring the hint in this last sentence. 'How horrible! Your mother too. So when will you meet your dad? Can you remember him at all?'

'Not much,' she said honestly. 'I'm flying off to try to track him down next week.' The decision to do so had coalesced seemingly of its own accord last night, following a long phone call with Paul Markham. 'He's in Sydney. At least, that's where he lives. He could actually be anywhere. Paul, the journalist that helped me, said he travels a good bit. He has overseas interests, apparently.'

'The whole thing's amazing,' Clemmy said. 'Everybody's talking about it. Should I be calling you Christine now? Or Chrissy, the way the papers do?'

'No. I'm keeping Sara. I'll have to change my surname eventually I suppose, but for the time being I'm still using Blake. It's on my driver's licence, my Medicare card, my bank account . . . Anyway, that's for later. How do you like my new hat?'

Clemmy grinned. 'Very much. You look a proper bushie now, or you would if you weren't so pale. I suppose with your colouring you never tan?'

'I can do red but that's all.' Sara removed the bone-coloured Akubra to examine it afresh. 'At least it stays on. With the straw one I was fighting every bit of breeze. The kids are keen on it anyway.'

Jack would have approved too, she thought, sighing. Clemmy heard and her focus sharpened.

'Are you okay?'

'Yes. Just a bit sad to be leaving, that's all. I've got fond of the kids and I think of you all as my friends – you and Helen and Beth, Len and Jack. I'll miss you all. What about young Nick? Has he finished up too?'

'Yes. He'd be happy to stay on but it's not up to us of course. You know the paper used that pic he took of you? He's really chuffed. Sees it as the start of his new life, apparently.'

'I live but to serve,' Sara quipped dryly, standing up. 'Maybe he should come to the concert and photograph it? Becky's waving. I'd better go see what she wants.'

41

Sara was frankly amazed at how well the concert turned out. The children had managed only two complete rehearsals in the time available. All had learned their parts separately but when the curtain went up on the show, the production came together easily.

'They're good,' she remarked to Beth who, like her, was clapping wholeheartedly as the cast crowded onto the stage at the end.

'Yes, they really throw themselves into it.' Beth's gaze was on her son, whose thin frame and bald head made him easy to spot. He bent at the waist, one arm before and the other behind him, awkward as the rest of them as they bowed to their audience. 'I'm so glad Sam was able to take part. He's missed so much through his illness. I'm taking him home now – no sense pushing our luck. Will you stay? Santa's coming later. You could collect Sam's present for him. Mum and Dad'll wait for Becky so you could ride back with them after the barbecue.'

'Okay. Tell Sam his present's safe with me. This will give me a chance to say goodbye to everyone.'

Beth got up. 'Horrible word! I don't like to think about you leaving.'

It was going to happen though, and soon. Tomorrow Sara would book her flight to Sydney and find accommodation there. She couldn't just rock up at her father's house and expect to be taken in, particularly if he was away and his wife came to the door. Of course it wouldn't happen like that. She would ring first, tell them she was coming. Would the second Mrs Randall welcome her or see her as a threat to her own children? She found herself wishing yet again that her father was just an ordinary man, with a wage and a mortgage like everyone else. It would make things so much simpler for all concerned.

After Santa's visit – he had arrived, fittingly, in the prime mover of a road train – and the mayhem of cheering and present-opening that followed, Sara joined Becky, Helen, and Jim and Rinky Hazlitt at one of the long tables set up on the school lawn for the evening meal.

'Bit different?' Jim asked. He was a lean slab of a man who normally had little to say for himself, perhaps because Rinky talked enough for two.

'Very,' Sara agreed. 'Wonderful though. Whose idea was the road train?'

'They try for something different each year,' he said. 'Snow and sleighs don't cut it much with our kids.'

'I guess not.' Neither, she imagined, would formal meals in a hall – not that a school without classrooms would have any use for such a gathering point. The stars were paler here above the town's lights but many were still visible and, glancing upwards, Sara thought that however her life turned out, she would always remember this night – Becky's joyful face and the aroma of roasting meat and the chatter of friends. The town was fairly quiet, the traffic noises muted by distance. A child with a Native American headdress whooped in circles brandishing a plastic tomahawk, and there was a faint wild tang on the breeze, from fires burning on the ranges surrounding the Alice.

Later, back at the house, Sara delivered Sam's gift to him in bed and she and his parents watched him rip it open. His eyes lit up at the sight of the chemistry set. 'Wow!' he cried, 'Thanks, Mum, Dad. Mrs Murray told me about some crazy experiments you can do with this stuff.'

'Just show some sense with it,' Len warned. 'No blowing things up. That apart, we're glad you like it, son.'

Sara winked at him. 'There's Christmas cake too. It's in the fridge.'

He grinned. 'Thanks, Sara. You're the best.'

'There's the phone.' Beth was rising from the bed. 'Okay, champ. Time you were asleep.' She kissed him and left. Sam lay back on his pillows, looking thin and spent.

'You were brilliant tonight,' Sara said softly. 'You all were. I never enjoyed a concert more. I'll see you in the morning. Good-night, Sam.'

''Night,' he said and yawned tremendously 'So tired,' he murmured as Len switched off the light.

'Big day for him,' he said gruffly, then Beth was calling her name.

'Jack.' Beth thrust the phone at Sara. 'He wants to speak to you.'

Joy surged through her and she took the handpiece. 'Jack, hello.' She could hear the sudden lilt in her voice and hastily turned her back on Beth to hide her face. 'How are things out there?'

'Pretty much the same. Kids having a good time?'

'Yes. I'm sorry you weren't here tonight. It was great. Everyone seems to be in town. What about you? What are you doing?'

His tone sounded flat and weary. 'All the usual stuff. Look, the reason I'm calling. Somebody from Randall's office phoned me earlier. Apparently they'd been trying to get me all day but I wasn't in. Your father's flying into the Alice tomorrow. He'll be at the Hilton anytime after midday, she said. Are you there, Sara?'

'I – yes.' She was suddenly breathless. 'Tomorrow, the Hilton. Who was it who rang?'

'His PA. Lillian Somebody. I didn't catch it. She said – here, hang on, I wrote it down. *Mr Randall will be pleased to meet his daughter if she cares to come to the Hilton. He expects to arrive in*

Alice Springs at noon, providing his flight suffers no delays. That's it. The DNA test must have decided him. *His daughter*, she said. So, you've finally got your life sorted out.'

'Yes,' she whispered. Only she hadn't. She had complicated it disastrously by falling in love with a man who didn't want her. The words were out before she thought. 'I'm scared, Jack. I wish you were here.'

'You'll be fine,' he said bracingly. 'Why would he even come, if he wasn't going to accept you? This time tomorrow night you'll wonder at yourself. This time next week you'll be living a fairytale. I've got to go now, Sara. Say hi to Mum and Dad for me, and take care of yourself. Bye.'

'Goodbye, Jack,' she said gently. She heard him hang up but continued to stand there, the silent phone pressed to her ear, picturing him leaving the office for the kitchen to wash up after his lonely meal. Or possibly to eat it, depending on what time he'd finished the many chores that would await him when he got in from the run.

'Everything all right, Sara?' Helen, passing, gave her an odd look.

'Yes.' She replaced the handset, concentrating on setting it straight before looking up to meet the woman's gaze. 'That is – I feel a bit – that was Jack with a message from my father. He's flying in tomorrow to meet me.' She lifted a hand to her face. 'I didn't – I'm —'

'Hornswoggled?' Helen suggested with a smile. 'That's marvellous, Sara!'

'And scary, and I don't feel ready,' she burst out.

'But come tomorrow you will be. It's a big thing, for you and for him. Trust me, he'll be every bit as hornswoggled himself! I would if, God forbid, I'd lost Beth the way he lost you. And believe this, no matter how long it had been, Frank and I would run barefoot over broken glass if we'd been given the chance he has, of finding a lost daughter.'

'I do.' Sara laughed tremulously, trying to calm her chaotic thoughts. 'Where did you get a word like that, anyway? What does it even mean?'

'Hornswoggled? I've no idea, but it sounds fitting. Come on. Frank's made tea. Let's have a cup before we sleep on the day. And tomorrow? Well, tomorrow you'll have your own family again.'

In the morning Sara woke foggy-headed, having lain wakeful for hours until she fell asleep, exhausted, some time after three a.m. The family was already at breakfast; Len had a list of businesses to visit, his bank manager among them, and Beth and her son were dressed for the day. Sam's appointment at the hospital was for nine. The station grocery order was ready. Frank had volunteered to pick it up, and would drop them both off before attending to his errands.

'Best of luck.' Beth touched Sara's shoulder. 'I'll hear all about it this afternoon. Be good, Becky.'

'I always am, aren't I?' The child appealed to Sara, who smiled and wrinkled her nose.

'Always?' said Sara.

'Mostly. Can I come with you to see your dad?'

'Maybe another time,' she said. 'You can help me pack though, if you like.' She bent to whisper in her ear. 'Can you keep a secret?'

''Course!' Becky's eyes widened and she shot a careful look at her grandmother, her own whisper sibilant. 'What sorta secret?'

'You'll see. Come on.'

Once in her room with her bag on her bed, Sara produced two small parcels tied with ribbon. 'Can you hide these in your clothes and smuggle them home? They're gifts for your mum and dad. You might give them to your uncle to keep for you till Christmas. You can tell him,' she cautioned, 'but nobody else. Okay?'

'Cross my heart and hope to die,' Becky agreed seriously. 'What did you get them?'

'That's another secret, and one I can't tell you. Right, you bring me the stuff in the drawers and I'll pack it. How's that sound?'

'Okay. Then what'll we do?'

'I'm going to do some washing. After that who knows?'

The morning crawled by. The washed clothes dried almost immediately in the hot sun and were duly ironed and folded away. Sara and Helen drank tea in the kitchen, both women preoccupied with their own thoughts. Helen's were of her grandson, Sara's a chaotic whirl of expectation and anxiety over the coming meeting. Frank, who'd taken Becky with him, arrived home carrying the morning's flight schedules and offered to drive Sara to the airport, but she declined.

'Thanks, Frank, but no. He mightn't be prepared. I mean, he made a place for our meeting, I think I'd rather just stick to it.'

She helped prepare lunch, then pushed the salad around her plate smiling weakly when Helen remonstrated, 'My dear, you have to eat.'

'I can't. I'm too nervous. Maybe later.'

Then finally it was time. Frank said, 'I'll get the car out.' The moment was upon her, and for all the time she'd had to prepare, she wasn't ready. Her fingers gripping the lipstick shook and she stared at her reflection, appalled. What had made her choose that skirt? And the top was wrong. It should have been the blue . . . She was rummaging in her carefully packed bag when Helen came in to get her.

'For heaven's sake, Sara, stop it! Nothing could matter less than your clothes. You look quite lovely in any case, so just get in the car and go.'

'You're right.' Pulling herself together, Sara swallowed, then hugged her friend and hurried out to where Frank was waiting with the engine already running.

The hotel was tucked discreetly behind a band of spreading shade trees and immaculate lawns. The wide sweep of gravelled driveway crunched under the little car's wheels.

'Flashest pub in town,' Frank said, and the matter-of-fact comment helped break the nervous trance that had fallen on Sara. She gave herself a mental shake and gripped the doorhandle, drawing in a fortifying breath as they stopped before the darkened glass entrance.

'Want me to come in with you? I could wait if you like,' Frank offered.

'No, I'll be fine.' She was pale but composed. 'Thanks for bringing me,' she added and turned towards the entrance. Glancing back from the tinted glass doors she saw that Frank was still there watching her. He waved and, drawing a deep breath, she lifted her hand in return and went in.

Inside, the lobby was a vast atrium. The air was refreshingly cold. Palms in large pots stood about the tiled space that was divided by pillars and sectioned with seating. A slate-fronted reception desk was set to one side with three stations along it, and some sort of attendant in a well-cut suit rested – it was the only word for it, Sara thought – like an automaton awaiting use in a little area beside a low chest where refreshments were laid out for the hotel guests. There to answer questions or to pour the cold drinks? The query bobbed into Sara's mind and vanished as she oriented herself and began the hike across the marble floor to reception.

Then a voice behind her said, 'Chrissy?'

It was the tone – doubtful, questioning – that halted Sara more than the name, which she scarcely registered. She swung about and saw a man rising from the lounge where he'd been seated in the shadow of a palm. He was tall, grey-headed and sparely built. He was neatly dressed without jacket or tie, in grey trousers and a short-sleeved shirt of pale blue. When she turned to him, his face suddenly whitened beneath the tan, making the straight line of his big nose loom even larger. 'Mother of Christ!' Pain, brief and sharp, crossed his features, then was gone again. 'You're the living spit of your mother,' he said. 'I'm John Randall. I'm your father.'

42

Sara stared at the well-groomed stranger, trying frantically to make something familiar out of the man before her. She smiled weakly.

'Hello, I'm Sara. I . . .'

She had no idea what she wanted to say except that this was not him, not the golden-armed laughing god of her dreams. He was old. Of course he's old, her mind mocked as her gaze moved over him chronicling the evidence. His brow was lined, his eyebrows grey, the column of his neck creased. He must be in his sixties, sixty-five or sixty-eight perhaps. Frank was older but this man had no right to be. She felt a sense of loss and realised as the silence lengthened awkwardly that the moment in which they might have embraced naturally had gone by.

John Randall realised it too. He came towards her, his right hand rising but not to shake hers – it would have been faintly ridiculous given the circumstances – but to take her elbow and lead her back to the lounge. They were close enough for her to smell his cologne, to see the crease in his earlobe, so unlike her own small, lobeless ears. His voice was a pleasant baritone but that too woke no echoes in her mind.

'My God, I can scarcely believe . . . Chris – or do you prefer Sara? But you *are* Christine Mary Randall. Never mind the scientific nonsense, your looks shout the fact. Seeing you just now gave me quite a shock. You're the image of her, of Mary.'

'Didn't Paul Markham send a photo?'

'The journalist? No. The media and I – well, let's say our relationship hasn't always been amicable. Here, sit. Would you like tea, or something stronger?'

'Tea would be nice, thank you.' Sara sank onto the couch, setting down her handbag and smoothing her skirt. Her mind was a complete blank, or at least speech seemed to have deserted her, for although a thousand questions teemed in her head like a ball of wool whose end had been hidden, she couldn't seem to tease out the strand that would free her tongue to ask them.

The man – no, her father – returned, from speaking to the automaton and seated himself at the opposite end of the couch. He leaned back and folded his hands over one knee, assuming a posture of ease. The pose flexed the muscles of his forearms that were blemished with sunspots. The hair along them was no longer golden. And something in her broke open. She looked at this stranger, all that was left to her of her own blood, and was suddenly six again, locked in that room without her twin, knowing that the night, which she must face alone, was coming, and if they heard her crying either the horrid man or the nasty lady would come in and beat her. The words hurtled from her, accusing and cold.

'You didn't come! I opened the window and broke the screen and jumped out because Benny was gone and I knew you would come and f-find me and you didn't!' She was horrified by the childish wail that was escaping her, but helpless to control it. Her throat tightened and her chest heaved and she bawled her heart out, blinded by the tears that flooded her cheeks and choked by the breath that caught in her throat. In the midst of it all she was unaware of the besuited young man who appeared with a tray of tea things, then discreetly vanished with it again. She sobbed for all the years of abandonment, and the pain of loss, for Benny and her mother, whom she now knew she resembled, for the father she had lost and, in a muddled way – because she was far past being able to differentiate between her feelings – for Sam's sickness, her heart-break over Jack and the horrors of the drought as well.

When it ended she was clutching a man's sodden handkerchief and John Randall's arm was around her shoulder holding her firmly against him. She hiccupped a final sob and sniffed, mopping damply at her eyes.

'Better now?' he asked tenderly, and it was as if a door had suddenly opened in her mind. She saw herself at the foot of the garden wall from which she'd tumbled, sobbing over a grazed elbow, and her father scooping her up in his arms to kiss the sore spot and ask that same question.

'I'm sorry, Dad.' Fresh tears sparkled in the green eyes that lifted to meet his. 'I don't know what came over me. I didn't mean – I shouldn't have said . . .'

'You did, and you were right. It's a father's job to keep his children safe and I didn't. I failed both you and Benny.' His arm tightened around her and his voice thickened with pain. 'Everything that happened to you I should have prevented. For that I can never forgive myself, any more than I can for Benny's death. I never dared believe that your body wasn't out there with his – my poor innocent little Bryant and May.'

The names triggered another memory. 'I remember you calling us that. I never knew what it meant.'

'Matches.' John Randall blinked something from his eye, and gave the ghost of a chuckle. 'Bryant and May made Redhead matches.' He nodded at the corner of the room. 'There's a ladies' behind the screen if you need a moment. I'll order us some fresh tea.'

Staring into the mirror above the handbasin, Sara discovered a face streaked with mascara and eyes almost as red as her hair. There was a container of small hand towels above the basin so she made a cold compress of one to clean and repair the damage, then reapplied makeup, taking her time. She felt shaken to her core, but curiously relieved as well, as if some titanic struggle she had been engaged in was finally resolved. After all, her father must have come here seeking a ghost too. If he was no longer the strong young giant of her dreams, then neither was she a six-year-old child.

They moved from the lobby into a cafe space beyond the lift where the tables were widely separated with banquettes about them. A waitress served them, and over the tea and little cakes they began tentatively to question and learn each other's history.

'Tell me about my mother.' Sara spoke first. 'You said I look like her.'

'You do, even to the way you hold your head. I never noticed it in you as a child. What do you remember of her?'

'Not much. Her smell: powder and cigarettes. She could stand on her head. And she used to blow fairy kisses. When we were in bed and she was going away, she'd turn and blow them to us from the door. *Blowing us dreams,* she called it. Why did she kill herself?'

Randall sighed, and ran his hands over his cropped grey hair. 'It happened when they found Benny's body. It took away all hope of ever getting you back. When I told her about Benny and that I thought you were both gone – and you do see, Chrissy, that I couldn't *not* tell her – she screamed like her mind was going, and I really think it did. The news broke something in her. She couldn't conceive of you separately, you see. Well, to be honest, neither did I then. That's why the memorial plaque has both your names on it.'

'I know,' Sara said. 'I saw it.'

'Did you? It was the last straw for Mary. A week later she was dead and I'd lost you all.' His gaze was on the tablecloth, his face so bleak that she was moved to touch his hand.

'Paul, the journalist who found me, said no ransom demand was ever made. Is that right?'

'There was nothing.' His hand clenched on the white tablecloth. 'Nothing! No reason, no demand. If there had only been contact I'd have given anything, everything. But the months went by and when Benny's body turned up, I knew it was over, that neither of you were ever coming back.'

'And yet here I am.' Sara sipped, put her cup down. 'You married again.' It came out more abruptly than she intended, like an accusation. 'What's she like, your wife?'

'Fran?' He lifted his shoulders. 'She's good for me. Kind, understanding. We have three children, Chrissy. A son, Justin, and two daughters. Mandy, she's ten, and Sophie the baby, she's eight. No redheads. The kids take after Fran, who's a brunette.' His small rueful smile twisted Sara's heart for something she couldn't share. 'Well, she colours it now. But you'll see them for yourself. It's why I'm here – not just to meet you, but to take you home, if you'll come.'

'But –' Sara abandoned the half-uttered protest. There was nothing to keep her here – the job at Redhill was over and Jack had made no attempt to prevent her leaving. The knowledge was bitter.

'Tonight. I've two seats booked on the evening flight. We've got till six p.m., so there's time enough to pack.'

'The packing's already done. I've been staying with friends – they're my employers, or they were. My job's over now; I've no immediate plans.'

He was pleased, she could see. 'Good, then. So you're free? I could send a car for your stuff now or we can call in and pick it up on our way to the airport. It'd be a bit early but we could probably get dinner here, or would you rather eat on the plane?'

'Oh, the plane because I have to see my friends before I go, Dad.' The name came out hesitantly this time and Sara's smile was uncertain. 'It's so odd to say that. I never called him by that name, you know, or Father – Vic Blake, I mean. I never called him anything.'

He grunted. 'I've called the murdering bastard a few things. I've killed him so many times and in so many ways – I used to fantasise about what I'd do to whoever took you both . . .' He shook his head. 'Enough of that. There are so many things I want to know about you, Chrissy. The journalist sent me his paper with the story in it – there was a grainy pic with the article but it gave no real idea. I want to know about your growing up, how those people treated you. And who you are now, what you do, all the things a father should know about his daughter's life. You're twenty-seven, so what about men? Is there someone special?'

'No,' she lied. 'But I've been married. It didn't work out.'

'I'm sorry about that. The paper said you work as a governess?'

'Yes, but only recently. It's a long story.'

'I'm listening.'

So she told him everything, re-examining the days of her life, going off on tangents at times as something prompted further memories to emerge. Her father was able to frame her six-year-old recollections with the background of their settings. He placed the garden, the dog and the stone wall at Vinibel Downs, a property outside Winton in Queensland, and the poultry and egg collecting on the sheep stud in New South Wales. Still talking, they moved from the cafe back to the lounge and later to the gardens, walking slowly over the grass in the shade beyond the pool, talking, talking . . . John Randall spoke of Benny and the closeness of the bond her twin had shared with her, of their secret language until the age of four when they suddenly began to speak properly.

'Mary was worried sick about your brains,' he said. 'She thought you'd both been damaged at birth. It took a nursing sister in Winton to convince her that it wasn't unusual in twins, though it mostly happened with identical ones.' Sara heard the pain in his voice when he spoke of his first-born son and she wept again, but these were gentler tears for her long-lost companion whose ghost had lived on in her heart.

'I think some part of me always knew – if not about him, then that *something* was missing,' she said slowly. 'It was like I was always listening, always waiting.'

'I can believe it. We marvelled, Mary and I, that as tiny babies each of you was so *aware* of your twin. Even fast asleep you'd reach out to one another. And when you both began to crawl, it was always towards the other. We could put you on opposite ends of the verandah at Vinibel, and you'd both continue moving till you met.'

'Did you sell the properties?' Sara asked abruptly then.

John Randall stopped his pacing and sighed. 'Yes, because there was no point in holding them. Land is there to pass on but I had no one left. Nothing mattered. As far as I was concerned it was all finished, the dreams, the planning, everything. Of course you learn in time that pain doesn't kill, and that's the worst bit. Around then I could so easily have ended it all – I thought of it more than once – or I might've drunk myself to death; instead Fran saved me. Made me see there might still be a future.' He scrubbed his hands through the short hair on his nape and looked at her. 'I'm an entrepreneur, Chrissy. I have a talent for turning a buck, always have – it's part luck, part know-how, part timing. So with Fran's help I put my life back together and success followed. Since losing you all I have had my share of fortune,' he said soberly. 'Don't think I don't know it. Having Fran and the children, now finding you again. Despite everything, I'm a lucky man.'

'Your children.' Sara stared at the pool, the surface of the sky-blue water trembling from the breeze that moved across it. 'Do they know about me yet?'

'Yes, I rang Justin before I left, and I imagine he's seen the papers by now. He was with his study group when we spoke. This is his senior year; he's a bright boy. He intends to do a degree in business studies at university.'

'And the girls?'

'Oh, Fran will have explained it to them. They're madly excited at the thought of a big sister. They were desperate to come along and see you, but Fran thought that we'd manage this first meeting best alone. She's a clever woman, Chrissy, and ready to welcome you. Don't worry about that. And the kids'll love you to death. They can't wait for me to bring you home.'

43

It was the first time Sara had flown business class. The hours since Frank had dropped her at the Hilton's entrance had sped by, a blur of emotion and half-assimilated impressions. Already the man beside her, seat semi-reclined now that their dinner trays had been removed, had assumed familiar proportions, as if their acquaintance really did reach much further back than a few hours. There was still so much unsaid between them, but for the moment her brain and bruised heart could hold no more. The final parting with the Ketch family had been wrenching. She relived it again behind closed lids and saw Becky's face, her tears brimming like translucent pearls and spilling from her swimming eyes. 'I don't want you to go,' she had sobbed, and at that moment Sara had not wanted to leave either. She had watched Len and Frank shake her father's hand, seen their quiet assessment of him. Jack's words, *You've got the Ketches in your corner now*, had whispered in the corner of her mind. She wanted them to like him, it was somehow necessary that they should not find him wanting in any way, and she was relieved when he and Frank had immediately found common ground. Helen had made tea. Sara had never felt less like taking refreshment but had seized the chance to spin out their time together. She chatted with Becky and promised Beth that she would write and keep them informed of anything she learned from the police.

When it was finally time to go, Beth, the most self-contained of women, had hugged her hard, murmuring, 'Dammit! I am *not* going to cry. Don't forget to write, will you? I want to know – we all will – how you get on.'

'Yes,' Sara answered fiercely. 'I'm coming back, you know. I can't see myself settling in Sydney. The Alice is much more my style. Let's not lose touch. I want to know how Sam's doing, and when the rain comes.'

She had found Sam himself resting in the lounge, thin and boneless-looking but quietly satisfied. 'My blood test was good and I didn't have the chemo, Sara. The doc said the next lot could wait, then we'd see.'

'Did he?' Sara felt an instance of fear for him then dismissed it. Beth hadn't mentioned his missing the chemo but that was good news, surely, if the blood tests were okay? The blinds had been closed and the air conditioner hummed quietly on the wall. 'Don't get up.' She patted his stick-thin leg. 'I just want to tell you goodbye and that it's very important that you work hard at getting well. Your family needs you, you know, Sam, and so does Redhill. Besides, I'm coming back out here and when I do I want you to be strong enough to give me riding lessons. You said you would, remember?'

'Yeah, and I will.' His gaze, so much wiser than his years, held curiosity. 'Do you like your dad, Sara? Uncle Jack said you'd be happy when you met him, but grown-ups lie sometimes when they don't want kids to know things.'

She caught her breath. 'Well, yes, I do like my dad. Of course, I don't know him properly yet, and that's why I'm going away now, because knowing anyone takes time.'

'But you aren't happy,' he objected. 'I can tell.'

She laughed shakily. 'Because I'm leaving you all. But I'll becoming back, you know, to tell you about Sydney and my new brother and sisters. And to see the country when the drought ends. Your uncle told me about how it changes but I want to see it for myself.'

His smile had bloomed at that. 'I'm glad, Sara. You'll see, it'll be worth the wait.' She had taken that gallant hopeful smile with her as Frank grabbed her bag and they all moved towards the door. There was another round of hugs from Helen and Beth while her father stood by and let Frank load her luggage. Last of all she felt the strong embrace of Frank's arm and the roughness of his aged skin against her cheek. 'You want me to kick that idiot son of mine for yer?' he murmured, and she'd given a little spurt of helpless laughter that could easily have turned to tears.

'Just tell him . . .' She couldn't find words for all she wanted to say. 'Never mind. I'll be back this way, Frank. I might get to tell him myself.' Then she was in the car, twisting in her seat, waving frantically as the house slipped behind them and the first of the streetlights came on. The sun had gone and the sky was deepening to violet above the solid line of range either side of Heavitree Gap. Soon, another hour or so, and the plane would rise and all the world she had recently known – the Alice, the sand country, the mulga – would slip away behind her, lost in the vast void of inland Australia.

'It's a long flight,' John Randall said. 'You should get some sleep.'

'Yes.' Sara was exhausted, her limbs too heavy to move. She had reclined the seat to its limit. 'I think I will. I feel . . .'

'I know.' His smile was rueful, understanding. 'Like a hill fell on you. Emotional overload. Rest yourself.' The stewardess came at his signal and returned almost immediately with a light blanket, which Randall spread over his daughter. 'Let it all go for now, just till we get there.' He dimmed the lights above them and her last impression as her eyes closed was an awareness of his gaze resting upon her, while the night slid by outside. A quiet joy slipped into her heart and spread there, like a tree taking root, as sleep carried her away.

Sydney airport was less crowded at night; the shops within the concourse were closed and it was mainly security people moving about. Feeling crumpled but somewhat refreshed, Sara and her father descended to the ground floor and waited for the carousel to produce her luggage. Outside the terminal the night air was sultrier than the desert but there was scarcely time to feel it before the taxi was swooping away from the kerb, darting through bewildering lanes of traffic that carried them into the city, then on towards Watson Bay.

'Where do you live?' Sara asked.

'Vaucluse. Fran and I chose the place just before Sophie was born. The kids love it because it's close to the beach. Justin's a surfer and Mandy belongs to the local life savers' club.'

'Oh, excuse me.' Sara tried to strangle the yawn that slipped out. The brief spurt of energy she had experienced on waking had passed and she longed only for bed.

'Not far now,' John Randall said. 'Ah, here's the street. Do you feel like food, Chrissy? Fran'll make you a snack if you want something.'

Sara yawned again. 'Oh, I can't seem to stop. No, thanks. I just want to sleep.'

'Then so you shall.' Her father leaned forward. 'The one on the right with the tall gate,' he told the cabby, and leaned forward pressing the remote opener he had taken from his pocket. The gates slid aside and a moment later they had arrived.

It was a big house, Sara saw, double-storeyed with metal balcony rails. A light burned behind long drapes in the downstairs front window and another switched on as they stepped between tall pillars into the portico. Behind them the cab wheels swept around the driveway, crunching over gravel, and somewhere water played amid a smell of humus and damp greenery. The air was filled with scent – roses or jasmine, Sara wondered? An outside light came on, casting the shadows of palm leaves onto a brilliant green patch of lawn. Randall was pointing his fist at the gate and as it closed the front door, inlaid with leaded glass, opened and Frances Randall stood there. She was a trim, vital figure in her early forties with broad cheekbones, dark eyes and black hair that swept to her jawline.

'Christine!' Her hands were out as if to embrace Sara. 'Come in. You're here at last. Welcome home!' Sara found herself clasped in a light embrace. 'The girls and I seem to have been waiting for you forever!' Frances confided. 'Hello, darling.' She kissed her husband's cheek and slipped an arm around him. 'How were your flights?'

'Good, and as you see, she's here. Chrissy, this is Frances. Which room have you prepared, love? She's tired. We'll go straight up and everything else can wait till the morning. The girls asleep?'

'Hours ago. And Jus rang. It's this way, Christine. You sure you won't have something? There's water and biscuits in your room, but if you'd like a hot drink . . .'

'It's kind of you but no, really, dinner was fine, very substantial. I'm just tired.'

'Then here we are. You've got her bag, John? Okay then. Your bathroom's through there and breakfast will be whenever you want it.' Frances took a quick look around the pretty, spacious room with its en suite facilities and floor-length curtains that matched the ruffled bedspread, and paused at the door to smile at Sara. 'I'm so glad you're here, Christine. You're living proof that miracles can happen. Sleep well, my dear.'

'Thank you, and for the lovely welcome,' Sara responded, gazing around. 'It's a beautiful room.' She patted the plump pillow sheathed in crisp linen. 'I'll sleep like a top here. Thank you again. Good night, Frances. 'Night, Dad.'

'Goodnight, Chrissy.' He brushed her cheek with his lips. 'Sweet dreams, poppet,' he murmured, then he too was gone.

Alone at last Sara unpacked her toilet bag, cleaned teeth and face in the luxuriously appointed bathroom, then undressed, located the light switch on the bedside lamp and was asleep the moment her head touched the expensive, incredibly soft pillow.

Sara woke slowly to the distant warble of birds, and something else. Half dreaming, she listened behind closed lids and heard it again, a scuffle and a breathy giggle. She opened her eyes to see two young girls peering at her, one from behind the lens of a camera.

'Hello.' She smiled at them and sat up, stretching. 'I'll bet you're Mandy.' She addressed the chubbier of the two who wielded the Polaroid camera. 'So *you* must be Sophie.'

The little one giggled again. 'Hello. You're Chrissy. Mandy took your picture. You want to see? It'll be ready soon.'

The Polaroid shot rapidly darkened and they crowded in to show her the result. Both girls had their mother's colouring, though Mandy's hair was in bangs across her forehead while Sophie's was held back into a side parting by a plastic slide. Both wore school uniforms. Mandy tilted the camera and pointed to Sara's curls, which showed vividly red against the white pillowcase. 'Is your hair really red or did you dye it?'

'It's really red.' She smiled at their enquiring faces. 'I got teased to death about it at school. Is it late?'

'It's not breakfast time yet,' Sophie said. 'Mum told us not to wake you but we didn't, did we?'

'No,' she assured them. 'I'm going to have a shower. You can wait if you like. I won't be long. Then you could show me where everything is. But it doesn't matter if you're busy.'

Visibly delighted, the girls perched on the bed, talking nonstop through the bathroom door while Sara showered and dressed. She missed most of the chatter about school and friends and the beach and emerged in time to hear the question Mandy aimed at her. 'Where did Daddy find you, Chrissy? He flew off to get you, Mum said. He's been to China, you know. Did you come from there?'

'Not from China. From a place way out in the desert where it doesn't rain. I was teaching some children there.'

Sophie's mouth dropped open. 'Are you a teacher?'

'Not really.' Sara pulled a brush through her curls, hung some clothes in the cleverly concealed wardrobe that Sophie opened for her, then made the bed. 'Shall we go and look for breakfast? You don't want to be late for school.' Sophie took her hand and she smiled down at her. 'You remind me a bit of the little girl I taught. Do you like school?'

'It's nearly finished,' Mandy cut in, anxious not to be over-looked. 'I'm glad, because then we can go to the beach every day! Come on, Chrissy. It's this way.'

Frances was in the kitchen slicing fruit. It was a large open-plan room, airy and cool, with black granite counters, a central island and yellow-topped stools at a breakfast bar. 'Good morning, Christine. I expected you'd need more of a lie-in.' Frances said. She wore white pedal pushers and a tangerine top. 'Come on, girls, sit up and eat. What would you like, Christine? There's fruit, cereal, toast, juice —'

'Juice please and some toast. Is Dad up?' The title sounded awkward in Sara's ears, but Mandy, mouth full of mango, was shaking her head as Frances looked up, surprised.

'Heavens, yes! He's gone. He always starts early and particularly now. He said to apologise to you but he had to go in today. He's been away overseas, you see, so there's a backlog of stuff for him to catch up on. I tell him to delegate but he's the hands-on sort. He'll be home about six.'

'Oh.' Disappointed, Sara helped herself to tea. 'I didn't realise. Of course . . . And Justin, where's he?'

'Staying over with his study group. He's got his last exams this week. He'll be back tonight though so you can meet him then.'

'How does he feel about my turning up?' Sara asked carefully.

'He's a bit older than the girls. Had he known before about us, about Dad's other family, I mean?'

Frances smiled wryly. 'He's a teenage boy. Who knows what he thinks or feels? Say anything you like to him at present and he'll probably answer, *Whatever.* So-o infuriating! But my friends with sons of a similar age assure me that it's normal, if there is such a thing as a normal teenager.' She drained a glass of juice and glanced at the clock. 'Now, come on, girls. Teeth, bags, then into the car. Would you like to come for the run, Christine? I can drive you round a bit after, show you where things are. Another day we can go to the beach or into the city. Have you visited Sydney before?'

'No. I've never been on the east coast. And I'd love to come, thank you. I'll just pop up and get my bag.'

In the car the girls fought over who would sit beside Sara until Frances settled it by putting them both in the back seat and giving Sara the front. The school was a private one, a large sandstone edifice set in green playing fields behind a stone wall.

'They break up in a week's time,' Frances said as they watched the two dark heads file in past a staff member standing by the tall wrought-iron gates. 'There'll be a concert – Sophie's in it – and an awards night. The girls would love it if you'll come. Mandy's in line for a prize. I think she'll be as bright, academically, as her brother. Were you a good student, Christine?'

'I worked hard,' Sara said. 'I did well enough.' For a perpetual outsider who had received no encouragement at home. This should have been her life, she thought, as the uniformed girls loitered and chatted their way through the school gates. Some, she saw, carried musical instrument cases. In high school she had earned her own money and there had been none to spare for extras. Studying for a career at university had been beyond her reach so she had settled for office work, then marriage. Her half-sisters would have very different futures and she felt a flicker of envy that passed when she remembered that Benny's had been lost, and Sam's hung in the balance. Viewed that way, she hadn't fared so badly after all.

Frances engaged the gear and swung the Volvo back into the traffic. 'I'll show you the coastline and the village; I have a couple of errands to run, then we might have some coffee before going back. Sound okay to you?'

'Lovely.' Vaucluse was a leafy suburb and Sara looked with appreciation at the greenery around her. 'It's so lush, so green! There's a drought where I was working; you cannot imagine how desolate the country is out there.'

'You're right about that, I can't imagine it. I'm city-bred. Your father was the country boy. I'm afraid I've no desire to step beyond the bright lights.'

'Where did you meet then, you and Dad?'

'Oh, I've known him from childhood. My father was his professor at Sydney University and he initially took pity on him because he knew nobody in the city. He used to invite him to tea. I was, I don't know, five, six? He'd play with us, my sister and I. It was certainly a first, in our experience. Most of the students my father brought home were far too grand to notice little girls.'

'So where did he live, then?'

'Your grandfather had a merino stud somewhere in the north of the state. John inherited it and that's where he met his first wife. I never knew your mother. He and I didn't meet again until after the tragedy. I was in my mid-twenties and he was forty-something but the age difference didn't matter to either of us. It never has. He's a strong man, your father. What happened would have broken most men and I can't tell you how happy I am that you've been found,' Frances said, turning in to park on a headland lookout. 'He deserves it. I'm sure you do too. I don't mean to make light of your suffering, Christine. It must have been awful, but it scarred your father in ways only I can see. So for that reason alone you'll always be welcome in my home.'

'Thank you,' Sara said inadequately. 'It's – just thank you.'

'That's okay.' Frances gave a crooked smile. He says you're the spit of Mary. She must've been very lovely. I hope we'll be friends. What do you think of the view?'

'Oh.' The sudden change of topic made Sara blink and for the first time she took in the sweep of ocean, blue and silver in the morning sun, with the dark bay curving around to the right. 'It's beautiful. What is it that they say up here, something about things being lovely one day and beautiful the next?'

'That's Queensland. *Beautiful one day, perfect the next*. It's not bad here either. If you look way round to the left where that tower is, that's Gibsons Beach. The kids practically live there in summer. So, back to the shops, and coffee?'

'Suits me.'

'Good. Your turn now. Tell me about this job you had in the desert. How on earth did you end up there?'

44

Sara moved carefully through the day, exploring the environs of her father's life, so radically different to the Calshots' own lot. They would be on their way home now, driving through the stark dry country, the bitumen swimming with the mirages that constantly retreated before them. Pulling in at Emu Creek for a breather, then taking the narrow track through the mulga. Back to Redhill, to Jack, and the daily grind of the drought, while she was here in this city of glass and steel, cossetted with every luxury. For a moment her treacherous heart longed only to be travelling with them but she reminded herself, marvelling at her contrariness, she also wanted to be with her father.

John Randall had an office in the city with branches in Melbourne and Perth from which his transport empire was overseen. He frequently travelled to Asia and the United States, and he owned a second property in the Hunter Valley, where an employee managed a small horse stud for him.

'It's his one link with the past,' Frances said. 'He's a country boy at heart still and he loves his horses, not that he has any time to spend with them these days. *When he retires*, that's his mantra, but I can't see it happening anytime soon.'

'Is his health good?'

'Yes, thankfully. And despite how often his work takes him away, he does enjoy it still.'

'That's important,' Sara agreed, her thoughts winging to Frank and his son.

'Yes, well, I'm off to pick up the girls. Will you come?'

'I'll stay, if that's okay, and just enjoy the garden.'

It was certainly worth the pleasure it gave, Sara thought as Frances left. A jacaranda tree had layered the grass with a blue skirt of fallen blossom, and a profusion of coloured hibiscus bloomed against the sandstone wall. The back garden was terraced with broad timber steps leading through islands of low flowering shrubs, none of which she could name. A bed of annuals was bordered by the blue of agapanthus, and in a green bower by a clipped hedge a fountain played, creating rainbows in the sunlight. She should write her impressions down while it was all fresh, Sara thought. She had promised Beth to keep in touch and right now a letter seemed a safer bet than a phone call. It would allow her to censor the thoughts that her tongue might otherwise betray. And it would give her something to occupy her time and soothe her longing for the life she had left.

Seated with pad and pen in the gazebo she had discovered behind the fountain, Sara wrote the address and date, then hesitated, lost for words. How could she describe the temperate fecundity of her surroundings to a woman trapped in the pitiless heat of central Australia? Or describe the luxurious home and lifestyle her family enjoyed when Beth's was struggling for survival? It was none of Sara's making and certainly Beth would not begrudge her situation, but after the comparatively spartan conditions of Redhill, might it not seem like the difference was being rubbed in? She tried sketching a letter in her head to Jack.

> Dear Jack,
> I think you would like my father. He has no pastoral interests now but he does keep a horse stud. Maybe I will see it one day. He has a nice home. It is cool here . . .

The words dried up. None of it mattered but she couldn't just write *I love you.* In the end she wrote:

> `Dear Becky,
>
> I am writing from the garden here in Sydney. It's very pretty, all the flowers are out and the weather is lovely. I went for a drive this morning and saw the sea – all silvery blue with little white caps on the waves, but I haven't been swimming yet.
>
> I think you would like my sisters, Mandy and Sophie. Sophie is nearly as old as you. They are both still at school and I am going to their concert next week. I wonder if it will be as good as yours and Sam's? My brother is away but he's coming home tonight.
>
> I miss you all lots, and Redhill too. I will write again soon. Heaps of love and kisses for you all (and for Nan and Pop when you talk to them next).
>
> Love from your best friend,
> Sara
> P.S. I'll send photos next time.*

Justin arrived home shortly after his sisters, riding a pushbike across the lawn and dumping it at the laundry entrance. He entered the kitchen, backpack over one shoulder, and went straight to the fridge to pull out a carton of juice. Sophie, tidily eating a quartered slice of bread and honey at the breakfast bar, let out a squeal at his appearance.

'Justin, guess what? Chrissy's come, and Mandy and me saw her first, before she even woke up this morning!'

'No kidding,' he said flatly just as Frances and Sara walked into the room.

'There you are, Jus,' Frances said. '*Don't* drink out of the carton, please! How many times must I tell you? Here's Christine. She and Dad got in late last night after you'd rung.'

'Hello, Justin.' Sara smiled, wondering whether she should offer her hand. He was a handsome boy, tall, his hair brown rather than black. He had eyes of a misty grey with a darker line around the iris, and was as gangly as adolescent boys tended to be. 'You look like your father,' she observed.

'Hi.' He didn't return her smile and the grey eyes were hostile. 'You don't.'

'No. I understand I take after my mother,' she offered.

'Yeah. Well, I've got to study.' He replaced the carton in the fridge and shouldered past the two women heading across the hall for the stairs.

Frances said, 'Justin!' but he was taking the steps three at a time and ignored her. 'Christine – I'm so sorry. It's not like Jus to be rude. He will apologise. I —'

'No, please, let it go.' Sara bit her lip. 'See it from his side. Nobody asked him if he wanted an interloper brought into his family to usurp his place. That's how it must seem to him. I'm sure he'll come round in time, but not if it's made into a big issue now.'

'You're not an interloper!'

Sara said wryly, 'And we're not seventeen. He's got enough problems, poor kid. I don't want to turn into another one.'

Frances sighed. 'You're probably right, though whether John will be as understanding I don't know.'

John Randall was home in time to sit down with his family at the big table in the alcove off the kitchen. He kissed his wife and smiled at his eldest daughter. 'I'm sorry I had to leave before you were up this morning. Did you have a good day?'

'Yes, thank you. Frances showed me round. We had a coffee and looked at the coast. It's very beautiful. I can't get used to the greenness after being so long with the drought.'

'Yeah, they're doing it tough out there, poor beggars.' He

turned his attention to Justin and the girls, enquiring after their activities. Justin, who was still to directly address Sara, said, 'Stu's folks are taking the boat out for the weekend. I'm thinking of going with them.'

His father shook his head. 'Another weekend, perhaps. Your sister has just come and I'd like for us all to spend time with her. God knows we've missed enough of it already.'

'Why?' Justin's brows creased in a scowl. 'I bet she's not planning to move out anytime soon. Anyway, Mandy and Sophie are my sisters. She's only half – if that.'

'Justin!' thundered John Randall. 'How dare you speak of Chrissy like that! She has every bit as much right in this house as you have. She's just as much my child. She was my child before you were born and I won't allow —'

'Oh, yes. Your sainted first family!' Justin leapt to his feet, face white and grey eyes blazing. 'The prodigy twins so tragically dead. Only it turns out she's not dead *or* a prodigy, after all. Just a scheming governess who saw a chance to screw money out of a rich man. Wake up to yourself, Dad. You're pathetic!'

Randall's fists had clenched and the veins stood out on his neck as he half rose from his chair. 'That's enough!' he roared. Frances looked appalled and Sophie burst into tears, while Justin wore an air of both defiance and fear.

Sara pushed her seat back and slipped quietly from the table and into the living room, closing her ears to the words her father was saying in a voice gone suddenly hard and cold as steel. She felt sick; she should never have come, she should simply have met with her father in the Alice and then gone her separate way. It had been selfish to want more of him and now she was witnessing the result, discord and resentment where there had been peace. She had broken the harmony of her father's house simply to soothe her own need to belong.

It seemed a long time that she sat huddled into the corner of the squashy leather lounge before Frances appeared with a tray. She set it on a glass-topped table and came to sit beside her.

'I've brought coffee,' she said. 'I'm so sorry! And so ashamed of my son, Christine. I —'

'No.' Sara shook her head. 'It's me. And my name is Sara. Perhaps I should keep the Blake too. It's still on my licence, after all. I'm sorry; you've been very kind but I see now that I shouldn't have come here.'

'Don't!' Frances raised her hand. 'Don't you dare let the words of an angry child drive you away. Your father deserves better than that! So do you. My son is spoilt and he feels lost and insecure at present – as you said, he's seventeen – but he'll get over it. Now please, won't you drink your coffee? John will be in directly and Justin, I can guarantee, will apologise in the morning.'

Sara took the proffered cup, observing dryly, 'That won't make him feel any better.'

'It's not supposed to, but that's his problem. I don't believe in rewarding bad behaviour.'

Beth had said something similar once of Becky. The memory brought with it a sudden shaft of longing sharp as a knife for Redhill, which cut through the dull ache of missing Jack that was a constant dirge in her heart. Then her father appeared, his mouth a grim line, and Frances rose to pour coffee for him. He carried a large cardboard box, which he handed to Sara, his face softening as he spoke. 'This is for you, Chrissy. I remembered it this morning and got it out of the bank. I lodged it there when I lost your mother.'

Justin's words fresh in her mind, Sara received it gingerly, hoping it wasn't jewellery.

'What is it?'

'Bits and pieces. I couldn't stand either to throw them out or keep them by me. Open it, that's the easiest way.'

Sara complied, lifting out first a framed head and shoulders studio portrait of a beautiful, red-headed woman, her curls crowned with a nimbus of light. A pale-blue scarf draped her shoulders and her head was tilted a little as she smiled at the camera. Her eyes were as green as moss. Sara gasped and laid a finger on the glass, half-recognising, half-intuiting the portrait's identity, grief rising afresh as she stared at the woman and that dimly remembered smile.

'She was lovely!'

'She was,' John Randall agreed. He looked at Frances, who was also staring at the picture, eyes wide. 'What do you think, did I exaggerate the likeness?'

'She couldn't be anyone else's daughter,' Frances declared.

Below it was another photo frame. Sara lifted it out and went very still. Her heart swelled in painful recognition and her eyes grew wet. It showed her and Benny dressed in matching shorts and tops, her shirt yellow, his red, holding hands and grinning at the camera. A section of white latticework was behind them and off to one side, as if it had just rolled there, was a large beach ball. They were hatless and her twin's hair was as red and curly as her own. Their faces were quite dissimilar, she saw. One of his cheeks had a dimple, and his chin was broader than hers, his eyes more hazel than green. They were the same height; she guessed their age to be around five years.

'Where. . .'

'The garden at Vinibel. Most of the others – there's a whole lot more – were taken there, or on holidays. We used to tow a caravan to the coast and live at the beach.'

'I remember. You swung me around above the waves. And we built sandcastles. The hairs on your arms were golden and I had a yellow bucket and spade.'

'That's right.' His smile was warm. 'Mary said pink would never suit you.'

'She was right,' Frances agreed as Sara, forgetting her cooling coffee, worked through the remaining pictures. There were other bits too: a handmade birthday card addressed *To Daddy* with both middle d's back to front. It was signed with a shaky *B & C*. There was a tiny teddy bear and a copy of their birth certificates. One of the photos, taken when she was a toddler, showed John Randall with a twin on either arm, and she caught her breath. 'That's how I remember you, big and strong. Though I could never call your face to mind.'

Randall sighed. 'It was another life. As is this one, now you're here.' His grey eyes studied her. 'You won't let Justin's silliness spoil it, will you? He didn't really mean what he said. And if he did, he knows better now. I told him about the DNA match.'

'I want to talk to you about that.' Sara packed the last of the photographs back into their box, choosing her words. 'Don't blame him too much. I don't . . . I mean, I half expected him to resent me. It's understandable in a way. I'm only guessing, but I'll bet you said nothing till you got the test results, then announced my existence and jumped on the plane to Alice. Is that about right?' She caught his nod. 'He didn't have much time to get over the shock of it. And it must have been a shock, so of course he thought you'd been conned. But what I wanted to say was that I can't stay here – not indefinitely. It's wonderful to have found you all, and I am never going to lose you again, but that doesn't mean moving in. I want to go back to the Alice, you see. I'll come and see you all quite often. And Frances said you have offices in Perth that you visit – so maybe you can fly there via the Alice. I'm sorry. It sounds ungrateful after you've just brought me here. I didn't really want to rush into telling you this but as it's come up, there's no point in not. And it might diffuse things a bit with Justin.'

'He's —'

'He's seventeen. Unsure of everything except his family, and his place in it, which suddenly seems to be threatened. He was the eldest child and now he's not. I don't want him to see me as an incursion into his family but as a separate person, someone there is no pressure for him to like or accept. It's best this way that I should appear as a visitor rather than a fixture. If he realises that I'm no threat to him, that I intend to live my own life, he'll come round more quickly.'

Randall looked torn. He opened his mouth, closed it, and looked at his wife. 'What do you think, Fran?'

She nodded thoughtfully, reaching to touch his hand lightly. 'I think Christine's right. We should have thought, prepared him more. And it's a bad time for him to be upset, with exams still to come. Your daughter's very wise and understanding, John. Of course this is still her home and always will be. I'll make that perfectly clear to Justin if you haven't already done so.'

Randall huffed out a breath. 'I think I might have.' He rubbed his neck. 'Very well, then. It will be however you want it, Chrissy.' His searching gaze met hers, hiding disappointment. 'You're not going to rush off immediately, though? You've only just got here.'

She smiled at him, a shadow in her eyes. 'How about I stay till Christmas? It would be wonderful to share that with you. Speaking of which, do you remember the year we got the rocking horse, Benny and I? Isn't it odd the things you remember? We always wondered how Santa got it into his bag.'

A reminiscent smile lit his face. 'By God, I do! You were only, what, five that year?'

'It was the last real Christmas I ever had,' Sara said. 'I can still see us riding him on the verandah.'

'With the boards squeaking like crazy. And your mother —' He broke off. 'Well, that was then.' His gaze was direct. 'There's something else in Alice Springs, isn't there? A man? I asked before but you turned it aside.'

Sara rose, holding the precious box. She wouldn't lie to him but her tongue was stiff and unwilling and the words rang dull with unhappiness. 'Yes, but it's not that. He doesn't want me. I just — I feel at home out there.'

45

The following morning Sara found her father and brother break-fasting on the balcony overlooking the front garden where the table had been set for six.

She greeted them both, adding to her father, 'I thought you'd be gone. Frances told me you usually started work with the sun.'

'Old habit.' He dabbed his mouth with a napkin and reached for the teapot. 'Tea?'

'Please.' She glanced at her brother, who looked uncomfortable under her regard. 'How are you, Justin? Do you have exams today?'

'Yeah.' He moved his plate aside but didn't look at her as he said stiffly, 'I apologise for what I said, okay? I didn't know about the DNA. I've gotta go, Dad, or I'll be late.' He pushed his chair back and left before she could formulate a response. In the silence he left behind they heard his feet clattering down the stairs. Somewhere in the garden a bird trilled, careless in the sunshine.

Sara sat down. 'That didn't go so well,' she said ruefully. 'I suppose it'll take time. What are you doing today?'

He passed her the cup, then slid the milk jug across the table. 'I'm going into the office to tidy up a couple of things. After that I was thinking of taking you out. I thought we could pick up Justin after his exam and go to lunch somewhere, give you a bit of time together. Would that upset anything you've already planned?'

'Not at all. What about Frances?'

'It's her day for tennis, after she's dropped the girls off.'

'Then I'm entirely at your disposal. Where are the girls?'

'They'll be down any minute. I dragged Justin out early. He's – the trouble is we don't have enough time together. I'm always travelling, home late, leaving early. It came to me I need to see more of him, perhaps explain my actions more. I don't want my son to be a stranger.'

'No,' Sara agreed, adding, 'I don't have much experience of families, except the Calshots, and things are different in the mulga.' Jack's phrase came naturally to her lips, bringing a glimpse of his face. 'I mean, they live and work together. Their lives aren't so fragmented as those of urban families. Good morning, Frances. Isn't it a beautiful day?'

'Good morning, did you sleep well? Eat up, girls.' Dressed in their school uniforms the two slid onto their chairs and shook cereal onto their plates. 'Careful with the milk jug, Sophie!' Frances admonished, helping herself to toast. Her hair was freshly styled and she wore tennis whites. 'Has Justin gone already?'

'Just now,' Sara said. 'Dad's taking us both to lunch later.' It still seemed strange to call him that. 'Will that fit in with whatever you've planned?'

'Perfectly.' Frances crunched toast and checked the sky. 'Beach weather; we shall have to get you down there soon. Come *on*, girls. Finish your juice, Sophie.' She sighed. 'Another week, thank God, and this morning rush will be over.'

Luncheon in a busy bistro in the heart of the city was a strained affair. Justin, under his father's eye, was mostly silent. He answered Sara's questions but made no effort beyond that. He exhibited no stress about his likely test results, dismissing the outcome with a shrug. 'It'll be cool.'

'Lucky you, then. I was never that relaxed about mine,' Sara observed rather tartly. The exchange depressed her. The thinly veiled disdain he exuded made her want to shake him but she couldn't win that way. For now it seemed best to let it ride – it was no more possible to force affection between siblings than to alter the shape of one's face. His DNA might proclaim their relationship but only his feelings could truly make him her brother. Unconsciously she frowned, flicking her finger against her thumb, and John Randall leaned across the table to tap her hand, with a little smile for his son.

'Look at that,' he said. 'She does it too. You two couldn't look more different, you've never met and yet you have the same mannerism. How do you explain that?'

'Genes.' Justin grunted at the same moment as Sara spoke while eyeing her hand as if it belonged to a stranger.

'I guess it must be *galli-galli*.'

'Which is?' Justin demanded, his tone somewhere between scornful and intrigued.

'A useful descriptive word for anything you don't understand.' She heard Jack's words as she spoke and pain squeezed her heart.

'It's just family.' Her father corrected obliviously, as he signalled a suave waiter. 'Well, what would you like to see next, Chrissy?'

'Anything,' she answered. 'You must know the city. Justin – do you have any suggestions?'

'I dunno. Touristy things. A ferry ride maybe.'

The days fled rapidly by. All the family attended the first end-of-year concert. It was held at the school and Sophie, as a shepherd seated next to the crib, was required to nurse a real lamb. Her first words after the event were *Ew! It peed on me, Mum!* The next was Sophie's ballet performance. Justin begged it off but Sara enjoyed it. Mandy criticised her sister's performance; her own interests lay with music and she was learning the violin.

'I'm sure you play better now than you did when you were eight,' Sara said diplomatically. 'So you have to grant Sophie the same licence.'

'Huh?' Mandy looked bemused. 'What's that mean?'

'That you shouldn't be unkind to your sister. Remember, she's younger than you,' Frances replied, clapping enthusiastically.

On the weekend, they all went to the beach. Sara was surprised at how quickly she had reaccustomed herself to city living, to the traffic and congestion and crowded pavements. Sydney had more of all these than Adelaide and, dreaming behind her sunglasses in the folding chair set up under the huge beach umbrella, Redhill seemed as distant as the stars.

'You're not swimming?' Frances, clad in a red one-piece, was slathering sunblock over her limbs.

Sara shook her head, glancing down at her long cotton pants and full-sleeved blouse. 'The shade's safer for me. Five minutes in a swimsuit and I'd look like a lobster.' She watched them from her seat – Justin had separated himself from them, vanishing the moment his board was unloaded. The girls shrieked and leapt amid the rollers, and her father had taken Frances's hand as they waded into the waves. His body, she noticed, was still firm even if his chest hair was grey. He looked to be in good shape for a man of sixty-eight.

Sitting alone, her thoughts turned again to Jack and the others, and the searing desert heat. Had the drought broken yet? The weather news, which she'd avidly followed since her arrival, told her nothing, concerned only as it was with New South Wales.

The sea breeze ruffled her hair and behind closed lids she thought of the way the blessed night breeze had blown through the French windows of her room at Redhill. And inevitably of Jack; he had never kissed her, but he had held her, helped her, cheered her. She had felt cherished by him, which made it the more hurtful when his interest had cooled so suddenly. Because he'd remembered her city background? Her heart railed against the unfairness of it.

Wanting him, his presence, his touch, affected everything that Sara thought and stole the joy from her days. She sifted sand through her fingers, caught between the need to be both here with her new-found family and back amid the daily struggle at Redhill. She had promised she would return but now, with the perspective that distance gave, she wondered how she could. They had problems enough without an extra mouth to feed, and one, moreover, who would need transportation from the roadhouse to the station. She could always stay with Frank and Helen in the Alice, but that wouldn't solve the problem of seeing Jack, who was seldom in the Alice. And if she *did* see him? There was no answer to that, save a stubborn conviction that just to do so would ease the pain of longing, if only for a little while.

Sighing, Sara stood up and dusted off her hands. There was still the problem of Justin. Clamping her hat to her head, she set off through the sprawled sunbathers to the section of beach where the board riders congregated. He might neither want nor know how to talk to her, she thought, because heaven knew she hadn't much idea what to say to him, so perhaps just sheer proximity would help remove the constraint between them. If nothing else her persistence would show him that she cared about his interests.

After a few days her father returned to his regular work schedule, though Frances said he had postponed an overseas trip that he had originally planned for before Christmas.

'There's some research he's looking at funding over there, but he tells me it can wait. I'm so glad. John is always dashing off somewhere. I've been wanting him to slow down for some time.'

'But you said he's fit, that his health is good.' Sara couldn't keep the sudden alarm from her voice.

'Oh, yes, no worries there,' Frances assured her. 'Do you feel up to some shopping? The girls have Christmas presents to buy, which will take forever. Sophie, bless her, is suggestible, but Mandy's not. The crowds will be horrendous but it'll only be worse next week. The closer Christmas comes the worse it is. I thought we could make a day of it, shop, lunch, cinema. That ought to wear them out. What do you say?'

'Lovely. The cinema will be my treat. Do you have a movie in mind?'

'Something called *The Lion King*. The girls have been talking about it forever. Half the school's seen it apparently and they're feeling disadvantaged.'

Sara laughed. 'Well, we can't have that, can we? *The Lion King* it is.'

They had a busy time of it. Sara, wandering through the crowded, glittering stores awash with Christmas decorations, bought presents for her sisters and after some thought selected a large backpack for Justin.

'Do you think?' she asked Frances. 'For uni. I know he has one but I thought something bigger?'

'An excellent idea,' his mother agreed.

For Frances she found a handbag of buttery soft leather, then a wallet for her father. That left only Becky and Sam, and a book and a puzzle respectively – neither of which were prohibitively expensive to post – settled them. She bought a card for Jack and nothing else, unable to decide how he might view a gift. Would he be reluctant to accept it? Would he take it, as she would hope, in the spirit of friendship, or feel obliged to reciprocate, and be annoyed at her for encouraging the bond he sought to break?

But the day was too busy for introspection, with the girls excited over their purchases and caught up in the hype of Christmas.

'This is fun,' Sara declared as they lunched in a crowded food hall. 'I've never bothered much with Christmas before. Except when I was married, but that wasn't for long.'

'Did you have a tree?' Mandy asked. Sara shook her head. 'We do, a ginormous one in the hall. When are we gonna put it up, Mum?'

'Well, I thought we could do it tomorrow,' Frances said and Sophie, mouth smeared with tomato sauce, clapped her hands.

'Oh, goody! I love doing the tree. You can help too, Sara, so you won't be sad. 'Cause I would be, if I couldn't.'

'Thank you, sweetie.' Touched, Sara reached to smooth back the hair that had escaped her clip. 'I don't think I'll ever be sad again now I've got a sister like you.'

'And me!' Mandy interjected indignantly.

'And you,' Sara agreed. Glancing at Frances she wondered if she would ever be able to say the same of Justin. 'So, when does this movie start?'

46

Once the school holidays began Sara had little private time, which was just as well, she silently acknowledged. Thinking about Jack, recreating his face in her memory, along with his walk, the shape of his skull, the quizzical glint that visited his grey eyes, did nothing to help her forget. She rang Redhill one evening, aiming for a time when dinner would be finished, and got Beth.

They were all doing fine, she was told, especially Sam. Sara heard caution and hope warring in her friend's voice as Beth said, 'Of course, we won't know for sure until his next appointment, but I think, I really think, Sara, that he's not just holding his own now, he's improving. He doesn't get so tired so quickly, and he's eating better.'

'That's wonderful! I'm so glad. How're Len and Jack?'

'Busy,' Beth said. 'You wouldn't believe it but we got a lightning strike in a patch of whipstick mulga this afternoon. It started a fire. They're out fighting it now.'

'Oh.' Sara was lost. 'Is that bad? What's whipstick mulga exactly?'

'Mulga that grows in thickets, practically solid. Burns like blazes.'

'Not good, then. But lightning? At least you're getting storms.'

'Uh huh, dry ones. Anyway, how's your life in Sydney?'

'It's fine, thanks; I miss you all, though. Give my love to the children, won't you? Tell Becky to watch out for the mail. I've posted a letter and some pics to her. I'll call again at Christmas, Beth.'

'Yes.' Her friend's voice, with the dry undertones that were so much a part of her, said, 'Who knows, maybe it'll be raining by then. Bye, Sara.'

'Bye,' she echoed, then sat for long moments with her hand on the phone, picturing the two men, black shapes against orange-red flames that roared into the night. Sara had only seen bushfires on television. Beth hadn't sounded particularly worried for them so it couldn't be that dangerous, could it? At the same time it seemed terribly unjust that a storm that should've brought life-giving grass would instead be burning the only fodder on the property. Sara found herself hoping desperately that they would be able to control it, then calmed her fears with the reflection that the men from Munaroo and Wintergreen would turn out for Len. *You can't survive alone out here,* Jack had said once when she'd asked why he spent so much time fixing others' gear. *We help each other.*

The Christmas tree was decorated and looked splendid, Sara thought, with its dark green boughs and shiny decorations set against the plain cream wall and embossed ceiling of the hall. The days ticked steadily away, marked off by the Advent calendar the girls rushed for each morning. Friends of Frances's dropped in for drinks and gossip; they had all seen the news stories about Randall's lost daughter, and their avid appetite for details of her life made Sara uncomfortable. The media had either lost interest or thought better of breaching John Randall's privacy. Having been spared their more searching attention, Sara resented the women's prying interest. She attended the gatherings because she was a guest there but was firm in refusing her father's invitation to the Randall Company's Christmas party.

'Take Justin,' she suggested. 'There's no point in introducing me to your managers and salespeople. He's the one they need to know by the sounds of it, given he's going to be studying commerce at university. Besides, I don't want him to see me as a threat to his potential future in the company.' She had begun making headway with the boy, mostly by doggedly persisting and refusing to take offence at his efforts to shut her out.

John Randall pondered the matter, then nodded. 'You're right. He'd probably prefer hanging out with his mates at the beach, but we could start a tradition of introducing the next generation. It's the sort of thing they do in Asia. Thanks, Chrissy – Mary was good with people too. She was useless with figures, but she understood people. Always knew and told me when I'd upset somebody.'

'If it comes to that I wouldn't want a business depending on *my* bookkeeping either.'

He looked thoughtfully at her, the chair tipped back to accommodate his long legs. His reading glasses lay folded on the desk at his elbow where a vase of summer roses scented the air of his home office. 'Would you like to change that?' he asked. 'Oh, not necessarily bookkeeping, but if there's a career you wanted to study for, you could. A university education is something else you were robbed of – but you could still have it.'

Sara shook her head. 'Maybe if I had a particular talent or a burning desire, but I haven't. Thanks all the same though.'

'Well.' He sighed. 'If you should change your mind . . . You had to scrape for books and stuff once, I know. But now you just have to say the word. I never want you to want for anything again.'

'Yes, I get that.' She smiled at him and rested a hand on his arm, still shy of greater displays of affection. 'It's all right though. I'm happy as I am.'

On Christmas morning Sara had reason to recall her father's words. As they unwrapped their gifts amid the litter of discarded decorations and torn wrapping paper in the hall, Sophie discovered an envelope decorated with a curl of scarlet ribbon.

'It's for you, Chrissy!' She gave it to Sara, then hung over her chair arm as Sara slit open the paper and tipped out a set of keys. 'Huh!' she exclaimed. 'That's a funny sorta present. What are they *for?*'

They were for nothing less than the tan-coloured Toyota station wagon parked in the second space of the double garage, Randall's own car having been left in the driveway to accommodate it. Sara, gaze switching between the gift and the giver, pressed a hand to her cheek.

'It's too much! You can't – I can't let you!'

'On the contrary, poppet. You can't stop me.' Her father grinned. 'It's not near enough. How many birthdays and Christmases have you missed? How many parties and celebrations are owed to you? If you're going to spend time in the bush, you need reliable transport. It's a diesel, it has a five-year warranty and they've fitted a bullbar. That's to protect the front end.'

'I know what a bullbar is,' Sara said faintly. 'It's – I don't know, Dad. It will certainly make getting around easier, but —'

'I wouldn't argue,' Justin said enviously. He was circling the vehicle, eyes bright. 'Nice one, Dad! Hey, will you take us for a spin, Christine? 'Course I'd sooner have something nippier and sporty, but it's not bad.'

'It's not bad at all.' She smiled at him, then laughed happily and flung her arms around her father. 'Thank you so much! I never expected – but oh, it's wonderful. I can go anywhere now!'

'With proper precautions,' he amended. 'There's a shovel aboard and a water barrel. I'll give you some lessons at four-wheel driving before you leave.'

'I'll hold you to that,' she said.

He was as good as his word and the following morning they set out for the Blue Mountains to spend the day familiarising herself with the Toyota. Watching Sara pack lunches, Justin was visibly torn between accompanying them and arrangements already made with his friend Stuart.

'There'll be another opportunity,' Sara told him.

'But you're leaving, you said.'

'So I'll stay a few more days,' she promised. An idea occurred to her. 'You don't have anything planned, do you, for the holidays?'

'No, well, the old man'll expect me to get a job.' He grimaced. 'Seems pretty pointless really. It's not like I'm gonna keep it up, supposing I fluke one, but he's got this thing about work being, I dunno, necessary?' He finished on an incredulous note.

Sara smiled at him. 'The bad news is that I've got it too, mate. Idleness isn't really very satisfying, you know. Anyway, I'm sure we'll find time for a drive before I leave.'

Later, on the freeway, relaxing into the feel of the vehicle, Sara said cautiously, 'I've had an idea, Dad. Justin and I were talking earlier – he tells me you expect him to get a job for the next couple of months?'

'Uh huh. What did he want, for you to talk me out of it?'

'Not at all. You do know that it won't be easy for him to land one? He's unskilled and one of a thousand school leavers all looking for a wage, most of them more committed than he'll be. No, I wondered – if I found something for him to do, would you pay his wage?'

John Randall's brows rose. 'Care to explain? What would I be paying for? I'm not objecting – yet.' His eyes twinkled at the driver.

'You'd be paying for his labour. I thought he could come back with me, just for three weeks or so. They've got this beautiful old homestead at Redhill with wooden floors. And it's suffering badly from years of neglect. Not that the Calshots wouldn't fix it, but they can't afford to. When I leave here I'm taking back a load of timber dressing or sealant or whatever you use to preserve flooring. Applying it is what Justin would do. What do you think?'

His first question caught her unawares. 'Can you afford this, Chrissy?'

'Yes – and it wouldn't matter if I couldn't. I owe it to them.' Sara's grip on the wheel tightened and she risked a quick glance away from the road. 'They were so kind to me; Jack particularly helped me to —' She broke off. 'Anyway, it's a thing I can do and it's not so costly that they won't be able to accept it.'

'Ah, yes. There's always that aspect,' her father agreed. 'So, it's Jack who . . . He's the one?'

Sara swallowed tears. 'Yes. But it isn't about him. It's Len and Beth's home and unique in its way. It's over eighty years old. It'll be quite hard work for Justin, I imagine, especially with the heat.'

'Well.' Randall rubbed his jaw. 'I'll talk to Frances. If she's okay with it, I'll ask him tonight. If he wants to go, I'll stump up his wage.'

Justin considered the proposal carefully. The idea of a long trip obviously appealed to him, but did it appeal deeply enough, Sara wondered, for him to accept her company?

'You want me to paint floors?' he said incredulously.

'It's a job. Free meals and accommodation, plus travel, maybe,' she added. 'If you've got your L plates, you'd have a chance to drive part of the way. Does that sound so bad?'

He straightened. 'You'd let me drive your car?'

'If you were careful.'

'Okay,' he conceded. 'So what's it pay?'

'The basic wage?' Sara suggested. 'Painting's not rocket science. You'll need a shady hat. It's hotter than you can imagine out there.'

'Heat doesn't worry me,' he said scornfully. 'I live for summer.'

The girls were immediately jealous of their brother, until Sara reminded them that there was no beach or ice-cream to be had where she was going. Mandy doggedly demanded proof of these statements.

'Show me,' she commanded.

Her father flattened a map on the dining-room table and Sara traced out the route they would take: north-west through Dubbo, on to Broken Hill and into South Australia, then north up the centre of the state to the Alice, along the Stuart Highway.

'But how can you live *there*?' Her sister was aghast. 'There aren't any towns. Where will you buy bread and milk and, well, *anything*?'

'We manage. You can make your own bread, you know. And there's plenty of goats' milk.'

'Ew!' Sophie grimaced. 'I'm glad I'm not Justin. Can we go to the beach today, Mum?'

47

That evening the television news was headlined with pictures of the devastation that Cyclone Nelson had wreaked along the Kimberley coast. Broome had caught the brunt of it: roofs had been torn off, trees uprooted and wind gusts of 170 kilometres an hour had been recorded. Kununurra had suffered too. Staring at the pictures of flooded fields and devastated plantations, Sara shook her head.

'It's either too much or too little.'

Over a metre of rain had fallen in two days; it seemed impossible. The cyclone had spent its fury and become a rain depression with a south-westerly trend, the danger of it reforming lessening with every kilometre that distanced it from the ocean.

'You won't have to worry about road conditions,' John Randall said. 'There's been no rain where you're heading. Tomorrow I'll show you and Justin how to change a tyre – just in case.'

'Stop worrying,' Frances commanded. She looked at Sara. 'Ring us, won't you? Otherwise he'll be imagining all sorts of disasters and heading off after you.'

'I will,' she promised.

They left on the first day of the new year. The evening before, Sara had rung Redhill without getting an answer. Her initial alarm died when she remembered that it was New Year's Eve, and she had let go of the breath she had unconsciously been holding. Of course! They'd all be in at Charlotte Creek. If she'd only had the number, she could've rung the roadhouse. It would have to wait. Tomorrow evening would be time enough to tell Beth they were coming.

The call the following night, however, also went unanswered. Sitting on the motel bed in Dubbo with the phone in her hand, Sara felt alarm flare within her. Something had to be wrong, badly wrong, if Redhill was deserted. Her thoughts flew to Sam and she screwed her eyes shut trying to remember Helen's phone number. She'd written it down, but where? A hasty search through her bag unearthed her new address book and she paged through it.

Justin had the sound turned off as he flicked through the television channels. He glanced up from where he was sprawled on one of the twin beds. 'You finished there yet?'

'No. I have another call to make.' Helen picked up immediately and Sara spoke quickly. 'It's me, Sara. I've been trying to ring the station but there's no answer. Is Sam okay?'

'Sara! How nice. Frank and I were speaking of you only today. Sam's well. It's rained, Sara! Redhill's phone has gone out, well, most of the ones in that area have. A lightning strike on the booster station, I believe. How's Sydney? Did you have a good Christmas?'

'Rain? Oh, how wonderful! I'm so pleased, Helen. Was it enough – is the drought broken, do you think?'

'I'd say four inches have put a fair dent in it.' Her tone served to bring the woman whole before Sara: wry, capable, with a glint of humour in those steadfast hazel eyes. 'And more to come, if you can believe the Met Office. It was that cyclone on the Kimberley coast, or at least the rain depression off it. It's sweeping clean across the Territory. Best rain in decades.'

'I'm so pleased. Look, I'm coming back, with a special passenger. Is it okay if I drop in on you when we get to the Alice? It'll be a few days yet. We're heading for Broken Hill next.'

'Of course. Come and stay, both of you. Who is it?'

'I'll explain when I see you,' Sara said, mindful of cost. 'Thanks heaps, Helen. Give my love to Frank. Bye.' She beamed at Justin. 'It's rained! The drought's over.'

'Wicked,' he said, bored. 'Can I turn the sound up now?'

'If you want.' Sara sighed. It had been a difficult day, with Justin treating her to long spells of silence. The only interest or eagerness he had shown was when she allowed him to drive for an hour between towns. She had refused to let it upset her, telling herself that she had known this was going to take time. If he wanted to shut her out, well, it just gave her more thinking time to anticipate their arrival at Redhill and her reunion with Jack and what she might say to him. And now there was the bonus of drought-breaking rains.

'Come on,' she said gaily, ignoring Justin's irritation at the interruption of his viewing. 'Let's go find something to eat.'

Alice Springs had also been the beneficiary of Cyclone Nelson. The town was green and refreshed, the sky beyond the ranges a sparkling blue. A soft green hue had settled like a quilt over the dusty red earth and the formerly searing heat had turned humid and sticky.

'Not much of an improvement,' Helen said, kissing Sara. 'But, oh, it's worth it. Who's this, then?'

Justin, looking different in his new, broad-brimmed felt hat, was introduced. As tall as Sara, he stood beside her a little diffidently, lost in the quick exchange of news. Helen was concentrating on the family, Frank on the rainfall garnered from local radio reports.

'So when are the phones likely to be fixed?' Sara asked. They were in the kitchen drinking tea under the ceiling fan, save for Justin, who had asked for a cold drink.

Frank shrugged. 'Day or two, they say. The techies can reach the booster station from the bitumen. In any case, you need to wait a bit for the country to dry out before you head off. You don't wanna get bogged.'

'We've got a four-wheel drive,' Justin announced. 'It handles really well, too. We've been sharing the driving,' he added casually.

'You can bog them too, lad,' Frank explained kindly, watching Justin mop his face. 'You reckon it's hot? The bad news is you haven't seen the worst of it yet.'

'You're kidding?' Justin paused his hand in horror. 'Sara said, but I didn't think she meant as hot as this.'

He had decided to call her Sara when she told him it was how she was known at Redhill. It seemed easier for him than using her birth name.

'You'll get used to it,' Frank said.

'He'll be too busy to notice,' Sara told them. 'He's going to sand and dress and seal the floors at Redhill. His holiday job. It's my Christmas present to Beth and Len. I've got all the gear and stuff in the back of the vehicle and the means of applying it right here. It might disarrange the household for a bit but it won't cost them a cent.'

'That's very generous,' Frank began. 'But —'

'No argument.' Sara interrupted. 'I cannot begin to count what you've all done for me and this is the only payment I can make. I couldn't stop the drought for them or cure Sam, but I can get their floors done.' She looked at Justin. 'I had nobody in the world and now I've got a gawky sort of brother, two gorgeous sisters and my Dad, so *nobody's* going to stop me fixing Beth's floors. You hear me?' Her voice trembled with passion and she turned aside to run a finger under her eyes.

'Right, we get it.' Justin eyed her uneasily and looked at his host. 'How come girls always cry? I've got two other sisters and they turn on the waterworks every time, too.'

Frank winked at him. 'I dunno, son, but if you find out, let us in on it, will you?'

It served to clear the tension and Sara laughed at Justin, deeply heartened by that *other*. 'I'm not crying, you twit. I'm just happy.'

Two days later they were on their way again. Now the country through which the Stuart Highway ran looked so different Sara scarcely recognised it. Even the ochre hills about the Alice were patched with the green of spinifex mounds while the flat country was a sea of brilliant feed, so bright it hurt the eye. It was a fortnight since the rain had fallen and already tiny white and yellow flowers had budded along the bitumen's verge. Water glittered still in some of the narrow creeks, and birds were everywhere. She saw ducks and bush turkeys and flocks of shrieking galahs. There was even a pelican, while the easily recognisable shapes of hundreds of budgerigars tore through the blue, swooping and turning like schools of fish.

'Where did they all come from?' Sara wondered.

Justin, listening to his Walkman through earphones, spared a glance for the emptiness beyond the window, unimpressed by the sameness of the view. 'Thought they lived here.' His attention returned to his music.

Even Charlotte Creek seemed fresher, renewed by the rain, the dusty ground grass-covered and the rubbish dump mostly hidden beneath a sprawl of paddymelon vines. One of the houses had a new coat of paint and the police station's front fence had been replaced. Sara parked between the half-finished hall and the roadhouse just as the Greyhound bus they had been following pulled away from it.

'What're we stopping for?' Justin pulled his earphones out.

'A cold drink. And to see some friends.'

Mavis was in front of the bar, opening the freight cartons the bus had brought. She looked up as they entered, seeing a gangly kid with city stamped all over him and a young woman, her red curls clustered beneath a pale Akubra. A smile split her face as she dropped the Stanley knife she was using. 'Sara – well, hang me up and call me a hat! I didn't expect to see you back here.'

'And I didn't expect everything to be so changed,' Sara said. 'It's all so *green!*'

'I know. It gets you like that. We had nearly six inches here and over five at the station, Beth said. The national park had a tad under seven. It always was a lucky spot for rain, Walkervale. Every dam in the country is full and the budgies are already nesting.'

'We saw them. Mavis, this is my brother, Justin. How's Alec, by the way?'

'He's good. Hello, Justin.' She shook hands, shooting a look at Sara as she did so. 'It all worked out, then – finding your family?'

'Yes. I've been with them since I left.' She took off her hat and moved to the bar. 'Any chance of a cold drink? Talking makes me thirsty. On second thoughts I think I'd sooner order tea.'

'I'll light the gas.' Mavis left her unpacking and vanished beyond the bar, her voice floating back to them along with the chink of crockery. 'Then I want to hear all about everything.'

'Me too,' Sara called. 'Is old Harry doing his run this week? And Clemmy, is she well?'

Justin sighed and replaced his earphones.

48

There were vehicle ruts in the road to Redhill, gouged deeply into the track, the tyre marks plain to see. Sara wondered if it was Jack's Toyota that had made them. The grass, taller through the sand country, literally shone in the sunlight and no dust rose behind them. The sky was the most amazing blue, as if it had been washed and polished that very morning. Water, tinged reddish brown, filled holes and declivities in the red clay and even the mulga looked fresher.

She pointed out the Forty Mile block and the different paddocks whose names she had learned. Justin seemed more impressed by the distance they had come.

'How far *is* this joint?'

'Oh, about an hour more.' The words conjured her first meeting with Jack and her lips curved in a little smile. 'Time is how they measure things out here.'

Justin shook his head. 'I don't get it. This sort of place is where you want to live. Why?'

She shrugged. 'Maybe because I started life on a property. I guess it's in my blood.'

He sniffed. 'Lot of trees and nothing is all I see. Where are the cows?'

'Scattered about. It's a big area. There's fifteen hundred square miles of Redhill. That gives them plenty of mulga to hide in.'

'So how do they ever find them when the round-up's due?'

'You should ask Len,' Sara said, 'or even Sam, come to think of it. And it's called a muster.'

'If you say so. Can I drive?'

'Not on this bit,' she said.

Sara had rung ahead and they were expected. Jess came barking to meet them and as she pulled up at the gate she saw a curious Becky skipping down the steps, Sam and Beth moving more sedately behind her. The oleanders made a vivid screen of colour and above the familiar roofline the bright vanes of the windmill glittered in the sun. Somewhere in the background an engine throbbed.

'The dog won't hurt you,' Sara told Justin. She got out and patted the bitch's head, then Becky was there, plaits flying, grabbing her waist in a hug.

'You're back, Sara! An' it rained! You shoulda been here, the lightning was *so* loud!'

'I told you I'd come, chicken. This is my brother, Justin. I brought him for a visit too.'

'Oh.' Becky glanced at him and into the empty vehicle. Her face fell. 'You said you'd bring the girls.'

'Not this time. He's all right though, for a boy. Only he doesn't know anything about stations.'

Becky brightened at that. 'I'll learn him, then.'

Sara was staring at Sam, whose head was covered in a brown fuzz of hair. 'Sam, you look great! Gracious, I'm sure you're taller too. And your hair is growing back!'

'Hello, Sara.' He smiled his contained smile. His face looked fuller and his eyes were bright as he studied the vehicle. 'Wow! Is that yours?'

'Yes.' She turned to hug Beth. 'It's so good to see you again. I've got stuff from Helen for you. But the grass! I can't believe the difference in the place. And Sam's got hair.'

Beth clutched her, laughing. 'It's like a miracle, Sara – no chemo for two months now. The cancer's in remission.' Her thin face was flushed, her smile brilliant. 'And then the rain on top of it. Some days I could just cry from sheer happiness.'

'Well, if anyone deserves it, you do. How's Len, and Jack?'

'They're good. Oh, and this is your brother. You're very welcome, Justin. We think a great deal of Sara, you know. You're very lucky to have found her. But come in. It's just on lunchtime; I'll pop the kettle on. Sam, run and tell your father it's time to eat.' She beamed at Sara, blinking over-bright eyes. 'I can say that now, because he can run.'

'Is Jack still here?' Sara asked, trying for a normal tone, as they climbed the steps.

'He's gone home, but,' she added, the word reviving sudden hope in her listener, 'he'll be back tomorrow, maybe even today.' Beth cocked her head at Justin. 'So, Justin, I hear you're heading for university?'

Nothing had changed and yet everything was different, Sara reflected, settling into her old place at the kitchen table. Every window showed a vista of green. New growth was bursting from the garden trees, and Sam's voice and steps rang as noisily and as quickly as Becky's. Later she would see the adorable newborn kids in the goat flock, and the empty horse yard where grass had grown over the dung-powdered dirt where Star and Lancer had stood so often to be fed. But for now Len was tramping up the steps and she rose to meet him as he entered.

'Sara!' His bloodhound face wore a wide smile as he grabbed her close for a moment. 'Good to see you – I like your hair short like that. How are you?'

'Great, Len, and it's great to be back. What do you think about this, then?' She leaned down for the Akubra beneath her chair and stuck it on. 'Complete bushie, huh?'

Len laughed and agreed, then began to tell her about the rain. Both the dams on the property were full and all the creeks had run. You could already see the improvement in the stock. 'Dozer's back in the shed,' he concluded. 'But enough about that. What are your plans?'

'Justin's here to do a job,' she explained. 'He'll fly home from the Alice once it's finished, but I'm staying on. Not at Redhill obviously, but wherever I can get a station job. I can cook, teach, do home help – somebody's got to want me. If not, I'll find something in the Alice instead.'

'She's nuts,' Justin announced tolerantly. 'Dad offered her a job but she turned it down.'

'I didn't want it,' she responded. 'Horses for courses, Jus.' It was the first time she had used the family's diminutive. 'Out here's where I want to be.'

'Like I said, nuts.' For the first time the mockery was absent from his tone. He might have been teasing his younger sisters, and Sara's heart was warmed by the change.

Beth hauled the conversation away from the personal. 'What job have you got, Justin?'

He jabbed his thumb at his sister. 'She'll explain,' he said, so Sara did.

It took time. Beth raised all the objections Sara had foreseen but once the meal was over and she had coaxed her out to the vehicle to view the carefully packed drums and paintbrushes, she knew she was winning the argument. 'It's a gift,' she said. 'Something I really want you to have. You can't turn down a well-meant gift! Dad's paying Justin's wages because he thinks it's good for him to work, and I do too. Also I want to get to know him and I've a better chance out here where he can't run off to the beach to avoid me. He wasn't very happy when I turned up, you see. He was sure it was a con job; and I think also that he was a bit protective of his position as the oldest kid in the family. Well, we seem to have finally got that sorted.' She rolled her eyes. 'Half the trip out either he wasn't speaking to me or he had his head plugged into the Walkman he carries. But he seems to be coming around. By the way, you said when I first came to work here that the floors needed doing but you couldn't afford it. So what's changed? The rain's wonderful but it hasn't made you rich, has it?'

'No,' Beth said ruefully. 'Oh, all right then! It's amazingly generous of you, Sara. It's true the floors are either going to warp or splinter if something's not done soon, but there's no way we can repay you for this.'

'Yes, you can.' Sara was pulling things out of the vehicle as she spoke. 'This is from Helen, and here're a few fresh vegies I picked up in town. You can put us up until the job's done and let the kids show Justin what real life is all about. He's a nice boy but his outlook's limited. A dose of Sam and Becky is just what he needs.'

'The kids will love to have his company. Of course we'll put you up! Thank you, Sara. It will be lovely to have the floors done.'

Len had gone back to the shed and the welder was growling again. Sara, with Becky in attendance, unpacked in her old room, while Justin, overseen by Sam, hauled the material and equipment he would be using onto the verandah. Afterwards Beth walked through the house discussing with Sara where and how the work should progress.

'We're all using mosquito nets,' she said, 'so we could shift the kids' beds out onto the verandah till their rooms are dry.'

'And Sara's,' Becky chimed in. 'It'll be fun. We can look at the stars. Does Justin know about them, Sara?'

'I shouldn't think so, chicken.' She frowned. 'Will the dining table be a problem? It's so big. Will it even fit through the door?'

'Well, somebody got it in there, so maybe when Jack gets back he and Len can sort it out. Still, we could just move it to one end of the room, then put it back. Oh –' she swung her arms energetically, stretching her lean torso – 'the timing's great! No dust to get into the new work. I'll have a proper spring clean, I think, maybe even make up that curtain material I've had waiting in the cupboard since before Sam got sick. That's getting on for three years now.'

'He looks so different. And so well!'

'For now,' Beth nodded, her next words a prayer. 'Maybe for good.'

Questions about Jack hovered on Sara's tongue – when would he arrive? how was his state of mind? had he mentioned her at all in her absence? – but she bit them back. She had returned to Redhill; what happened next was his choice.

Chiming in uncannily on the thought, Beth asked, 'Are you happy, Sara? With your dad and the rest of them? It must be strange to be pitchforked into a family you don't know. Should we be calling you Christine now?'

'Dad calls me Chrissy, but I'd quite like to stay Sara out here. Justin's picked it up too – I like that. I'll change my surname next time my licence comes due. And to answer your first question, yes, I am happy. For the first time in my life I feel . . .' She searched for words to explain. 'I don't know. I feel grounded, I suppose. When you don't belong anywhere, when you think you haven't any blood ties, it's hard to believe that you matter.'

'What's your stepmum like?'

'Frances? Funny, I never thought of her in that light, just as my father's wife. She's great. I really like her, mainly because you can see she loves Dad. She wants him to be happy, and finding me has done that.'

'A sensible lady, then.'

'Yes, but with a generous spirit too. She might've worried that I'd be taking something from her own children, whether it was his love or attention or just his time but it doesn't seem to have occurred to her.'

'And the press?' Beth asked. 'There was a news headline about you meeting him in "an exclusive Alice Springs resort". We saw it on the news the following day but apparently by the time they'd got a cameraman round there you'd already gone.'

Sara laughed. 'He probably planned it that way. No, I'm yesterday's sensation now, nobody's bothered me.'

'That's good.' Beth grinned suddenly. 'It's going to be great, having you here again. It took your leaving to make me realise how much I miss having another woman around.'

'And I've been thinking,' Sara said, 'maybe we could take a day and visit Clemmy while I'm here? After the spring clean maybe?'

'It's a deal.'

49

Late in the afternoon the two children took Justin with them to bring in the goats. Sara, declining to accompany them, watched his lanky form pacing off between the two. He was tanned from the beach but wilting in the heat, as she was herself after the weeks she'd spent away from it. It was cooler in the garden; she carried a chair out under the lemon tree, breathing in the sweet scent of its blossom. Beth was showering, Len still at the shed, she presumed, though the welder had ceased its bellowing some time since. She felt tired, let down. All through the long drive to Redhill the thought of arriving, of seeing Jack, had buoyed her spirits. She had pictured a dozen possible ways that meeting might go but had never imagined that he wouldn't be there.

Now all she could do was wait and worry. Thanks to the phones being out he didn't know to expect her. Perhaps that was for the best. His first reaction would most truly reflect his feelings for her – if they existed, Sara reminded herself. She dropped her hat on the grass and pushed her hair back, feeling the way the damp curls clung to her fingers. Somewhere far off a plane droned; above her head the leaves of the lemon tree glittered silver-edged as she searched for the plane amid the patches of blue but without success. The drought skies had shown a fiercer light but today's was still brilliant enough to make her eyes ache. Sara dropped her chin and blinked, to rest them. She picked up her hat, then shot to her feet as the distant drone suddenly metamorphosed into the steady beat of a diesel engine. A vehicle – coming to the front of the homestead.

When it pulled up she was already there, standing beneath the glossy-leafed oleanders as Jack killed the engine and got out, staring as if he'd seen a ghost. Or an unwelcome reminder from the past? Sara banished the treacherous thought and spoke first.

'Hello, Jack.'

'Sara.' He said blankly. He seemed to be frozen to the spot, arms hanging at his sides as he gazed upon her, and her heart sank. Coming here had all been for nothing after all. She had been wrong. He didn't want her.

Then, as if a spring had turned within him, he cried, 'Sara!' on a gladder note. 'You're back. What? Why?' He stopped speaking, his hands reached for her and he grabbed her into a hug.

She clung to him, feeling the comfort of his strong, lean body against her own, while taking in the dear familiar essence of his smell – a hint of diesel and sweat and man skin – knowing again the absolute security his presence had always brought. Nothing could harm her now, all her worries were baseless, her uncertainties abandoned. His arms tightened so possessively around her that she was forced to gasp, 'You're squashing me.'

'Sorry.' His grip slackened, but only slightly. Held tightly against him she could feel the rapid leaping of his heart. 'That hat suits you really well.' The words came in his usual unhurried delivery, with the hint of a smile in them.

'I'm glad you like it.' Sara tugged it off and let it drop, then lifted her face to his. Her own heart was hammering and she could feel the blood pulsing under her skin. 'Kiss me,' she commanded, amazed at her own boldness. 'You irritating wretch.'

He cupped her face with his hands, staring down into the green eyes. And then gently, tenderly, he kissed her deeply and then did it again, the light rasp of his stubble against her soft skin a benison.

'I have missed you so much. The place has been dead without you.' He kissed her again, his hands sliding up over her shoulder-blades to cradle her skull, sending little ripples of delight through her. 'You didn't tell me you were coming.'

'I tried,' she murmured as his lips moved from her earlobe to the hollow of her throat, 'but the phones were out.' She welcomed him back to her lips then pushed him away. 'Jack, we're standing in the sun. I'll be as red as a beet if we don't move.'

'Can't have that.' He scooped up her fallen hat and led her by the hand into the garden, seeking the shade of the lemon tree. 'So it turned out all right with your family? I've wondered so often.'

'But Beth knew. Didn't she tell you? I rang her at Christmas, and before that, and said —'

'She did.' He was holding her hands, his thumbs caressing her knuckles. 'And an independent wench like you I'm necessarily sup-posed to believe it? Would you have told her you were unhappy, supposing you were?'

'Well, no,' Sara admitted. 'She's had so much to contend with herself up till it rained.'

'Yes,' he agreed, gathering her to him again. 'But the drought's over now, hers and mine.' He kissed her cheeks and chin and eyes, lips moving towards her own again, as he murmured, 'If you knew how long I've ached to do this . . .'

'Then why didn't you?' Sara demanded, the hurt she had nursed so long finding sudden utterance. She jerked her head free of contact with him. 'You let me leave without a word, as if I was truly no more to you than the governess. You broke my heart, Jack Ketch, and why I'm letting you kiss me now I don't know!'

'Whoa! Hang on a moment. You were never *just the governess*. Not to me. And as for letting you go, of course I had to. Surely you can see that?'

'Why?' she flashed, and suddenly her anger was no longer half pretence. 'Because you've got a hang-up about city women?'

'Jesus,' Jack muttered. 'It's true what they say about temper and redheads. What about city women? Mum's a city woman, for God's sake – or she was. She was born in Sydney, you don't get much more citified than that. And I might have let you go, but I was coming after you. Next week, in fact.'

'You were coming to the city? To see me? Really?' Her face broke into a smile.

'Well, mainly to deliver a letter.' But she had caught the tilt to his mouth and smacked him hard on his arm.

'What letter?'

'This one.' He fished it from his pocket. 'From that journo, Markham. Probably wants a follow-up story: *My life as a millionaire's daughter.*'

'He sent it here? He must know I'd left. Beth said it made the headlines – the meeting with my father, that is.'

'Territory headlines,' Jack agreed. 'They could've had a better story that day in Adelaide. And I suppose he knew we'd forward it.'

'But you didn't.' Sara consulted the date stamp, still smiling. 'It was posted three weeks ago.'

Jack rasped a hand over his jaw. 'Roads have been too wet for the mail. And I was heading after you, anyway. Whatever it was, I reckoned it could wait.'

'So why were you coming, Jack?'

'Because I wanted to know you were okay.' He reached a hand to cup her nape and she shivered under his touch. 'I know that dreams can be realised, Sara, but in my experience it's rare. There's no law says families have to get on.'

'Oh, Jack.' Her anger melted, she kissed him swiftly. 'You've always cared about me, helped me. I've never met anyone as generous-hearted.'

'Maybe, but self-interest came into it too. Forgetting you wasn't working, as you've seen.' He brushed a stray curl back from her brow. 'You've got beautiful hair, Sara, did I ever tell you that? By the time I got to Sydney I reckoned you might've worked out what you wanted to do with your life. That's why I wasn't in a real hurry to get there. If you were all set up for a future in the city, the plan was to deliver the letter and clear out.' He grimaced. 'The truth is you're heir to some part of a very big fortune, Sara, and I didn't see how that was going to work when my life's out here.'

She stared at him, absorbing this. 'Then it wasn't Marilyn?'

'*Marilyn?* What's it got to do with her?'

'I thought –' Sara felt suddenly dizzy, as she perceived her error – 'that you didn't – that you gave up on me because you'd made a mistake falling for her and didn't want to repeat it with another city woman.'

Jack made a sound between a laugh and a groan. 'How can you be so blind? I love you.' He released the hand he was holding to scrub his own across his jaw and grimace. 'So much for good intentions. You're still your father's heir – you could, I imagine, have anything you want. How can I ask you to give that up and stay out here in the scrub with me? Even though I love you, Sara, and in the blood and bones of me I know I always will.'

'Oh, Jack.' The green eyes misted over. 'It's all I want. Not some grand home. Money only buys things. It's useful but it's not real the way Sam and Becky are, or you, and Beth and Len. I loved you long before that trip to the canyon and everything else is incidental. I want to live with reality, like your parents do – with love, not with money or power.'

This time his arms crushed the breath from her. When the kiss stopped he spoke against her cheek, and she felt his breath stir the tendrils of hair about her ear. 'Then do. Come live with me and be my love. Stay out here in the dust and heat and flies. You're sure it's what you want, Sara?'

'I want you,' she said. 'Especially when you quote poetry at me. I don't care about a bit of dust. And I can put up with the flies.' Joy enfolded her like a hug. 'I love you, Jack Ketch. You gave me back the life they stole from me, and I intend to spend it with you.'

'I've been warned, then.' There was a smile in his voice as he bent to pick up her hat, which they had dislodged again, and place it on her curls. 'What does the letter say?'

'Oh.' Sara had forgotten about it but there were only a few lines. She read them swiftly. 'The police have arrested Stella Blake. Actually I knew that, my father told me. The police contacted him just before New Year. Paul says she's since been arraigned on charges of kidnapping and an accomplice to murder.' Her eyes sought his. 'That means I'll have to go to court . . . Or wouldn't the testimony of a six-year-old count?'

He shrugged. 'She might plead guilty anyway. But you'd want to see her punished, wouldn't you?'

'I suppose. She deserves it for Benny.' But somehow Sara couldn't muster the hatred she should have felt for the woman she had once called mother. 'I think Dad suffered most,' she said slowly. 'I mean, I didn't enjoy life with Stella but I'd forgotten what I'd lost, whereas he's had to live with it all this time. I doubt he'd be in a very forgiving mood. It cost him so much. This too.' Her gesture took in the land around them. 'He was a bushman, from choice, but he left all that behind when the Blakes stole us. So yes, Stella has much to answer for. The harm people do,' she said sadly. 'It's like there's no end to it.'

'I know.' His hand slid down her arm to circle her wrist and their fingers entwined. 'You want to come for a drive?'

She was startled. 'What, now? It's getting late.'

'It won't take long. Just to Kileys and back. What do you say?'
'Why?'

He heaved a sigh. 'Yes, or no, my love?'

Sara melted at the endearment. 'Then yes.' She glanced around at the deserted front of the homestead. 'I'll have to tell Beth first. She doesn't even know you're here. Neither does Len, and the kids are getting the goats in. Shall we take my vehicle?'

'Yours, is it? Might be a bit flash – the road could be boggy still. Don't worry about Beth – she'll figure it out. Let's go.'

The track was actually better than before, the rain having filled the potholes and firmed down the dust. When they neared the fringe of mulga that opened to the sand country round the bore, Jack slowed. 'Okay, close your eyes. No peeking permitted.'

'Why?' Sara repeated, but did as she was bidden. She held the door as the vehicle swayed round a curve. 'Can I look now?'

'Not yet.'

The vehicle slowed, and stopped. Galahs shrieked and as Jack cut the engine she heard the splash of water falling into the stock tank. He came round to her side of the vehicle, opened the door and took her arm.

'Out you get. Okay, you can look now.'

Sara gazed upon a fairyland.

She gasped in delight and he slid his arm around her shoulder. The shadows lay long across the ground in the slanting golden sunlight. She saw the tank, mill and trough nestling in a sea of herbage, the shimmery-surfaced spill of the overflow where three wild ducks paddled, and the familiar creek bank fenced by white-trunked gums. But it had been bare before, the land stripped to its bones. Now colour flowed in every direction. Great blazes of golden yellow, seas of pink and white, rivers of purple, rippling away across the sand flats between the whitewood clumps and the stark trunks of the gums.

'This is what rain can do.'

'I never imagined. Surely this doesn't always happen?'

'Not every time. Conditions have to be just right to get this sort of show. You might see it this way once in thirty years.'

'I'll be getting on for sixty next time, then,' she said. 'It's breathtaking, Jack! There should be angels or trumpets. Oh, I never want to forget this! I have to walk among them, to make sure I don't forget. It could take a little while.'

'We've got time,' he said comfortably. 'We can do it together.' He glanced down at her, a glint in the grey eyes. 'You realise that another man might have claimed that he'd arranged it specially to dazzle you? Not me. I just wanted you to see it.'

'How noble.' Her lips quirked. 'And you're not even calling it *galli-galli*.'

'There's that too. Damn but you're sharp!' He nodded at the palette of colour stretching to the horizon. 'I reckon there's memories enough for anyone here.'

'For everyone,' she corrected fervently.

'And afterwards,' he suggested, 'shall we start making some more?'

'Oh, yes,' Sara murmured and kissed him. 'Let's do that.'

His hand slipped down from her shoulder and she spread her fingers to accommodate his, feeling a goosepimpling instant of deja vu as she did so. A memory of an older bond, and a smaller hand that had once linked with hers just as naturally. Without releasing her grip, Sara curled her other arm about Jack's neck, pulling him close to bring his body against hers, so close that she could feel the regular beat of his heart against her ribs. It was a strong, relentless beat from a heart that would not easily quit, but it was kind too, she thought, and as tough and enduring as the desert land upon which they stood.

Out of Alice

DISCUSSION NOTES FOR BOOK CLUBS

1. *'I want you to come back to Kings Canyon, to the scene of your abduction. It's the only way to get to the truth. If you see it again, the memories of what happened might return. Surely you want to know how your twin died?'*
   Do you think Sara had any real choice in returning to Kings Canyon?

2. Jack tells Sara that in the mulga, the definition of an optimist is 'any mug on the land'. Do you think that the farmers in this novel are optimists?

3. The drought features prominently in the book. Discuss its significance in this story, including the ways in which it influences the course of events and the social, economic and psychological impact it has on the community.

4. *'The bush holds many secrets. People vanish, perish, are murdered . . .'*
   This is a work of fiction, but it could well be true.
   Discuss the role of the harsh landscape in other infamous cases of human disappearances in the Australian outback.

5. In one of Sara's earliest interactions with Justin, she invokes the term *galli-galli*, which she learned from Jack. It is a delicate term, in her words 'a useful descriptive word for anything you don't understand'. On what levels does *galli-galli* operate in the novel?

6. Paul Markham's plays an integral role in *Out of Alice* but he is not characterised sympathetically. Do you believe Paul Markham is a hero or a villain in this story?

7. Discuss the theme of family as it is explored in this novel. What do you think it takes to make a 'real' one?

8. Helen says, 'There are times when this country could get you down if you let it,' but do we ever see her being down? Even in the face of enormous adversity, what do you think keeps her strong?

9. Identify times in the novel when bush humour is used. What role does it play in the lives of the characters and do you see its use as a means to survive the landscape? Do you ever witness it in the city characters?

10. Would Sara have been better off if she had never confronted the truth about what happened to her and Benny?

11. How does Sara's union with Jack influence her wellbeing? How does it echo the relationship that she shared with her twin, Ben?

12. Kerry McGinnis's prose is often described as being like poetry. Can you identify any such passages in this latest novel?

Acknowledgements

Gathering background for Sara's story involved a journey through the desert and I would like to thank Lyn Conway of Kings Creek Station, Northern Territory, for her willingness to answer my questions about road conditions in the area and other historical information from the seventies that I have used in this book.

Also my grateful thanks to the many people at Penguin Random House who helped in the preparation of the manuscript, most notably Ali Watts and Clementine Edwards. What writer wouldn't be lost without editors? Thanks heaps, everyone.

Secrets of the Springs

The past can't stay buried forever ...

When Orla Macrae receives a letter asking her to return to the family cattle property where she grew up, she does so grudgingly. Her estranged uncle Palmer may be dying, but he is the last person she wants to see, not when she's made a new life far away from where she lost so much. But on his deathbed he utters a few enigmatic words about a secret locked away and a clue as to its whereabouts.

Intrigued, Orla decides to stay, reconnecting with old friends and taking a chance on a long-time dream of opening the homestead to tourists. Continuing the search for her uncle's elusive secret, she discovers far more than she bargained for – a shocking truth about her parents' marriage, and the confession of a chilling murder.

Set in the stunning countryside north of the Barrier Ranges near Broken Hill, this is an authentic tale of life on the land and a gripping mystery about old family secrets and finding love in the harsh Australian bush.

COMING IN JULY 2017

Tracking North

Kelly Roberts finds refuge in the rugged and remote cattle country of northern Australia, but when tragedy strikes she is forced to find a new life for herself and her children outside of Rainsford Station.

She retreats to the family's only asset – a freehold block of land owned jointly by her eccentric father-in-law, Quinn. In the valley at Evergreen Springs, Quinn hopes the fractured family might all come together to start over again.

Life in Queensland's far north is unpredictable – especially with the wet season, in all its wild majesty, to survive. But when twelve-year-old Rob makes a gruesome discovery in the valley, real peril comes far too close to home.

'Vividly transports you to the Gulf Country. Settle in
for a really enjoyable read.'
SUSAN DUNCAN

'Kerry McGinnis writes like poetry . . .
She stands out among Australian authors.'
FLEUR McDONALD

'The setting is *beautiful* . . . I am definitely
adding her other books to my to-be read list.'
ALL THE BOOKS I CAN READ

Mallee Sky

When it all goes wrong, where is there left to run to but home?

Kate Gilmore hasn't been home in years, but with her marriage over and her job in jeopardy she doesn't know where else to turn. Desperate for comfort, Kate retreats to the Mallee, a place crawling with dark secrets and lingering childhood memories.

When she's offered a carer's job on the isolated Rosebud Farm, Kate soon meets old Harry Quickly, an intriguing young boy called Maxie, and a handsome harvest contractor who's not shy about making his intentions known.

Under the endless Mallee skies, Kate discovers that she might just have a future in the place that has haunted her past. But are some family secrets better left in the grave or can new friendships heal old wounds?

'Hard to put down.'
NEWCASTLE HERALD

'A moving and evocative novel of mystery,
heartbreak and courage.'
MILDURA MIDWEEK